DICK LIGHTHEART;

OR,

The Scapegrace of the School.

BEAUTIFULLY ILLUSTRATED.

VOLUME I.

LONDON:
HARKAWAY HOUSE, 6, WEST HARDING STREET, FETTER LANE,
FLEET STREET, E.C., AND ALL BOOKSELLERS.

DICK LIGHTHEART

THE SCAPEGRACE OF THE SCHOOL

Mr Harlequin
Miss Columbine

DICK LIGHTHEART;

or, The Scapegrace of the School.

"'I'LL HAVE A LARK WITH THE GOVERNOR NOW,' SAID DICK."

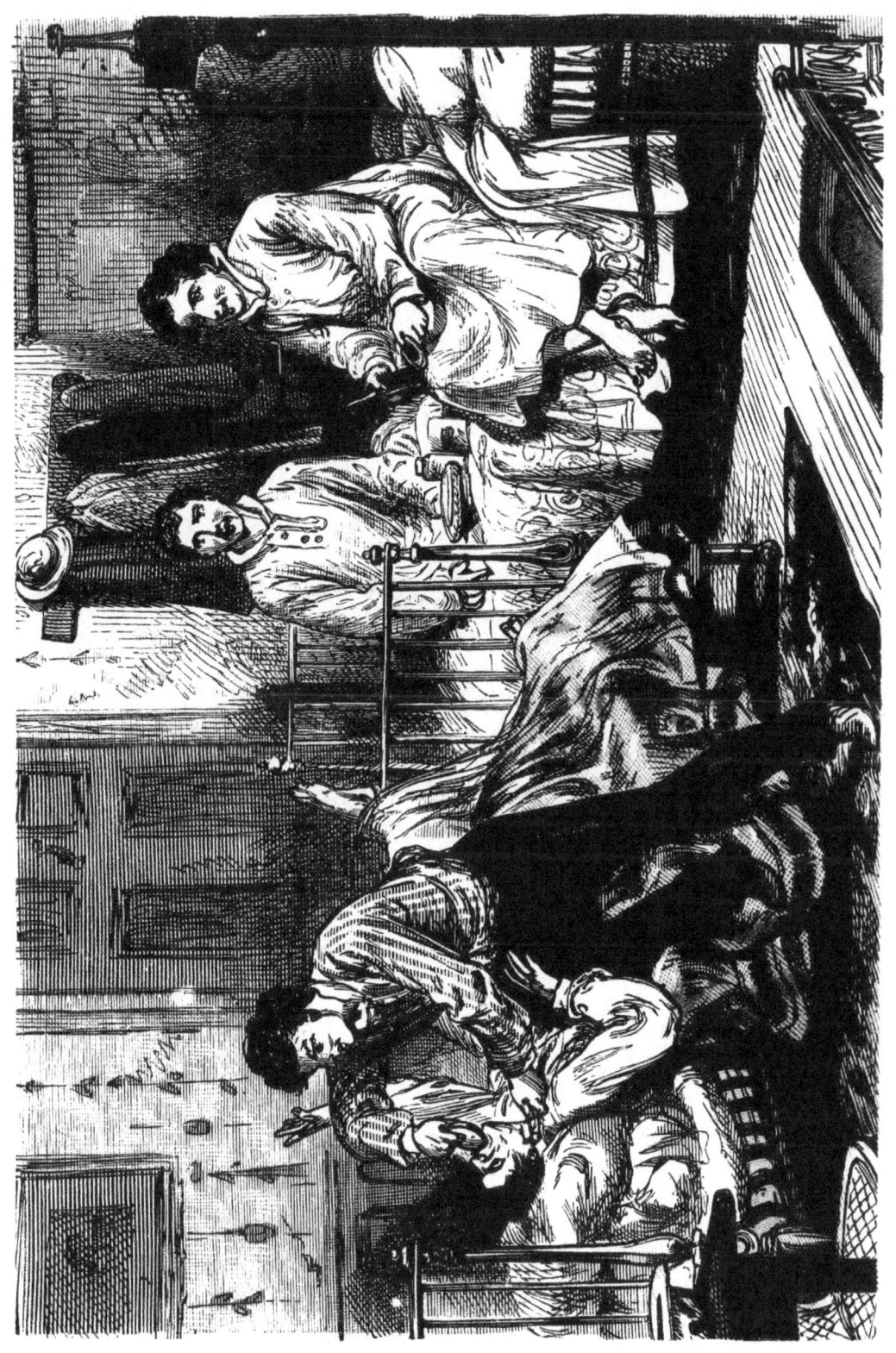

"Open your mouth and shut your eyes," cried Dick.

DICK LIGHTHEART;

Or, THE SCAPEGRACE OF THE SCHOOL.

BY THE AUTHOR OF "JACK HARKAWAY."

CHAPTER I.

THE TUTOR'S TROUBLES.

THE Reverend Septimus Lightheart, Rector of Ingarstone, near Hayward's Heath, was very much in favour of educating children at home.

He did not like schools.

In his opinion, all that was bad and irreligious was picked up at school, by both boys and girls.

But, then, he had never been to school himself, which made a great difference.

He had been educated by a private tutor, and he determined that his children should not be exposed to the temptations of schools, but be privately instructed at home, as he had been.

At the age of thirty the Reverend Mr. Lightheart had been inducted into a living worth a thousand a year by a rich relation.

He soon afterwards married.

His wife was of an amiable disposition; kind and charitable, knowing as little of the world as did her husband.

In fact, their world was comprised within the limits of their parish.

At the time our story opens they had five children.

Two girls and three boys.

The eldest boy, Richard, being nearly fifteen, Harold and Arthur, each a year younger, and the girls, Emily and Agnes, sixteen and seventeen respectively.

Harold and Arthur were what is called very good boys, and Emily and Agnes were very good girls.

The boys had a tutor living in the rectory, named Mr. Smiles, while the girls had an elderly lady for a governess, whose name was Miss Bodmin.

Dick, however, was an exception; he did not submit to control as did his brothers and sisters.

He exercised an independent spirit, which all around him in vain endeavoured to quell.

Frequently Mrs. Lightheart would say to her husband, with tears in her eyes—

"Mark my words, Septimus, that boy Dick will be the scapegrace of the family."

"I don't recognise the necessity, my dear, for there being a scapegrace at all in the family," the parson would answer.

"Oh, yes," Mrs. Lightheart replied, "there is always a black sheep in every flock."

Mr. Lightheart sighed, and wondered how it was that any boy of his could threaten to turn out badly after the careful education he was at the pains to give them at home.

Yet he would not yield to the solicitations of his friends and neighbours, and send the lad to school.

Mr. Smiles, the tutor, was the constant victim of Master Richard's jokes.

He, at least, would have been very glad to have seen him sent anywhere.

Once he suggested the propriety of selecting the sea as the proper profession for him.

"Our mercantile marine," he ventured to say, "offers splendid opportunities to spirited but wayward boys."

A severe frown from Mr. Lightheart silenced him.

"No," said the clergyman; "the lawlessness and profanity of those who go down to the sea in ships is proverbial. No son of mine shall be a sailor. I intend Richard for the ministry. He shall be a clergyman like myself. Those escapades of his will wear off as he has more sense; and the wildness of youth will be followed by the refined wisdom of manhood."

Mr. Smiles hoped it might, but he did not say anything.

One morning, in summer, Mr. Lightheart said to the tutor—

"You have not taken the boys out lately, Mr. Smiles, to explain to them the beauties of nature; do so to-day. I empower you to give them a half holiday. Go to the cook; see what cold provisions she can supply. Pack a basket, and picnic in the open air under the shade of some spreading beech tree, as Virgil has it. Botanize, sir; explain to their young minds the nature and properties of trees and plants."

Mr. Smiles gladly agreed to the proposition, and the boys, no less pleased, set about making their preparations.

Nevertheless, there was an inward tremor about the heart of the tutor, for, as Dick had let him alone for a week or two, he thought it was about time for him to play him some trick or other.

After walking some distance, they selected a shady spot, where they decided to dine.

There was a hedge and an oak tree, beneath whose aged boughs they spread their cloth.

Some cold lamb and a jar of cider, a salad, cream cheese, and bread were an excellent repast.

"Observe this tree," said Mr. Smiles, pointing upwards. "It is one of the noblest specimens of forest grandeur. For centuries it may have braved the storm, and grown green in the sunshine. Our ships were made of oak, which is a wood of all the most durable. Let me apply history. King Charles II. once hid in an oak, and thus baffled his pursuers."

"Thank you, sir. Will you carve?" exclaimed Dick, who did not care much about this lecture on oak trees.

"I will, gladly; and you, Richard, say grace. But stay; where am I to sit?"

"Here, sir," answered Dick, indicating a particular spot.

Mr. Smiles, his face overflowing with satisfaction and good-nature, accepted the position.

He was hungry.

The prospect before him was inviting.

Dick said grace, and Mr. Smiles began to carve.

Suddenly the knife fell from his hand, and he uttered a sharp cry of pain.

"Dear me! how unpleasant. A wasp," he exclaimed.

"Did it sting you, sir?" asked Dick, keeping some distance off.

"It did; and I declare here is another—and another; the place is alive with them; and—am I sitting upon a thistle, or—dreadful thought!—are these wasps beneath me?"

Scarcely had Mr. Smiles spoken than he essayed to rise, but he had hardly struggled a foot above the ground when he was constrained to sink down again.

His coat tails were firmly fastened, by means of two split pieces of wood, to the ground.

A perfect swarm of wasps now surrounded him, and began to sting him in various places.

"Help! help!" he cried, wildly, plunging about, and beating the air with his hands.

He had sat down upon a wasps' nest, and the savage little insects were resenting his intrusion upon their domain.

When he partially rose, he liberated some of them, and they assisted in the attack.

By a desperate effort he got free, and, rushing to a small trout stream which flowed at the bottom of the field, plunged his burning face and hands into the cold water.

"How odd that he should have sat on a wasps' nest," said Dick to his brothers.

"I believe you knew all about it, and I'll tell of you when we get home," replied Harold.

"Sneak away," retorted Dick; "and if you do, I'll give you a thrashing the first time I catch you out alone."

Harold held his tongue.

"Let us move these things. I object to wasps in connection with cold lamb and salad, and if Smiles has lost his appetite, there will be all the more for us to eat," continued Dick.

The things were quickly removed to

another spot, and spread under the shelter of a haystack which had been erected near the stream.

It had been partly cut, and Mr. Smiles was lying in considerable pain upon a ledge close to the water, and under the boughs of a sycamore.

He had been stung in six or seven different places.

Dick took him some dinner and a mug of cider.

The latter he drank, but he could not touch anything to eat, for a wasp had stung him inside his lip, which was much swollen.

"I am sorry for this, sir. Wasps are nasty things to meddle with. Shouldn't do it again if I were you, sir," said Dick.

"Go away; leave me," replied the tutor, who spoke with difficulty, owing to the injury to his lip.

Dick retired and joined his brothers, whom he assisted in demolishing the dinner.

"That's a very good tuck in," said Dick, drinking some cider. "Now, you two fellows, clear up the fragments, and put everything away in the basket."

Accustomed to obey their brother, Harold and Arthur did not refuse.

They knew that a refusal on their part might be attended with unpleasant consequences.

"I wonder if Smiles would give us a little more botany," remarked Dick.

"I think he's gone to sleep," said Harold. "Do let him alone, Dick. It must be so bad to be stung as he was."

"What could he expect when he went and sat down on their nest? I don't blame the wasps a bit. I say, if Smiles was suddenly startled, which way would he jump?"

"Jump?" echoed Harold.

"Yes."

"Why, into the river, of course. It's just before him. Why do you ask?"

"Oh, nothing; never mind," replied Dick, who disappeared behind the sycamore tree.

In a few moments he was back again, busying himself in helping his brothers to wash the plates in the stream and pack up.

All at once Arthur exclaimed—

"Look at that smoke. Is the rick on fire?"

"Perhaps," answered Dick, coolly. "I have heard of such a thing as spontaneous combustion in hot weather."

"That's no reason why Mr. Smiles should be spontaneously combusted, or whatever you call it," replied Harold.

"He'll find it out presently," said Dick, who was evidently enjoying what he considered the fun.

Harold ran towards the rick, which was already smoking and burning in an alarming manner.

"Hi, sir! look out. The rick's on fire! Hi, hi!" he cried.

Mr. Smiles had sought a passing relief from the stings of the wasps in sleep, but the noise made by Harold effectually roused him.

Looking behind him, he saw fire and smoke; before him was the shining stream.

His determination was taken in a moment.

With a terrified cry, he leaped into the water, and sank like a stone.

When he came to the surface, being a good swimmer, he struck out and reached the shore without difficulty, landing, dripping with water, and presenting a pitiable spectacle.

Meanwhile, Dick, who had only set fire to some loose hay which he found lying about, proceeded to beat out the flames with a pole, and, by dint of dragging the burning mass, by many a poke and shove, away from the rick, he soon extinguished it.

The most amiable of men would have lost his temper under these repeated annoyances.

Mr. Smiles was not naturally irritable, but he rushed upon Dick, and pulled his ear.

"That's one pull for the wasps, and another for the fire," he exclaimed, at each tug. "I'll tell your father, you bad boy, and have you sent to sea."

"Shall you go too?" asked Dick, wriggling himself away, and standing out of reach.

"No; you will be entirely amongst strangers."

"Oh, I don't care so long as you are not one of the party," answered Dick, adding, "Good-bye."

"Where are you going to?" cried Mr. Smiles

"I've had my dinner, and I'm going home. Besides, I should not like to be seen with you in your present state."

"You young rascal!" shouted Mr. Smiles. "Who is to carry the heavy basket and the cider bottle?"

"You must do it between you. I did my share in coming, and would not have shirked it going back if you'd been civil, and not pulled my ears. Perhaps you want to make them as long as your own."

Mr. Smiles was speechless with indignation.

Leaving the tutor and his brothers together to get home with the remains of the picnic as well as they could, Dick walked slowly along the bank of the stream, wishing that he had a line with him to tempt the speckled trout he saw leaping after the flies, and splashing in the sparkling water.

He had not gone more than half-a-mile, before he came upon an elderly gentleman, fast asleep under a tree.

His line was in the water, and his rod rested upon a forked stick stuck in the ground.

He had evidently fallen asleep while fishing.

"The governor, by Jove!" exclaimed Dick, recognising his father, who frequently stole an hour or two from his parochial duties to go and fish in the stream.

A can to put fish in, which contained two small perch, was near the rod.

"I'll have a lark with the governor now," said Dick, as he seized it.

Pulling up the line, he tied the can firmly to the hook, casting it into the stream again, when it instantly sank.

He then threw a stone at his father's gouty toes, which woke the old gentleman up.

Rubbing his eyes, he looked around him.

"Been to sleep," he murmured. "Heat of the sun. I suppose. What woke me? Strange pain in my right foot. Cramp, I suppose. Hullo! float under. Got a bite—big fish, I should imagine. Very careless to go to sleep—very."

Getting on his feet, he seized his rod and began to haul in the line, which he did with difficulty, owing to the weight at the end of it.

"Dear me; heavy fish," he said. "Wonder what it is. Something must have bolted the bait. It pulls like a twenty-pound pike. Gently; mustn't break the line. I'll play him a bit. Gently, gently."

He let go the line, and the can rolled down the shelving bottom just as if a fish was running away with it.

Then the old gentleman hauled in again, and again he played his big fish, thinking he was acting with consummate skill.

Thus half-an-hour passed, and he fancied he had exhausted the strength of his large capture.

With a desperate effort he pulled the can on the bank, and looked eagerly at it.

A groan burst from him, which was nearly followed by a naughty exclamation.

But he checked that.

"Some one has played me a trick while I slept," he exclaimed. "I wish I knew who it was."

Dick, who had watched this with much amusement, could restrain his mirth no longer, and burst into a loud roar of laughter.

But he made off without being seen, although his father felt sure he recognised his voice, and put down his disappointment, as usual, to Master Dick.

These pranks were usually followed by a long lecture, for which the culprit cared very little.

The next day being Sunday, Mr. Lightheart had carefully selected his sermon, which was printed and bound in a little book.

The text was taken from the Old Testament, and had reference to the sons of Anak, the argument being that if there were men in those days who were bodily gigantic, in the present age we outdid them in our mental attainments.

Seeing the sermon on his father's library table, Dick looked at it, and, tearing out the front page, substituted for it a page of the history of Jack the Giant Killer.

The trick was not discovered, and the unsuspecting parson got into the pulpit, gave out the text with great solemnity, and proceeded—

"In the early days of the history of this island, there were many great and grim giants, who caused much misery to the people, and it was a great consolation to all when a deliverer arose in Cornwall who, from his prowess, was known as Jack the Giant Killer."

"Eh—what! What is this?" stammered the unhappy clergyman. "I fear, my friends, I have made a mistake."

Here he turned over a few leaves of the sermon.

All was hopeless confusion.

"Yes," he continued; "there will be no sermon this morning," and he proceeded to dismiss the congregation.

It soon got known that Master Dick had been at his tricks again, and many a good laugh was indulged in by the villagers at the rector's expense.

Mr. Lightheart, however, was not to be pacified.

He had been made to look supremely ridiculous in the pulpit.

On Monday morning he said to his wife—

"I am going to walk over to Thorpe Hamlet, my dear."

"Who on earth are you going to see there?" asked Mrs. Lightheart.

"Mr. Deacon, of the school. It's only a two-mile walk, and Dick could go there every morning."

"But I thought you said——"

"That I disapproved of schools. Quite right. Yet, let me ask you, what we are to do with such a boy? There is Mr. Smiles laid up with a bad cold through his ducking, and his face not fit to be seen through wasp stings, and I the laughing-stock of the whole parish. The boys call me Jack the Giant Killer in the streets. It's a nickname that will stick to me all my life. I know they'll call me the Giant Killer or Old Jack, or something of that sort to the day of my death."

"Very well, dear. Go and see what you can do. I think I'd let him go a voyage; that might tame him," replied Mrs. Lightheart.

"I don't like the sea. Sailors are desperately wicked. That shall be a last resource."

So Mr. Lightheart walked over to Thorpe Hamlet, to see Mr. Deacon.

CHAPTER II.

FURTHER VEXATIONS.

DICK had long wished to pay off an old score he had against Miss Bodmin, his sisters' governess, who, on one occasion, had detected him in the midst of one of his misdeeds, and straightway informed against him.

He disliked her, too, for the severe way in which she punished his favourite sister, Emily, keeping her in, time after time, and making her learn more geography in a month than she would ever have use for in a lifetime.

Getting hold of Emily, he said—

"I want you to imitate Miss Bodmin's handwriting, and write a letter to Mr. Smiles, asking him to meet her under the cedar tree on the lawn at dusk this evening. Say she has worked hard, and saved up some money, and Smiles might do worse than listen to the voice of affection. If you write this, Emmy, I'll imitate Smiles's hand, and entreat her to

keep the same appointment, and when they're together, I'll go and tell mamma. It will be such fun, and they will look such fools."

"Capital!" exclaimed Emily. "Perhaps she'll have to leave."

"I shouldn't wonder."

"How glad I should be to get rid of old Bodmin," said Emily. "I'll write the note. You go and write ours, and come to me in half-an-hour."

The conspiracy prospered very well.

Mr. Smiles received a letter, which took him considerably by surprise, but he resolved to keep the appointment asked for, and see how much money the governess had saved.

Miss Bodmin, on her part, was ravished with delight at being asked to meet Mr. Smiles, who declared that he could no longer remain silent. If he did not give utterance to the promptings of love, his overcharged heart would break.

At dusk two figures stole on to the lawn, and disappeared in the shadow of the cedar tree.

They were Mr. Smiles and Miss Bodmin.

At the same moment Dick, leading his mother by the hand, hid behind a laurel bush, where they could hear what passed.

"A very pretty flirtation," muttered Mrs. Lightheart. "I must have been blind not to have seen what was going on. Nice people to be entrusted with the care and education of children."

"Dear Miss Bodmin," exclaimed Mr. Smiles. "How can I thank you for this proof of your esteem?"

"Is it possible," she murmured, softly, "that we can have lived so long in the same house without suspecting that we were dear to each other?"

"Ah, I have worked, but I have not saved," said the practical Smiles.

"Nor I. My slender stipend has gone to support an aged mother," answered Miss Bodmin.

"What, no money!" cried the astonished and mercenary tutor.

"Not a farthing; but I can work."

"This is a misrepresentation; but no matter, I am warned in time," continued Mr. Smiles.

"What is lucre to hearts that love? Oh, that letter of yours! I shall wear it ever next my heart."

Mrs. Lightheart rushed forward.

"I can bear no more of this," she cried. "The two simpletons!" adding—

"Miss Bodmin, I am ashamed of you; at your age you ought to know better. And as for you, Mr. Smiles, I can only say that this clandestine love-making is not in any way creditable to you."

"She wrote to me, ma'am," said Smiles.

"It's false! He wrote to me," said Miss Bodmin.

"I have her letter."

"I have his."

"You need not quarrel over the matter. Go to the house, if you please. I will speak to you, Miss Bodmin, in your own room," said Mrs. Lightheart.

Thus ordered, they went away, and it was not for some hours that it was discovered how they had been hoaxed.

When all was explained, they had a hearty laugh, and Dick, as usual, came in for the abuse of all parties.

That evening the governess retired to rest early, to indulge in a good silent cry, as the best means of giving vent to her vexation.

Scarcely had she entered her room, when she beheld a shadowy figure enveloped in white garments, having great staring eyes, as red as fire.

Uttering a series of shrieks, she fell forward insensible.

Her fall caused the apparition to tumble over.

It was a long pole enveloped in a sheet, with a hollow turnip for a head, in which burnt a piece of candle.

The latter fell against the valence of the bed, which quickly took fire.

Fortunately her cries alarmed those below.

The Rev. Septimus Lightheart, followed by Mr. Smiles, rushed into the room just in time to prevent a serious conflagration.

The water jug and a blanket were brought into use, and the fire extinguished before it could do much mischief.

"Thank goodness we arrived upon the spot," said Mr. Smiles.

"It's that dreadful boy again. He'll do something desperate some of these fine days," said Mrs. Lightheart, who busied herself in attending to the inanimate governess.

"He shall go away," said Mr. Lightheart; "and this very night I will see what virtue there is in a sound caning."

"No," cried his wife; "we have always been opposed to corporal punishment. Try moral suasion."

"I have tried it," answered the parson, in a rage, "and what good has it done?"

"Sleep over it, dear. You should never correct a child while in a passion."

Mr. Lightheart said nothing, but went into the room in which the boy slept.

Dick had just crept into bed, after enjoying the fruit of his practical joke, and pretended to be fast asleep.

"Get up," said his father, shaking him by the arm, and brandishing a riding whip.

Dick trembled, but did not move, whereupon the parson turned down the clothes, and holding the boy down on his face, administered a castigation which made Dick bellow as lustily as a bull.

In a moment his mother was in the room, and snatched the whip from her husband's hand.

"You shall not do it," she exclaimed. "This violence is unmanly. Poor boy!"

"How can you expect him to respect me when there is this deplorable conflict of authority?" said the parson.

"He shall not be hurt," answered Mrs. Lightheart, kissing her boy.

The clergyman retired to his study in a passion, and gave way to most unchristian-like reflections.

That last scene decided him, and the following day he walked over with Dick to Mr. Deacon's school at Thorpe Hamlet.

"Keep him all the week," he said, "and let him come home from Saturday to Monday, if he is good enough to deserve such an indulgence."

"He will soon improve under my parental rule," answered Mr. Deacon. "I have had many unruly and unmanageable boys, but I have contrived to tame them all."

"So much the better," replied Mr. Lightheart.

And he retraced his steps, much pleased at having got rid of his constant tormentor.

During the remainder of that day and the next there was peace at the rectory.

"This is delightful," exclaimed Mrs. Lightheart, after supper, on the evening of the second day.

"Yes," remarked Miss Bodmin, with a vindictive look. "One does not now go about in fear and trembling."

"He cut all my bootlaces before he went," observed Mr. Smiles.

"I am inclined to believe that school is a good place for some boys, but not for all," said the parson.

At that moment the door opened, and in marched Dick.

"Hullo!" cried his father.

"You here, Richard?" said his mother.

"Bless my heart!" exclaimed Mr. Smiles and Miss Bodmin, in chorus.

"Good evening. Glad the supper hasn't been cleared away, because I'm hungry," said Dick, sitting down and preparing to help himself to some cold beef.

His sisters looked frightened, and his brothers grinned.

Dick had told them he didn't mean to stop long at Deacon's.

"If you have run away from your school, sir, you have made a mistake," exclaimed Mr. Lightheart; "I will take you back again, and have you publicly punished, and made an example of."

"I didn't run away," answered Dick.

"What then, sir? Why are you here?"

"Because they wouldn't have me any longer," replied Dick, with his mouth full of beef and bread.

"You have been expelled then?"

"I believe that's what they call it," said Dick, coolly.

"What did you do?" demanded his father.

"Nothing much."

"Tell me."

"Oh, I daresay you will hear all about it in the morning," Dick replied.

"I wish to know."

"I'm too tired to talk to-night; besides, no man is bound to criminate himself."

Neither threats nor persuasions could induce Dick to tell his family anything that night.

So he was allowed to have his supper, and join in family prayers, after which he went to bed as usual with his brothers.

Loud laughter was heard in their dormitory for some time afterwards, and it was supposed that Dick was entertaining Harold and Arthur with an account of his adventures.

The Reverend Septimus Lightheart, however, did not feel at all inclined to laugh.

He lay awake the best part of the night, wondering what his son's future would be, and having a presentiment that he would give him a great deal of trouble before he was much older.

CHAPTER III.

A SHORT STAY

IN his strong advocacy of home rule and home discipline, Mr. Lightheart had forgotten that boys are too much with grown-up persons.

They become little men almost before they are boys, and this makes them self-opinionated, conceited, and wilful.

He began to see that he had made a mistake, and wished he knew how to remedy it.

It was not long before he heard from Mr. Deacon's own lips why Dick's stay had been so short at Thorpe Hamlet school.

From the first moment of his arrival Dick had exercised his ingenuity to discover in what way he could signify his dislike to the new control under which he was placed.

The master's desk was placed at a height of about four feet above the level of the schoolroom floor, and approached by six steps, like a throne.

While playing about in the room, Dick found a loose plank, and, pulling it up, saw that the ground beneath the floor was nearly three feet deep, it having been excavated so far to prevent damp.

He knew that Mr. Deacon ascended his desk every morning at ten o'clock, and, standing up in a particular place, read prayers.

At once he conceived the idea of loosening the supports of the platform on which the master stood, in such a way that he should gradually sink, and fall into the hole which he knew to be underneath.

Accordingly, he got up in the night, went to the schoolroom with a lighted candle, a hammer and a saw, and in an hour or two had cut away the boards and arranged them in such a manner that he felt confident of the success of his scheme.

Mr. Deacon did not suspect anything.

He ascended his desk, as usual, smiling blandly upon his pupils.

The usher advanced and handed him an open Bible, according to custom.

Mr. Deacon took up his usual position in front of his desk.

Suddenly **he began to disappear.**

He grew gradually smaller and smaller.

With frantic efforts he clutched at his desk, but its surface was treacherous and slippery, and it afforded him no material support.

"Help! help!" he cried.

"My dear sir, where *are* you going?" asked the usher, in a tone of mild remonstrance.

Presently Mr. Deacon vanished from the scene altogether.

The usher ascended the steps, and peeped cautiously into the hole.

In the darkness below he was just able to discover his principal, seated upon a heap of shavings.

The boys were about to leave their seats, when the usher, recovering his presence of mind, said—

"Sit where you are. Don't dare, one of you, to move."

Then he leant over the hole, and said—

"Below there, sir."

"Is that you, Mr. Jinks?" inquired Mr. Deacon, in a sepulchral voice.

"It is, sir. What can I have the pleasure of doing for you?"

"I have fallen upon a tender part, and I am in pain," said the principal. "The boards must have been purposely cut, or they would never have given way. I am portly, Mr. Jinks, and I fell heavily. Tenpenny nails, with their points upwards and firmly embedded in the hard earth, are not nice things to fall on, Mr. Jinks."

"Decidedly not, sir," answered the usher.

"Can you get a ladder?" inquired the hollow voice, like one risen from the dead and speaking from the tomb.

"A pair of steps can be easily procured."

"Procure them then, if you please. I am anxious to be liberated from this thraldom."

Mr. Jinks went after a pair of steps, and in a short time Mr. Deacon was enabled to emerge from the dreary vault into which he had been precipitated in such an extraordinary and unexpected manner.

He was very dusty and hot, and looked flurried when he again made his appearance upon what remained sound of the dais.

A glance sufficed to show that a hole had been recently and designedly cut in the planking.

Occasionally he put one hand behind him, as if he was conscious of a painful sensation.

"Boys," he exclaimed, "one of you has been guilty of the commission of a diabolical outrage upon my person. I, your preceptor, am the victim of an infamous practical joke. It is a mercy, a providential mercy, that I did not break my limbs or dislocate my neck. I have had a narrow escape, but that is no reason why I should feel inclined to be merciful to the culprit—the wretched, contemptible culprit! Now I appeal to this individual to give himself up, in order to save the remainder of you boys from condign punishment, for—mark me well—if I don't find out the offender, I will severely punish every boy in the school. Do you understand me?"

The schoolmaster paused and looked around him.

The boys whispered one to another, and appeared much puzzled.

"A boy who is wicked enough to invent such a pitfall as that into which I have unhappily fallen is, I am convinced, too much of a coward to own his misdeed," Mr. Deacon continued.

At this Dick Lightheart rose up in his place.

Every eye was fixed on him.

"I never was afraid to own my share in anything," he exclaimed, "and I fully admit that I did what you are complaining of."

"You, Lightheart?" exclaimed Mr. Deacon.

"I, sir."

"Alone?"

"Quite alone."

"You have no accomplice?"

"None whatever," replied Dick.

"This takes me by surprise. I fear I shall have to expel you, as an example to the other boys; but I will do nothing hastily. Mr. Jinks, you will be good

enough to conduct the business of the school this morning without me. I am too much shaken to do anything myself. I must retire to my study, and consult a physician. Before nightfall I will deliver my decision with regard to the misguided and vicious boy."

With this speech he withdrew, and Dick was left to his own reflections.

Mr. Deacon did not make his appearance again until the evening, when Dick was told that in the morning he would be ignominiously expelled with all the disgrace attendant upon the solemn ceremony of expulsion.

But Dick did not see why he should wait for that; and finding the door unlocked, quietly walked out, and appeared at the rectory, as we have related.

For some days his father preached to him, his mother talked to and entreated him, while Mr. Smiles and Miss Bodmin told him stories of celebrated criminals who all had been bad boys.

The end of it was that Mr. Lightheart went to Brighton.

There he had an interview with Professor Simcox, of Harrow House, Kemp Town.

This gentleman had established a school on principles of his own.

He believed in corporal punishment amongst other things, and did not put faith in expulsion.

"I will make something of this scapegrace of yours, Mr. Lightheart," he exclaimed; "and I shall be glad of the opportunity of testing my principles and method upon such an unruly subject, but you must leave him entirely to me."

"Entirely," answered the parson.

"If I am compelled to whip him, you must not listen to his complaints, and if he escapes my vigilance and runs away, you must send him back again."

All which Mr. Lightheart promised faithfully to do.

On his return to the rectory, the parson said to his wife—

"My dear, get Dick's box ready. I flatter myself I have found a school which will do for him, though I have had to sacrifice all the principles upon which I have hitherto trained him."

"When does he go?" asked Mrs. Lightheart, acknowledging to herself that it was impossible to keep him at home.

"When you like. Say to-morrow. I will accompany him myself."

The announcement being made to Dick, he smiled, and did not seem in the least alarmed at the prospect before him.

When he was asleep at night, Mrs. Lightheart stole into the room, and kissing him tenderly, let a tear fall upon his face, murmuring—

"My poor boy, I will pray that you may meet with as much kindness among strangers as you have in your own home."

CHAPTER IV.

THE SCHOOL AT KEMP TOWN.

IT was difficult to know why Simcox called himself a professor.

Being a great believer in the art of telling a boy's character from the bumps on his head, perhaps he may be called a professor of phrenology.

Once his usher, Mr. Snarley, hit a boy on the head with a ruler.

Mr. Simcox passed by and said, "Come here, boy. It seems to me that you have a new bump of unusual development," and retired disgusted when he found it was the result of the ruler and not of nature.

Mr. Simcox was a little man; short, stout, and fussy, appearing always in danger of apoplexy.

He had a great idea of his own importance, and was proud of his position of schoolmaster.

In early life he had married his cook, an amiable but vulgar woman, who did not appreciate the letter H at its full value.

Her knowledge, however, of what ought to be done in the kitchen was of great use to the boys, who had to thank her for many a savoury dish, and through her care and management, they had plenty of good substantial food.

Mr. Simcox employed a master to come in and teach Latin and Greek twice a week.

He confined his efforts to preserving discipline and teaching English, while Mr. Snarley, the usher, attended to mathematics and managed the school generally, during study and recreation.

A tall, thin, spiteful-looking man was Mr. Snarley.

The boys dreaded as much as they hated him, for a more persistent tyrant never lived.

When Dick arrived, he found thirty boys inmates of the school at Kemp Town.

They all seemed cowed and crushed, wanting life and energy, which was one of the admirable results of Mr. Simcox's discipline.

"I shall have to wake them up a little," Dick thought.

There were only a few boys bigger than himself, and as he was naturally quick and had been well taught at home, he was put in the second class, the head of which was named Messiter.

After reading a lesson, the boys in each class were asked questions bearing upon it, and those who answered correctly were passed up over those who failed to do so.

On the second day of his stay at the school, Dick took the third place, only having Messiter and Fowler above him.

Mr. Simcox had been into his private room in the evening of the second day, and said, "Sit down, Lightheart. Since your father left you here yesterday, I have heard a good report of you. That is right. You must retrieve your character during the time you are with me."

"I did not know that I had lost it, sir," said Dick.

"Ah! well. We will not go into bygones. What you did before you came here does not concern me, though I know more about you than you think I do, possibly. Remember that I am not to be trifled with. Go on as you have commenced, and you will return home at Christmas laden with prizes, and bearing with you the commendation of your pastors and masters, as well as the esteem of your companions. Take this piece of cake and go and have your supper."

Dick thanked him and returned to the schoolroom, where the boys were preparing their lessons for the next day.

"Well," said Messiter, "what did he say?"

"Buttered me awfully," answered Dick with his mouth full of cake.

Mr. Snarley, who was reading a novel borrowed from a circulating library, and had just become much interested in the details of a double suicide, looked up.

"No talking there," he exclaimed.

"Say it was Smiff," whispered Messiter.

Smiff was the nickname of a half silly boy, whose real name was Smith.

Owing to some impediment in his speech he called himself Smiff, and if a scapegoat was wanted for anything, the boys always declared that Smiff had done it.

In fact Smiff was to the school what the cat is to a lodging-house.

"Please, sir, it was Smiff," exclaimed Dick.

Mr. Snarley put down his book, and coming up to Dick, said, with a deep frown—

"Why do you tell me such a falsehood?"

Dick grew red in the face, and did not know what to answer.

Mr. Snarley repeated his question.

"I only did it in fun, sir," Dick said.

"Then that will teach you not to indulge in such doubtful fun again!" exclaimed Mr. Snarley, giving him a stinging box on the ear, which knocked him off the form on which he had been sitting on to the floor.

For a moment Dick was stupefied, but when he recovered, he rushed at Mr. Snarley and kicked him violently on the shins.

"That will teach *you* not to hit me in that cowardly way again!" he cried.

It was the first time that he had ever been struck in such a manner.

"Why," he continued, "my father never did such a thing, and you shan't."

"Oh!" said Mr. Snarley, while the tears came into his eyes, "he has kicked me in a sore place, just where I fell down on the beach the other day. But I'll pay him out. Hold him tight, you boys in the first form; hold him for me!"

Such was the discipline amongst the boys at Harrow House that the six in the first form got up directly, and seizing Dick, held him down on the ground in spite of his struggles.

Mr. Snarley had lost no time in going to his desk, in which was a peculiar-looking garment of a yellow colour.

This was a straight waistcoat.

Once Mr. Snarley had been a keeper in a lunatic asylum, and he had brought this instrument of torture away with him.

Professor Simcox approved of its use, and the boys knew what was coming the moment they saw Mr. Snarley go to his desk.

In a very short while Dick was helplessly clothed in this thing, which rendered him perfectly powerless, as he could not use his hands.

"You'll kick me again, will you?" asked the usher, boxing first one ear and then the other.

Dick was no sooner made by the blows to sway on one side than he was knocked up again on the other.

"I think you're a great coward," he gasped.

"Silence, sir, and beg my pardon!" exclaimed Mr. Snarley.

Much against his will, Dick was obliged to do so, when he was seated on a chair in the corner with his face to the wall, remaining there till supper time, when he was turned round to see the other boys eat, though allowed none himself.

He was glad when he got into his bedroom, for this sort of thing was so different to anything he had been accustomed to that he felt low and wretched.

Mr. Simcox was obliged to make up beds in the different rooms as he could, and all the large rooms being occupied, he had put Dick in a double-bedded room on the ground floor with Messiter.

They were by themselves, and after Mr. Snarley had seen the candles put out, they did not fear any interruption.

To occupy the same bedroom together is always enough to make two boys friends.

It was very nearly the only chance of unrestrained conversation they had.

"I don't like this place," said Dick, when they were alone.

"Mind what you say," observed Messiter.

"Why?"

"Because Snarley has a way of listening."

"At the keyhole?"

"Yes. You don't know who is a spy and who isn't here."

"What must one do then? Mayn't we talk?"

"It is safer to do so in whispers."

"I tell you what. I should run away, if I wasn't afraid of being sent back," continued Dick, in a lower tone.

"You'll get used to it in time. I thought as you do once, but I've got sly," replied Messiter.

"The way in which we're treated would make anyone sly. One can't even get out."

"Yes, you can."

"How?"

"I found out the dodge," said Messiter. "Write home and ask permission to learn gymnastics, and to use the swimming bath at Brill's."

"Do you?"

"Yes; twice a week I go to Mohammed's gymnasium in Castle Square, and three times a week to bathe at Brill's."

"Do all the fellows do it?"

"No. Only about a dozen, and as Snarley can't leave the school, we go together. If we are back at our time, it is all right. We do have a spree sometimes; we can go into the shops and buy what we like. It's—what shall I say?—a gleam of sunshine in a coalhole."

"I'll write to-morrow. Thank you for the hint."

"It's no use being cocky here," Messiter went on. "The professor prides himself upon our obedience. Be sly, and you'll get on.'"

"Yes. That's all very well, but I have always been taught to be straightforward and open," replied Dick.

"Won't do. It's a mistake. Pretend to be good and quiet."

"I'll make that beast Snarley sorry for what he did to-night before long," said Dick, rather vindictively.

Mr. Snarley pretended to be very fond of Dick after this affair, and let him off little punishments occasionally, but Dick was not easily deceived.

Messiter whispered to him—

"You look out for squalls, now Snarley's shamming kind."

"Dry up," answered Dick, with a significant smile. "You needn't teach your grandmother to suck eggs. He won't get a rise out of me."

The usher tried his hardest to be kind.

Taking Dick out for a walk with him, he led him into a pastrycook's, and pointing to the counter, which was covered with all sorts of delicious jam and pastry preparations, said—

"Have what you like, Lightheart."

"Thank you, sir," replied Dick.

In a few minutes, he had eaten about ten twopenny raspberry and cream tartlets.

"You see I am not such a bad fellow, Lightheart," continued the usher. "It is only my position that makes me appear harsh."

"Yes, sir," answered Dick, with his mouth full.

"Boys must be kept in order. It would not do to let them return to their parents like young savages, would it?"

"No, sir."

Dick now began his fifth cheesecake.

"But come, boy, let us return home."

"There's two and six to pay, sir," exclaimed the shopkeeper.

Mr. Snarley paid it, not without a groan, murmuring—

"There's two and sixpence out of my hard-earned salary gone into his maw. I do hope he will have a pain after it."

After that the usher gave up being kind to Dick, as the part of Judas Iscariot was difficult to play and produced no result.

Mr. Lightheart promptly accorded Dick permission to learn swimming and gymnastics, so that he was able to accompany Messiter and the other boys.

"It will be jolly to be all by oneself," remarked Dick to one of his friends.

"Will it?" exclaimed Mr. Snarley, who happened to overhear the observation. "I shall go with you. Boys ought not to be left to themselves."

Much to Dick's annoyance, Mr. Snarley went with them to Brill's and stood on the side while the boys were bathing.

Dick played about in the water for some time, and suddenly began to splash and kick.

He covered Mr. Snarley with water, and making a dash at his legs, succeeded in pulling him into the bath.

The unfortunate usher fell in head first, and was nearly half a minute before he came up, spluttering and half suffocated.

His hat floated gaily on the surface until a boy carried it under and tore it to pieces.

"You young rascal!" cried Mr. Snarley, whose voice was drowned by the roar of laughter that came from all sides of the bath.

He presented a most ludicrous appearance as he stood dripping like a waterfall, and shaking his fist at Dick.

"I don't know what came over me, sir. I thought I was drowning," said Dick.

"I'll drown you, you vagabond!" exclaimed the usher.

"I'm the son of a gentleman," answered Dick, "and I'll write home to my father if you call me names."

"Very well, my young gentleman, it will be my turn next."

"Hadn't you better go home, sir? You might catch cold," said Dick.

Mr. Snarley shook with rage.

"I'm well again now, sir; don't stop on my account. It was only a passing fit, or something of that sort. Have a cab, sir?"

All this time Dick kept at a respectable distance from the usher, who would certainly have beaten him had he been able to reach him.

Presently he left the swimming bath to go home and change his clothes.

The boys crowded round Dick and applauded him for what he had done.

"I couldn't help it. He looked so tempting," said Dick.

"He'll never forgive you for it, or for chaffing him," exclaimed Fowler.

"I vote we all have fits like Lightheart; and he won't be so fond of coming with us wherever we go," said Messiter.

"I'll have him again before long," remarked Dick, quietly.

As they walked home they passed a shop where birds and other live stock were sold.

"Hold hard," said Dick, to Messiter. "I'm going to buy something."

He went into the shop and was gone about a minute.

When he rejoined Messiter, his handkerchief was hanging out of his pocket.

"What have you got?" asked Messiter.

"Wait a bit and you'll see. It's something for Snarley," answered Dick, with a merry twinkle in his eyes.

There was an hour's school before dinner, and Dick took his accustomed place.

Mr. Snarley had changed his clothes, and looked very pale.

Dick cracked a nut.

"Will you have some?" he exclaimed, addressing his nearest classmate.

Mr. Snarley heard the crack, and advanced at the double.

"Who's eating in school?" said he.

No one answered.

"It's you, Lightheart. You're eating nuts," continued the usher, with the air of a man who says to himself, "Now I've got him."

"No, sir; I'm not," replied Dick.

"How dare you say so, when I see the shell in your hands?"

"It was only one nut, sir, and that's not nuts," Dick exclaimed.

"That is a quibble. I believe you've got a pocket full. Look at your right-hand trousers pocket. It is distended with something. Empty it this instant. I shall report you to Mr. Simcox."

"What for?"

"You'll see what for. Empty your pocket."

"I'd rather not, sir."

"Why?"

"I'm afraid."

All the boys began to titter, except those who were too much alarmed lest they should be noticed.

But everyone was pleased.

Dick was beginning to wake them up, as he said he would.

"Do as I tell you!" exclaimed Mr. Snarley.

"You may, sir, if you like."

"Very well; stand up. Why, your pocket is bloated with nuts, as I suspected."

"Take care, sir," said Dick.

"Of what?"

"Mind he doesn't bite."

"Bite! what nonsense. Do you think I am to be made a butt of by you? Do you want to be considered the privileged buffoon of the school? If you do, you will have to pay dearly for it, I can tell you, if you make your jokes at my expense."

Dick turned his left side to Mr. Snarley, who pulled out the handkerchief.

Then he plunged his hand in.

Expectation was at its height.

Suddenly, and with a sharp cry of pain, he withdrew his hand, which was dripping with blood.

"You've done this on purpose! You put a live thing in your pocket," he exclaimed, furiously.

"I told you to mind it did not bite, sir," said Dick, "and I did not know it was against the rules of the school to keep animals. If I like to put a pet in my pocket, that is my look-out."

Mr. Snarley could not deny to himself that he was in the wrong.

"Very well; we shall see. What animal is it?" he said.

"Only a ferret, sir."

"A ferret!"

"There are rats in my bedroom. I heard one outside the door near the keyhole the other night."

Messiter was here seized with such a violent fit of coughing that some one had to slap him on the back to prevent him from choking.

"Go out into the yard and put the creature in some place of safety," exclaimed Mr. Snarley.

Dick departed, and the usher, binding some plaister round his injured finger, went on with the morning's work.

In the evening Mr. Snarley often enjoyed the luxury of a cigar with the professor.

During these hours of idleness they compared notes, and talked over the business of the school.

"I wish," the usher said, "that we could do something to check the mischievous propensities of that new boy, Lightheart."

"What has he done?" asked the professor.

Mr. Snarley told him, concluding—

"He tried to drown me at Brill's, and I have a strong suspicion that he bought that ferret to bite me."

"For neither of which things can I justly punish him."

"I don't say you can, sir; but it is hard for me to have to put up with it."

"So it is. You'll catch him tripping before long, and I will cane him within an inch of his life. I had his character from his father," said Mr. Simcox.

"Some boys don't care for caning," remarked Mr. Snarley.

"They may pretend they don't, but in my opinion the effects of a caning are more lasting than those of the birch. A good caning must make itself felt for days afterwards, and if it does not affect him, we will put him in our black hole on bread and water for twenty-four hours. We've tamed a few unruly spirits by that means, Snarley."

"Yes, sir, we have, and that will be the thing for this Lightheart."

All at once a shower of sparks came into the room through the keyhole, amidst a great fizzing and smoke.

"Good Heaven, what's that?" cried Mr. Simcox.

"Someone's stuck a lighted squib in the keyhole," answered Mr. Snarley, darting out.

At the end of the passage he heard a scuffling.

In a moment he was lending his valuable aid to Mrs. Simcox, who had hold of a boy in his night shirt.

"Who is it, ma'am?" cried Mr. Snarley.

"I don't know. The young Turk knocked the candle out of my hand, but I collared 'old of him, thinking he was up to some mischief."

"Quite right, ma'am. It is lucky you were coming this way. Give him to me."

The usher gripped hold of the lad tightly, and dragged him to the light.

"Don't scuff him too 'ard," said Mrs. Simcox.

"Never fear, ma'am."

He took him to the study, followed by Mrs. Simcox.

"Have you got him?" asked the professor.

"Fast, sir."

"That's right; let's have a look at him. Who is he?"

Mr. Snarley flung the boy's face round full to the gaslight.

"Lightheart," exclaimed Mr. Simcox.

It was Dick, who was caught at last.

DICK LIGHTHEART; OR, THE SCAPEGRACE OF THE SCHOOL.

"'I'LL DROWN YOU, YOU VAGABOND!' EXCLAIMED THE USHER."

CHAPTER V.

CAUGHT AT LAST.

"SO, sir, it is you, is it?" exclaimed Mr. Simcox, regarding Dick with a stern look, not unmixed with triumph.

"I thought as much," remarked Mr. Snarley, whose face glowed with pleasure.

He would rather that Dick should have been captured than any other boy in the school.

"I'm in for it," thought Dick. "I shall catch it; but there's one comfort, they can't kill me."

"Dear me!" said Mrs. Simcox; "who'd ha' thought it? Hif I'd been hasked, I should 'ave said that Lightheart 'adn't got it in 'im."

"Not got it in him!" repeated the professor, indignantly. "Why, he's the very imp of mischief himself. It's his character. We had it with him from his own father. He's one of the unruly ones, and was sent here to be tamed."

"I'm sure I don't like to see a boy beat," replied Mrs. Simcox. "But if that's his character, and such is his wicked nature, why, I must be one of the first to say, give 'im all he deserves. Fancy putting fireworks through the keyhole! Himp's just the word for 'im. I'd himp him."

"Leave him to me, my dear. Are you master of this school, or am I?" exclaimed the professor, who did not like his wife's interference.

"Hoh!" cried Mrs. Simcox, who was not in a yielding mood, "hif I'm to 'ave my nose snapped off in that way, I'd better go."

"Go, madam, at your pleasure," answered the professor.

Mrs. Simcox sank into a chair and put her feet firmly on the floor, as if she meant to intimate that she had taken root, and nothing but brute force should move her.

Taking no further notice of her, the professor pulled one of Dick's ears so severely that he winced under the pain.

"What do you mean, sir, by such behaviour?" exclaimed the professor. "Do you think it is seemly to dare to put fireworks in your master's keyhole?"

"Only a squib, sir," said Dick, humbly.

"Only a squib! Do you know that people have had their eyes put out with squibs?"

"Indeed, sir!" said Dick, as if he was highly interested in this important fact.

"My wife, with the rashness of her sex, has urged me to punish you, and you deserve punishment."

"Yes, sir," replied Dick, trembling in his shirt.

"I am glad to see you penitent. Where there is shame there may be reformation. You may have heard that I am severe, but I know how to temper justice with mercy. It depends upon yourself entirely whether you become acquainted with the means I have at my disposal for conquering bad boys. At present you shall not say that I have erred on the side of severity. This is your first fault."

"Not exactly, sir," said Mr. Snarley, who saw the offender slipping from his grasp.

"Do not interrupt me, if you please, Mr. Snarley. I believe I am master here."

The professor looked round with the air of a king.

No one contradicted him.

"Very well," he continued, "I say it is the first fault of this boy which has come directly under my notice, and I shall let him off with a warning."

A groan of intense disappointment broke from the usher.

"Did you speak?" asked the professor.

"No, sir," answered Mr. Snarley.

"Very good. Lightheart, you will return to your dormitory, and thank your lucky stars that you have escaped a deserved caning; another time you will not find me so merciful. Let this be a warning to you. No more pranks in this house, or you'll regret it."

He released his hold of Dick's ear, and that young gentleman ran away, congratulating himself upon the "close shave" he had had.

Messiter had been waiting for his return in the greatest anxiety.

"Did they nail you ?" he asked.

"Yes. But the governor was in a good humour and I got off, as it was my first fault."

"That's spiffing," said Messiter. "I thought you were in for a good leathering, and I expected every moment to hear your sweet voice crying out, 'Oh! please don't, sir. No more, sir. I won't do it again, sir. Let me off this time, sir. Oh! sir! Oh! don't, please, don't.'"

"Thank you," said Dick, dryly. "You seem to know all about it."

"I've had a taste of it in my time."

answered Messiter, "and I find that the more you holloa, the more they lamm into you."

"I should sing out as if they were murdering me," replied Dick, "and I think they would leave off to get rid of my noise."

"You'll have a chance of trying the experiment before long, if you go on as you have begun," replied Messiter, with a grin.

"All right, we shall see by and bye. I'm off to sleep," Dick said, turning over on his pillow.

In five minutes the boys were asleep such is the elasticity of youthful nature.

CHAPTER VI.

OUT IN THE FIELDS.

THE quarter glided on, and, for a wonder, Dick Lightheart kept out of mischief.

Perhaps his busy brain was plotting something new, but at any rate, he showed no sign of it.

"See the effect of my discipline," said Mr. Simcox. "I am positive that, when a boy is not hardened, more may be done by kindness and persuasion than by flogging."

Mr. Snarley shook his head, as if he did not quite agree with the professor.

The boys used to play in a meadow at the back of the house in Kemp Town, which was tolerably large, and occupied by three or four schools, who all paid a small sum for the privilege, each using a particular corner.

In the autumn hockey or football were the games in vogue.

The Harrow House boys played hockey sometimes and at others football, preferring hockey, for which they had long, stout sticks, with curved handles.

Mr. Snarley did not often join the boys in their sports.

There was nothing congenial between him and them.

While they played he usually read a book, or indulged in a pipe in some quiet corner.

One day the Harrow House boys went as usual to the field to play at hockey.

Mr. Snarley condescended to play with

them for a short time, but Dick contrived to hit him on the shins with his stick and send him away limping, begging his pardon loudly, and protesting that it was the purest accident in the world, when all the time he had done it on purpose.

"Getting tired of the game ?" Dick said to Messiter, who was his invariable companion. "Let's stroll about. I've had enough of this."

"So have I," replied Messiter.

"I can see Rumcovey over there, selling things to Ginx's," continued Dick.

"So can I. Have you any tin ? We'll have some tarts."

"I've got a bob," answered Dick.

They walked towards another part of the field where the Reverend Mr. Ginx's boys, a rival school in the neighbourhood, were playing.

Rumcovey was a Jew, who carried about with him a tin case with a door to it, and three shelves inside, on which rested some very decent pastry.

And this he sold to the different schoolboys whom he found out playing, or stood on the Parade and took his chance of custom.

He was tall and thin, and sallow as to his complexion, and had corkscrew ringlets very highly greased, and spoke with the peculiar intonation of the sons of Israel.

When they came up to him, Dick said—

"I say, our tutor wants some jam tarts. He's taken rather bad, and you're to go to him with sixpenn'orth. Leave your tin here."

"Yes, ma young shentleman," answered Levey Rumcovey; "yes, ma goot poy, but who ish to mind it?"

"I will. You know me," answered Dick.

"Vell, I don't like to keep a shentleman a-waitin', and I don't see vat harm you can do, ma poy, as I lock up my little tin of cakesh. So I vill go to your usher, and take sixpenn'orth wid me."

Accordingly Rumcovey took out some tarts and locked up his tin case, which he placed on the ground.

Dick pointed out a part of the field in which he knew Mr. Snarley was lying down, and the Jew set off at a run.

"I think I've got a key that will open that lock," said Dick.

"Have you?" exclaimed Messiter delightedly. "Now, then, for a lark."

Dick took out a small bunch of keys which he happened to have in his pocket, and tried the lock.

After one or two attempts the key turned in the lock.

"Hurrah!" he said.

"Does it fit?" asked Messiter.

"Beautifully."

The door came open.

"I say, you *are* a fellow!" cried Messiter, lost in admiration.

"Tuck in, and look sharp," said Dick, himself setting the example.

Levey Rumcovey happened to have done a good business that day, and there were not more than a couple of dozen tartlets in his case.

These, as a matter of course, quickly disappeared before the united exertions of the boys.

"Now fill it up with stones," said Dick.

Messiter took the hint, and shortly the shelves were lined with stones picked up from the field.

Presently the Jew came back, looking very irate.

"The shentleman did not vant any tarts. You shall not play me any more tricks, ma poys!" he said.

Just at this moment Ginx's boys left off playing and crowded round the pieman, some to buy his pastry, and others to drink the gingerbeer which he carried in a basket.

"Plenty of tarts to-day, sir," Rumcovey answered an intending customer. "Everything of the very besht."

He unlocked his case, and drew out first one tin and then another.

"Why s'help me never!" he cried in dismay. "Vat is thish? My tarts have turned into stonesh!"

"It's Simcox's boys," exclaimed the captain of Ginx's; "I saw two of them here just now. Where are they? Pound into them. Give it them, the brutes. We'll teach them to steal your tarts, Levey."

Dick and Messiter were standing by, enjoying the effects of the joke.

It was too late to run, and, putting a good face on the matter, Dick went up to the pieman, and said—

"I did take your tarts. What are they worth? I am willing to pay for them."

"Ah!" replied Rumcovey, "I always shaid that Mr. Shimcox's boys were the shoul of honour. Give me five shillingsh, sir, and we'll cry a go. They're worth more, but I'll take that."

It was nearly all the money Dick had with him, but he freely gave it the Jew, considering that he really owed it him.

"Are you satisfied?" he asked.

Levey Rumcovey expressed himself highly so.

Then Dick turned round to Jackson, the captain of Ginx's, and said—

"I think you spoke to me just now."

"Well, what then?" answered the captain of Ginx's.

"You said something about stealing."

"So it was stealing."

"Do you feel inclined to apologise?"

"Certainly not," answered Jackson, in a decided tone.

"Oh! you don't? Take that, then."

As he spoke, Dick hit at him straight from the shoulder.

Jackson sprang back, and the blow grazed his forehead.

In an instant they were at it hammer and tongs, Jackson having the advantage in being older and taller, but Dick was heavier, and his muscular frame made him look as if he could last.

Messiter was much alarmed.

He did not see the first blow struck,

and his impression was that Dick was being ill-treated by the whole of Ginx's.

Thinking that he would best serve his friend by apprising Simcox's boys of what was taking place, he started off for that purpose, knowing that his single arm would be of little use against thirty or more opponents.

Simcox's hated Ginx's.

There was a feud of long standing between them, and it was reported that the last time they encountered one another in battle array, Simcox's got the worst of it, so that many of the Simcoxians burned for revenge, which the Ginxites were not at all slow to allow them to try to take.

"I say, you fellows," exclaimed Messiter, arriving out of breath, "Ginx's are half killing Lightheart."

"Are they?" said Fowler. "Let's rescue him."

"Rescue! Rescue!" cried a dozen boys, in a breath.

As if with one accord, they ran quickly, sticks in hand, to the other part of the field, just as in days of old the stalwart shopboys of London answered to the cry of "'Prentices! 'prentices! Clubs, clubs!"

In the meantime, the fight had gone in Dick's favour.

Jackson had been knocked down twice, and to do Ginx's boys justice, they had made a ring, and looked on to see fair play.

Just as Fowler and the others arrived, Jackson had fallen for the third time, and Dick was standing over his prostrate foe, with a bleeding nose, and an eye beginning to puff and blacken.

"Has he had enough of it?" exclaimed Dick.

"If he can't come to time, I'm game to fight the lot of you, one down and the other come on."

"Now, then," suddenly cried Fowler, in the rear. "Go in and win, lads. Give it the cowardly brutes hot and strong."

"Wire in, wire in," said Messiter, dealing one of Ginx's a blow on the back of the head with his hockey stick, which sent him sprawling.

Directly all was confusion.

The Ginxites defended themselves as well as they could, and a small Donnybrook Fair commenced.

"There, darlint. Just taste this sprig of shillelagh," said O'Shaughnessy, an Irish boy at Simcox's. "By the powers, an' we'll see which is the thickest, your head or a yard of good blackthorn."

The fight waged furiously for some time, but the Ginxites, taken by surprise, were no match for their opponents, who in about five minutes, drove them in an ignominious rout from the field, carrying with them some broken heads, and leaving their badly wounded on the ground.

"Hurrah!" exclaimed Fowler, "we've licked them. That will teach them to ill-treat one of our fellows again."

Mr. Snarley had arrived on the scene of action, and was much scandalized by what had taken place.

He was met by Ginx's usher, a Mr. Cooper, who said—

"What is the meaning of this disgraceful scene, sir?"

"Just what I was about to ask you, sir," answered Snarley.

"Do you see how my boys have been treated?"

"I have seen nothing."

"But I have."

"Why didn't you stop it, then?" said Snarley, with a sneer.

"Because I couldn't, unaided. We were set upon by a gang of ruffians."

"Ruffians in your teeth, sir. I can fight, sir; come on," said Mr. Snarley, growing valiant, doubling his fists, and turning up his coat cuffs.

"I do not fight, sir," answered the rival usher with dignity. "I am not a blackguard."

And turning on his heels, he beat a retreat after his boys, leaving Snarley the master of the field.

Never had Snarley behaved in a manner more calculated to raise him in the esteem of the boys under his control.

They declared that he was a brick, and that he possessed qualities of which they had hitherto been ignorant.

All were loud in his praise as they returned to school, the play hour being now over.

No notice was taken of Dick's black eyes, which was discreetly overlooked.

He was the hero of this adventure, which raised all the Simcoxians very much in their own estimation, and also in that of their antagonists, who in future gave them a wide berth.

CHAPTER VII.

THE BRANDY-BALL MAN.

EVERY boy who has been at school in Brighton knows the brandy-ball man.

That eccentric-looking personage, with a velvet cap and a long tassel, carrying, slung over his shoulders by a strap, a tray containing sweets of a round shape, supposed to be mysteriously concocted of sugar and brandy.

Who can forget his wonderful corkscrew ringlets, and the peculiar intonation of voice with which he sang—

> "Come, buy my fine brandy-balls;
>   To young and old,
>   They're hourly sold,
> Are these fine brandy-balls.
>   Come in a trice;
>   They are so nice—
>   *So* nice—
> And buy my brandy-balls."

One evening Dick had been indulging in this enticing refrain, and he said to Messiter—

"I wonder if we could give Snarley the slip, and get out to buy some brandy-balls."

The boldness of this proposition almost took Messiter's breath away.

"Get out!" he repeated.

"Yes. Why not?"

"Such a thing has never been heard of at Simcox's since it was a school."

"All the more reason why it should be done."

The boys were in the schoolroom, getting up their lessons for the next day.

Mr. Snarley was nodding over a book at the upper end of the room.

Again was heard the refrain—

> "Buy my fine brandy-balls."

"I must have some of them, or else I shan't sleep," continued Dick.

"I should like some," said Messiter, wistfully.

"Are you game to come with me?" asked Dick.

"Ye-es," said Messiter, half afraid.

"All right. I'll slip out first, and wait for you in the passage. We can get out of the front door, and I daresay one of the servants will let us in at the area."

"The cook's a stunner; she won't split."

"That will do, then. If I can once get out, I have no doubt I can get in again. Come quietly, and Snarley will not be any the wiser."

Messiter nodded.

Dick got up, and managed to leave the room without attracting attention.

Then he stood in the passage with a beating heart, waiting for his companion.

Presently Messiter joined him.

"Quick," said Dick, under his breath.

At this moment Mr. Snarley looked up.

"Who is that just gone out of the room?" he asked.

"Messiter, sir," said some one.

"And Lightheart, sir," said another boy.

"Oh!" remarked Mr. Snarley, scenting mischief afar off.

He rose from his seat, put down his book, and went out of the room.

As he reached the passage he heard the street door slam.

"Hullo!" he muttered, "can those boys have gone out?"

Taking down his hat, which hung on a peg, he went into the street.

Under a lamp were two boys talking to the brandy-ball man, who was serving them with his wares.

"My boys," said Mr. Snarley. "Here, I say, what is the meaning of this?" he exclaimed, in a louder tone.

Dick heard him.

"Run," he whispered to Messiter. "Snarley's twigged us. Cut along."

"Where to?" inquired Messiter.

"Follow me."

Dick ran along the Parade, closely followed by Messiter, and Mr. Snarley scudded along after them in full chase.

After going some distance, they came to a flight of steps leading to the beach.

"This way," said Dick, hurriedly. "It is dark on the beach, and we shall fog him there."

They darted down the steps at the imminent risk of their necks, but the usher was after them; and as his legs were the longest, he was rapidly gaining on them.

The stars were out and it was a fine night, but there was no moon.

The tide was just on the turn, and the waves plashed mournfully on the beach, retreating with a sullen roar.

"Stop, stop! It will be better for you," cried Snarley.

The boys paid no heed to this admonition.

"I know who you are," he continued, "you, Lightheart, and you, Messiter, do you hear me?"

It was difficult to run on the shifting shingle, and Messiter, slipping down, sprained his ankle slightly.

"I can't run any more," he said.

"Why can't you?" asked Dick.

"I've hurt my foot."

"I won't be caught. Blow that beast Snarley! We should have been in again, and at our desks all right by this time, if it had not been for him," Dick said, with determination.

"Here's a boat. Suppose we get into it?" Messiter suggested.

It was an ordinary rowing boat, fitted with a small mast and a sail.

"Jump in," answered Dick.

Messiter did so.

The beach here was of a shelving nature, and taking advantage of this formation, Dick, exerting all his strength, pushed the boat down.

It fell at once into deep water and floated.

Giving it one more push, Dick sprang in and sank down in the bottom, where Messiter was already reclining.

Mr. Snarley looked here and there, and was considerably puzzled.

"They were close to me a minute ago," he muttered. "Where on earth can they have got to?"

It never occurred to him that they were in the boat.

"Perhaps they are hiding behind the bathing machines," he muttered again.

Acting upon this idea, he went to a row of machines drawn up on the beach, and carefully ransacked their interiors, looking inside, outside, and under the wheels, consuming more than a quarter of an hour in this agreeable pastime, without, of course, making any discovery.

"They've given me the double and gone home, I should think, hoping to get in before me," he said.

Giving up the search as a bad job, he returned home in the worst of tempers.

"I'll have their jackets dusted for them," he went on savagely.

Mr. Simcox was apprised of what had taken place, and a strict search was made throughout the house for the two runaways.

It was supposed that they would return when they fancied all were asleep, and attempt to get in at some window at the back of the house.

Their absence created no real alarm.

While preparations were being made for their reception, and the punishment to be given them was talked about, the boys were laughing at their escape.

For nearly six minutes they lay immovable at the bottom of the boat.

They thought that Mr. Snarley might see them if they showed a head.

"Have a brandy-ball?" said Dick.

"Have you got some? I hadn't time to take mine, though I paid old Brandy-balls for them," answered Messiter.

Dick gave him one.

"He's gone by this time," said Messiter; "at least I should think so. Take a squint round."

Dick did so.

"By jingo!" he said, with a whistle

"What is it?" asked Messiter.

"We've left the land," answered Dick.

"Left the land!" repeated Messiter, in dismay.

"Yes, and a good way, too, behind us. Look at the lights of the town, and the chain pier lights. We seem to have got away from that."

It was true.

The tide was going out, and it had drawn the boat with it.

"Oh! What shall we do?" said Messiter, inclined to cry.

"Have a brandy-ball," said Dick, coolly.

"Ain't you in a funk?"

"No."

"Why not?"

"I never am," Dick replied, with a laugh.

"You're the coolest fish I ever saw; but perhaps there are oars in the boat, and we can pull her in."

"A good idea."

Dick looked carefully all over the boat, but to his consternation, there was nothing in the shape of an oar to be seen.

"Sold again," he said.

The owner of the boat had withdrawn the oars when he beached her.

"Here's a go!" exclaimed Messiter. "What is to become of us?"

"We shall have an opportunity of enjoying a life on the ocean wave, as the song says."

"Oh, do be serious."

"Shall I sing you 'I'm afloat'?" asked Dick.

"Oh, no. How can you think of singing when we are in such a mess?"

"You won't have a song? Try a brandy-ball then," replied the imperturbable Dick.

His countenance was a trifle graver, however, although he would not allow his companion to see it.

"What a fellow you are! We may be drowned, I tell you! Oh, I wish I hadn't come! I'd give anything to be at school again!" groaned Messiter.

"And get whalloped by Simcox? Thank you. Not for me!—not much!—next week! I'd rather be where I am, ever so much!" answered Dick.

"But think of being drowned."

"That's better than being hanged. It's an easy way of going out of the world."

Messiter was silent.

"I call this lovely," exclaimed Dick. "Look at the beautiful stars, and the sky, and the lights of the town, and see the waves sparkling. It's awfully jolly. If I could smoke, I think I should enjoy a cigar."

"If the beastly boat goes on rolling like this, I shall be sick," said Messiter.

"Try a brandy-ball," replied Dick.

"Hang your brandy-balls! Oh, I do feel so bad."

"If you won't, I will. These brandy-balls are not to be sneezed at. But a little brandy without the balls is the thing for a sea voyage."

As he spoke he ate a brandy-ball, crunching it between his teeth instead of sucking it leisurely, which was a sign that he was not at his ease.

In spite of his levity he knew that the boat was drifting out to sea.

And this, at ten o'clock on a not particularly bright night, was anything but a cheering prospect.

CHAPTER VIII.

DRIVEN OUT TO SEA.

A STIFF breeze was blowing from the shore, and without the aid of oars it was clearly impossible for the boys to regain the land.

Messiter was much alarmed.

He had not the natural courage of his companion, and had never studied to acquire the self-reliance that always stood Dick in good stead.

Lying at the bottom of the boat, he did nothing but cry.

"Come, I say," exclaimed Dick, cheeringly, "don't blub. What's the use of blubbing?"

"I can't help it," sobbed Messiter.

"Suppose you cry all night. Will that bring us back again?"

"No, no."

"Shut up then. If it wasn't dark, I should call it a good spree."

"We've nothing to eat."

"I've got one brandy-ball left," replied Dick.

"You always laugh at things. I wish I were like you," answered Messiter.

"Pull yourself together. Perhaps we shall be picked up by some passing ship."

"And taken to Australia."

"Not likely."

"Or cut to pieces by a steamer."

"That's more probable," answered Dick. "But we must take watch and watch, as the sailors say, and keep a good look-out. I'm going to make the best of it. There ought to be a rudder on board. I shall look for it and ship it."

A few minutes' search showed him what he was in search of, and without much difficulty he attached the rudder to the stern of the boat.

"Can you steer?" asked Messiter.

"Rather. We had a little sailing boat on a lake near the governor's house, and I often used to go out in her. One winter she got swamped, and leaked so ever afterwards that we were obliged to turn her up. It's very easy. If you want to go right, you pull the right string; if left, pull the left, unless you have the ropes crossed, and then it's *vice versa*."

"What is to become of us?" moaned Messiter.

"You are a milksop," said Dick, almost angrily. "We shan't come to much grief, for with the rudder I can keep her head to the wind, and prevent the waves breaking over us, as they seemed inclined to just now. If you were a girl, you couldn't funk more than you do."

"I'll try to be brave. Tell me what to do."

"Catch hold of the tiller. We have no ropes. This piece of wood, I mean. I want to explore the ship. There ought to be a sail somewhere. Here's the mast."

As he spoke he handed the tiller to Messiter, telling him to hold it in a particular way, and seizing the mast, stepped it in the place appointed for it.

In the bows of the boat was a locker, and this he proceeded to open by unfastening the button which kept the door fast.

"Hurrah!" he exclaimed; "here's the sail!"

"What's the good of it?" asked Messiter.

"It will enable us to run over to France."

"To France! Oh, Lord! what nonsense!" groaned Messiter.

"What rot you talk."

"Can't we tack, or something? I don't know what they call it, but there is a way of going against the wind; I have seen sailor fellows do it. Let us tack, Dick, and get back again."

"No, thank you; I am not such a nincompoop as you. I mean to have a spree now, and go to France for a day or two."

"But we have no money."

"Never mind; we'll get some. You've no go in you. I should like to see you turned upon the world to get your own living. Why, you'd be just nowhere—not in the hunt," answered Dick, in a tone of disgust.

"I call it foolhardiness."

"I don't. The Channel is not so very broad here, and we shall be able to make Dieppe with this wind before noon to-morrow. I wish we had some grub."

He dived into the locker again as he spoke, and was half lost to sight for a short time.

When he emerged, he exclaimed—

"This is fizzing."

"What?" asked Messiter.

"There is grub in this locker."

"What have you found?"

"Some sandwiches, half a Bologna sausage, and a small pigeon pie, as well as something which smells very much like ale, if I'm not much mistaken, in a stone jar."

"How do you account for that getting there?"

"I should imagine that some fellows had made arrangements with the owner of this boat to go out fishing in the morning, and they had put away their breakfast over night."

"Very kind of them, I'm sure," said Messiter, partially regaining his spirits at the prospect of a feed.

"Won't they be sold?" said Dick, with a grin.

"Rather."

"What'll you have? Here are all the delicacies of the season. Pigeon pie. It ought to be pigeon by the claws sticking up through the crust. I hope they haven't put too much steak in."

"I'll try a bit."

Dick raked out a knife, and cut his friend a huge hunch of pigeon pie.

Messiter ate this with a keen relish.

"It's better than old Simcox's Dutch cheese," he said.

"I should think it was, by a long chalk, or old Mother Simcox's bread and scrape."

Dick raised the beer bottle to his mouth, and took a hearty draught.

"Have a swig?" he asked, extending it to Messiter.

"Thanks," replied the latter, adding, "I say, this isn't half so bad, is it?"

"Bad! I call it rattling good fun. Peg away. When you've done tucking in, I'll put the sail up, and you'll see how we'll cut along. How is the pie?"

"The pigeon's good, but the crust is rather chunky."

"Never mind; any port in a storm. Hold on tight to the tiller, and keep her well to larboard."

"What's that?"

"Larboard's left, and starboard's right."

Dick knew something about sailing, and soon got the sail up; then he took the tiller from Messiter, and said—

"You have a sleep somewhere. Pitch on the boards with your head in the locker, and you won't feel the wind so much."

Messiter followed his instructions, and was soon asleep.

The night was chilly, though clear and bright.

There was little difficulty in steering, and the little craft rode over the waves splendidly.

Dick had been on the sea before, and was what is called a pretty good sailor; that is, he did not suffer from sea-sickness, but the motion of the boat soon had an effect on his friend.

Messiter woke up feeling very uncomfortable, and made a rush to the side.

"Holloa!" cried Dick, "not going to commit suicide, I hope."

"I'm so ill. I think I shall be sick," replied Messiter.

"Go ahead, then. Feed the fishes. I daresay they won't object," Dick said, with a laugh.

Messiter made no reply for some seconds.

"Oh! I'm so bad; I think I shall die," he said. "It's all very fine for you to chaff. You can stand anything. You've got the best of it."

"I don't know so much about that," Dick replied. "It's jolly cold, and I'm getting sleepy, but if I don't keep a good look-out, we shall capsize, and it will be a case of stump. Here are you, my first mate, knocked into a cocked hat at starting, and all the work falls on me. Have I the best of it?"

Messiter had been very sick, and felt a little better, though his head was light and dizzy.

He crept into the locker again, and for some time Dick heard him groaning and grumbling to himself.

"I shan't take him to sea again," he muttered.

The hours passed slowly.

Dick knew that the Continent lay exactly opposite, and kept the boat in the proper course as well as he was able.

Towards five o'clock he got very drowsy.

He nodded, and his eyes closed.

Suddenly a peculiar sound fell upon his ears.

It was the measured beat of a steamer's engines.

In five minutes more he would have been under her bows.

She must have run him down and cut his boat in two.

"This won't do," he said, waking up.

In a twinkling he put the boat about and ran past the side of a huge outward-bound, having a tonnage of not less than two thousand register.

Her lights were distinctly visible, and he could hear the officers on board giving their orders.

"A narrow shave that. What I call a squeak for it," observed Dick to himself, as he found his little boat tossing in the heaving, hissing water in the wake of the big ship.

He took a pin out of his shirt collar and ran it into the calf of his leg.

"That will wake me up," he said.

Soon day broke, and he watched the sun rise with undisguised interest.

It was a magnificent sight.

"The cruise is worth all the trouble, if only to see that," he remarked.

Then he had his breakfast, some sausage and a draught of beer.

In the daylight there was little danger of being run down, as he could see the numerous ships which studded the expanse of the Channel, ploughing their way to distant lands.

Messiter felt a little better after his night's rest, and volunteered to take the helm.

"No, thank you; my life's precious, and I don't feel inclined to trust it to you," answered Dick.

"But I'll be careful," said Messiter.

"So you say. By Jove, what an object you look."

"What's the matter with me?"

"You look washed out, that's all."

"I don't feel very lively, but my sleep's done me good. I haven't got that beastly feeling of sea-sickness now. Aren't you tired?"

"A little. I'm not made of cast-iron, but I shall hold out till we land, and then I shall knock up.

"I don't mind when I'm between the

sheets in a good hotel, with the prospect of a jolly dinner when I wake up."

"Hotel! I should say the workhouse—that's what I'm looking forward to when we get into some port," said Messiter.

"There are no workhouses in France," answered Dick. "So you needn't fret about that. I shall say that I am a private gentleman's son, come over for a trip. We can enjoy ourselves till the bill comes in, and then I'll tell the landlord to telegraph to my father for the coin."

"Can you speak French?"

"Well enough to be understood, I'll bet. If you're a good boy, you shall have some frogs for dinner. I'll order them for you."

"Frogs?" said Messiter with a shudder.

"Yes; they're the natural food of the country."

"Now you're laughing at me."

"Am I? Wait till we get there," replied Dick.

Towards three o'clock in the afternoon they sighted the French coast, and Dick followed in the wake of some fishing smacks, which he imagined were going into harbour with their cargoes.

Nor was he mistaken.

About six he sailed into smooth water, and brought up his boat at the side of the quay.

Several French sailors and a custom-house official or two came up to him.

"It's a pretty-looking town," observed Messiter.

"What place is this?" asked Dick, in French, not taking any notice of Messiter.

"Dieppe, monsieur," was the reply.

"Thank you. Which is the best hotel?"

"Hotel de Lille et d'Albion, monsieur," some one hastened to say. "It is close by. Shall I take your luggage?"

"I have none. We only ran over for a day or two. Show us the way to the Lille et d'Albion, and I shall be obliged to you; and, I say, who'll mind our yacht?"

"Monsieur's yacht?" answered a custom-house officer; "Pierre will see to that."

"Who's Pierre?"

The officer pointed to a hairy-looking Frenchman, who had a most vile smell about him of stale fish.

Pierre bowed and jabbered away in French, not one word of which Dick could understand.

"All right, old cock; so long as you're honest and won't run away with her, as we did," Dick said, in English.

They were now conducted to the hotel, where English was spoken by the head waiter, who had himself been in England at the time of the first Exhibition.

The boys asked for apartments, and ordered a few oysters and a cup of tea, after which they expressed their determination of going to bed early, as they were fatigued with their voyage.

"I'm as tired as a dog, and shan't want rocking," said Dick.

"I'm sure I ought to be very thankful to you for the way in which you have looked out," remarked Messiter.

"There are no bones broken," answered Dick. "Finish those oysters, and then let's go to sleep."

Scarcely had their heads touched the pillow than they were fast asleep and snoring.

CHAPTER IX.

A STAY AT DIEPPE.

IN the morning the boys awoke like giants refreshed, and descended to the private room they had engaged for breakfast, which was provided in a liberal manner, the table being covered with cold meat, besides fish, etc.

"Fire away," said Dick, sitting down before the tea-urn. "It will be charged for all the same, whether we eat much or little."

"How is it to end?" asked Messiter, who was always timid.

"Oh, the governor or some one will come over and fetch us. I shall telegraph presently."

"I thought you had no money."

"No more I have."

"How can you telegraph without tin? Will they tick?"

"Not much," answered Dick. "I shall send to the landlord and ask him to lend me a nap or two. The telegram will go down in the bill."

"What's a nap?"

"Napoleon. Their sovereign, you know. It's twenty-five francs. They call them naps over here."

"Will he do it?"

"Of course he will."

After breakfast Dick spoke to the waiter, and said—

"I want this message sent by telegraph to my father. Give it to the landlord, and tell him to lend me a couple of napoleons. We came away in a hurry and forgot our purses."

Dick had written out the telegram, which ran thus—

"Hotel de Lille et d'Albion, Dieppe, France. From Dick Lightheart to the Rev. Septimus Lightheart, The Rectory, Ingarstone, near Hayward's Heath, Sussex. Dear father,—We have arrived here in a boat. Will you kindly come and fetch us, and bring some money to pay our hotel bill? By 'we,' I mean my friend Messiter and myself. Will explain all when we meet. Do not be anxious about us. We are well and jolly. Perhaps you had best call on Mr. Simcox. You know I always tumble on my feet."

The waiter bowed and went away, returning in about ten minutes with two pieces of gold on a silver salver, which Dick took up.

"That's plummy," he exclaimed, when they were alone again. "I was pumped out. Only had sixpence half-penny, a knife, an old button, and a bit of slate pencil."

"But you had some brandy-balls," said Messiter, smiling for the first time since they left Brighton.

"Yes, I had forgotten. Have one?"

"Don't mind if I do."

Dick handed his friend the paper containing the brandy-balls, the effort to get which had caused them to run so much risk.

"You see, we couldn't have got on without money," Dick continued. "I have a weakness for a clean shirt, and I am rather limp in the matter of collar, to say nothing of buying a tooth brush, enjoying a bathe in the sea, and having a drive in a fly."

"You're a genius, Dick," exclaimed Messiter, lost in admiration. "You'll get on in the world. I envy you, but I say——"

"What?"

"Shan't we get it when we return home?"

"Hot, I should say, but we shall have the comfort of knowing that we've had our spree, and that's something," Dick answered.

"I've had a welting before now, but I don't mind, if you don't," Messiter said, with a mournful look.

"And I haven't, which perhaps makes me think less of it than I otherwise should, but it's silly to spoil one's pleasure, by thinking of disagreeables before they come. Bother Simcox, let's go out."

They put on their caps and made a few purchases, such as a pair of gloves, shirts, collars, tooth brushes, etc., and going back to the hotel, made themselves tidy, Dick observing that he felt decent, like a Christian.

They then sallied forth again, and had ices, and tarts and cherry brandy, which was a combination of luxuries that made Messiter quite brave.

"I think I should punch Snarley's head, if I saw him walking on the parade," said he.

"Perhaps you'll have the chance," Dick answered. "Snarley may come over with, or instead of the governor."

Messiter's countenance fell again.

"Do you think so?" he asked.

"It would not surprise me."

"After all, Snarley's too big to punch," Messiter answered. "I might run behind and kick him."

It was a charming morning, and the little picturesque French watering-place was crowded with visitors, who disported themselves all over the town.

The boys had a bathe, and declared that it was the pleasantest bathing they ever had, but every now and then they grew grave, for the thoughts of going back to Harrow House, and Mr. Simcox's rage, would intrude upon them, like the death's head at the banquet, though neither of them liked to confess it one to the other.

"How about dinner, Dick?" said Messiter, who was growing hungry.

"I told the waiter we should dine at the table-d'hôte at six—that's the public dinner, you know, at which everybody dines, so if you feel peckish, we must make up with something out of doors. What do you say to a blow out of oysters?"

"Oysters and stout?" said Messiter.

"Yes. Here's a shop. *Huitres*—that's oysters."

Accordingly they went into a shell-fish shop, and had some fine fat native oysters at three francs the dozen.

After which they hired a fly, and drove about for a couple of hours.

To give themselves an appetite for dinner, they took a blow on the pier.

"I should like to astonish the natives," said Dick, "and I think I know how to do it."

"How?" asked Messiter.

"You leave it to me."

"Don't do anything dangerous. I shouldn't like to be locked up."

"Nor I," answered Dick. "I can do it all myself, and you can keep out of it altogether, if you like."

"Oh, no, I won't do that. I can't leave you in the lurch. I'm not such a selfish, cowardly beast as all that comes to. Don't think that of me."

Seeing that Messiter was really hurt, Dick replied—

"I didn't mean it. You're a trump, Bob, and I have always said so, only you want bringing out. Your education isn't complete yet."

"It soon will be if I am much with you," answered Messiter, laughing.

Dick did not reveal his plan to his companion, though he several times begged him to do so.

He made some mysterious purchases at a chemist's, and when at the hotel, he mixed several powders together, putting all into a large paper bag when he had finished his preparations.

"You're not going to blow the town up, are you?" said Messiter.

"No, you donkey. Not likely," answered Dick.

"But I heard you ask for some salt-petre."

"Possibly."

"And charcoal and brimstone, and things like that."

"What then? Wait patiently, and you'll see what you will see," Dick rejoined, with an air of the closest secrecy.

At dinner their appearance created a little sensation, as it had been rumoured that they had crossed the Channel in the night, in a small boat all by themselves.

But they were English boys, and the English do such funny things in the opinion of all foreigners, that the curiosity was not very great.

Nevertheless they were asked several questions, which Dick answered with the air of a man of thirty.

He said they often took cruises in their yacht.

He meant to go to America some day in her—all the way from Brighton to New York, across the Atlantic.

The ladies fell in love with him, and their admiration was so great, that many of them kissed him, and called him a pretty, fair-haired, brave English boy.

"Ah!" said Dick, in his best French, to a lady of title, who was petting and making a great fuss with him; "ah, madame la marquise, your brave country-men can do what they like on the land if they are not betrayed, while we English take to the sea naturally, and make our-selves masters of it."

This compliment pleased the French vastly, and they drank his health, and he drank theirs.

"Let's get out of this," he whispered to his friend. "I shall get screwed, or have a stomach-ache, or something, if I go on drinking their beastly wine like this."

"All right, I'm ready," replied Messiter.

They rose and bowed to the company, and taking up their caps in the hall, strolled arm in arm along the parade towards the pier.

As the season of the year was approaching autumn, the evenings began to draw in, and the pier was deserted about eight o'clock.

Though the people retired, Dick lingered, though Messiter did not know why.

"Now's the time," said Dick, as the shades of night began to fall.

"Time for what?" asked Messiter.

"To surprise the frog-eaters."

He put his bag down on the woodwork of the pier as he spoke, and opened it a little.

Then he placed a long strip of brown paper partly inside, and let the remainder hang out.

"What's that?" inquired Messiter, who was very curious about the proceedings.

"A slow match," answered Dick. "It will burn ten minutes, and I reckon we can get to the end of the pier comfortably before that time if we run."

"But——"

"Don't jaw," exclaimed Dick. "I'm busy, and you put me out."

Messiter was silent while his companion placed the bag in a conspicuous position, struck a match and set light to the slow match.

"Now then run," he cried.

They started off as fast as their legs would carry them, and being last on the pier, did not encounter anyone.

"Gently now," said Dick. "I don't want the sentries at the end to see us."

There being a regiment quartered in the town, a sentry was on duty at the end of the pier near the custom-house.

Messiter was making efforts to recover his breath.

"Don't puff and blow like a grampus," exclaimed Dick.

"I can't get my wind," answered Messiter.

"Go without it then."

They walked on to the quay without exciting the attention of the sentries, and joined the people walking up and down from the custom house to the *Etablissement* and *Grande Rue*, and back again.

"Come into this wine shop," Dick exclaimed, "and we'll have some cherry brandy, and I say——"

"Well?"

"Keep your eyes on the pier-head."

"Never fear," answered Messiter. "I'm as anxious as possible to know what your little game is."

They had not long to wait.

Suddenly a lurid flame burst out on the pier, shining with the utmost brightness.

And as it was at the back of the lighthouse—that is to say, facing the town, the little tower reflected it with the utmost brilliancy.

"I say, Dick!" cried Messiter; "the pier's on fire!"

"Is it?" said Dick. "What's that to us?"

"It's you. I know you've done it. It must be that stuff you had in the bag."

"Hold your row!" exclaimed Dick, between his teeth, "unless you want me to scrag you! Do you wish to see me locked up by those red-legged French soldiers?"

"No, but——"

"Shut up, I tell you!" Dick interrupted, squeezing his arm till he hurt him.

Messiter said no more.

The flame, which was as red as that of the setting sun, burned brighter and yet more brightly every moment.

Crowds assembled in the street, and talked excitedly to one another.

The *générale* was beaten at the guard-house, and a company of soldiers advanced to the beat of the drum.

The whole of the houses on the quay were lit up by the glare of the fire.

When excited by any strange occurrence, the French people can excel any other in gesticulating, talking, and making a noise.

It was generally supposed that the pier was on fire at its extreme point.

The firemen, or *pompiers*, came out in a body, and advanced with the citizens to the fire, buckets in hand.

The military kept the crowd back with their bayonets crossed.

"Oh, do let us go and see it!" said Messiter.

"There's nothing to see. It will go out directly," answered Dick.

"What is it, then?"

"Red fire, that's all. We made some at home last November on Guy Fawkes' Day, and as I recollected the recipe, I though it would be a good dodge to get up a sensation over here amongst these benighted frog-eaters."

"Is that all?" said Messiter, much comforted.

"Won't it do any harm, then?"

"Not at all—only make them all mad and wild when they find out they have been hoaxed."

As Dick spoke, the fire went out all at once, and the change from the lurid glare to blank darkness was quite as striking as the outbreak of the flame had been.

The firemen had rushed up to the pier to extinguish the conflagration, and when they got there, all they found was the remains of some chemical compound, which, in a brief space, had burnt itself out without doing any more harm than slightly scorching the woodwork.

Their annoyance was extreme.

When the fact became known, the people laughed, and declared that it was a good joke, but that the perpetrators of it ought to be punished, and the authorities of the town offered a reward of five pounds (125 francs) for the discovery of the offenders.

The people of Dieppe were in a state of commotion for about half an hour, and during the remainder of the evening nothing else was talked about.

It was half-past nine when the boys started to return to their hotel.

" I shall have some supper and turn in," exclaimed Messiter.

" So shall I ; but I shall go into the smoking-room with the men for a short time, to hear what they say."

" Do you think they will suspect us ?"

" Never in a blue moon. Why should they ?" answered Dick.

" I don't see any reason. But it was awfully daring of you."

" It was well done, and we didn't get bowled out, which is all I care about."

" I can't do it as you do."

" No, because you haven't had the practice that I have, and you don't love a joke as much as I do. I am so fond of joking that I don't care what risk I run, and as long as I can remember, I liked playing tricks upon people."

" Here's the 'Lille et'— what do you call it ?" said Messiter.

" ' Albion,' " supplied Dick.

They entered the hotel, and the waiter exclaimed—

" Gentleman to see you, sir."

" Eh !—what ?" cried Dick.

Messiter felt as if he could sink into his boots.

" Came by the steamer an hour ago, sir, from Newhaven."

Dick thought he detected a grin upon the waiter's face.

" What sort of a gentleman is he ? " he inquired.

" Tall—thin—not very old, sir—wears a white tie."

" Oh, by Jove ! it's a case," muttered Messiter. " I'll swear that's Snarley."

" My governor wears a white tie, too," said Dick.

They hesitated a moment.

" What shall I say, sir ?" exclaimed the waiter.

" Where is he ?" said Dick.

" In the coffee-room, sir."

" Did he ask for us ?"

" He brought your telegram with him, sir. I suppose he went at once to Newhaven, caught the boat, and came over."

" Oh, very well. I shall be very glad to see him presently, but I have a purchase or two to make, so we must go out again for a short time. Tell him to make himself comfortable, and let him have anything he likes to eat and drink."

" Very well, sir."

Dick took Messiter's arm and moved towards the door.

But his progress was impeded by a figure which, coming from the coffee-room, interposed itself between him and his going out.

„ Not so fast, young gentlemen !" exclaimed a voice, alas ! but too well known.

It was Mr. Snarley.

Messiter was in such a fright that he sank into one of the hall chairs, the picture of misery and despair.

" How do, sir ?" said Dick, preserving his serenity.

" ' How do, sir ?' What do you mean, sir, by such impudence ?" cried Mr. Snarley, white with rage. " I have heard all about you ! I have been listening !"

" Not for the first time," muttered Dick.

" What are you mumbling about, sir ! Don't incense me ! Tell me to make myself comfortable, and give me what I like to eat and drink, while you get away ?"

" I couldn't be more hospitable, and if you don't like the 'Lille et d'Albion,' you'd better go somewhere else. I shall stay here."

Dick put his hands in his pockets, as he spoke, with a determined air, and stared the usher hard in the face.

Mr. Snarley was literally speechless with rage, and could only glare at him, being utterly unable to say anything.

"'STOP! STOP! IT WILL BE BETTER FOR YOU,' CRIED SNARLEY."

DICK LIGHTHEART; OR, THE SCAPEGRACE OF THE SCHOOL.

CHAPTER X.

MR. SNARLEY'S ARRIVAL.

WHEN Mr. Snarley found his voice, he had had time to reason with himself, and he then saw the necessity for curbing his anger, which, in the place in which he was, would only make him ridiculous.

Already some of the people staying in the hotel, and the waiters, had lingered in the hall to listen to what was going on, though, as the conversation was carried on in English, they were not much the wiser.

"Wait till I get them home again," was Mr. Snarley's mental exclamation.

"What I want to say, sir," exclaimed Dick, "is that while we are here, you must not let people think that you are the master and we the pupils."

"Why not?" asked the usher, smiling in spite of himself.

"Because we have a character to keep up. We have said that we were going to send to my father to come and fetch us, and that we were in the habit of going out in our little yacht, only we got blown a little too far, and made for the coast of France."

"Very well. You have a private room, I suppose? Let me be your guest. We can talk better in private," answered Mr. Snarley.

Dick led the way, followed by the usher and Messiter, and the gathering crowd dispersed.

The waiter brought up some tea and a couple of cold fowls, which made an excellent supper.

Mr. Snarley did not attempt to bully them as at first, but talked to them more as if he had been a parent than a tutor.

"Of course you will be punished when you return to Harrow House," he said. "But that is Mr. Simcox's affair, not mine."

"What will he do to us, do you think, sir?" asked Messiter.

"I cannot tell. He will probably decide upon your degrees of guilt, and see who was most to blame. That you deserve punishment I do not deny, for you must admit that it was a most fool-hardy thing to cross the Channel in such a cockleshell of a boat as I hear you had."

"We could not help it," replied Dick. "We only went out to get some brandy-balls, and to avoid being taken back by you, we got into the boat, and pushed off, only thinking we should float a little way, and be able to scull back."

"Why did you not?"

"Because there were no oars. The wind and tide were against us, so we set the sail, and stood over to France."

"How did you manage to steer?"

"Well enough," answered Dick. "You have taught us geography, and I knew we should get to Dieppe. Our only danger was the chance of being cut in half by a steamer. In fact, sir, we took French leave. It was more my fault than Messiter's. I told him what to do."

"Then you take the blame on yourself?" said Mr. Snarley.

"Entirely, sir. It is no use for both of us to be in the row."

"I admire your generosity, and shall report what you say to Mr. Simcox. And now what do you think of going to bed, as we shall have to get up early to catch the first steamboat?"

The boys made no objection, as they were tired with roaming about all day.

Dick told Mr. Snarley of his obligation to the landlord, and the usher promised to see the debt of the two napoleons paid.

They were up early, and down at the quay at eight o'clock, seeing their luggage put on board the boat.

By their luggage we mean the little craft they had come over in, which the owner was very anxious might be restored to him, and the cheapest way of getting it back was to take it with them.

While the steamer was getting up steam, and the usher was purchasing the tickets at the bureau, a man came up, with something in a tub which he showed to Dick, asking him to buy it, foreigners having an idea that English men and boys are insane enough to buy anything.

"What is it?" inquired Dick.

"An electric eel," replied the man.

"Hang your impudence," said Dick. "What do I want with electric eels? Stop a bit, though, what does it do?"

The man explained that, if you put your hand in the water, you received a slight shock, and if you touched the slimy thing, you felt as if you had come in contact with a galvanic battery.

"Oh, that's it, is it? How much?" said Dick.

"Ten francs," replied the man.

"Ten humbugs!" exclaimed Dick. "I'll give you five."

"Say six, monsieur, and the eel is yours."

"All right. Go down to the boat and put it on board, tub and all. Here's the *l'argent*," said Dick.

The man pocketed the money, and the boys followed him to the *paquebot*, to see it safely bestowed.

"What a funny fellow you are," said Messiter.

"Am I?" answered Dick, unconcernedly.

"Yes. What on earth can you want with such a thing as an electric eel?"

Dick bent down and whispered—

"Snarley!"

Messiter comprehended his meaning in a moment, and grinned with delight.

"That's spiffing," he replied. "Oh, my! won't he jump!"

"He may jump overboard for what I care. I hate the beast," remarked Dick, with the same low tone, but with a vindictive energy which showed that he meant what he said.

In a short time the steamboat started, and clearing the bar, began to cross the Channel, in the direction of Newhaven.

Dick sat on deck, near the boat in which they had crossed over, which was called the " Lively Polly."

He was silent, and meditatively sucked the last but one of his brandy-balls.

Mr. Snarley approached him.

" Well, Lightheart, what are you thinking of? Pleasant thoughts, eh?—a penny for them," exclaimed the usher, grinning malevolently, as he fancied that Dick was down on his luck, and melancholy at the prospect of the thrashing in store for him on his arrival.

"Money first, sir, and you shall have them." answered Dick.

Mr. Snarley gave him a penny, saying—

"There you are; but don't speak with your mouth full."

"It's only a brandy-ball, sir. Have one? I've got one left."

"Goodness me, no. I wouldn't put such trash into my stomach," answered the usher.

"If you won't, I will, though you might have said thank you," Dick exclaimed, as he put the last of the sweets into his mouth.

"Now for your thoughts."

"I was thinking of the ' Lively Polly,' sir."

"Good gracious me! Is it possible that you have formed some acquaintance of that name during your short stay in Dieppe? What a precocious boy!"

Dick laughed.

"It's not a woman or a girl, sir. It's the boat here, and a neater and tauter craft never ploughed the bosom of the deep," he said.

"You're becoming poetical," observed Mr. Snarley, with an air of disappointment. "What have you got in that tub?"

"That's something livelier than Polly, sir," replied Dick. " It's going to be my pet. I mean to keep it in the schoolroom near my desk."

"But what is it?"

"A tame eel, sir."

"A what?—a tame eel! I never heard of such a thing," said Mr. Snarley.

"We live and learn, sir; men as well as schoolboys," said Dick, demurely.

"And you propose to keep such a thing as that?"

"Certainly, sir."

"It is unfortunate for you, that you did not ask my permission before you made such a silly purchase, and threw your money away on such rubbish."

"Won't you let me keep it, sir?" asked Dick, with an air of assumed regret.

"By no means."

"Poor old boy," exclaimed Dick, putting his hand in the water, and pretending to touch it, which he took good care not to do.

The eel remained quiet at the bottom of the tub.

In an instant Dick felt a very strange tingling all up his arm, and withdrew it, feeling rather uncomfortable.

"Aren't you afraid of it?" inquired the usher.

"No, sir. It's quite tame, and won't bite because it's had its teeth drawn. Do let me keep it. Poor old Nap! It's christened Nap, after the Emperor, and was intended for the Prince Imperial."

Messiter was hiding his face, as he was bursting with laughter, and did not want to be detected in the act.

"I shall throw the nasty thing overboard. You shan't take it to school, that's flat," said Snarley.

He turned to lift the tub, but it was too heavy.

"Very well, sir," exclaimed Dick, with a sigh of resignation. "I deserve that you should be a little harsh with me, for I have been very bad and disobedient, but I'll try and be better in future, and earn your good opinion. Take the eel and throw him overboard. Hold him tightly by the neck, or he'll slip through your fingers."

"Come," said Snarley, soothed; "you are not so hardened as I thought you."

"It's only the devilment I've got in me, sir."

"Where there is shame, there may be reformation. You have heard that before, I suppose."

"No, sir. Thank you for telling me. I'll try and remember it. Was Henry the Eighth ashamed of himself for having so many wives, and was his shame the cause of the Reformation we read about in his reign?"

"Nonsense!" said Snarley.

"I did not know, sir. I beg your pardon. You may have the eel, sir. Will you ask Mr. Simcox to let me off?" Dick replied, in the same penitent voice.

"I hope he won't go on like that any longer. I shall have a fit if he does," muttered Messiter.

Dick heard him gurgling in the distance, with suppressed laughter, and taking the half-sucked brandy-ball out of his mouth, threw it at him, and hit him in the eye by way of warning.

"I can't go so far as that, Lightheart," said Mr. Snarley. "But I will try and beg you off some part of your punishment."

"Thank you, sir. Will you have the eel now?"

"Yes. You are sure he is harm-less?" answered Snarley, tucking up his sleeves.

"Quite, sir. He's like a baby. Old Nap wouldn't hurt a child. That's right, sir; take both hands to him, one for the head, another for the tail. Won't he be glad to get into the sea again? His native element, I may say."

Mr. Snarley bent over the tub, and looked at the eel, which was not a very formidable monster, being about four feet long, and just thick enough to grasp easily with the hand.

The day was somewhat cloudy, but fine, there being little or no wind stirring so the ship did not roll, and the passengers were all on deck, enjoying the passage, which was pronounced a good one so far.

"Now, sir. Go in and win," said Dick.

"Oblige me, Lightheart, by not addressing me in that slangy way," remarked the usher.

"Beg pardon, sir. Now or never. Hold him tight. Poor Nap!"

Mr. Snarley dived into the tub, and dexterously seized the eel with both hands, bringing it into the air, and holding it very tightly in spite of its wriggling, which was excessive.

Suddenly he stopped short on his way to the side of the boat, and becoming rigid, uttered such piercing cries, that the passengers and some of the crew came up to him.

The eel had slipped from his grasp, and was sliding about on the deck.

"Oh! oh! my poor arm, my poor body!" groaned Snarley.

"What's the matter? asked the captain, who had descended from the bridge.

"He's caught the sea-serpent," said Dick.

At this there was a general laugh.

Mr. Snarley bestowed a look upon him, which seemed to say—

"I'll 'sea-serpent' you, my young gentleman, when I get a chance."

"What is it?" asked one gentleman, who was a doctor.

"It's the devil," answered Snarley, who had received a succession of strong electrical shocks from the creature, and was in great pain and trembling all over.

Never having heard of an electrical eel, he could not understand it.

"Pitch it overboard," said the captain to one of the sailors.

The man touched it, but recoiled instantly with aggravated pins and needles up his arm.

"Blow me if I touch the beggar again!" said the man, rubbing his arm.

"Here's a lark," said Messiter, who had joined Dick.

"Hold your row. Listen to Snarley," answered Dick.

"The thing seemed to sting me," said Snarley to the doctor. "I don't know how I feel. I'm all over a tingle. I've got sharp shooting pains all over me. I believe my system's poisoned."

"Nonsense," replied the doctor. "It will wear off. Have some brandy and water. It's an electric eel—that's what it is. You'll feel the effects for some time, but you will sustain no lasting injury."

"Oh! oh! oh!" was all Snarley could say, as the pains continued to dart through him.

"You're galvanised," exclaimed the doctor.

"Am I?" said Snarley, as if the fact was a matter of perfect indifference to him.

"You are indeed. I shall send a report of your case to the *Lancet*, which is our principal medical paper. Will you take the eel up again? I should like to be able to report your symptoms after the second shock."

"Not if I know it," said Snarley, savagely.

"In the interests of science," urged the doctor.

"Bother science! Do you want to kill me outright?"

"Let me persuade you, my dear sir."

"I'll be hanged if I do. Oh, oh! As if I hadn't had enough of it, and to spare."

Then Snarley's gaze fell upon Dick, who was enjoying the scene with sparkling eyes.

"All right, my boy," exclaimed Snarley, with concentrated hatred. "That's another chalk to you. I'll not forget you."

"Thank you, sir. But wouldn't it be better if you did not set us the example of talking slang? What is a chalk?" said Dick.

Mr. Snarley shook his fist at Dick, and allowed himself to be led below by the doctor, who, during the remainder of the journey, plied him with brandy and water, which he made the steward put down to Snarley's account, and bothered him with a variety of questions as to his sensations at the time of contact with the eel and afterwards, until Snarley was scarcely aware whether he stood on his head or his heels, and began to entertain a firm opinion that he had had an encounter with the great sea-serpent, in the middle of the vast Atlantic, and had come off victorious after slaying his adversary.

At last he fell off to sleep, as tipsy as he could be, and the doctor, closing his note book, left him.

Meanwhile, the eel had been swept overboard with a broom, and his tub thrown after him, the latter act being Dick's doing.

"You have thrown my eel overboard," he said, "without my permission, and I choose to throw his tub after him."

"But it's a good tub, and worth something. It'll come in handy," said the captain.

"Never mind; it's my tub. I paid for it, and I shall throw it after my eel. He may want it," replied Dick.

So over the tub went, and Dick sat down once more near the "Lively Polly" as if nothing had happened, with Messiter by his side.

"I say," exclaimed Messiter.

"Well?" answered Dick.

"Snarley will have it ready for us after this."

"We were in for it before. Whatever Snarley may say won't have any influence over old Simcox. I expect, though, I shall catch it, and you'll get off."

"I don't know."

"But I do. I shall say it was all my doings, and get you off. What's the use of both of us being licked, eh?" replied Dick.

"No," said Messiter. "But it's very kind of you, Dick, and very generous to think of me in such a way. Most fellows would like to have a companion in misfortune."

"I'll make it all square and smooth for you, never fear."

Messiter took Dick's hand, and wrung it heartily.

"If ever I get the chance, I'll return

your kindness, and stick to you like a brick. You're a wonder, and I never saw a fellow in my life I liked so much as I do you," he said.

Dick smiled, and returned the pressure of his friend's hand.

He had a large heart, and was not a sneak, if he was the scamp of the family.

CHAPTER XI.

THE BLACK HOLE.

THE arrival of Dick and Messiter at Harrow House caused no little sensation.

It had leaked out that the boys had gone to France, and it was known that Mr. Snarley had been sent over to fetch them back, because Mr. Simcox had told one of the housemaids so, and she had told one of the head boys.

But the particulars of their strange voyage were not known, and much speculation was rife.

Dick and Messiter were sent into the schoolroom about tea-time, and surrounded as soon as they entered, each having his circle, and they told their story exactly as it had occurred.

The boys admired them immensely, and they were naturally the heroes of the hour.

In a short time Mr. Simcox entered, and took his place at his desk.

There was a dead silence.

Unlocking his desk, the professor took from it a long, lithe, glistening cane.

With this he struck the desk three times.

Those who knew him well saw from his face that he was annoyed, if not seriously angry.

The tea had not yet been announced, and it was presumed that it had been postponed.

Mr. Snarley leaned against the door, looking very limp and fishy about the eyes.

"Young gentlemen of Harrow House School," began Mr. Simcox, after the third rap of the cane.

Everyone looked at the professor.

"An event of rare occurrence has taken place in our midst," he went on. "Two boys have dared to set an example of the most flagrant disobedience. They shall stand forth. Lightheart and Messiter, stand up on that bench in front of me."

The culprits thus designated got up on the bench, and stood with their hands behind them and their eyes cast down.

"Your offence," continued Mr. Simcox, "is one which it is impossible to overlook, nor have I any inclination to do so, because I can see no extenuating circumstances in your case."

"I am willing to bear all the blame, sir," said Dick. "Messiter acted under my advice throughout. In fact, he couldn't help himself, and it would not be fair to do anything to him."

"Very well, that simplifies matters," said Mr. Simcox. "I do not wish to confound the innocent with the guilty. Go to your seat, Messiter, thanking your stars for your good fortune, and let this be a lesson to you as long as you live."

Messiter sprang down and was gone in an instant, though he looked pityingly at Dick when he got to his place.

"At most schools," Mr. Simcox went on, "you would be expelled, Lightheart; but I adopt a different system.

"I pronounce no boy irreclaimable, however wicked he may seem to be. Far from it, I give him another and another chance.

"The black sheep may become white—*nil desperandum;* and now, instead of sending you home to your father's house, which I have no doubt would delight you extremely, I am going to cane you severely."

Here he flourished the cane, and brought it down with a sounding thwack on the desk.

"And, having done that, you will be put in the black hole for four and twenty hours, on a diet of bread and water, when your aching back, and the solitude which will surround you may, let us trust, bring you to a proper sense of the duty you owe to those who are set in authority over you. You hear your sentence. Now what is it for? We want to hear your confession."

Dick remained obstinately silent.

"I will speak for you, though I have no doubt we shall make you find your voice presently."

The professor laughed, and looked around him for applause.

"First of all," said the professor, "you go out at night without leave; you run away from the usher, who goes after you; you get into a boat which does not belong to you; you set the sail and go to France, and behave like a fast young scamp, showing symptoms which must be knocked out of you, if we wish you to turn out an honest, steady man, and a respectable member of society. Venner, do your duty."

Venner was the biggest boy in the school, though not at the top of the first class.

Indeed, he was nearly at the bottom of the second, for his superiority was in his bodily, not his mental strength.

Whenever a boy was caned, it was Venner's duty to " horse " him; that is, to take him on his back, and, holding his wrists round his own neck, keep him in a favourable position for the head-master's blows.

Stepping out from his companions, Venner went up to Dick, and told him to put his arms round his neck, which Dick did, seeing that resistance would be useless.

In an instant Venner gave a jerk, and Dick found himself perfectly helpless, and tightly held.

Then Venner turned round, and took up a position in an open space, so as to give the professor's arm full play.

Swish went the cane through the air, descending on the offender's back with a dull thud.

At first these were the only sounds to be heard, but as the pain increased to positive torture, and the elastic cane bent double and twined round his jacket, actually cutting the cloth, Dick began to add his cries to the noise.

At length he screamed with pain, and kicked violently, receiving the blows on the calves of his legs, but he was unable to liberate himself, and it was not until the cane broke off at the top, by coming in contact with the boy's boot, that the professor desisted from his efforts.

Venner let him slide down on to the floor, where he rolled about for more than a minute, writhing in uncontrollable pain.

"That is the first lesson," said Mr. Simcox. "You see, my young friend, I am not to be trifled with. I shall be prepared to repeat the lesson if you give me cause. There is nothing like a good caning to bring a boy to his senses. It hurts, and the pain lasts. You are bruised all over, and you will feel your hurts for some time. Now, Mr. Snarley, your aid, if you please, to convey him to the Black Hole. *In carcere duro*, literally, in a hard prison, he will remain until to-morrow at this hour."

Snarley had been enjoying the scene, for it was a pleasure to his mean and narrow mind to see Dick suffer, because he had played him so many tricks.

Though still very shaky from the effects of his sea voyage and the brandy and water, he advanced with alacrity, and, raising the boy up, half pushed, half dragged him from the room.

Dick's face was flushed, and his cheeks stained with tears.

Sobs broke from him at intervals, and it was evident that he had gone through a severe castigation, which was no joke.

Messiter pitied him sincerely.

They took him downstairs, past the kitchen, into a long passage, at the end of which was the coal cellar.

A light which Mr. Simcox had taken from the cook enabled them to see a door with a key in it.

Throwing this back, a dark and gloomy vault of narrow dimensions was disclosed.

It had the appearance of being a disused wine cellar.

In one corner was a small mattress, looking rather mouldy and damp.

Mr. Snarley gave him a spiteful push, and he fell upon this rough sort of bed.

"Lock him up," exclaimed Mr. Simcox.

The usher pulled to the door, and turned the key.

Dick was alone in the dark.

The professor and his satellite went upstairs together.

"I think we shall cure him, sir," said Mr. Snarley.

"It shall be kill or cure," answered the professor. "I never allow myself to be beaten by my boys."

Given away with No. 3 of]

[" Dick Lightheart ; or, The Scapegrace of the School."

"Open your mouth and shut your eyes," cried Dick.

"Quite right, too, sir."

"Have you given him his bread and water, Mr. Snarley?"

"No, sir; I forgot it."

"Please do so before you go to bed. He must not be starved. The mind does not suffer so acutely when the body is attacked by the pangs of hunger and thirst."

"I'll not forget, sir," Mr. Snarley replied.

After this, tea was served in the dining room, and the boys trooped in to enjoy their "sky blue and bread and scrape."

The discipline inflicted upon Dick had so far affected them that they all spoke in a subdued tone.

"Didn't the governor lay it on?" one would remark.

"Rather. I never saw him so savage," another would reply.

"They haven't licked him yet," Messiter observed to Venner, after tea.

"What did he holloa for then? That looked as if he gave in," answered Venner.

"So would you sing out," said Messiter, "if you were lammed into at that rate. Wait till Lightheart recovers, and he'll be worse than ever. I know him better than you do."

"He'll catch it again then."

"I don't think he will; he'll bolt first. But it's no use talking to you," replied Messiter; "you like to horse fellows You're like the sworn tormentor of the old Tower of London."

As he spoke Messiter dived under the table to avoid having his ears pulled, coming up on the other side, and at a safe distance from Venner's burly form.

He was right, however, about Dick, who was only shocked and stunned for the moment.

It would take a good deal more than that to beat the devil out of him, as will be seen shortly.

CHAPTER XII.

ALONE IN THE DARK.

PERHAPS few sensations are so disagreeable as that of being plunged suddenly into total darkness.

Though in the midst of solitude as profound as possible, you fancy a thousand kinds of noises, and fret the mind by imagining things that exist only in the imagination.

We have proved that Dick was brave, but after all he was only a boy, and when he found himself alone in the dark, and remembered that he had to put up with such confinement for four and twenty hours, a feeling of despair seized him.

This was joined by terror, and the two combined drove him pretty nearly frantic.

He began to cry out at the top of his voice, and utter the most unearthly shrieks; but no one could hear him on account of the thickness of the doors, and the remote position of the cellar.

Then he fancied he was being stifled and could not draw his breath, though this was really fanciful, as a current of air was introduced through a hole in the wall, which communicated with the larder, a place always kept cool and fresh.

"They have put me in here to kill me," said Dick to himself, giving way to his panic fear.

"I know I shall die. Oh, this is horrible," and again the cell resounded with his shrieks.

The echoes of his own voice sounded like the mocking voices of demons, and his hair grew stiff, as he thought the place haunted.

For nearly two hours his agitation lasted, and no one but himself knew what he suffered during that time.

When the panic was over, he sat down on the floor to think calmly over his situation.

"What a fool I was to think I should be suffocated, and that there were ghosts," he said. "Of course it is not their interest to kill me. Simcox only wants to break my spirit, and if I give way again, as I did at first, he'll do it. I shall be all right if I keep quiet. How thirsty I am, though."

He was consumed by a burning thirst,

and made a search round the cellar for some water without finding any, though Mr. Snarley was on his way with a pitcher full at that very moment, and a not very appetising hunch of dry bread.

There was a click, as of a key in the lock.

"Some one coming," said Dick.

He guessed it was Mr. Snarley, and an idea struck him.

Standing up near the door, he waited the appearance of the usher.

Mr. Snarley threw open the door, and allowed the light to enter.

It dazzled Dick, who put his hand over his eyes.

"Here's some bread and water for you," said Snarley, brutally. "It's all you'll have."

He looked at him with a sort of pleasurable satisfaction, and seemed to enjoy the position in which he was.

"Why don't you lie down?" he asked.

"Because there's a young rat in the straw, sir. It's got a nest there, and bit me," answered Dick.

"Young rat? Nonsense! But if there is, it is only what a wicked boy like you must expect. You may think yourself lucky there are no snakes, as there are in some prisons."

"It's bad enough to be in the dark, sir, without being bitten by rats, and if I were to write home, and tell my father that you shut me up to be eaten and frightened by rats, he wouldn't like it. I only ask you to drive it out for me, sir," said Dick.

"Oh, please do! I shan't care so much then," he added in an imploring tone.

Moved by this piteous appeal, and thinking the request, after all, a reasonable one, Mr. Snarley said—

"I will see what I can do.'

"Oh, thank you, sir!" cried Dick, gleefully.

"Hold the candle, and stand away from the door, while I kick the straw, and start the animal on its travels."

Dick did as he was told, and waited till the usher began to kick the straw about.

Then he made a sudden dive through the door, which he instantly shut and locked, the key being on the outside.

In his hand he held the candlestick.

Snarley was in the dark, shut up with his bread and water.

"Let him hunt rats," said Dick, smiling.

The kitchen clock struck eleven.

At that hour the servants had all gone to bed, and he knew that the house was still.

The usher had put off his visit to him till the last thing.

Dick had acted upon a sudden impulse in caging the usher, and had not considered what he should do afterwards.

Now he stood still and thought.

He fancied he could hear Mr. Snarley's voice through the thick oaken door, but he could not distinguish what he said.

"What a lark!" thought Dick; "everybody to-morrow will be saying 'Where's Snarley?'"

It was rather cold in the passage, and Dick, being hungry and thirsty, determined, before he did anything else, to satisfy his appetite.

He opened the door next to the Black Hole, and was delighted to find himself in a spacious larder.

In a bowl stood some delicious milk, which he was able to drink by stooping down, and he took a good draught.

On a shelf was half a cold chicken, left from the professor's supper; on another plate was some cut ham and cooked sausages.

"These will do finely," said Dick, helping himself to each of the dainties, using his fingers for want of a knife and fork.

"Old Simcox will go short to-morrow, and cookey will think the cats have been in the larder, but she won't know it's a two-legged cat. How hungry that Black Hole has made me. I hope Snarley will have to eat all his bread and drink his water."

At that moment a deep groan startled him.

He jumped up, and nearly dropped his plate.

It was followed by another, and he then saw that it came from a hole in the wall.

"What an ass I am," he muttered; "I might have recollected that the Black Hole is next to this, and the sound comes from Snarley through some air-hole or other."

Putting his mouth to a slit he saw in the wall, he exclaimed, "Snarley!"

"Who calls?" replied a sepulchral voice.

"It's Lightheart. I'm in the larder, and pegging away at the governor's prog. Wouldn't you like a bit of cold chicken, sir, or a nice thin slice of ham, or what the vulgar boys call a 'sassage?'"

"Dick; my dear, good boy, Dick! what have you done?" exclaimed Mr. Snarley. "I am rejoiced at this opportunity of conversing with you. It is a fortunate chance. You will let me out, will you not?"

"And get put back myself; no, thank you," answered Dick.

Each time he spoke he put his mouth to the hole, and then placed his ear there to receive the answer.

"The punishment will be dreadful—I do not hesitate to say dreadful, if you leave me here," answered the usher.

"I'll chance that. Did you find the rat, sir?"

"Dick, listen to reason. You will be found out, and then you will be sorry. I will undertake that you shall be pardoned, and sleep in your bed to-night."

"I fully intend to, sir. But about that rat?"

"You young rascal, I'll rat you!" cried Mr. Snarley. "Let me out, or I'll know the reason why!"

"Don't get excited, sir. It's no use running your head against a brick wall. Shall I put something through the ventilator?" asked Dick.

Without waiting for an answer, he pushed a chicken bone through the hole.

"Oh, my eye!" cried Mr. Snarley; "he's poked my eye out."

"Good night, sir," said Dick. "I hope that rat won't disturb your rest. Very nice straw, clean and dry. Very wholesome bread and water. Good night, sir; see you again to-morrow."

Regardless of the usher's cries and exclamations, he had another drink of milk, and overhauled a plate that contained some cold veal, to which he paid his respects.

"I haven't done so badly," he said; "and now to have a look at Messiter. The old boy will stare when he sees me."

Taking off his boots, he proceeded cautiously upstairs, pausing as he went past Mr. Simcox's study.

The professor had a light burning, and was correcting some English exercises for the fourth class.

"I'll wake him up presently," was Dick's muttered exclamation as he went by.

Pushing open the door of his room, he heard Messiter snoring. He had previously put out the candle and the room was in darkness.

Shaking Messiter's arm, he whispered—

"Time to get up."

"Is it?" answered Messiter, rubbing his eyes. "Is that you, Dick? I thought——"

"What?" asked Dick, waiting for him to collect his thoughts.

"Why, they hyked you off to the Black Hole, didn't they?"

"Yes, and I've got out again."

"Did you really, though?"

"I think my being here is the best proof of that," replied Dick.

"Is it really you, though?" asked Messiter, grasping his arm.

"If it isn't, it's my ghost."

"Oh, don't talk of ghosts; the very idea makes me shivery."

"Ghosts don't generally talk. I tell you it is me; all as right as ninepence."

"How did you get out?" inquired Messiter.

"Snarley came with the bread and water, and while he was hunting for an imaginary rat I had talked about to him, I popped out and locked the door."

"Is Snarley inside?" asked Messiter, grinning with delight.

"Rather. He might as well try to get out of Newgate, as out of where I have left him."

"You are a fellow!" cried Messiter. "But ain't you hungry?"

"Not I," rejoined Dick. "I've had a stunning good feed in the larder; cold chicken, and ham, and milk, and sausages, and veal. I haven't had such a regular buster since I've been here. Somebody will have to suffer through it."

"It's the governor's grub, I suppose?"

"It was, you mean; it's gone now. But I don't care whose it was. I've polished it off, and I'm all the better for it, I can tell you."

"Wasn't it awful in there?" Messiter inquired with a shudder.

"Awful isn't the word for it. You know I'm not easily funked, but I thought I should have had a fit for the first hour. It'll do Snarley good."

And Dick laughed heartily at the idea of the usher being shut up in the Black Hole.

"I'm so jolly glad that Snarley's in for it. He did joke to the boys about your being shut up. He said he'd cure you of running off as you had done; and he was at me all the evening, throwing off all sorts of nasty things."

"Perhaps he'll let me alone for the future, and think I'm a match for him."

"What a fuss there'll be when he's missing to-morrow. But what do you mean to do?"

"I shall go and hide in the larder or the coal cellar," answered Dick. "But I mean to turn in to-night, and have a good warm sleep. Simcox never comes round to the boys' room, and because they shan't see my bed's been upset, I shall turn in with you, if you have no objection."

"Objection!" exclaimed Messiter. "Is it likely? You're welcome to half my bed. Come in."

"Not yet."

"Why not?"

"I want to give the professor a turn. He's in his study, smoking and looking over exercises. He looks so jolly happy with his fire and his grog, that I couldn't rest in my bed if I didn't make him miserable."

"How are you going to do it?"

"That's just what I was thinking. Haven't you got a mask in the press that you used last fifth of November?"

"Yes."

"I thought I remembered you showing it me. Get it out. I'll put that on, and my night-shirt over my clothes."

"I say, what a shame to make a fellow get out of his warm bed," said Messiter.

"Do as you're told, or I'll serve you as I served Snarley," answered Dick.

Messiter laughed, and did as he was asked.

The mask was a very hideous one, representing the devil with two horns, a wide mouth and a prodigious nose. Its colour was black and red.

"If this don't give the professor fits, I don't know what will," said Messiter.

"We live in hope," answered Dick coolly.

He quickly put on his nightshirt and the mask, which prevented his being recognised, and altogether he presented a very ghostly appearance.

"Wish you luck, Dick," said Messiter.

"Don't you worry yourself," answered Dick.

"If I'm collared, I shan't come in here to get you into a row. I shall bolt to the lower regions. I don't want to let Snarley out, and if they see who I am, they'd guess the trick directly, and the bird would get out of the cage."

"I can fancy him," said Messiter, "biting his nails and pulling at his stumpy whiskers; I know his ways so well. His snubby nose will turn up more than ever. You know how he says, 'You boys! you boys, there! less noise, if you please.' Oh! it's grand to think that he's coopered up in the Black Hole. I shall love you for ever, Dick, for that."

"Shut up now, and keep your ecstasy for another time," answered Dick. "I've got work in hand, and I'm off to do it. I wish I had not eaten so much of that chicken and stuff, though; I'm gorged, and feel too lazy for practical joking!"

"Have a try; you're sure to pull it off; you always do," said Messiter.

"I'll go in a good un," answered Dick, shaking his friend's outstretched hand; "and it won't be my fault if I come to grief."

CHAPTER XIII.

MR. SIMCOX IS PUZZLED.

DICK wished Messiter good night, in case he was not able to come back as he intended, and went along the passage to Mr. Simcox's study. The master was still at work, and Dick watched him through the half-open door for a while.

"Three more to do," he said, as he put down an exercise; "and then I shall be able to retire to my well-earned rest. The fourth-form boys are improving; so is this brandy and water. Each glass I take seems better than the other. Ha! ha! If Snarley only knew there was brandy and water going on, he would not have gone to bed so soon. Snarley's got a nose for anything good. I fancy he enjoyed his trip after those boys to Dieppe. The rascals! That boy Lightheart is a perfect fiend!"

"Take care what you say," said Dick in a sepulchral voice in the passage.

He darted under the hall table as soon as he had spoken, and was out of sight.

"Dear me, what was that? It's very odd," exclaimed Mr. Simcox.

He got up and looked with the light outside the door, but, seeing nothing, returned to his seat at the study table.

"I could have sworn I heard somebody," exclaimed he. "Perhaps it's the wind; these houses are very badly built, and we are getting into winter. Yes, I repeat that Lightheart is a bad boy. He is the sort of lad that breaks his mother's heart and brings his father's grey hairs with sorrow to the grave. I'm glad he isn't my son."

"So am I," exclaimed a voice outside.

"Bless me!" cried Mr. Simcox. "There must be someone outside, or else it is the echo of my voice. I must cure myself of the habit of speaking aloud when I'm alone."

"The sooner the better," said Dick.

"There it is again! Some one spoke; I'm sure I heard a voice."

He got up a second time, and made an exploration of the hall and passage.

Dick no sooner saw his back turned, as he went down the passage with the candle in his hand, than he slipped into the study and sat in the professor's arm-chair.

Mr. Simcox returned, considerably puzzled.

"No one there," he said, still indulging in his favourite habit of speaking aloud. "My senses must have deceived me. Can brandy and water have the faculty of so muddling a man that he fancies he hears sounds which are not?"

His eyes fell upon Dick, who looked most ghostly in his hideous mask and white shirt.

"Oh, Lord! oh, Lord!" gasped the professor, as he fell on his knees.

"Bad man, repent!" exclaimed Dick in a hoarse voice, unlike his own. "You are cruel to your boys, and vengeance will overtake you. Repent—repent, and——"

"What?—oh, what?" asked the unhappy professor, as the ghost hesitated.

"Get rid of Snarley," continued Dick.

"I will! I will!" answered the schoolmaster, half overcome with brandy and water, and wholly collapsed with fright.

Dick blew out the lamp, and taking up a roll of exercises, hit the professor violently on the head as he passed him, scattering them all about the room.

Then he ran away as swiftly as he could, and made for the larder, where he lay hid for some time.

Mr. Simcox soon recovered from his fright, which, indeed, was but momentary.

"Ghosts don't hit, and if they talk, it's something new," he muttered "I'm a fool."

Here he drank some more brandy.

"I'll go and look about the house. I've been tricked. If it wasn't that Lightheart was in the cellar, I should say it was he who had done it. The others haven't courage enough. They have been here till I have broken their spirits, as I will his before long."

But Mr. Simcox had overrated his courage.

He did not like to go and wander about the house by himself.

His wife had gone to bed, so he drank more brandy, and at last fell asleep on the hearthrug, where he remained till morning.

It was five o'clock when he woke, and he crawled, shivering with cold, upstairs, and crept into his wife's bed without waking her.

This was the most clever and judicious thing he had done for some time.

For had Mrs. Simcox known all about his excess, and his nap on the hearthrug, the probability is he would not have heard the last of it for some time to come.

When Dick heard the house quiet, he stole up and got into Messiter's bed, making him laugh heartily at what had taken place.

In the morning, he woke as soon as the school bell rang with its dismal clatter, and dressing himself, went to the lower part of the house.

He had some difficulty in getting past the kitchen, but the cook was engaged in lighting the fire, and he gained the larder without being observed.

There were some old butter tubs piled up in a corner, and he found a nest behind them.

His position was irksome enough, and, after being there some time, he thought he would rather exchange places with Mr. Snarley.

"At least," he said to himself, "Snarley has got some straw to lie upon. This won't do; I must hook it."

The voice of the milkman was heard at the area, and he knew it was eight o'clock.

"I'll get out of this," he said.

Getting up, and emerging from his shelter, he helped himself to some cold veal, and, seeing the hole communicating with the cellar, couldn't resist the temptation of speaking once more to the usher.

"I say, sir!" he exclaimed.

"What is it?" answered Mr. Snarley. "Thank goodness some one has come! My bones ache, and I am half beside myself."

"You will be wholly so, before long," answered Dick.

"Is it you, Lightheart?" exclaimed Mr. Snarley. "Be a good boy, and let me out."

"But, I say, sir!" said Dick, with a chuckle.

"What?" asked Snarley.

"Have you caught that rat?"

"Rat be ——!" cried Mr. Snarley, losing his temper, and adding—

"No, I don't mean to be cross, but it is really enough to try a man's temper to be shut up here like this. Let me out, Dick, there's a good boy."

"Next week," answered Dick. "There you are, and there you'll stop, as far as I'm concerned. I'm going into the town now to enjoy myself. I've got a friend who's staying at the 'Bedford,' and we'll drink your health, and success to your rat-catching. Good bye, sir! Don't be too hard on the rats."

He heard Mr. Snarley grate his teeth with rage, and slipped out of the larder, up the area steps, and gained the street, up which he walked, towards the Old Steyne.

When he said he had a friend staying at the Bedford Hotel, he did not exaggerate, for he had received a letter from his sister a short time back, in which she announced two items of news.

The first was, that Lieutenant Harry Smart, of Her Majesty's Navy, was about to visit Brighton, and would be found, for some time to come, at the "Bedford."

The second was, that Agnes—his youngest sister—was coming to school at Brighton, and would be living at Kemp Town, near Mr. Simcox's.

Lieutenant Smart was a young man with a tolerably good income and some interest at the Admiralty, but he could not always get a ship. The vessel in which he had sailed had been paid off, and he was enjoying what he called a cruise on shore.

The lieutenant had paid several visits to the rectory, and, with the sharpness of a boy of his age, Dick fancied that he was paying attentions to his sister Emily.

Nor was he mistaken.

"If he's spooney on Emily," thought Dick, "he'll be glad enough to be civil to me."

So he went boldly to the Bedford Hotel, and asked for Lieutenant Smart.

"I mustn't look down on my luck," said he to himself. "These naval men give themselves airs, and he'll look upon me as a milksop if I show the white feather."

True to his early training, Mr. Smart was an early riser, and was at breakfast as Dick was ushered into his room.

"Oh! how do you do?" he exclaimed.

"Sit down, Master Dick. I meant to call upon you to-day."

"'Mr. Lightheart,' or 'Dick,' plain 'Dick,'" answered our hero; "or, when you have occasion to write to me, 'Richard Lightheart, Esquire.' I can't stand the 'master!'"

"Thank you for putting me right," said the lieutenant; "and to what fortunate circumstance am I indebted for the honour of this visit, Dick?"

"I've had a bit of a kick-up at our school, and thought it would be better for my health if I left the authorities to themselves for a little while."

"Indeed!"

"It's nothing much; you need not interest yourself about it," added Dick.

"How did you know I was here?" asked Harry Smart.

"Give me some breakfast, and I'll talk to you. Show your hospitality, or Emily shall never speak to you again," said Dick.

"Really!" exclaimed the lieutenant, laughing; "you seem to know how to get to windward of me. What will you have?"

"I like ham, honey in the comb's not bad, potted beef is good, anchovy paste is cheerful, partridges are appetising, but prawns for choice, to start with. I like them to begin with; they are a penny apiece, and therefore a luxury. Secondly, each time you eat a prawn, you can fancy you're eating ten shrimps, and they're not half the bother to peel. I'll start with the prawns decidedly, and you can order me a fried sole and some cocoa."

The lieutenant did so, and contrived to get Dick into conversation by degrees.

He learnt how he had been over to Dieppe with Messiter, and how Mr. Snarley had come to him, and subsequently incarcerated him in the black hole.

He heard how he had frightened the worthy pedagogue with his ghost trick, and how he had shut up the usher in the cellar.

"You ought to go to sea, my boy," said the lieutenant; "you're just cut out for a seafaring life. You'd get some of the liveliness knocked out of you with the rope's end, I'm thinking."

"Don't you make any mistake," answered Dick; "I'm too wide awake to go to sea, either in the merchant service or Her Majesty's, though I believe the former is better than the latter."

"Thank you for the compliment," said Smart.

"I didn't mean anything personal," remarked Dick, "though I believe you're a favourable specimen of the officers of the Royal Navy. Why don't you wear your uniform and let everybody know you're R. N.? You would get such a lot of credit in Brighton."

"You impudent young whelp!" exclaimed the lieutenant; "I'll take you back to your school and stand by while they flog you, if you are not more civil."

"Just like you fellows," answered Dick, putting his legs on a chair. "I always said the navy brutalised men."

"If you came here to abuse me and take possession of my rooms, I'll vacate them in your favour."

"Please yourself, my dear boy," replied Dick. "I'm very jolly if you won't bully me. Shy the *Times* over here, will you? I want to look at the Police Intelligence."

"You're a cool fish," said Lieutenant Smart, who could not help smiling, "but I was just the same at your age."

"Was you?" said Dick. "Then you must have been a highly interesting pup. But look here, old boy, I don't want to have a row with you. Make me jolly. I don't understand cigars and sodas-and-brandies yet, but I like a drive. The governor trots you about when you come to Ingarstone. Return the civility, or I'll crab you with Emily."

"I'll do anything you like," answered the lieutenant, "if you'll only condescend to tell me what you mean to do. You can't expect me to keep you away from school altogether."

"Certainly not. Under exceptional circumstances I have taken a day's holiday. All I want you to do is to entertain me to-day. Take me about, give me a good dinner and a glass of wine, and try and make me forget my troubles."

"And then?"

"Well, then, you must go to Harrow House School and say, that as a friend of the family, you protest against my being shut up in a dark stifling cellar, and you think that I have been sufficiently punished by being caned."

"If the master does not see it?" continued the lieutenant.

"Threaten him with a summons at the Town Hall, and an exposure for ill-treating me; the law will let you do that. And—Harry—oh! you can get me out of the scrape if you like! There are lots of ways. Old Simcox is an old woman, and a man can twist him round his finger.

"Very well," rejoined Mr. Smart, "I'll do what I can for you. You will find a Robinson Crusoe on the sideboard. Read that and give me the paper. It is too early to go on the beach. I've got a cave there."

"A cave!" said Dick.

"Yes, I rent it. A sort of a cavern in the sea wall, with a door. My friends and I smoke and have beer there. It's awfully jolly."

The lieutenant rather liked Dick, who found, by conversing with him, that he was intelligent and agreeable, though he was somewhat offhand.

About eleven they strolled towards the beach, and Dick wondered how Mr. Snarley was, and what Mr. Simcox thought of the situation.

Mr. Simcox was puzzled.

But we must reserve his speculations, and what happened at Harrow House, for the next chapter.

CHAPTER XIV.

IN THE CAVE.

THE cave Lieutenant Smart had spoken about to Dick, and which he was taking him to visit, was a sort of vault in the sea wall, a little below the "Bedford."

This he rented by the month, and kept in it some chairs, a table, a box of cigars, and some bottled beer and spirits, for the friends whom he asked to come in and spend an hour or two with him.

It was a curious fancy this, of having a vault of his own, when he could have had a comfortable room anywhere.

But naval men are peculiar, and it suited the rollicking tastes of this thoroughly good-hearted sailor to have a cave all to himself, where he could do as he liked, and neither landlord nor landlady could interfere with him.

At night, when the winds blew, and the stormy sea dashed its spray against the wooden panelling which shut in the front of the vault, he and his friends would burst into a noisy chorus which would drown the tumult of wind and wave.

When Dick and his conductor reached the beach, they walked a little distance along the wall.

The lieutenant stopped short before a small door, which he opened with a key.

"Open, Sesame!" he exclaimed dding, "Now, my young Cornelius Nepos, you see my den."

"A gloomy-looking den too," answered Dick; "had you not better light the gas?"

He said this jestingly, and was surprised to see Smart strike a fusee, and actually light four burners of a chandelier, which gave an excellent light.

"Don't you be in too much of a hurry, young Vulgar Fractions!" exclaimed the lieutenant. "At a vast outlay I had the gas laid on, which reminds me that I have the unpaid bill at this moment in my pocket. This is not the Temple of Vesta, and the fire cannot always be kept burning, though if we had known you were coming, we would have had the Saturn illuminated in your honour."

"Don't chaff, Harry. I'm not in the humour for it, old boy," said Dick.

"It's my nature. 'What's bred in the bone will come out in the flesh.' I once chaffed a nigger in Otahiti to such an extent that he immediately went and drowned himself, and his melancholy example was followed by his whole family; but as niggers are plentiful in those parts, they were not missed, and the king of the country gave me a testimonial."

"What a crammer!" Dick observed, laughing.

"It's a fact," answered the lieutenant, solemnly; "and now," he added, "what will your youthful mind delight in, in the way of drink? Some beer? I thought so. Look in that box on the

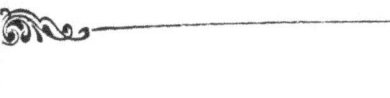

"MISS BODMIN APPEARED ON THE SCENE WITH A POLICEMAN."

left. No, not that one, stupid, that's champagne! Here's an intelligent animal from the scholastic world, who don't know a champagne from a beer bottle."

"Yes, I do!" said Dick, producing one.

The cork was drawn, the door was shut, and the gas burned brightly.

Lieutenant Smart lighted a cigar and smoked placidly; he was thinking; Dick sipped some beer, and thought too.

"Look here, young Bread-and-Scrape," said the lieutenant suddenly.

"Well?" said Dick.

"It is not well! What is to be done with you? You have bolted from your ship—cut and run, as we say."

"I suppose I'll have to go back again," Dick said, with a sigh.

"And be put in that black hole, but that won't do. I must get you out of that; still, it's a good thing to stick to your ship, even if the skipper is a rank bad un; I must get to windward of him somehow. I've got an idea in my mind."

"What is it?"

"I'll go to-night about tea-time, and say I have been sent to inquire for you by your father; then they will say you are in the cellar, and I will insist upon being taken down to it at once. So I shall see Snarley come out, and pretend to be very indignant at you being minus. It will be a rare lark. I know I shall laugh till my sides ache; Snarley's appearance is sure to give me fits."

"I'll sleep here to-night, with your permission," said Dick.

"Have a room at the hotel."

"No, thank you, they might find me out; I have been taken away from one hotel, and it makes one look such a fool. This cave is just the place to hide; lend me a rug and an old boot for a pillow, and I shall be right enough."

"Very well. But I want to get this Snarley down here," answered Smart, his eyes twinkling with anticipated fun.

"That would be splendid. How can we do it, though?"

"Leave it to me. I've got a dodge," said the lieutenant.

Dick did not ask any questions.

After a little more conversation, and another bottle of beer, they strolled about the Parade and on the West Pier.

After this they went into the hotel to dinner, which was provided in sumptu-

ous style, and Dick enjoyed himself immensely.

"This is better than hot and fat," he said with his mouth half full of turkey and sausage.

"What's that?" asked his friend.

"Why, we generally have mutton at Simcox's, and he asks us, 'Hot and fat for you, hot and fat?' meaning, will we have hot meat or cold, and have it cut lean or fat, for we are not allowed to waste anything; we must eat all on our plates."

"You may do what you like here. So pitch in and take in cargo for a long voyage."

The dinner over, the lieutenant looked at his watch.

"Just time for a weed," he said, "and then I must be off. I wouldn't miss seeing Snarley come out of that hole for anything."

At length he started and travelled in a cab to Harrow House, Kemp Town, and knocked at the door of Mr. Simcox's establishment for young gentlemen.

The principal received him kindly, but apologised for keeping him waiting a short time, saying—

"The fact is, sir, I am short-handed to-day. I only keep one usher, and he has mysteriously disappeared."

"Indeed!" said the lieutenant, stifling his laughter.

"I sincerely trust that nothing of an unpleasant nature has happened to him. He was a most estimable man. Can you inform me if you have heard in the gossip of the town of anyone being found drowned?"

"Can't say I have," answered Smart.

"But it seems to me I have not yet explained the business I have come upon."

"You have not, sir; though if you are desirous of placing one or more sons at my establishment, a reduction will be made for two. I need not say that."

"Hold on," interrupted the lieutenant. "How can a man want to send sons to school when he isn't spliced?"

"Ah! true; forgive me, sir. It is a brother, I presume."

"No; it isn't."

"Or a cousin? Ah! I perceive—a dear, yet distant relation, presumably an orphan. How Mrs. Simcox will cherish the poor friendless creature!"

"You run on so fast, Mr. Greek and Latin," said the lieutenant, "that I can't get an oar in edgeways. I've come here to see Dick Lightheart. His father is anxious about him, and you will oblige me by sending him in here."

"I must tell you about that boy, sir!" exclaimed the professor, becoming grave, and he told his visitor the whole story of his running away, and that he was in the black hole. "But," he added, "as the time is nearly up, we may as well let him out. I will let him off the remainder of his sentence, and say that my clemency is due to your intercession."

"Is that how you treat the poor little orphans your wife is so fond of?" asked Smart, but the professor pretended not to hear him, and they went downstairs together, the lieutenant insisting upon attending at Dick's restoration to liberty.

"I do believe that Mr Snarley has the key," exclaimed Mr. Simcox, as they stood outside the heavy, ominous-looking door.

"Send for a locksmith," suggested Smart.

"What's this?" asked the professor, as his foot kicked against something hard.

It was the key, which Dick had dropped in the passage.

"I hope that the hardened boy will show some signs of penitence," observed the master, as he put the key in the lock.

Behind him stood a servant with a light, which enabled them both to see the figure of Mr. Snarley emerge slowly from a dark corner as the door fell back.

"Why, what is this?" said the professor, rubbing his eyes, "Mr. Snarley! Can I believe the evidence of my senses?"

The usher made signs to the effect that he was too exhausted to speak, and wanted something to eat and drink.

Putting his arm in that of the usher, the professor supported him in this way to the kitchen, where he had a chair given him, and was supplied with a jug of ale.

"How did you get in there, my dear sir?" asked the professor.

"It was the cunning of that artful boy," answered the usher, speaking slowly; "when I went to give him his bread and water last night, he said there was a rat in the straw. I went to kill it; he popped out and made me a prisoner."

"What impudence!"

"How did you like it?" asked the lieutenant.

"Horrible!" answered Snarley.

"If it was so to you, how much more so must it be to a mere boy?" continued Smart. "You have had a good lesson, and it serves you right, and if Mr. Simcox does not promise me that place shall never be used again for the same purpose, I will expose him in the newspapers."

"Well, on consideration, I will give the undertaking," said the professor; "Mr. Snarley reports badly of the system, and it shall be discontinued."

"Now, where is the boy?"

"Ah! where indeed?" answered Simcox.

"Gone again?" asked Snarley.

"We have seen nothing of him; he must have run away a second time."

"It will be best for you to find him," said the lieutenant, "as his friends are very anxious about him, but I daresay he will be found somewhere in a short time, and I will not write to his father until to-morrow evening, when I will come up and see you again. Good night. I hope you liked your quarters, Mr. Snarley. By the way, if I should by any chance run up against Dick, shall I tell him you caught that rat?"

"No, sir, I did not catch it, but I believe I can smell a rat now," replied Mr. Snarley, with dignity.

"What do you mean?"

"It's my impression you know where the boy is, and have only come up here to gloat over me and my sufferings."

"I gloat over you?" cried the lieutenant. "In the first place I don't know how to gloat; if I did, I shouldn't over a contemptible gerund-grinder and boy slave-driver. Don't say a word to me, sir, or I shall be tempted to spoil the beauty of your figure-head, and knock you into the middle of next week."

"The law will protect me from your violence," replied Snarley, emboldened by the beer he had imbibed.

"I have punched a man's head, and been fined forty shillings for doing it, at Portsmouth, once when I had come ashore from a cruise, but I considered it a cheap luxury at the price."

"Sir, I must request you to leave my kitchen and my house. This riotous behaviour is unseemly," observed Mr. Simcox.

"Oh! And you want to have a go-in at me too?" said the lieutenant. "Well, I'll be off; but I must have a parting shot at that old mummy in the chair."

Seeing a bag of flour on the dresser, he took it up and threw it at Mr. Snarley.

It struck him on the head; the paper broke, and the flour fell in a whole cascade all over him.

"This is an outrage, sir!" said Mr. Simcox, seizing the lieutenant by the arm.

"Don't touch me, old Fireworks!" cried the fiery lieutenant.

There was a tub of dough standing by, and, grasping the professor by the waist, he tipped him over right into the trough, where he lay floundering and plunging, crying loudly for help, and joining his threats to those of Mr. Snarley, who was vainly endeavouring to get the flour out of his eyes.

Mrs. Simcox, alarmed at her husband's position, took up a spit and rushed at the lieutenant, who parried the thrust with his umbrella, and made his escape by the area.

His cab was at the door, and, jumping in, he was driven away, laughing heartily at his successful attack on the "gerund-grinders," as he called the professor and his assistant.

When Dick heard the story, he was delighted, and said he should have liked to be there.

"But," he added, "it will make him all the more savage when I get back."

"I shall stay here some time, and you can always come to me. I'll protect you, my lad, and now suppose we go somewhere? Go to the theatre and see the horsemanship. That's about your line of country, isn't it? Do boys like a circus?"

"Stunning!" said Dick. "Will you treat me to the circus?"

"Like a shot—pick up your cap, and come on." They left the hotel together, and walked along the Parade, and turning up a side street, came to the building in which the horsemanship was going on.

The place was not crowded, so they got two good seats in the stalls.

There was some riding and bare-backed feats. Then came the Bounding Brothers of the Caucasus, and Mr. Merriman, and a sprite, who popped up out of a trap in the floor in the most marvellous manner.

After that the appearance of the star of the evening was announced.

This was Miss Agatha Mountserrat, who was pronounced by all the crowned heads of Europe as the most accomplished and peerless horsewoman in the world.

At least this was what the bills said about her. She came on riding a splendid black horse, and looked a very pretty, well-made, fair-haired girl of seventeen, or thereabouts, sitting gracefully in the saddle, smiling at the jokes of the clown, while she waited for the band to begin.

The horse held itself in readiness, and she stood up on its back, bowing to the audience.

There was a crack of the whip, and the horse started suddenly. Dick said to his friend—"What's that?"

He pointed to the stage.

There was an indication that the trap up which the clown had come had not been properly fastened.

The lid hung down a little, and it was clear that if any great pressure was put upon it, it would go down.

For instance, if the horse trod on it, he would fall and perhaps break his fair rider's neck.

"What is it?" asked Smart, looking at the girl with admiration, and not paying much heed to his companion.

"The trap is down. I don't know much about stage business, though I was always very fond of theatres; yet I can see that it is dangerous. Miss What's-her-name will come to grief."

The music struck up and drowned his voice. For a moment he hesitated.

The horse and its rider, increasing their speed, approached the perilous spot.

CHAPTER XV.

MR. SNARLEY IS SOLD AGAIN.

BEING a boy of courage and ready resources, Dick did not stay to consult his friend any further. Delay was dangerous.

In a few moments the horse would be at the spot, and the accident would happen.

He could not bear the idea of such a pretty girl being carried away on a stretcher, bruised, mangled, and bleeding—maimed for life, perhaps. So he determined to act at once.

Standing up in his seat, he put one foot on the railing which divided the orchestra from the stalls, and sprang right over the heads of the musicians into the circus.

"Hallo! Dick. Here, I say, what are you up to?" cried the lieutenant.

He thought he was mad.

Dick paid no attention to him, but, standing in front of the horse, waved his hand, and shouted—

"Back! back! for your life!"

Miss Mountserrat saw something in Dick's earnest manner which made her feel sure all was not right.

She reined in her steed with some difficulty, and brought him to a halt just in front of the trap. At the same moment the clown seized Dick by the arm, and said—

"What is the meaning of this, young gentleman?"

The musicians stopped, and the audience stood up to see what was going on.

"Look at that trap," said Dick.

"What do you mean?" asked the clown.

As he spoke, he moved his position, and stood on the trap.

Only for an instant, though, for the trap gave way, and down went the clown.

"That's what I mean," said Dick, laughing at his disappearance.

Being used to trap-work, the clown caught hold of something in his descent, and was not much hurt; he soon climbed up again.

Bowing to the audience, he said—

"Here we are again!"

The trap was made fast, and the performance went on.

"Come with me," said the clown, who led Dick off by a side entrance.

When they were out of the din and bustle of the circus, and in a small room, which was used as the green-room, the clown said—

"You have done me a service, sir. That girl Polly is my daughter, and if the horse had stumbled, there is no saying what might have happened to her. My name's Hopkins. Polly shall thank you herself presently. As for me, Tom Hopkins is your friend for life."

"I am very glad I was lucky enough to stop the horse," answered Dick. "I thought something was wrong."

"You've very likely saved my Polly's life."

"Miss Agatha Mountserrat?"

"Yes. That's her professional name, you know. 'Polly Hopkins' wouldn't look half so well in the bills."

"Oh! I see."

At that moment Polly came in, having finished her performance, and the hall rang with plaudits. Going up to Dick, she took his hand and kissed it gratefully.

"I can never thank you sufficiently, sir," she said, "for your presence of mind."

"Don't say any more now," said Dick. "I am proud to make your acquaintance I shall come and see you again."

"Do, sir; ask for Hopkins at the stage door, and he'll give orders that you are to be shown behind at once."

"Perhaps you can do something for me some day. There is no telling," said Dick; "I may run away from school and want to go into your business."

The clown shook his head.

"Better keep out of it, sir. It's little pay and hard work," said he.

The bell rang, and father and daughter had to go on again—the former to make the audience laugh, the latter to appear in a new trick act.

They took leave of Dick, and begged him to return again, and one of the officials led him round to the front, where he joined his friend. But before he parted with the pretty Polly, he had begged one kiss, which she laughingly let him take.

"So you go in for saving people's lives?" remarked the lieutenant. "You are developing, young Fractions, your character is showing itself. I'm proud of you, and I'll have an account of this in the Brighton papers to-morrow."

"She's very pretty," said Dick, abstractedly.

"In love, eh! Well, there's no knowing what folly a schoolboy may be guilty of."

"Were you never in love?"

"I'm never out of it," laughed the lieutenant. "I began when I was a naval cadet, and wanted to run away with a publican's daughter; but he found me out and gave me a good hiding with an oak plant. I thought my heart was broken, but it wasn't."

When the performance was over, they went to the cave, and Dick curled himself up in a rug.

"Are you fond of your bed?" asked Smart.

"I don't know," answered Dick. "I'm never awake long enough to know. When I get into bed, I fall asleep, and in the morning I have to turn out when the bell rings."

The lieutenant wished him good night, and went to the "Bedford."

Dick dreamt of pretty Polly, and thought that Snarley paid her some attention, whereupon he knocked the usher down; but he slept well nevertheless, and was at the hotel for breakfast at eight.

The lieutenant thought all day long how he could play some trick on Snarley.

"I've got it," he said, at last.

"What?" asked Dick.

"Never mind," was the answer. "You stop here, my young and intelligent friend, and you shall see what you shall see."

Dick sat down in the cave, and the lieutenant went away.

In an hour's time he returned with Mr. Snarley, whom, to Dick's intense dismay, he introduced to the cave.

"I have been to Harrow House," he said, "and told them there that I met you this morning, and Mr. Snarley has come with me to take you back."

Dick groaned; but a wink from

Harry Smart gave him to understand that there was something going on which he did not comprehend.

"Misguided boy!" said Mr. Snarley, with a pious snuffle. "This gentleman has shown that he is your friend by coming to us and giving you up: prepare to accompany me to Harrow House."

"Not yet," said Smart; "you must have a social glass first, Mr. Snarley. We have to make up our little quarrel of yesterday."

"It is forgotten, sir," replied the usher; "you covered me with flour, but you have promised me another coat, and I am satisfied; but this black sheep——"

"I say, Mr. Snarley, don't you call me names. If you throw bricks, so can I!"

"Truly," answered the usher. "The ways of the ungodly are devious. However, I will drink the cup of peace with you."

"What's your liquor?" asked Smart.

"All spirits are invigorating, but rum for choice."

"That's your sort," answered the lieutenant, mixing a stiff tumbler of rum and water.

He slipped into it a little red powder he had obtained from a chemist, who was a friend of his, and who had assured him that it would, if mixed with a spirit, produce drunkenness in ten minutes.

Mr. Snarley drank the mixture, and with a sigh of satisfaction, held out the glass for more.

"What, another dose? You're going it, old Beat-the-boys. But I like gin, old Spankem, and here's your health," said the lieutenant.

Mr. Snarley sat down, and this time sipped his rum and water.

"It is not often that I indulge, but we have scriptural authority for saying that it is a poor heart that never rejoices. Wine was given to glad the heart of man."

"Truly, this man is repenting," said Snarley.

"I've squared it with the governor for you, Dick," said the lieutenant. "You are to receive a free pardon when you get back, and on the understanding that you will be a good boy in future, the past is to be forgotten."

"All right," said Dick.

Suddenly Mr. Snarley became vivacious, and was seized with a desire to dance.

"You have been in the navy, sir?" he said.

"I have. What of it?" replied Smart.

"In my youth I could dance a sailor's hornpipe. Push aside the table, and I will oblige you with an attempt to do so once more. Can you whistle the tune?"

"I've got a fiddle in the cupboard, and I can play it on that."

"Good again," answered Mr. Snarley, smiling blandly.

The table was pushed on one side and the violin produced.

Mr. Snarley began to dance and indulged in such serious contortions that the spectators were choked with laughter.

This made the rum get into his head, and presently he sank down on the floor insensible.

"He's tight," said Dick.

"Tight as a fly; and so would you be if you had taken what he has. I've drugged him," answered the lieutenant.

"What are you going to do with him?"

"You don't suppose I brought him here for nothing, do you? Unfasten that bundle. It contains a complete clown's dress, which I bought this morning at a costumier's I mean to dress him in it, and send him home like an ass as he is. I've got something that will revive him, though it won't make him sober."

"What a lark," laughed Dick, unfastening the bundle.

The lieutenant prepared some paint to ornament the usher's cheeks with, and arranged a wig which he had obtained expressly for him.

Meanwhile the unfortunate Mr. Snarley was wholly unconscious of what was going on.

CHAPTER XVI.

STRICT DISCIPLINE.

WHEN Mr. Snarley was rendered quite incapable of protecting himself, or knowing what was going on, the lieutenant proceeded to dress him in the gay theatrical dress he had procured for the occasion.

The clown's wig fitted him to perfection.

They powdered his face, and put a few streaks of paint on it, and then he was ready to go home.

"I think he'll do," said the lieutenant, looking admiringly at his work

"Just another dab on the nose," suggested Dick.

The dab was applied, and the unfortunate usher pronounced perfect.

"Go and bring two flys," commenced the lieutenant, "and I will apply the restorative. I only want him to be fuddled; if he is quite stupid, there will be no fun."

Dick went out of the cave, and his friend gave Mr. Snarley a draught which brought him to himself.

He did not know what had been done to him; but he had a vague idea that he ought to go home.

"So you shall; lean on my arm," said the lieutenant.

"And the boy?" said Mr. Snarley.

"Will come with us? Leave it all to me. Am I not your friend?"

"You are," replied Snarley, pressing his hand. "I know it; I feel it. And this night is one of the proudest passages in my life. Lead on, sir, I will follow you."

They met Dick at the entrance to the cave, and he supported Mr. Snarley at the other side.

In this way they proceeded to the cliff, where the flys were waiting.

Mr. Snarley was handed into one, and though the light was imperfect, the flymen could not help laughing.

"Is there anything ridiculous about me?" asked Mr. Snarley.

"Nothing, I hope," replied Dick.

"Why then are those men indulging in vulgar laughter?"

"It is their way," said the lieutenant, as they helped him into a fly. "We will follow you, sir. You must go first, and prepare Mr. Simcox for our arrival."

Mr. Snarley's head was in such a confused state that he scarcely knew what he was doing.

His chief idea was that he wanted to go home and get to bed.

So the flys started, and quickly came to Harrow House.

That in which the lieutenant and Dick were, stopped short of the school, but Mr. Snarley was driven boldly up.

The knocker sounded, and Mr. Snarley entered, walking straight into the professor's sitting room, where the latter and his wife were.

They had just finished supper, and their surprise at beholding the apparition that burst upon them may be easily imagined.

"Who are you, sir? How dare you intrude upon me at this hour?" said the professor, who did not know him in the least.

"Yes, how dare you?" echoed Mrs. Simcox, with equal indignation.

"What! not know its own Snarley—its favourite usher?" said that gentleman, in a maudlin tone.

"Are you Mr. Snarley, and in this guise? Why, your gait is unsteady; your breath smells most alarmingly of rum. It is the voice of Snarley, but it has the appearance of a clown."

"Giv'sh some wine," said the usher, seizing the decanter of sherry and helping himself.

"Mr. Snarley, you shall not," said the professor, taking the bottle from him; "you forget yourself, sir!"

"Fal, lal, la; fal, lal, la," said Mr. Snarley.

"What *is* the meaning of this extraordinary conduct?" said Mr. Simcox, in perplexity.

"Fal, lal, la. It's a way we have in the army."

"Mr. Snarley!"

"It's a way we have in the navy. Fal, lal, la. Jolly fellows, navy men."

"Bother the navy," cried Mr. Simcox.

"We, sir, do not bother the navy," said Mr. Snarley, gravely. "Navy is our great safeguard."

"Mr. Snarley!"

"Sir, to you."

"This behaviour is most reprehensible."

"It's all right, sir. It's only a way we have in good company. Fal, lal, la. 'What jolly dogs are we.'"

Mr. Snarley began to gracefully pirouette in front of the window, and eventually did a break down in the most approved burlesque style.

Mrs. Simcox had a keen sense of the ridiculous; she laughed till the tears ran down her cheeks.

Not so her husband.

He was furious, and pursued Mr. Snarley round the room, trying to catch him; but the usher dived under his arms, and reappeared in another part of the room, throwing out his huge arm, with a "Fal lal la, fal lal la, what jolly dogs are we!"

Dick and the lieutenant had mounted the railings outside, and were able to peer into the room, through the corner of the window, which was not quite hidden by the blind, and they enjoyed the spectacle immensely.

At length Mr. Snarley missed his footing, lost his balance, and fell back on the table, which was one of two leaves.

As he fell in the centre the screws gave way, the two halves tilted, and all the supper things fell with a crash upon the unhappy man, who lay in the midst of cold meat, pickles, bread, and a fine dry dinner sherry at thirty-six the dozen!

"Mr. Snarley, get up, sir. Are you hurt? How do you feel now?" said the professor, shaking him.

"I feel happy, sir," answered Mr. Snarley, smiling blandly. "I feel as if some one had died and left me a boarding school, replete with pupils, furniture, and all the stock-in-trade of a successful seminary It has always been my dream. Let me sink calmly to my rest. Adieu! In the language of the poets, sir, I say, solemnly, adieu, sir! adoo, Samivel! The time has come. But no matter."

His eyes closed, and he began to snore loudly.

Ringing the bell for the servants, who were as much surprised as any one else at the usher's condition, it was with the utmost difficulty that they got him to bed.

When the scene was over, Dick and the lieutenant returned to their hotel, and laughed heartily over the adventure.

"And now, Dick, what is your little game?" asked Lieutenant Smart.

"I shall go home to-morrow."

"Home?"

"Yes," said Dick, "and see if I can't make some arrangement with the governor to go somewhere else."

"Do you know what he'll do?"

"No."

"Of course I cannot speak with certainty," continued the lieutenant. "But from my knowledge of your father's character, I will bet a pound to a pinch of snuff that he sends you back again."

"If he does, I suppose I must go," said Dick, "though I am determined I won't stop long at Simcox's. I hate the place. A public school is the place for me."

"And Mr. Lightheart dislikes them very much. I have heard him say so. However, take your chance."

They went to bed, and Dick, in pursuance of his plan, borrowed some money from his friend to pay his fare to Hayward's Heath.

He thanked him very much for his kindness, which he declared he should never forget.

They shook hands at the station and parted, for some time to come, as the lieutenant went to Portsmouth in a few days, and they were wide as the poles asunder.

Dick could not help feeling a little nervous as he walked over to Ingarstone, and neared the Rectory.

Looking into the study window, he saw his father engaged in writing; and thinking it best to take the bull by the horns at once, he walked in.

"Oh, it's you, sir," said his father, laying down his pen. "Where have you been?"

"Been, father?" replied Dick.

"Yes, been, sir! I have received a letter from Mr. Simcox, detailing your conduct, and saying that you had absented yourself from his control."

"I have been staying at the 'Bedford' with Lieutenant Smart."

"A nice companion, upon my word. Well, what are you here for?"

"Because I don't like Simcox's."

"As a rule boys generally dislike their schools," said the Rev. Septimus Lightheart. "But I'll tell you one thing, you will have to like it; expect no encouragement from me. I am a believer in strict discipline, especially for wayward boys like you. I shall have your idleness punished, and I will take you back myself, at once."

"Let me have some dinner first," said Dick.

"Well, I have no objection to that. Go and see your mother and sisters; at three o'clock we will start."

Dick, looking rather crestfallen, left the study, disappointed at being so coldly received by his father, but his good sense told him that he deserved the reception he had met with.

Mrs. Lightheart was delighted to see him, as were his sisters, and when he told them some of his adventures, they could not help laughing heartily.

"Your sister Emily is going to school," said his mother.

"Indeed. Where?"

"At Brighton. Miss Bodmin, our governess, has taken a school, which, oddly enough, is at the back of Mr. Simcox's house; your playgrounds will join one another."

"And we can talk over the wall, Dick," said Emily.

"What fun," said Dick.

"Miss Bodmin is a good creature," answered Mrs. Lightheart, "and I hope she will succeed in her new venture. Emily is to be one of her first pupils, and, perhaps, Agnes will go afterwards. I would not trust the dear girl with anyone else, but Miss Bodmin has my perfect confidence."

"I don't mind going back so much now," Dick said to Emily. "You and I will see what we can do to assist the old girl."

Emily smiled and told him not to be a bad boy.

Mr. Lightheart was as good as his word.

At three o'clock he started for Brighton with Dick, whom he lectured all the way, and said that he hoped his master would make an example of him as he deserved.

CHAPTER XVII.

"DO UNTO OTHERS AS YOU WOULD BE DONE UNTO."

THE Rev. Septimus Lightheart was received with open arms as it were by Mr. Simcox, whose eye brightened still more when he saw Dick.

"Come in, sir; you are very welcome. I opined that your son had sought the refuge of your home, and that you would bring him back again," he exclaimed.

"Can I talk to you?" asked the parson.

"Certainly, my dear sir; let us hold a little friendly converse. Come in."

"Dick," said his father.

"Yes," replied Dick, a little sulkily.

"Stand in the hall till you are called."

Dick sat down, and his father went with Mr. Simcox into his private room, where there was a good fire, and the two gentlemen sat down and began to talk.

Dick's ears tingled, and he felt that he was the subject of their conversation.

Presently Mrs. Simcox came into the hall, and started at seeing Dick.

"What! have you come back again? —and where have you been?" she asked.

"Up a tree, ma'am," said Dick.

"What on earth does that mean?" inquired the good lady.

"Never mind, I've got down again; and my father is in the library with Mr. Simcox."

"Your father! Is he here?"

"Yes, ma'am, and he says I'm to be better treated in future. I told him about having mutton for dinner four times a week, and the black hole, and all that, and he says if I'm not better treated, he shall take me away."

"Dear me; you are treated as the other boys are," said Mrs. Simcox.

"Yes, ma'am, but they're strong and I'm not. I've been delicate from my birth," replied Dick.

"Have you really? Why did you not tell me so before? Did you dine before you came?"

"Just had a snack, ma'am. I could eat something, but nothing coarse; I'm so delicate. If you had a pheasant now——"

"Just the very thing," answered Mrs. Simcox. "I dined in the middle of the day, but Mr. Simcox, you know, Dick, always dines late. There's a pheasant for him, and a very fine one too. You can partake of it, but leave some for him, or else he will have to put up with the cold mutton. Poor boy, I did not know you were delicate."

"Dreadfully, ma'am," answered Dick, putting his tongue in his cheek when she wasn't looking. "But I'll try and eat a wing of the pheasant. Is there any bread sauce?"

"Oh! yes. I made it myself."

Mrs. Simcox led Dick into the kitchen and put before him the bird which had been prepared for the professor.

She told him not to cut it about much, and to enjoy himself while she went to the top of the house.

Dick set to work with a will, and began to demolish the pheasant in a manner that would have struck terror into the heart of Simcox.

The bird happened to be a very nice one, and done to a turn.

"In for a lamb, in for a sheep," said Dick to himself, "I'll polish the beggar off, and the professor will have to put up with cold mutton, as his wife touchingly observed."

While he was engaged in this pleasant manner, his father and the schoolmaster were engaged in earnest conversation.

"I don't think he is a bad-hearted boy," observed the Rev. Septimus Lightheart, after he had listened to Mr. Simcox's catalogue of evils; "I admit that he has done what he ought not to have done, and I confess, also, that had he not been a very bad and mischievous boy at home, I should not have sent him to school, yet I think he can be reclaimed, and made a respectable member of society; your studious boys do not always make great men."

"That is true, they do not," said Mr. Simcox. "But you remember the fable of the hare and the tortoise. The tortoise won the race, though the hare was the swifter of the two. This lad has set me at defiance, and he is so mischievous and full of tricks, that I am never safe. Fancy his bringing home my usher in a state of intoxication, and dressed like a clown."

"That was not altogether his fault. I know his cousin, Lieutenant Smart, well, and he is just the one to think of such a thing, and enjoy its execution. However, I have brought the boy back, and leave him in your hands."

"Very well, Mr. Lightheart. I will do my best with him, for your sake. You are a gentleman whom I respect, and whom I have to thank for the reference in my prospectus. Can I offer you any refreshment?"

"None, I thank you. By the way, my girls' governess, Miss Bodmin, is about to become a neighbour of yours."

"So I heard," said the professor.

"A very worthy lady."

"I hope she may get on, though Brighton is so overstocked with schools that great interest is required."

Mr. Lightheart soon afterwards took his leave, and Mr. Simcox called his wife.

"Well, my dear, so the runaway has come back; and now for dinner. What have you?" said he.

"A fine pheasant; I only took off a wing," said his wife.

"A pheasant, very good," said Mr. Simcox, rubbing his hands, "send it up, I am hungry."

Presently Mrs. Simcox returned in dismay.

"What's the matter, my dear? Nothing wrong with the pheasant, I hope?" remarked her spouse.

"Indeed, there is. I found Dick Lightheart shivering in the passage, and he told me he was very delicate, and his father had said he was to have something nice to eat, so I told him to take a bit of your bird, and——"

"What?"

"He has eaten it all up."

"The wretch!" said the professor, angrily. "He shall suffer for this! eat my dinner! delicate indeed! He shall live on bread and water for a week."

"I am very sorry," said Mrs. Simcox, "but I did it for the best, and did not know he was such a glutton as to go and gorge the lot. He must have done it out of spite."

It was no use to grumble, and the professor had to put up with the cold mutton, much to his disgust.

During the unsavoury meal, he reflected how he should deal with Dick.

Mr. Snarley came in to say that Dick had made his appearance in the schoolroom, and was talking to the boys with as much impudence and assurance as ever.

"It was as much as I could do to keep my hands off him, sir," he said.

"You were quite right to restrain yourself, Mr. Snarley," answered the professor.

"But what's to be done with him?"

"Caning has no effect. We have put him in the black hole, and that did not result successfully. What have you done with the clown's dress?"

"I have it in my press, sir."

"Very good. Suppose we sentence him to live on bread and water for a week and to wear that dress. Will not that be punishing him on the principle of 'Do unto others as you would be done unto?'"

"A bright idea, sir," answered Mr. Snarley. "I think we shall hit him if we make him ridiculous, and hurt his pride."

"It shall be done. Go and bring the dress, and follow me to the schoolroom," said Mr. Simcox.

The principal had looked forward to a good dinner, and was dreadfully irate at being cheated out of it.

He was angry, also, at the pranks Dick had played on the school, which was as quiet and orderly and well-conducted an establishment of its kind as could be found in the town.

The boys were kept in such a state of subjection that they had lost all spirit, as we have said, and it was only owing to Dick's indomitable temperament that they began to pluck up a little courage.

When Mr. Simcox entered, Dick was making all the boys roar with laughter at his account of Mr. Snarley's return dressed as a clown, of which occurrence they had been studiously kept in ignorance.

"Lightheart, stand forward," exclaimed Mr. Simcox, in his most awful and commanding tone.

"Yes, sir," replied Dick, coming to the front.

"You have been guilty of the grossest breaches of discipline, and no ordinary amount of correction seems to do you any good. Therefore I am about to punish you in an extraordinary way."

"My father says he won't have me hit, sir," replied Dick, inventing a falsehood, for his father had said nothing whatever about it.

"No matter what your father said," answered the professor; "for in my school you are under my discipline, and if I chose to cane you, I should certainly do so. But I have resolved to adopt another course. 'Do unto others as you would be done unto' is a golden motto, is it not?"

"Yes, sir."

"Very well; out of your own mouth will I condemn you. You ate my dinner. For one week you shall have the usual breakfast, tea, and supper, but at dinner time, while the savoury steam of roast or boiled is rising gratefully to the nostrils of the other boys, you shall have nothing but bread and water to eat."

"Please, sir," said Dick.

"Listen," thundered Mr. Simcox; "you dressed Mr. Snarley in the attire of a clown; for one week in school, and during vacation, you shall wear the self-same dress."

Dick sank back in a seat.

This declaration quite took his breath away.

Nothing for dinner but bread and water, and to go about dressed as a clown; the punishment was as severe as it was merited.

He had expected to be caned; that he was prepared to submit to.

He had thought of another night in the black hole, and that he did not care much about.

"Perhaps you will be cured in time of your mischievous propensities. If you are not, it will not be my fault," continued Mr. Simcox.

Mr. Snarley now made his appearance with the clown's dress, which Dick was compelled to put on, much to the delight of the boys, who laughed loudly at the comic appearance he presented.

"No laughter," shouted Mr. Simcox. "Go on with your work, and, Dick Lightheart, sit here on this form in the centre of the school-room. It will be your place for one week."

Mr. Simcox retired to digest his cold mutton, by the aid of a cigar, and the boys went on with their lessons till tea time.

Dick waited till Mr. Snarley's back was turned, and then put his hands in his large pockets, just as he had seen the clown do it in a pantomine, and he made a grimace at the same time.

All the boys were looking at him; in fact they could not take their eyes off him, he looked so funny, and when he made a face, they had the greatest difficulty to refrain from laughing.

Mr. Snarley heard stifled laughter.

"Who's that?" he cried. "Messiter, were you laughing?"

"No, sir," said Messiter.

Dick put his tongue in his cheek, and Messiter roared; a box on the ears rewarded him for his trouble, and Mr. Snarley advised all the boys to be careful.

But no sooner had he silenced one than another began, and his arm ached with hitting them.

He could not catch Dick in the act, for he looked studiously at the book whenever the usher turned round or came near him.

Tea time was a relief, and the boys could indulge their merriment, which they did freely.

"Oh!" said Messiter, "I wish you wouldn't make me laugh so. Snarley has half killed me."

"Somebody must suffer for it," answered Dick. "I can't be rigged out like this for nothing."

It was some time before the boys got used to him, and Dick reflected that whenever he met his friends of the circus again, he would have acquired quite a comic turn, and might make himself useful in the show.

Three days afterwards he was in the playground, and he heard laughter on the other side of the wall.

"Miss Bodmin and her girls have come," he thought.

Messiter, as usual, was with him, and he told him to go and get the steps.

"The steps! What for?" asked Messiter.

"There is a girls' school over the wall, and I want to go and see them."

"All right," said Messiter.

And he went for the steps, which were kept in an out-house.

Dick mounted them, and, springing

lightly over the wall, dropped gently down in the midst of about twenty girls.

They were astonished beyond measure at his strange appearance.

Taking off his cap, which had made him seem still more grotesque, he bowed politely.

"Here we are again!" he said.

CHAPTER XVIII.

THE NEW GOVERNESS.

DICK was not long before he discovered his sister, who was holding a skipping rope for the other girls.

"Emily, dear, don't you know me?" he said.

"Don't 'dear' me," she replied. "I will call Miss Bodmin! How dare you come into our playground?"

Dick laughed.

"Well," he said, "my disguise must be complete if you don't recognise me. I'm your brother Dick, just come over the wall from Simcox's to have a look at you. You asked me to, you know."

The other girls left off playing and looked curiously at him.

"I saw him jump down from the wall," said one, named Fletcher.

"Did you?" exclaimed Emily. "Perhaps it is Dick, after all! He is full of his tricks."

"Don't disown me, Emily. Look at my mole," said Dick.

"Your what?" echoed the girls in chorus.

"My mole. Emily knows I've got a mole on the left side of my nose, just under the eye."

"So he has," remarked Emily.

"Oh, do look, Miss Lightheart," said Miss Fletcher.

"If he has got the mole under his left eye by the side of his nose, it must be Miss Lightheart's brother," observed Miss Stonor.

"How interesting," remarked Miss Grey, who was of a sentimental turn of mind.

"Very much so," said Miss Jarvis, who was quite a big girl. "But I am afraid it is awfully improper."

"What's improper?" asked Dick.

"Looking for moles on strange people's faces."

"You go to Jericho!" answered Dick. "Not that I mean to be rude, but if you never do any more harm than looking for moles, you won't hurt."

"Oh, the wretch! I'll go and tell Miss Bodmin. Oh! I never did!" said Miss Jarvis.

"Dreadful!" ejaculated Miss Grey.

"Come on, Emmy, or else the old un will come, and I shall be turned out," said Dick.

Emily Lightheart approached and looked at Dick.

"Oh, yes, he has got the mole, and it is Dick. Oh, Dick!" said Emily.

"Oh! oh!" cried all the girls, and then looked quite excited at the advent of a boy in their playground, who was disguised as a clown.

"What does it all mean, Dick?" asked Emily.

"This is the reward of merit," answered Dick. "Whenever a boy distinguishes himself, Mr. Simcox dresses him up in this dress."

"Really!"

"He's so pleased with me that I've got to wear it for a week. It's called the philosopher's costume, and I'm to have a medal, and lots of books as prizes; I can tell you I'm a big swell."

"What a funny thing! You don't know how odd it makes you look."

"Ah! my dear, you must work hard as I have done, and attend to all your duties, and then you'll reap the reward of merit."

"I always thought you were clever, Dick," said Emily.

"People don't know half what I can do yet. They've been obliged to send away the mathematical master because he can't teach me any more," said Dick.

"Indeed! Miss Bodmin was saying this morning, that she must engage a lady to teach us mathematics, because she has so much to do and is such a bad hand at figures."

"Did she? Come here. Emmy, I have got an idea. You won't say anything?"

He whispered in his sister's ear.

"Will you really?" cried Emily.

"Won't I?" answered Dick; "you see if I don't, but you mustn't get chatting and spoil the fun. It will be a lark."

"Run, Dick, run," exclaimed Emily. "Here's Miss Bodmin coming. That horrid Miss Fletcher has been and fetched her. I shall be so wretched. Do, please run."

"All right."

Dick was off in an instant, after making a face at, and then kissing his hand to the girls, who were delighted at his impudence.

A friendly tree enabled him to gain the top of the wall, and he slipped over into his own playground.

He moved his arms up and down like a bird flapping his wings, and said—

"Cock-a-doodle-do!"

"Well," asked Messiter, "how did you get on?"

"I saw my sister, and I'm going after a situation," answered Dick.

"What's that?"

"Mathematical mistress at the ladies' school."

"Nonsense!"

"I am, though. The next time I can get out I shall buy some things at a second-hand shop, and dress up like a governess, with mittens, and all that sort of thing, and have a wig, you know, so that I shall make up stunningly."

"Does Miss Bodmin want one?"

"So Emily says. The hours are from twelve to one three times a-week, and I shan't be missed out of the playground when I get rid of this clown's tomfoolery. I wish Simcox had it on."

"I know how you could get rid of it," said Messiter.

"Do you? Eternal gratitude, and all that sort of thing, if you will tell me," said Dick.

"You know the cistern at the bottom of the playground?"

"Yes."

"Well, it's just over the dust heap. Let you and I play at bat and ball, and send the ball into the cistern. You go after it, and fall in. It isn't deep enough to drown you. Then get out and slip into the dust heap. That will ruin the clown's clothes,

and they will have to give you some brandy and water, put you to bed, and give you your own togs. Mr. Simcox won't mind much, for you have worn the things some time, and the joke's becoming rather stale."

"So it is; get a trap. I've got a ba somewhere in one of these big pockets, said Dick.

In a short time they were playing at bat and ball, and the ball was skilfully directed by Messiter into the cistern, which had no lid.

"There's a clever thing you've done," said Dick.

"What's that?" asked Mr. Snarley, who happened to be prying about the playground.

"Why, he's sent my new prize ball into the cistern, sir."

"I'll get it. It can't have had time to sink yet," Dick continued.

"Take care," said the usher; "the water is cold and the cistern's deep."

"All right, sir," said Dick, singing "'He bravely bore, mid snow and ice, a banner with the strange device, Excelsior! 'Take care,' they said, 'the water's cold, the cistern's deep, be not too bold.' But he answered, as he grasped firm hold, 'Excelsior!'"

"What a boy that is," remarked Mr. Snarley.

"I never supposed he was a girl, sir," replied Messiter.

"Silence. I don't want any of your impertinence. Hullo! What's that? He's gone. He's in the cistern. Bless my soul!"

Mr. Snarley ran to render what assistance he could, for Dick had vanished in the depths of the cistern.

He quickly reappeared, however, but without the ball.

Stumbling as he reached the dust-heap, he rolled over and over, and reached the ground covered with ashes.

"Are you hurt?" asked the usher.

"Save me, save me!" cried Dick, as he rushed into Mr. Snarley's arms, and clung round his neck, hugging him until he was half suffocated and as dirty as himself.

"Drat the boy!" exclaimed Mr. Snarley, as he shook himself free, "he's spoilt my new Melton cloth black coat. Drat him! I say."

"Oh, sir, I'm very sorry," Dick said,

penitently. "I didn't mean to do it, but getting into the cistern gave me such a turn you don't know."

"Bother the cistern."

"What am I to do, sir?"

"Go to your dormitory and take off your clothes. Really you boys are such a plague that I would rather beg bread in the streets than be continually persecuted by you," replied Mr. Snarley, surveying his dirty plight with ineffable disgust.

By this plan Dick got rid of the obnoxious dress which had caused him so much annoyance, and appeared in school in the evening in his usual clothes.

The next day, instead of going to Brill's to have a swimming bath, he went to an old shop near the theatre and purchased a dress, a shawl, a bonnet, kid gloves, &c., and took them home in a bundle.

His next difficulty was how and where to dress himself, but he contrived to make friends with Sarah the housemaid, who told Polly the cook, and they both agreed, for the fun of the thing, to help him.

"I don't want you to get into trouble," said Dick.

"It don't matter much if we do lose our places," said Sarah; "it's all hard work. I never was in a school before, and I'll take very good care I never go into another."

"So say I," remarked the cook, "and if Master Lightheart likes to have a bit of fun, why, we'll help him."

"If you could just help me to dress," exclaimed Dick, "say in the scullery—I could pop these clothes over my own, and get out at the side door, don't you see? No one would be any the wiser. If Mr. Simcox saw me come in, you could say I was your sister."

"So I could, but a nice sister you'd be," said Sarah, with a laugh.

"Now, Sarah, mind what you're about, or I shall take a kiss," said Dick,

"Take two, if you like," she answered, tossing her head impudently.

Sarah was not a bad-looking girl, and Dick took her at her word. He did kiss her. Cook got jealous, and he had to kiss her too before she was satisfied; and, after the kissing had been satisfactorily accomplished, they were both in good temper, and it was agreed that Dick should the

very next day put his plan in execution.

With the assistance of the servants, Dick had little difficulty in dressing himself.

He went out at the kitchen door, and walked demurely to Miss Bodmin's, which was only round the corner in the next street.

He walked a little stiffly, but that was in his favour.

He was shown into Miss Bodmin's parlour, and the good lady did not keep him long waiting.

The wig he wore was dark, and though she might remember his features, he did not think she would find him out.

"Good morning, madam," he said, making his voice as soft and low as possible. "I hear you are in want of a lady to teach mathematics."

"I am," said Miss Bodmin. "Your name, if you please."

"Miss Sharp."

"Ah, thank you. From whom did you get your information?"

"From the Rev. Septimus Lightheart, the Rector of Ingarstone, in whose family you lived so many years," he replied.

"Indeed. It is a strong recommendation to me. I have the utmost regard for Mr. Lightheart, and one of his dear daughters is under my charge at present. I hope to have Agnes, the younger one, soon. Have you known the family long?"

"Well, ma'am, to tell you the truth, I am a distant relation of Mrs. Lightheart, but I don't want that to go any further," said Dick.

"This is interesting," cried Miss Bodmin. "Did you bring me a letter from Mr. Lightheart by way of introduction?"

"No."

"It is usual in such cases."

"I am aware of that; but Mr. Lightheart said I had only to mention his name."

"Have you any testimonials?"

"I had several," Dick said, "but I have come from Yorkshire, and was robbed of my—my reticule in the train."

"What part of Yorkshire? I too, come from that county."

"Beverley, near Leeds."

"SETTING HIS TEETH TOGETHER, DICK CLIMBED OVER THE GARDEN GATE."

No. 5

"Bless me! my native town," said Miss Bodmin, rapturously. "We must have a little conversation."

Dick had spoken at random, and felt rather uncomfortable. However, he smoothed down his dress and put on a pair of spectacles with which he had provided himself.

The situation was becoming embarrassing.

CHAPTER XIX.

MATHEMATICS EXTRAORDINARY.

"ARE you short-sighted?" inquired Miss Bodmin.

"Very, ma'am. I have worked hard," replied Dick.

"You are young to have defective sight. May I inquire your age?"

"Three and twenty."

"Dear me, you do not look it; but study will affect the eyes. You remind me about the face of some one I have seen. Oh, Mr. Lightheart's eldest son. There is a strong similarity about your features and his own, Miss——"

"Sharp, madam."

"Thank you. I have such a bad memory for names. But we were talking about Beverley."

"Yes, Beverley, near Leeds," replied Dick, feeling more and more uncomfortable.

"Did you know the Smiths?"

"Oh, yes; lovely girls the Smiths," answered Dick.

"So they were. But the boys—oh, the boys were such Turks. How they used to kiss me under the mistletoe at Christmas. Did they ever attempt their impudence with you?"

"Once."

"Only once?"

"That is all, and then I slapped their faces."

"Quite right," sighed Miss Bodmin. "I once thought that the eldest Jones would—but no matter, 'tis a dream of the past. Now to business."

Dick breathed again.

"What salary do you expect?"

"I have other engagements in Brighton, and I will leave that entirely to your discretion, ma'am," replied Dick. "Take me for one week on trial, and then we will talk about terms."

"That will suit me very well," replied Miss Bodmin. "I engage you without making any inquiries, as I consider Mr. Lightheart's reference perfectly satisfactory and quite sufficient. Will you give the dear girls a lesson this morning? Just half an hour to commence with. I must tell you that I am classical, and biographical, and geographical, but not mathematical."

"Thank goodness," Dick mentally exclaimed.

"Follow me, Miss Sharp. But first of all, will you join me in a glass of ginger wine?"

Dick said he would.

They had ginger wine together, and Miss Bodmin kissed Miss Sharp.

"How rosy your cheek is, dear. Do you paint?"

"No, Miss Bodmin," replied Dick.

"Not a little bit?" said the schoolmistress. "Ah, now, confess. You *do* paint a little bit, or you would never have that colour. As for me, I powder and paint too."

"Do you?" thought Dick. "I'll remember that."

"You dear little thing. I know we shall be good friends. It was so kind of Mr. Lightheart to send you to me," cried Miss Bodmin.

She wanted to kiss him again, but Dick backed out of it, pretending to cough.

"If it was that Miss Stonor who was with Emily yesterday, I shouldn't mind," he muttered; "but I can't stand this old frump."

Miss Bodmin led the way into the school room, where the girls were assembled.

She called out half a dozen names, and said—

"The young ladies whose names I have called will stay and be examined as to their proficiency in mathematics by Miss

Sharp, whom I now introduce for the first time. The others may go and play."

The girls got up and went away, only those whose names were mentioned staying.

There was a sly twinkle in Emily Lightheart's eye. and Miss Stonor also seemed amused.

The other girls appeared to take little interest in the advent of the new governess, though they looked spitefully at her, and made critical remarks about her.

"Young ladies," said Miss Bodmin, "I will leave you with Miss Sharp, who has come with a high—I may say very high recommendation from an old esteemed friend of mine. If I hear of any breach of discipline, rest assured it shall be severely punished."

With this announcement Miss Bodmin left the room, and shut the door behind her.

The girls began to talk amongst themselves.

Dick was at first embarrassed, and did not know what to do, but soon recovered his courage and resolved to assert his authority.

"Silence!" he exclaimed.

All the six girls looked at him.

"Young ladies," he said, "I have come here to teach the young idea how to shoot. I am not now speaking of archery, but of the mind. I hope you have all mathematical minds, because if you have not, it will be a serious obstacle to our intercourse. Now, Miss Lightheart, oblige me by telling me what is a straight line?"

"Oh, Dick!" exclaimed Emily.

"How dare you, miss?" exclaimed Dick, sternly; "my name is Miss Sharp."

"But we all know it isn't," observed Miss Stonor; "we are aware that you are Emily Lightheart's brother."

"Who let the cat out of the bag?" asked Dick, laying down a book he had taken up, and resuming his natural manner.

"Emily did."

"Oh, Emily, thou false deceiver," exclaimed Dick. "What shall I do to you? Shall I kiss you all round?"

Murmurs of dissent arose.

Girls don't like being kissed all round.

They like to have to themselves whatever kissing they indulge in.

"Let's have a game at hunt the slipper; the old porpoise won't be in again for half an hour," Dick said.

"Capital!" exclaimed Miss Stonor; "I don't mind, if all the other girls are agreeable."

"Who's got a slipper?" Dick went on. No one answered.

"You have, Emily," he said, "and it's down at heel for a sovereign—they always used to be."

"Oh, Dick!" said Emily, in her tone of mild remonstrance.

"Pull it off."

She did so, and they all sat in a ring.

Dick was the hunter, and soon the fun grew fast and furious.

The girls passed the slipper from one to the other, and were too quick for him.

At last he got hold of it, and Emily had to hunt, while he sat down between Miss Fletcher and Miss Stonor.

"How nice!" he said; "I haven't felt so jolly for I don't know how long. Toss up which shall have a kiss, darling."

"Don't go on so," said Miss Davis, laughing.

"Oh, you are rude," said Miss Stonor.

"I've got the slipper, Emmy," said Dick, and he tossed it to the other side.

Suddenly the door opened, and the slipper, which was thrown as a boy throws a ball, struck Miss Bodmin in the face.

"Oh! my eye," she said, putting her hand to her face; "oh! my eye, my eye!"

"It's a case of bolt," thought Dick to himself. "I'm stumped this time. Just like my luck."

The door was the only means of exit, and Miss Bodmin was standing on the threshold.

It was wonderful to see how quickly the girls got up and sat on the stools, looking at each other just as if nothing had happened.

Dick was the only one who was at all disconcerted.

"Miss Sharp," said Miss Bodmin, in her most stern voice, "what's the meaning of this?"

"Girls will be girls, ma'am," said Dick.

"What do you mean?"

"They suggested a game at hunt the slipper, and I was weak enough to acquiesce. It shall not occur again, I assure you."

"But my eye?" said Miss Bodmin, feeling the injured optic.

"I hope the injury is not severe, ma'am."

"Whose is this slipper?"

"Mine, ma'am," answered Emily.

"And you threw it?" said the schoolmistress.

Emily did not like to get her brother into trouble, and she determined to say that she did.

"Yes, ma'am," she said.

"You, miss, go to your dormitory and get into bed, and wait till I come to you. Such conduct must not be passed over lightly," said Miss Bodmin, addressing Miss Sharp. "Oblige me by coming to my private room; I had no idea that my girls were so unruly. This behaviour in school hours demands some explanation."

"Certainly, ma'am," said Dick. He winked at the girls.

There happened, unfortunately for him, to be a disagreeable one amongst his class.

This was Miss Fletcher, who had called Miss Bodmin when he had jumped over the wall in his clown's dress.

She advanced to Miss Bodmin and said —"Can I say a word to you, Miss Bodmin?"

"Well, what?" said Miss Bodmin, impatiently.

"Miss Sharp is not Miss Sharp."

Miss Bodmin stared.

"I'll never kiss you again," whispered Dick, who was close by.

"What do you mean?" asked Miss Bodmin.

"She is Emily Lightheart's brother."

At this declaration, Miss Bodmin turned red, green, and blue.

She gasped for breath.

"It cannot be him! Have I lived to be deceived in this way?" she said.

Dick winked at the girls, and made a stiff curtsey. "I did not come here to be insulted, Miss Bodmin. My name is Sharp, as I have the honour of telling you, and my profession is that of a teacher of mathematics. I wish you a very good morning, and inform you that our agreement is at an end."

Miss Bodmin did not know what to do; at one moment she was inclined to believe Miss Fletcher, and, at another, she fancied he really was Dick Lightheart.

Emily was questioned, but she would not confess anything, merely replying vaguely that she did not know, and Miss Fletcher was cut by all the girls for telling.

In the meantime, Dick walked gaily back to the kitchen entrance of Harrow House; as he opened the door, he almost ran into the arms of Mrs. Simcox, who was going to look at the larder.

"Take care, young woman. Mind where you are running," she exclaimed.

"Beg pardon, I'm sure," said Dick. "Are you the cook?"

"Cook! bless me, what an hinsult," cried Mrs. Simcox, who as we have said, often confused her H's, when excited. "Me the cook! Who are you?"

"Well, my name's a secret," said Dick, mysteriously.

"Who have you come to see?"

"The governor."

"What governor?" cried Mrs. Simcox, trembling with rage.

"Mr. Simcox; he met me in the street yesterday, and asked me to come up and see him in the middle of the day. I was to take care and not run up against his wife, who, he said, was hideously ugly."

"Hugly! Me hugly?"

"Well, it can't be you," continued Dick, "because you are not at all bad-looking for your age."

The compliment mollified her.

"No," she said, "hi'm not Mrs. Simcox, only a friend; but what did Mr. Simcox say to you?"

"He told me he loved me, and we went into a pastrycook's shop, and had some soup and sherry—so nice—and then he kissed me. So nice. He is a delightful man. I love him so; tell him I'm here, will you?"

"I'll tell him. Oh, yes," continued Mrs. Simcox, grating her teeth with rage. "You wait here, miss, till he comes back. I'll tell him. Won't I?"

Bursting with rage, Mrs. Simcox went away to summon her husband, and left Dick half strangling himself with suppressed laughter.

"The fat's in the fire now, and no mistake," he muttered. "Won't it be a spree when old Simcox says he don't know me? She'll tear his hair out by the roots. I know she will."

CHAPTER XX.

MRS. SIMCOX IS JEALOUS.

DICK had not long to wait before Mr. Simcox made his appearance.

Fear was mingled with astonishment in the countenance of the worthy professor, who was dragged rather than led by his angry spouse.

To be told that a young woman wanted him was an overwhelming announcement, for the professor prided himself on his moral life and unexceptionable character, and when it was added that he had taken her into a confectioner's shop and treated her, afterwards telling her to come to his house and mind she did not meet his wife, he could not help fancying there was some mistake.

"There must be some mistake. I will soon put it right, my dear," he exclaimed, advancing quickly along the passage to the back door.

Dick put his finger to his lips and with a significant air nodded his head in Mrs. Simcox's direction.

"I'll call again," he said. "It's all right. We understand one another."

"What do you mean, you brazen hussy?" exclaimed Mr. Simcox.

"Another time will do," answered Dick.

"Thomas," said Mrs Simcox, addressing her husband in her most excited manner, "I hask you hif you know this 'ussy."

"Know her! I'll swear that I never saw her before in the whole course of my life," answered the bewildered schoolmaster.

"Oh, Tom, Tom!" exclaimed Dick, putting his handkerchief to his eyes, and pretending to cry. "Not know your own Fanny. You'll break my heart."

"There!" cried Mrs. Simcox, "she calls you Tom just has I do, and says she's ' your own Fanny.' Wretch, how you have wronged me. 'Ere 'ave I been slaving for years to keep hup your school, and this is hall the reward I get."

"That's just what he says. You're too much of a scrub for him. He does not like a drudge," Dick remarked.

Mrs. Simcox seized the professor by the left whisker, and administered a hearty box on the ear.

"Did you say so? Oh! you villain! I'll have your life, I will," she screamed.

"As Heaven's my witness, I never said anything of the kind," cried the professor "She's made a mistake. She's come to the wrong house."

"No, I haven't, Tom, but I'll say so if it will save you from getting into trouble," Dick exclaimed. "Good-bye, old man, we shall meet again some day, and then for sweet kisses. Oh, the dear little man, he does kiss so nicely."

This was more than Mrs. Simcox could bear.

Letting her husband go, she rushed at the supposed young woman, who had begun to beat a retreat, and caught her on the pavement.

"No, you don't," she exclaimed. "Hi 'aven't done with you yet. I'll teach you to creep into respectable 'omes like a viperish beast, and render man and wife miserable. I'll give you something to remember me by."

Strong as Dick was, he was unable to hold his own against Mrs. Simcox, who was a muscular woman, and her strength was increased by her fury, which had reached an ungovernable pitch.

Thump, thump, her blows descended upon Dick's back and shoulders.

His gown was torn into shreds, and after the lapse of about a minute and a half, Mrs. Simcox was leaning against the wall in strong hysterics, holding up in triumph a flaxen-haired wig.

"I knew it hall halong. I was sure hit was a wig," she gasped at intervals.

Blinded with rage, she did not scrutinise the person of her victim, who certainly presented a most peculiar appearance.

Deprived of his wig, his own hair stood up in a wild sort of way.

Blood oozed from scratches on his face; his bonnet hung round his neck by the strings, and rested on his back, which, through the rents in his dress showed his jacket, and his trousered legs were apparent through the awful tears in his once trim and pretty skirt.

"Why, it's not a woman at all!" exclaimed Mr. Simcox, "it's a man dressed up! No, it's a boy! We've been hoaxed."

"Hoaxed?" faintly repeated his wife.

"Yes; it's a boy. It's Dick Lightheart; he's been playing a trick upon us. You ought to have known I could never be unfaithful to you, my dear, after all these years, too. Oh! Martha, Martha, what a fool you've made of yourself!"

"Oh, Tom!" cried Mrs. Simcox, as the truth dawned upon her, "come to my harms! Oh!"

With a spasmodic cry, she threw herself into his by no means eager embrace, and with two or three hysterical shrieks, suitable to the occasion, fell into a faint.

"Case of carry me out, sir," observed Dick.

He had begun to recover his serenity, and, with mock modesty, gathered up his skirts with a mincing air, which made the servants who had come up to the area steps of the different houses to see the fun, shake with laughter.

"Confound your impudence!" cried Mr. Simcox, who did not know what to do with his wife, she being a good weight. "You shall leave my house at once and for ever!"

"That will suit my complaint exactly," answered Dick, unconcernedly, as he kissed his hand to the tittering servant maids.

The professor would have shaken his fist at Dick had not his hands been engaged.

"Take her in," answered the latter, "and shut her up. She is not fit to be allowed to run about loose. Look at my dress."

Handing her over to the care of the servants, who assisted her into the kitchen, Mr. Simcox returned to Dick.

"How long, sir, is this disgraceful scene to continue outside my house?" he said.

"I may do as I like in the street, I suppose? It's not your street," replied Dick.

"Do you recognise my authority or do you not?"

"Does it look like it? I ask you as a sensible man," Dick said.

"What am I to do?" cried the professor, dragging at his hair frantically.

"Apologise for your behaviour, and talk calmly. We may then come to some arrangement," replied Dick, adding, "Ah, here is a mutual friend. Miss Bodmin, how pleased I am to see you."

It was the proprietress of the ladies' school who had come to see Mrs. Simcox and discover if she had been tricked, as Miss Fletcher said, or not.

"What is it?" she exclaimed.

"What is what?" inquired Mr. Simcox, rather ungrammatically.

"I am Miss Bodmin, your neighbour," answered the lady. "I keep a school for girls, and I have reason to believe I have been shamefully imposed upon by one of your boys. I allude to that object, that thing with its bonnet off and its dress torn; is it masculine or feminine?"

She pointed to Dick.

"It's a boy, Miss Bodmin, and a very bad boy too. It's Dick Lightheart, the scamp of the family. What has he done to you?"

Miss Bodmin recounted her grievance.

"Infamous!" said the schoolmaster. "But I will exert my authority, if I die for it."

Dick had gathered up his torn skirts, and was performing a dance in the middle of the road for the benefit of those who were looking out of the windows or standing in the street.

"You vagabond!" cried Mr. Simcox, laying hold of him. "Come inside with you. I'll teach you a lesson. Come in. You shan't do this with impunity. Come in, I say! Come in!"

And every time he said "Come in," he cuffed him unmercifully.

By dint of superior force he dragged him into the house, and tore his clothes off, leaving him in his own, so that he was a boy once more.

"There," he exclaimed, flinging him from him in the passage, "that will do for you, I think. Go to the schoolroom. Take your Bible, and write out in a clear, legible hand the Book of Genesis. Be off!"

Dick "pulled himself together," as he expressed it, and went away singing—

"'It seems to me but yesterday since we were boys together.' Chorus. 'Jolly little boys, happy little boys, since we were boys together.' "

Mr. Simcox returned to Miss Bodmin.

"Madam," he said, " will you come in? Anything my poor establishment can offer you is very much at your service."

"Have you triumphed over that boy?" asked Miss Bodmin.

"I have. The wild beast is tamed."

A head was protruded from the passage window.

"Is he?" said a voice; "that's all you know. Don't count your chickens before they're hatched."

It was Dick.

Mr. Simcox took up a stone, but he had disappeared.

He uttered a dismal groan.

"That boy will be the death of me," he said, with a sigh. "I am reluctant to give up the sixty pounds a year that his father pays for his board and tuition, as my school is not a large one, but I do wish they'd take him home."

"I know him of old," remarked Miss

Bodmin, "and I sympathise with you very heartily. I was governess in his father's family. You will never do anything with him, sir, and he will never do you any credit; the boy is naturally a scamp and will come to a bad end. I am sorry to speak in this apparently unkind way of anyone, but it is my duty, and what I say is the result of painful experience."

"I will have him strictly watched, and he shall not annoy you again if I can help it."

"Thank you very much. How I feel for your poor wife. What a scene!"

"Will you come in and speak to her? Perhaps a few words of consolation from one of her own sex——"

"Certainly," replied Miss Bodmin; "I will do so with pleasure."

And the governess was ushered into the house by Mr. Simcox, finding his wife in the kitchen drinking brandy and smelling sal volatile and burnt feathers alternately, while she kicked and struggled one minute, and screamed the next.

CHAPTER XXI.

DICK FALLS IN LOVE.

MR. SIMCOX took secret counsel with Mr. Snarley as to how he should deal with Dick.

He did not like to be too severe with him, because he might run away.

When the irritation natural upon Dick's last freak had died away, neither the usher, nor the principal, nor even Mrs. Simcox could help laughing, the whole affair was so comical.

Over a bottle of good old port and a pheasant in the evening Mr. and Mrs. Simcox positively made love to one another as they used to do in the old times, when he was an usher and she was the cook with savings in the bank.

"How could I have doubted you?" said she.

"As if I would deceive you, my own!" replied he.

And putting down two pheasant bones which they were respectively picking, they allowed their lips to meet in a greasy kiss.

The professor decided that Dick should not be beaten, and that when he had written out the book of Genesis, he would not say anything more to him.

Dick took his time over the book of Genesis; and when he had done six chapters, the thing was forgotten, and he did no more.

During his brief visit to Miss Bodmin's the bright eyes and pleasant smile of Miss Henrietta Stonor had made a deep impression upon him.

He fell in love.

"I shall never be happy," he said to his friend Messiter, "until I marry that girl."

"But you're too young!" replied Messiter, who had some idea of the proprieties.

"Never mind that!"

"How will you keep her?"

"I have written to my sister Emily, and she has written back. Here is her letter. She says Miss Stonor is an heiress, and has thirty thousand pounds. Moreover, she is an orphan. Isn't it nice to love an orphan?"

"I don't know," replied the practical Messiter. "I never tried."

"Poor, unfriended, defenceless thing. She has only an uncle!"

"That's like the babes in the wood. They had an uncle."

"Yes," answered Dick, with a sentimental sigh, "and he sent them out into the wood to starve, and the robins buried them. I remember that."

"Affecting tale, isn't it?" said Messiter, with a smile.

"Don't chaff. I love Henrietta."

"Really!"

"Yes, and I'm going to throw a letter over the wall."

"Mind Miss What's-her-name don't get it."

"I asked Emily to look out for it, and I expect that both she and Henrietta are looking out at this moment. It's such a letter! It's full of love. Emily and Henrietta are bosom friends, and you know what that is with girls."

"Yes," replied Messiter. "They think they'd die for one another."

"Give us a leg up," said Dick, forgetting to speak in the language of love.

Messiter hoisted him up on the wall.

There was nobody there.

The girls were playing about in another part of the ground, but the note unfortunately slipped from his hand.

"I've been and gone and done it," said Dick, as he dropped from the wall.

"Done what?" inquired Messiter.

"The letter has fallen over. Suppose it is picked up by the Philistines?"

"What have you said in it? That's the thing."

"I have told her she is the dearest thing in creation, and that I would give the world for a kiss from her ruby lips, and I have asked her to slip out and meet me this evening in her playground under the wall at half-past-ten."

"Has she got a watch?"

"Don't be so beastly practical," said Dick, in a tone of annoyance; "you are always trying to throw cold water on a fellow. Of course she can guess the time. Suppose they go to bed at ten, can't she count successive sixties, and so make the seconds into minutes, and

shan't I be there and wait for her if she is late?"

"I think it was rather imprudent of you to get on the wall," said Messiter.

"Why?"

"The old dragon may have been looking out of the window."

"Bother the dragon. Who cares for her?" answered Dick, contemptuously. "She was Emily's governess, and I have played her so many tricks that she swears I turned her hair grey before its time."

They turned away and joined the other boys in a game at prisoner's base.

But Messiter's apprehension was well founded.

Miss Bodmin was on the look-out, and she happened to see him mount the wall.

She also chanced to see the little fluttering piece of paper fall to the ground.

"A note," she muttered. "For one of my girls, no doubt, and from that scamp, Dick Lightheart. I must see into this at once."

Accordingly she walked into the playground, and, speaking to one or two of the girls, hoped the young ladies were enjoying themselves.

She picked up the note without being observed and retired into her drawing-room to read it.

At present her school was not large enough to permit her to keep a governess.

She managed the dozen girls she had under her care all by herself, and so she had no one to talk to her about her little troubles.

Opening the note, she read it without scruple.

"Dearest Henrietta," said Dick, "to have seen you once is to love you for ever. My sister will have told you of the deep impression you have made upon me. I shall never be happy without you. Meet me by moonlight alone this evening. The almanac tells me the moon rises at ten. I will be in your playground at half-past, waiting for you. Do, dearest girl, come, or I shall die of disappointment and vexation.—Ever yours, DICK.

"P.S.—Don't mind that old frump, Miss Bodmin, she can't hurt either of us."

"Well, I never!" ejaculated Miss Bodmin, when she had finished the perusal of this precious epistle. "Don't mind that old frump, Miss Bodmin; that's me.

Old frump! I've come to something to be called old frump. That's a bad boy, and his ingratitude is base. I taught him his A B C. I held him when he first tried to walk, and I think I was the first to slap him when he told a story and said the cat drank the milk, while I saw him do it myself."

Walking again in the playground, she tried to contain herself by talking to the girls.

As she passed Miss Stonor, she purposely dropped the note which she had picked up.

Henrietta and Emily Lightheart were walking together. The latter stooped and picked it up.

"Oh, Henrietta," she said, "here is a note for you in Dick's handwriting. How ever *did* it come here?"

"Let me read it," replied Henrietta, eagerly.

The girls retired and read the note.

Scarcely had they finished it before Miss Bodmin came up and snatched it out of their hands.

"Young ladies," she said, "this conduct is unbecoming. Who is the writer of this letter?"

They were silent.

"Emily," said Miss Bodmin, sternly, "you never yet told me a falsehood."

"It's from my brother Dick," said Emily.

Miss Bodmin pretended to read it, although she knew its contents well.

"You both sleep in the same bedroom," she said; "go there with me at once. You shall go to bed, and I will lock the door. That is how I punish girls who behave in such a forward manner as to encourage bold, bad, rude boys."

The girls followed her without a word.

They were locked in their bedroom, and, as the window was many feet from the ground, escape was impossible.

"Dick will be sure to come. What a bother," said Miss Stonor.

"Sure!" replied Emily. "I know him so well. He will dare anything if he has made up his mind."

"Miss Bodmin will catch him."

"He won't care much for that," replied Emily.

"Oh, Emily!" continued Miss Stonor, rapturously, "I do love your brother so. He is so handsome and so daring. I could do anything for him. Do you think he loves me?"

"Yes."

"Have you ever heard him say he loved any other girl?"

"Never!" answered Emily.

"I must meet him. I will tell him how sorry I am his letter miscarried, and do you think if I gave Emma, our servant, five shillings, she would take in a note for me?"

"I should think so."

"That is what I will do then," continued Miss Stonor. "I will write to him, and get her to post the letter, and make an appointment in the playground this day week. I wish Miss Frump—I shall always call her Miss Frump after this—had not taken his letter away that I might kiss it."

Emily approved of this plan, and it was carried into execution.

Both of the girls languished for the rest of that day on bread and water, but when they were released they began to plot.

Emma, the servant, readily offered to post a letter for Miss Stonor, and in a short time Dick heard how and why he had been disappointed.

He had kept the appointment, and after waiting nearly half-an-hour in the cold, Miss Bodmin appeared on the scene with a policeman.

The policeman took hold of Dick and marched him back to his own house, in spite of his protestations.

Mr. Simcox opened the door when the policeman knocked.

"What is it?" he asked.

"Miss Bodmin, sir, next door, has found one of your boys in her playground, and she has got me to take him back to you, instead of giving him in charge," replied the policeman.

"Who is it?—show a light. Dick Lightheart! I thought so," said the professor

"Thank you, policeman; accept this shilling," he added, after a pause, during which he was engaged in hauling in Dick, and getting him in the passage.

The constable muttered his thanks, and retired.

"One shilling!" said the professor to

himself. "But I will stop it out of his pocket money."

"So, sir," he said aloud, "you've been at it again."

"Yes, sir," replied Dick, coolly.

"You did Genesis last; now go and write out Deuteronomy. Go to bed, lest I be tempted to cane you."

Dick slunk off to bed and shed tears when he thought of his dear Henrietta.

But her letter the following day consoled him, and he looked forward to their next meeting.

The reason that Dick got off so easily was that Mr. Simcox was afraid of him.

His most severe punishments had no deterring effect upon so bold and hardened an offender.

Dick, with his usual skill, continued to keep up communication with Henrietta.

She was not sixteen, yet she was madly in love with him, and he, with the romance of youth, thought he could gladly die for her.

He contrived to meet her often in the playground, in spite of the vigilance of Miss Bodmin.

She admitted that she loved him, and he urged her to elope with him.

"What are we to do, dear Dick?" she asked, as she stood by his side in the bleak playground, shivering in the cold.

"Get married," he said.

"When, and how?"

"We can go to some inn. I have a little money, and you——"

"I have just seventeen and sixpence," replied Henrietta.

"I'll get the banns published," said Dick.

And he did.

The next Sunday and the two following ones, the banns were put up between Dick Lightheart and Henrietta Stonor, in one of the churches at Brigton.

This done, he continued to urge her to run away with him on Saturday night, stop at an inn, where he had engaged two bedrooms, one for her, and one for himself, and leave the rest to Providence.

Henrietta consented.

Dick made all his preparations, and they met as usual at half-past ten in the playground.

She had her bonnet and shawl on, and he opened the door leading into the street.

It was an anxious moment.

They walked arm in arm along the Parade.

The night was dark, and the sea roared sullenly on the beach.

"Courage, darling," whispered Dick. "Courage, my own little wife; we shall soon be able to defy the world."

Henrietta clung closer to him, and they hurried away from their schools, looking behind them at times, as if they dreaded pursuit.

It was a foolish undertaking; but they were young, and what is more, they fancied they were in love.

CHAPTER XXII.

RUNAWAY LOVERS.

SOON after the lovers had taken their departure in the romantic manner we described in the last chapter, Miss Bodmin made a discovery.

She had become extra vigilant of late, and went round to the different bedrooms to see if the girls were asleep, before she retired to rest herself.

Miss Stonor's bed was empty.

Emily occupied the bed on the other side of the room, and pretended to be asleep, though she knew very well where her friend had gone and with what object.

Holding the candle to her eyes, Miss Bodmin tried to rouse her, but Emily would not be disturbed until she was violently shaken.

There was no further excuse for pretending to sleep.

"Emily," exclaimed Miss Bodmin, "where is Miss Stonor?"

"I don't know," replied Emily.

"If you do not know where she is, you at least are aware where she is gone."

"No, miss."

"You can't be ignorant of the reason why she has quitted her room at this time of night," continued the school-mistress.

Emily did not answer.

"Emily!" said Miss Bodmin, more sternly, "I have known you from a child, and you must not pain me by continuing to feign ignorance of Miss Stonor's movements. You are not consulting her interest in doing so. You will save her and me too by confessing all you know."

"It would not be right to tell," said Emily.

"Indeed it would. I appeal to you as a young lady of honour to let me know the meaning of this mysterious disappearance."

Still Emily did not speak.

"Oh! my dear child," exclaimed Miss Bodmin, with something like a groan. "How deeply pained your mamma and papa would be if they knew how you are behaving in what is perhaps the crisis of your little friend's life. Tell me, is she in the playground with your brother Dick?"

"No," answered Emily.

"Where then?"

"She is with Dick."

"Having admitted so much, you cannot refuse to tell me something more."

"I will not say anything more, miss, because I promised not to, and you have always taught me that a promise is sacred."

"Not in a bad cause; you are justified in breaking it in a bad cause. Speak, child."

"I will not say another word," replied Emily.

"Then you are a naughty, wicked, bad girl, and I will see how severely I can punish you in the morning," answered Miss Bodmin, angrily.

Seeing that she was losing valuable time in questioning Emily, and believing that what she had admitted was the truth, she resolved to go over to Mr. Simcox.

That gentleman was reading his paper, when the schoolmistress knocked at the door.

Mrs. Simcox let her in.

"Come inside, Miss Bodmin. How flustered you look," said Mrs. Simcox. "I 'ope nothing 'as 'appened."

"Indeed, something has occurred which has quite unnerved me. Can I speak to your husband? Time is valuable, and a pursuit must be organized at once," replied Miss Bodmin.

Without a word Mrs. Simcox ushered her into the dining room.

The professor got up and handed her a chair.

"It's that boy Dick Lightheart again, I'll lay my life!" he exclaimed.

"You are right, sir. One of my young ladies has disappeared—Miss Henrietta Stonor, and I have elicited from a friend of hers that she has gone somewhere with Dick."

"The young Turk!" observed Mrs. Simcox; "what hare we coming to?"

There was a knock at the door.

"Come in!" said the professor.

It was Mr. Snarley, who had come to make his report for the night.

"Well, any news?" asked Mr. Simcox.

"Lightheart is missing," replied the usher.

"We know it. He has run away, so it is presumed, with one of Miss Bodmin's young ladies. What shall we do?"

"Go after them, sir."

"I think that I and Miss Bodmin might take a fly, and drive up and down the principal streets. We may see them. If not, we can communicate with the police. There is no train to London to-night, and they may be in the town. In fact, they must be."

Both Mrs. Simcox and Mr. Snarley thought this a good idea, and the professor put on his hat and coat, and, offering his arm to Miss Bodmin, they went away together.

After going a short distance, they met a fly, and drove along the Parade, through Castle Square, and up East Street.

There were few people about.

The night was dark and cold, and they scrutinised carefully all the faces they saw during their progress.

Suddenly Mr. Simcox exclaimed—"There they are."

Dick, not being very well acquainted with the streets of Brighton, had lost his way, and was looking for the inn at which he had engaged beds.

Had it not been for this unfortunate occurrence he would have been safe from pursuit.

Miss Stonor was getting frightened at being out so late, and began to cry.

She almost wished she had not quitted her school.

Dick was endeavouring to comfort her to the best of his ability.

"Stop," said Mr. Simcox, touching the driver of the open fly on the shoulder.

He assisted Miss Bodmin to alight.

The next moment he had seized Dick by the collar, while Miss Bodmin grasped Henrietta firmly by the arm.

"You young rascal," cried the irate professor, "what do you mean by this?"

"You bold, bad girl!" exclaimed Miss Bodmin. "How dare you behave in such a manner? Where do you expect to go to?"

"Let me loose!" said Dick, struggling violently. "I'll kick."

He was as good as his word.

Mr. Simcox felt his shins violently attacked, and pummelled the lad severely in self-defence.

Miss Bodmin dragged Henrietta into the fly, and, boxing her ears, held her down by her side.

"Oh, Dick, Dick, dear Dick, help me, save me!" the girl cried plaintively.

This appeal maddened Dick, and he struggled so strongly that Mr. Simcox could scarcely hold him.

"Let me go. You have no right to hold me like this!" he exclaimed.

"I'll let you know whether I have a right or not (cuff). I'll teach you to defy me (punch). I've been too lenient with you (kick). You shan't go on like this (box). You young scamp, you shall learn who is your master (hit). Your father gave me authority over you (punch), and told me to do as I liked with you (kick), and I will, too" (punch).

Dick's cries attracted the attention of some passers by, and one amongst them seemed inclined to interfere actively on his behalf.

This was an elderly man, who, looking at Dick by the light of the gas lamp, said—

"I know that face."

Looking up at the sound of the voice, Dick said—

"Of course you do, Mr. Hopkins. I saved your daughter Polly from falling down the trap at the circus."

"That's it. That's what I was trying to remember. I thought I knew you," replied Tom Hopkins.

The old clown was returning home after the performance at the circus.

Fortunately or unfortunately he had arrived just in time to be of service to his young friend.

"You saved Polly and I'll save you," said the clown. "Let him go, governor."

"Go about your business and don't interfere with me, my good man," replied Mr. Simcox. "He is one of my pupils, and I as his schoolmaster have a right to take him home."

"And I dispute that right."

"My name's Simcox. Professor of—"

"I don't care a dump who you are. Let the boy go," thundered the clown.

Mr. Simcox said he wouldn't.

Tom Hopkins wasn't a man to stand any nonsense, and letting out with his left, Mr. Simcox rolled over into the gutter and lay in the mud half stunned.

"Now then, come along with me," said Hopkins, laying hold of Dick's arm.

"But Henrietta——" began Dick.

"Oh! bother Henrietta!"

"I love her, and she loves me."

"If she does, she'll find a way of getting at you. Don't stop, the police will be up directly. To-morrow's Sunday, and I don't care about being locked up in quad till Monday. Come on."

Thus constrained, Dick took a despairing look at Henrietta, and suffered himself to be drawn away by his rescuer.

CHAPTER XXIII.

DICK TAKES MONEY.

LEAVING Miss Bodmin and the professor to get home as best as they might, with the captive and weeping Henrietta, Tom Hopkins and Dick hurried along until they reached one of those small and comparatively cheap thoroughfares in the neighbourhood of Church Street.

Here the clown lodged with his daughter, having the three rooms on the ground floor.

Agatha had quitted the circus before her father, and had changed her gorgeous dress as the " Fair Maid of Circassia," for the homely-looking cotton print of everyday life.

She was engaged in the interesting occupation of cooking tripe and onions for her father's supper as he arrived with Dick.

The onions gave out a most savoury smell.

" Ha!" said the clown, " supper is nearly ready; you will join us, my young friend ?"

" No, thank you," replied Dick.

" Tripe—good—do," urged the clown.

They now reached the sitting-room, and Agatha Mountserrat, or Polly Hopkins, as she was called off the stage, was laying the cloth.

She gladly welcomed him, and when he told his story, and related how he had run away with Henrietta, they both laughed heartily, though to Dick it was no laughing matter.

" It's your first love. You'll soon get over it," said Tom Hopkins. " First love is calf love. Ahem! Polly there wants a sweetheart."

" Go along, father!" replied Polly, with a blush.

Just as they sat down to supper, which Dick was easily prevailed upon to partake of, a tall, gentlemanly-looking man, with whiskers and moustache, dropped in.

" Captain Hanger, our manager, our proprietor, I may say," exclaimed the clown, by way of introduction.

" Who have we here ?" asked the new comer, looking at Dick scrutinisingly.

Tom Hopkins explained how they first met, and how he had again encountered him that evening, and rescued him from his schoolmaster.

The captain laughed, and said—

" I ran away from half-a-dozen schools, but I was never such a fool as to go away to get married. That would have been out of the frying pan into the fire, wouldn't it, Polly ?"

" Don't ask me," she replied, tossing her head.

Supper proceeded, and such is the inconstancy of the human heart, that before the savoury meal was over, Dick believed that Agatha, *alias* Polly, was prettier than his lost Henrietta.

The men filled their pipes and mixed their grog, while Polly cleared away the things.

" Are you all ready for a start to-morrow, Tom ?" asked the captain.

" Quite; where is our next pitch to be ?" replied the clown.

" Lewes, for a night or two, and so on round the coast to Folkestone, Ramsgate, Canterbury, etc."

" Are you going to leave Brighton ?" asked Dick in dismay.

" Yes; the route is decided on, as we used to say when I was in the army," answered Captain Hanger.

" What am I to do ?"

" Go home, I should think, or back to school, or get a ship and go aboard. What did you expect to do ?"

" I thought I could have made myself useful to your company in some sort of way," replied Dick.

" You've got a father, I suppose ?"

" Yes."

" What is he ?"

" Vicar of Ingarstone, near Hayward's Heath."

" I know it," said Captain Hanger, " and a very good living it is. What can you do in our line ? Can you ride or tumble ?"

" No."

" I'll tell you what he might do," remarked the good-natured clown. " He could take money."

" So can all of us, when we get the chance," remarked the captain, with a laugh.

"What's that?" asked Dick.

"Stand at the door, and receive the people's money, as they come in, and put it in the till as you give them their tickets. We're short-handed, and the captain had to do that himself lately."

Captain Hanger thought for a brief space, then exclaimed—

"I don't mind putting him on to take money, just for a start, as he's in a fix."

"Oh, thank you very much!" Dick cried, rapturously. "I'd rather do anything than go home or be sent back to school."

"Consider it arranged then. Tom, you'll make him up a shakedown in your crib here, for the night, and as I shall give him ten shillings a week when we start at Lewes, he'll be able to remunerate you for your kindness."

"I don't want his money," answered the clown. "He saved the girl from being seriously injured, and I owe him something for that."

This arrangement relieved Dick's mind considerably.

Captain Hanger asked him a variety of questions, and appeared to have taken a liking to him, which, on the whole Dick could not be said to have returned.

There was something about the captain's face and manners he did not care about.

It was handsome, yet it was a bad face.

He learnt afterwards that Captain Hanger had been in the army, but was obliged to leave the service on account of his misconduct, being sentenced to dismissal by a court martial.

Having no visible means of subsistence, he lived upon his wits in various ways, until at length a relation died, and left him a small sum of money, with which he became proprietor of the show in which Tom Hopkins played the part of clown.

Being a thorough Bohemian, he got on with his troupe, who regarded him as a clever, though unscrupulous man.

One thing was very much in his favour.

He made the entertainment so far successful that they were all paid on Saturday night, and with theatrical people it is a great thing to have a Saturday.

The next morning Dick accompanied the strollers by train to Lewes, and helped them to make arrangements for a performance in the evening.

Messengers sent on before had placarded the town, and when the evening came, and Dick took his place in the money-taking box, there was a goodly shower of half-crowns, shillings, and sixpences, these being the charges for admission respectively.

Tom Hopkins and Polly treated him with the utmost kindness, and during the day he amused himself by going among the men in the stable or attending the rehearsal.

Polly tried to teach him to ride a bare-backed steed, in which he was not very successful, as he tumbled off more than once, to the imminent danger of his neck, and the "Flying Sons of the Desert," the "Bounding Brothers," and the "Flashes of Human Lightning," as the artists called themselves, advised him facetiously to get inside, and draw the blinds down.

On the fourth night they had what Captain Hanger called a bumper house.

Many of the gentry who had been called upon had bought tickets, and the seats were all full.

The captain came into the box where Dick was at ten o'clock.

"Well," said he, "plenty of coin?"

"Rolling in," replied Dick.

"That's right. How much have you taken?"

"I should say about thirty pounds."

"That's my idea. I put it down at a thirty-pound house," said the captain. "Keep on. I've just stuck up a notice outside that half-price to the pit has begun. There is standing room at the back, and we may as well collar the sixpences of the rustics."

"All right, sir!" replied Dick.

As he went away Captain Hanger dexterously placed the cash-box in which Dick put the money under his coat, which was a heavy Inverness cape, and with it retired to another part of the house.

At half-past eleven the performance was over. Dick was in great trouble, because he had missed the cash-box, and did not know what had become of it.

He could not get out to communicate his loss to any one, and waited with impatience for the appearance of Captain Hanger, who generally came to relieve him of the cash as the lights were lowered.

The captain came in as usual.

" Well !" he exclaimed. " Taken much more ?"

" No," replied Dick, " only seven-and-six."

He pointed to the money which lay on the counter.

" Why didn't you put it in the box ? It is careless to leave it exposed in that way !" cried he.

" I would have done so, but I couldn't find the box !" Dick said in perplexity.

" Not find it ? That's all nonsense ! That tale won't do for me, my boy. This is the best house we've had, and it's my opinion you have stolen the money !"

Dick looked at Captain Hanger as if he could have flown at him and strangled him, but a moment's reflection showed him that the contest would be an unequal one, owing to the disparity of their ages.

Still, a terrible accusation of which he knew himself to be perfectly innocent, had been brought against him.

It was a dreadful thing to be called a thief !

" I give you my word of honour I know nothing about it, sir," he replied tremulously.

" Has any one been in your box ?"

" No one but yourself."

" It isn't likely I should steal my own property, is it ?" said the captain, with a sarcastic smile.

" No, it is not ; but——"

" What ?"

" How could it have gone ?" said Dick.

" Don't try to humbug me. You have either stolen the money-box or handed it to some confederate. I had no great opinion of your character from the first. A man, or rather a boy, who could run away from school and play the pranks I have heard you say you did, is capable of any villany."

Dick cowered before the denunciation, which he did not expect from such a quarter.

He saw now the value of a good character, which he had forfeited by his bad conduct at Harrow House under the care of Mr. Simcox.

" Come ! who is your confederate ?" shouted Captain Hanger.

" I haven't one !" said Dick.

" You won't give him up ! I've a good mind to call in a policeman, and have you locked up for your impudence, but I might have expected to be robbed, when I picked you up as I did."

At the prospect of being dragged off to a police cell on suspicion of having committed theft, Dick trembled in every limb.

" Wait till to-morrow !" he exclaimed. " Do please wait. Something may be discovered by then which will acquit me."

" That is as much as to say that if I give you till to-morrow, you will speak to your accomplice, and try and recover the money. You're an artful young dodger, and no mistake !"

" I haven't taken it, and I know nothing about it," Dick persisted.

" Of course not. Stick to that ; lie it out. However," replied the captain sarcastically, " I'll give you till to-morrow. I shall not say anything, and I advise you to hold your tongue also. Come to my room at the hotel at ten in the morning, and then we'll talk the matter over."

With this Captain Hanger went away, leaving Dick overwhelmed with shame and apprehension.

He went to the lodging he occupied in the town, which was in the same house with Hopkins and his daughter, and retired without speaking to either of them.

For hours he lay tossing restlessly on his squalid bed, and he began to contrast his present position with that he had so rashly quitted.

A hundred times over he wished himself back again at Mr. Simcox's.

That some one had stolen the cash-box he did not doubt for a moment ; nor, on calm reflection, did he blame the captain for accusing him.

He never supposed that Captain Hanger had for his own purposes abstracted it ; all he could do was to bewail his unhappy position, and lament that he could have been such a goose as to leave his school, where he was well fed, well housed, well taught, and well cared for.

The morning came, and with it renewed misery.

He could scarcely touch his breakfast, and with a heavy heart he wended his

"CHAPMAN LAY ON HIS BACK, HAVING A VERY CONFUSED IDEA OF THINGS IN GENERAL."

way to the inn at which Captain Hanger was staying.

The proprietor of the show was smoking a cigar, standing with his back to the fire as he entered.

"Well," said he, "have you come to confess?"

"No," said Dick, "and for this reason, I have nothing to confess. I do not know any more than you do how the cash-box disappeared."

"Do you mean to deny that you were responsible for its safe keeping?"

"Not at all."

"It is a serious loss to me. What am I to do?" asked the captain, with his hands in his pockets, and blowing the smoke through his nose.

"I am entitled to a thousand pounds when I come of age. It was left me by my grandmother, and if you will wait a few years, I will make it up," Dick said.

"But I want it made good now, my fine fellow. I can't afford to lose it. Does your father keep any money in the house?"

"At the Rectory, do you mean?"

"Yes," said the captain.

"He generally has a hundred pounds or more in his desk," answered Dick. "You see he keeps the money that comes from the offertory on Sundays, and as he has frequent payments to make, and gifts to dispense to the poor, to whom cheques would be a nuisance, he keeps the cash by him, but he would not give me any. It isn't likely, when I have run away from school, and led him such a life as I have for so long past."

"You'll come to the gallows," said the captain, bluntly.

"Thank you," replied Dick. "Perhaps you'll go first."

In spite of the unpleasant and desperate position he was in, his old spirit was alive, and he could not allow himself to be insulted without saying something.

"Do you mean to defy me?" cried the captain, angrily.

"You may do what you like," said Dick, sullenly. "I won't be bullied."

"Who's bullying you?" answered the captain, in a different tone. "All I say is, that as I have lost my money, you ought to do what you can to get it back for me."

"That I am willing enough to do," Dick replied, cheerfully.

"You say you are entitled to a thousand pounds when you are of age. This money your father holds in trust for you, I presume?"

"Yes."

"Very well. You further say he keeps money in his desk, but will not give it you. Why not go to his desk and take out what there is in it? It is in reality only taking your own money."

"It would be stealing," said Dick.

"That's what you must do, or I shall hand you over to the police."

Dick was much troubled.

"Take your choice," concluded the captain. "If you do not——"

"Rob my father?" put in Dick.

"I don't call it robbing him at all. It is only taking your own money after all. But if you do not get me the sum I require, I shall prosecute you on suspicion of stealing my cash-box. That's a certainty. You can't get out of that. If you take your own money, as I call it, out of your father's desk, you will not get into trouble. The most your father could or would do, if he found you out, would be to lecture you on the impropriety of helping yourself. But, as I said before, take your choice. I will give you five minutes. One touch of the bell-rope will call the police, and you will be taken off to prison, my boy."

The captain held his watch in one hand while with the other he grasped the bell-rope.

A thousand thoughts rushed pell mell through Dick's brain.

Better, he thought, to accept the terms of Captain Hanger than to have his name in the county papers and to be branded as a thief, even if he were acquitted of the charge.

He little knew that the captain had invented this accusation as a plan for making him rob his father in order to put the money into his own pocket. If he had only suspected the real character of his accuser, he would have defied him, but he did not know that he was a notorious swindler and blackleg.

All that he had got to find out.

"Time's up," said the captain, replacing his watch in his waistcoat pocket

"I'll do it," said Dick, in a strange voice.

"Very well, my lad," answered the captain, "I'll drive you over to Hayward's Heath this evening. Some one else shall be put in your place, and I suppose the show will go on without me for once."

The blood went and came to Dick's cheeks, and he felt sick at heart.

What would he not have given never to have left his school in so rash and reckless a manner, which had brought him into contact with Captain Hanger?

At present, though suspected, he knew he was not a thief, but in a few short hours——

He dared not think what the future had in store for him.

It was too dreadful.

CHAPTER XXIV.

CAUGHT IN THE ACT.

ON the following day Captain Hanger made all his arrangements for being absent in the evening, and after the circus was filled, he told Dick to take a seat beside him in a dog-cart, and they started together for Hayward's Heath.

Dick sat, still and sullen, like a criminal being taken before a magistrate for examination.

He was fast in the toils, and thought it would do him no good to struggle.

The captain spoke to him occasionally, obtaining a short answer in return.

"You needn't be downhearted, my lad," said Captain Hanger, when they had traversed about half the distance; "what you are going to do is not very dreadful. You are entitled to money when you come of age, aren't you?"

"Yes," said Dick.

"Well, your father has the use of that, and you are going to help yourself to a portion of it."

"You said that before."

"Did I?—then I say it again," said the captain sharply, "and I'll say more. It is only through my kindness you get out of the scrape so well."

"What scrape?" asked Dick.

"Stealing my money."

"I did not steal it."

The captain laughed in his own peculiar way.

"I have only your word for that," he said.

"All I know is this; you were, through my generosity, placed in a position of trust, and you had not been there a week before I was robbed; you took the money and put it in a cash-box. When I came for that box, it was missing. Is that so or is it not?"

"Yes."

"Very well, you will not deny that you were answerable for that money?"

"No."

"If I had handed you over to the police, it would have gone hard with you. I have given you an opportunity of putting things straight, and you ought to be thankful. However, we will not talk any more about it; the time has come for acting, so put the best face you can on the matter, and let's have no more sulking."

The captain spoke severely, and Dick did not answer him; he was far too miserable and frightened to do anything of the sort.

They drove on in silence, until they reached Ingarstone, and Captain Hanger rather surprised Dick by his knowledge of the road.

"Here we are," exclaimed he. "This is the Rectory; the lights are out, and I suppose all are in bed."

"You seem to know the place, and the way to it," remarked Dick.

"I ought to," said the captain, drawing up the dog-cart under the hedge which fringed the lawn of the Rectory; "and when you come out, I shall hear your footstep. If anything goes wrong, whistle and I'll make off. I don't want to be seen in this business. It wouldn't look well, and, indeed, I only do it for your sake. You are the son of a gentleman. I am poor. I should not like to see you in the hands of the police, but at the same time I cannot afford to lose my money, either through your fraud or carelessness."

Setting his teeth together, Dick climbed over the garden gate.

Dick was pleased to see that there were no lights in the rectory windows.

This was not surprising, because the members of his family retired to rest early, and if his father did sit up, it was to write a sermon for the ensuing Sunday.

He looked at the study window.

The lamp was on the table, but its flame burned very dimly, and the light it gave was hidden by a shade.

The fire flickered in the grate, and cast fantastic shadows on the floor.

Getting upon the window-sill by the aid of a box tree which grew outside, he pushed up the window and entered.

His father was sitting asleep in an armchair.

Apparently fatigued by work, he had taken a little rest.

The sheets of his sermon were lying upon the table just as he had written them and thrown them on one side when they were finished.

Attracted by an irresistible impulse, Dick approached the table.

He looked over the half-finished folio.

"To you who are young and inexperienced, I appeal specially," the reverend gentleman had written. "The Almighty sends you temptations for which you are little prepared; but if you remember the lessons which have been taught you, and have faith in earnest prayer, you will be spared the sin of falling. Serve thy Creator in the days of thy youth, and he will not forget you in your old age."

Dick read those lines, while the blinding tears forced themselves into his eyes.

He was of a mind to forego his enterprise.

But the reflection that Captain Hanger was outside, and that he would pursue him relentlessly, urged him on to the completion of his crime.

He had left his school, thrown up his home, and estranged himself from his loving friends to throw in his lot among strangers, from whom there was no mercy to be expected.

"I must do it," he groaned.

The cash-box, in which Mr. Lightheart always kept a considerable sum, was placed in the table drawer.

In the drawer was a key.

Turning this, Dick drew out the box, which, from its weight, was well filled.

Suddenly his father moved restlessly in his chair.

Dick remained, as it were, rooted to the spot.

A minute passed, and it seemed an age to him.

Then he glided, serpent-like, to the still open window.

The Rev. Mr. Lightheart nodded again, and Dick breathed more freely.

But as he proceeded, he stumbled over the hearthrug, and the heavy cash-box fell from his hand with a crash.

Mr. Lightheart awoke with a start.

By the pale dim light of the waning lamp, and the flickering gleam from the fire, he recognized his son.

"Dick!" he said. "Am I dreaming?"

The cash-box on the floor and the open window met his gaze, and he comprehended all in a moment.

Rising to his feet, he walked towards Dick, who was so overwhelmed with shame that he could not answer.

Shutting the window, he placed his hand on his son's shoulder, and said in tones of sorrow rather than of anger, "Has it come to this?"

Dick bowed his head.

Never in his life had he experienced such pain as he felt at that dreadful moment.

"Have you come like a thief in the night to rob your father?" pursued Mr. Lightheart.

Dick made no answer.

The old man could say no more.

He sank into his armchair and sobbed like a child.

"He will break my heart," he murmured, adding fervently, "Oh, Lord! may it please you to take this cup of bitter affliction from me; for sharper than a serpent's tooth it is to have a thankless child."

Dick could bear no more.

He was a good-hearted boy, and his father's grief afflicted him ten times more than a severe reprimand or an outburst of anger would have done.

"Oh, father!" he cried, throwing himself on his knees before him, and seizing him by the hand, "Forgive me; hear what I have to say!"

"What can you say?" said Mr. Lightheart, looking at him; but his pale and haggard features startled him, and he added, "Speak; I am willing to hear you."

"They told me that as you were my trustee for what grandmother left me, I might take some of your money, because, in reality, it was only taking my own."

"Who told you this, and where have you been since I had a letter telling me you had left your school, after a series of bad actions which had shocked and disgusted your master?"

"I ran away with a friend of Emily's," answered Dick, "and we went to get married, but Mr. Simcox and Miss Bodmin overtook us, because I had lost my way, and then I met some people connected with the circus, which was going to Lewes, and they engaged me at ten shillings a week to take the money; but last night someone stole the money-box, and they said I did it, and he told me that if I did not go and get your cash-box, he would prosecute me in a police court."

Dick's agitation made him talk in a rather rambling sort of a way, but his father caught the gist of it.

"Who is he?" asked the parson.

"The proprietor of the circus—Captain Hanger."

"Hanger," repeated Mr. Lightheart. "I seem to know that name."

"He said he was born in this parish, as we came along."

"I have it," exclaimed Mr. Lightheart. "His father was a very respectable man —a retired officer in the army, and this man of whom you speak brought his grey hairs with sorrow to the grave. This Captain Hanger was expelled from the service into which his father's long service and interest had introduced him. He has suffered more than one term of imprisonment, and is a ruffian of the worst description. He told you to do this?"

"Yes."

"If you refused, the penalty was to be——"

"He said he would hand me over to the police."

"Do you know anything about his money-box? On your honour, now, Dick; our future friendship and intercourse depend upon the truthfulness of your reply."

"On my word of honour," Dick answered, "I know no more of what became of it than you do, father."

"I believe you," said the old man.

"I may be bad and wild, father," Dick cried, "but I would scorn to tell you a lie."

"That is enough, my boy. Sit down in that chair and thank Heaven that you have this night been rescued from the commencement of a life of crime, which might have ended you know not where."

Dick sat down penitent and humbled, but more hopeful than he had been for some time.

A weight was removed from his heart, which had oppressed it terribly.

He watched his father anxiously as he got out of the window with more agility than he expected from a man of his age, and gradually receded from sight in the distance.

CHAPTER XXV.

DICK GOES TO A PRIVATE TUTOR.

THE reverend gentleman was absent nearly a quarter of an hour, and Dick heard the sound of wheels dashing over the gravel, which gave him the impression that the captain had taken his departure.

"He's hooked it," he muttered; "and a good job too."

What passed between Mr. Lightheart and Captain Hanger Dick did not know, for his father contented himself with saying—

"I have spoken to the bold, bad man, and he has gone, never to trouble us again, I hope. Ah me! what a change a few short years have made in him. Verily, the descent of Avernus is easy."

He did not speak much to Dick that night.

He led him up to his own little bedroom, which was just as he had left it.

Kneeling down by the bed, the good old gentleman asked a blessing on his son, and left him, saying—

"The affairs of to-night, Dick, shall remain a secret locked in my breast. It would pain your relations, and especially your mother."

"Thank you very much. It is just what I wanted to ask you, father, but I scarcely dared," answered Dick, with tears of gratitude in his eyes.

All that was said the next day was that Dick had come home unexpectedly.

He was received with open arms.

Mrs. Lightheart thought that the restraint of a school life was too much for Dick, as he had been always accustomed to a certain amount of freedom.

"Send him to a private tutor's," she said.

"I had been thinking of the same thing myself; the idea is a very good one, my dear," said the parson; "and thank you for the suggestion, as I think he is much more likely to get on with say three or four youths of his own age or thereabouts, who are placed under the care of some competent gentleman. I will look out for something of the kind."

For the next week he made inquiries and carefully read the advertisements, one of which at length engaged his serious consideration.

It ran thus—

"To parents and guardians of unmanageable youths.—The advertiser, an M.A. Cantab., third wrangler, prepares half-a-dozen young gentlemen for the army, civil service, and the universities. A judicious system of discipline is enforced which has had most satisfactory results in numerous cases of self-willed boys and young men. For terms, &c., apply to Mr. M., Highfield Terrace, Hove, Brighton."

Mr. Lightheart went over to Brighton the next day with the advertisement in his pocketbook, and called upon Mr. M., who was a gentleman named Markwell, residing with his sister, an elderly lady, who kept his house.

He had under his care at that time four boys about sixteen, and agreed to receive Dick.

His terms were high, but he spared no care, and kept a liberal table.

When Dick heard of this arrangement, he made no objection.

"You must promise me that you will not run away or disgrace me and yourself," said his father, "because I want you to remain at Mr. Markwell's till you can go to a university."

Dick gave the required promise.

"So you are an unruly boy," said his sister Agnes, with a smile.

"Not more than usual," replied Dick.

"Emily has told me all about you and Henrietta, and they mean to write to you when they can post a letter without Miss Bodmin seeing it; Henrietta has been so punished. They have kept her in and even whipped her, I believe."

"The wretches! What a shame," said Dick, indignantly.

"But that's not what I meant by being unruly. It's the advertisement," continued Agnes.

"I haven't seen that. Whose advertisement?"

"Mr. Markwell's, where you are going. Here it is. Papa showed it ma, and I picked it up."

Dick read it.

"Oh!" he said, in a significant tone, "they might have told me this. I'll let Mr. Markwell know whether his system of discipline will have satisfactory results with me or not. Thank you, Aggy. I had intended to be a good boy, but I shan't now. They won't let me be good when I want to."

"Oh! but you must. Papa says you shall go up to Oxford as soon as you can pass the examination, and then he hopes you'll take to the church, as you can have his living when he retires."

"I shall go into the army," Dick said; "but it's no use talking now. They'll find it all out in time."

"You won't run away, dear, will you?" exclaimed Agnes.

"No, I won't. I've had enough of running away; but I shan't be idle. Mr. Markwell shall admit that I am a most diligent boy."

He smiled again.

"That means that you will play tricks. If you do, write to me and tell me all about them. You are so funny when you begin, Dick."

Dick kissed his little sister, and soon afterwards went to Mr. Markwell's.

This was a quiet, middle-aged gentleman, with a benevolent aspect.

He always liked to trust to the honour of his young gentlemen, and, if obliged to speak severely to them, he did it more in sorrow than in passion.

His was the soft and gentle manner of dealing with refractory boys, and he found it answer.

The boys at present at Mr. Markwell's were Mr. Lawless, the Hon. Henry Brabazon, son of Lord Broadacres, Mr. Burrell, and Mr. Chapman. They were always addressed as Mister, as Mr. Markwell treated them like young men, and made them responsible for all their actions.

Mr. Lightheart did not accompany Dick to the private tutor's.

He gave him some money and the address, and wished him good bye, saying, "I shall expect to hear a good account of you, Dick. I have written to your old school, saying you will not return there. Try and conduct yourself well, for my sake."

"And mine, too, Dick," said his mother.

Dick said he would, and muttered as he drove to the station, "Promises don't cost much. It pleases them and don't hurt me."

At first he had felt deeply grateful to his father for his kindness, but that feeling soon wore off, and he became as independent and callous as before, though he could not repress a shudder when he reflected upon the disagreeable situation in which the unscrupulous Captain Hanger had placed him.

When he drove up to Highfield Terrace, Mr. Markwell came out to welcome him.

"Ah!" he said. "Glad to see you."

"Sorry that I can't return the compliment," replied Dick.

"Ahem! you are Mr. Richard Lightheart, I presume."

"I'm an unruly youth."

Mr. Markwell looked surprised.

"You advertise for them, you know," continued Dick; "so you ought to be pleased when they come. But I am very unruly, indeed. They can't do anything with me anywhere. I've run away from three schools, and been sent away from six more. I'm dreadful. You will have

a time of it with me. I like to be candid."

"Strange boy," said Mr. Markwell, with a smile. "You are a character."

"I haven't got a good one, if that's what you mean."

"Never mind, we shall be good friends, I know," said Mr. Markwell.

"I have my doubts about it, for you'll find me very trying. Just order my things to be taken in, will you?—and, I say, what time do you dine?"

"At two—always punctually at two."

"It is now one," said Dick, looking at his watch. "I shall take a stroll along the Parade. Hove is rather inconvenient for getting into Brighton. It is a pity you don't live more central. Ta-ta! see you at dinner."

As he spoke, he strolled off with his hands in his pockets.

"Here! my dear young sir, stop. This will never do," cried Mr. Markwell.

Dick turned round.

"By the way," he said, "just settle with the cabman, will you? I'm rather short, and you can put it down in the bill, dear boy—stroll on."

Mr. Markwell was astounded.

"Settle with the cabman. Put it in the bill—calls me 'dear boy,' and says, 'stroll on,'" repeated he.

"What is the world coming to?"

But it was useless to try and bring Dick back.

So he paid the cabman, and had Dick's things taken upstairs by the servant.

Miss Priscilla Markwell, the sister, had overheard this scene from the passage, and was as much amazed as her brother.

"What a young imp," she said.

"We must be patient with him," said Mr. Markwell, in his benevolent way. "His father gave me to understand that he was unruly, but do I not advertise for refractory youths? I shall triumph in the end, for though he be like a roaring lion and I like a meek sheep, yet my strength is in my weakness. My system will conquer him."

Miss Priscilla shook her head as if she had her doubts, but as the dinner required her personal supervision, she retired to the kitchen, while Mr. Markwell went upstairs into Dick's room with a bunch of keys, one of which opened his boxes.

He carefully overhauled everything, and was glad to find nothing of an objectionable nature except a pistol which Dick had bought for shooting cats.

In the meantime Dick proceeded towards the Parade. He had not gone far before he met a well-dressed young gentleman, who, as he neared him, did not seem inclined to make way.

The pavement was rather narrow in one part, owing to the erection of a hoarding, during some repairs to one of the houses.

"Get out of my way," said the young gentleman.

"Get out of mine," said Dick.

They glanced defiantly at one another.

"I never make room for a blackguard," said the first speaker.

Dick lifted his hat slightly, and replied with a bow, "I always do," and stepped into the street.

He walked on.

"Here! I say, you fellow," cried the young gentleman.

"Well, you blackguard," replied Dick; "what do you want?"

"I like you—let us exchange cards. I am the Honourable Henry Brabazon, and I am being coached at Mr. Markwell's, near here."

"Indeed, Honourable Henry Brabazon. It's a pity your coach does not teach you manners. I'm Dick Lightheart, son of a parson."

"Are you? Well, here's my pasteboard. I like your pluck. It's rather fun to be shut up as you shut me up. Glad to know you. Let's have a liquor."

"All right," said Dick.

There was an hotel near, and they went into the billiard room, where three young gentlemen were drinking and playing billiards.

"These are our fellows. We are all at Markwell's, and this crib is our headquarters."

"Ah!" said Dick; "very fine training indeed for the army, the universities, and civil service examinations, and for all unruly youths."

"Have you seen that in the governor's advertisements?" replied Mr. Brabazon "It annoys us, I can tell you. We don't like it."

"It's as bad as being ticketed," remarked Dick.

"I'll introduce you. Nice fellows, all of them. Mr. Richard Lightheart——"

"Son of a parson," whispered Dick.

"Ah! yes. Son of a clergyman. My friends—Mr. Chapman, Mr. Burrell, and Mr. Lawless."

The young men bowed.

"Marker," cried Brabazon, "agitate the communicator. Our internal organizations are in a state of exhaustion, which can only be revived by the beer of the country in the pewter of the period."

The bell was touched and the waiter entered.

"I'll toss you who pays," said the honourable, when the beer arrived.

"I'll pay, but I never toss; it's low," answered Dick, throwing a shilling to the waiter, and telling him to keep the change.

"That will do just as well," said Mr. Brabazon.

"Thank you, Honourable Henry Brabazon," answered Dick.

"You must not give me my title every time you speak," whispered Brabazon; "it's caddish."

"Is it?" said Dick, with apparent innocence. "I never met a nobility before. How's your father?"

"All right; but I say!"

"What?"

"You're an odd fish."

"So I have heard before. It's a way I have. Spiffing good bitter, Honourable—I mean Brabazon. How's your mother?"

"Her ladyship was quite well when she wrote last."

"That's gratifying. I feel better," Dick answered.

Mr. Brabazon looked at him with a puzzled expression, as if he could not quite make him out.

"He's getting in a fog," thought Dick. "It's all a lark."

CHAPTER XXVI.

AN UNRULY YOUTH.

DICK looked on at the game which was proceeding, and when it was over, Mr. Markwell's young gentlemen prepared to go home to dinner.

"I'll walk with you: I'm going your way," said Dick.

"All right; buckle to," replied Brabazon, giving him his arm. "We always walk arm-in-arm, and shove the town cads into the street, and the private schools."

"That's your sort," said Dick. "How about the old women?"

"Oh, they have to go too."

"Here's one coming: shall we charge her?"

The old lady, however, saw them ahead, and perhaps knowing Mr. Markwell's unruly boys, crossed over, and got out of their way.

The boys laughed.

"You're a nice set of young men for a small tea party. I should think they'll get up a testimonial for you—tea pot or a medal," observed Dick.

"We let them know a thing or two," answered Lawless.

"Gentlemen should always act as such," continued Dick.

A young man, who looked like a shopman, came by, and, putting his shoulder well forward, Dick gave him a shove which sent him cannoning up against a lamp post, from which he fell on his knees in the gutter.

"Saying his prayers," observed Lawless.

The young man resented this treatment, and came up to Dick with his fists clenched.

"What's the row?" asked Dick, coolly.

"You shoved me into the street!"

"That was your fault, my good lad. We are gentlemen," said Dick. "We've got an honourable amongst us, and I'm the son of a clergyman."

"Take that, Mr. Clergyman," replied the young man.

But Dick slipped back, and cleverly pushed Brabazon forward, who received a severe blow on the nose, which he did not like.

"Come on, all of you!" cried the excited clerk, putting himself in a fighting attitude.

"Gentlemen don't fight with cads," said Brabazon, putting his handkerchief to his nose.

"Oh, don't they?" answered Dick. "Then I shall put my gentility on one side for once. There's something for you, Mr. Tradesman! And when a gentleman hits you another time, take off your hat, and say, 'Thank you, sir!'"

The young man and Dick indulged in a fair fight, which ended in Dick leaving him on his back in the street, in about three minutes, not knowing where he was, and having very confused ideas of things in general.

Brabazon smiled, and they walked on.

"Are you hurt?" he asked of Dick.

"Not got a scratch."

"You polished him off well, but we don't like street rows; they are vulgar."

"You go the right way to get into them," answered Dick. "I shall understand your ways soon. I'm sorry you got that prop on the nose. He knew how to prop, but so did I. Does it hurt?"

"Well, it is painful," answered Brabazon.

They now reached Mr. Markwell's.

"Good bye," said Brabazon, "I can't ask you in."

"Don't apologise, I can sit in the hall," replied Dick.

The young gentlemen stared at him.

"If you've got a bit of cold meat or a hunch of bread you don't want, I shall be thankful," continued Dick.

Brabazon laughed.

"You are a funny fellow, anyhow," he said.

"Regular lick, ain't I?" answered Dick, whose object was to be as peculiar and vulgar as he could, just for the fun of shocking the young gentlemen who, he knew, would enjoy the joke when they found out who he was.

"There's the dinner bell," said Burrell, "we must go and wash. If he likes to sit there, let him."

The others acquiesced, and they all went away, leaving Dick alone.

Presently Mr. Markwell came into the hall.

"Oh, Lightheart," he said, "why are you sitting there? Come into the dining-room. I will introduce you to your future companions."

"Thank you, sir," said Dick.

He was led into the dining-room and given a seat near Miss Priscilla.

Dick saw at once that she wore a wig.

He remembered he had in his pocket a fishing line with a hook attached.

This he carefully got out and unrolled, contriving dexterously to slip the hook into Miss Priscilla's back hair without being perceived, as he got up to shake hands with her, on her brother's introducing him as "The new pupil, my dear."

The line he allowed to fall down upon the ground, but he held it between his knees for instant use when necessary.

The young gentlemen now entered the room, and stared very considerably at seeing Dick.

"Our new pupil, Dick Lightheart," said Mr. Markwell; "you must know one another."

"This is the Honourable Brabazon," interrupted Dick. "I know him. How do, Brabazon? Same to you, Burrell. Wish you luck, Chapman. Servant, Lawless."

"Dear me, how strange! You seem old friends," observed Mr. Markwell.

"Quite old pals," replied Dick. "Honourable Brabazon and I are like Siamese twins, ain't we, Brab?"

Mr. Brabazon was horrified at being called "Brab," and said—

"The fact is, sir, we met accidentally this morning, but none of us knew that Mr. Lightheart was the new pupil, nor did he think fit to enlighten us."

"Funny boy!" remarked Mr. Markwell.

"You'll say so when you get to know me," answered Dick. "I'm all there."

"Vulgar brute!" observed Brabazon to Lawless.

"Ploughboy! Clodhopper! Beast!" answered Lawless.

"Well, silence," continued Mr. Markwell. "'For what we are going to receive,' etc. Miss Priscilla has roast mutton, but I think I have pheasants.

Young gentlemen, you will take your choice."

"Mutton for me, and cut it fat, mum," said Dick.

Miss Priscilla shrugged her shoulders. The new boy's vulgarity was really dreadful.

She assisted him to mutton, and Dick helped himself to mustard.

"He's eating mustard with mutton!" whispered Lawless to Brabazon.

"Awful!" replied Brabazon. "I've heard of it with beef and pork."

"Stunning!" said Dick, with his mouth full, "and real good mealy 'taters.' This is what I call plummy, and no flies!"

Miss Priscilla could bear this no longer.

"Mr. Lightheart," she said, "your education seems to have been neglected, and as you came here for improvement, you must not be offended if I speak to you for your own good."

"No, mum. A little more fat, please; there's a dollop on that side," said Dick, who could himself only with difficulty refrain from laughing.

"You will please to wait," she replied, with dignity; "we pride ourselves here upon our gentility."

"So Brab said, mum, when he drove the old lady across the street and left me to fight the grocer."

"I am sure the Honourable Henry Brabazon is far too gentlemanly to do anything of the sort."

"He says it's caddish to give him his title. But never mind, go on, mum, I ask pardon."

"You must not talk so much at dinner," said Miss Priscilla, "and when you do talk, try to model your conversation upon that of the other young gentlemen whom you have the good fortune to have for your companions."

"Yes, mum; but touching the fat?"

"Be silent, sir! Really, Phillip," she added, addressing her brother, "this boy is shocking!"

"Oh, I'm a treat, mum! I'll bet you didn't bargain for a chap like me. I'm Sussex all over. Sally more 'taters, and pick 'em out crummy, like yourself."

The servant smiled, and handed him the vegetables.

"What shall I do? My ears ache

already. He is excruciating!" cried Miss Priscilla.

"Let him alone, dear. We will soon teach him better manners," observed Mr. Markwell.

"I for one protest against such companionship being thrust upon me," said the Honourable Mr. Brabazon.

"And so do I," said Lawless.

"Ain't I genteel enough?" asked Dick.

"No."

"Not by a long way, eh? Well, I'll try to cut it a bit finer," said Dick, adding, "Governor, I'll trouble you. Birds is fine now, and I do dearly love a pheasant. Bit of the breast and a wing will do me first-rate, and don't forget the bread sauce. My! it makes one's mouth water!"

"He hasn't even washed his hands or brushed his hair," said Miss Priscilla.

"Please, mum, it's a wig," said Dick.

"What's a wig?" said Miss Priscilla, nervously.

"My thatch, mum. I had a fever, and have worn a wig ever since. Don't you like 'em, mum?"

"Horrors upon horrors accumulate! Fancy a boy with a wig! Fancy anybody being so base as to wear other people's hair!" cried Miss Priscilla.

"Suppose you've got none, or very little of your own, mum?" said Dick.

"Don't address me in that way!"

"Beg pardon, mum; didn't say you wore a wig. Do you?"

"Do I? Oh, this insolence! Vulgar little boy, know that I do not wear a wig, and would scorn to do such a thing!"

Here Miss Priscilla looked fondly at the Honourable Mr. Brabazon, who was an especial favourite of hers, and who she fancied in return rather liked her.

"Oh, my! ain't she making eyes at Brab?" said Dick, winking at Sarah, the housemaid, who was waiting at table.

Sarah, being human, could stand no more; she rushed out into the passage and leaned against the table, fairly roaring.

"The impudence of that girl," said Miss Priscilla.

"Ain't it awful vulgar in a genteel family, mum?" said Dick.

"I'll speak to her, that I will. I'll give her notice," answered Miss Priscilla.

"My dear, be patient," said Mr. Markwell.

"I cannot bear it, Phillip."

"Go in and win, mum," said Dick.

Miss Priscilla rose.

Dick grasped the string tightly with his left hand.

He knew the catastrophe must come as soon as she moved any distance.

CHAPTER XXVII.

THE COMMANDER-IN-CHIEF'S NEPHEW.

MISS PRISCILLA moved with dignity towards the door.

Dick felt a pull at the string and gave a jerk.

Off came the wig.

Miss Priscilla stood for a moment wigless, the few hairs she had standing out in bold relief on her yellow-looking head, and her glorious curls were lying at her feet.

She gave a shriek—a piercing shriek of agony, and rushed from the room in a fainting condition.

Dick ran forward, picked up the wig and took out the fish-hook, which he replaced in his pocket without being observed.

"Give me that—that thing," said Mr. Markwell, snatching it from Dick's hand.

And he followed his sister.

"That's neat," observed Dick, sitting down.

"Don't address yourself to me. I am a gentleman!" said the Honourable Mr. Brabazon.

"Your gentility will kill you if you don't look out," answered Dick. "But don't cut up rough, Brabazon; pass the bird."

"I shall do nothing of the sort, sir!"

"Please yourself. You'd rather punch my head, wouldn't you?—only it is not genteel," answered Dick, getting up and helping himself.

THE SCAPEGRACE OF THE SCHOOL.

"You are an infernal cad," replied Brabazon, "and if you are to stay here, I shall go."

"I shan't miss you, and I dare say we shall not have to put the shutters up," Dick said, with his usual coolness.

Brabazon drew his chair near the fire, as did the other pupils, and they lighted their pipes.

It being an understood thing that when Miss Priscilla retired, they might smoke in the dining-room until work began in another apartment, and Mr. Markwell superintended their studies.

The servants cleared the dinner things away, and Dick took up a book.

Just then, there was a knock at the door, and a gentleman was announced.

"Lieutenant Smart," said the servant, "to see Mr. Brabazon."

"Show him in here," answered Brabazon.

Dick pricked up his ears at this, and wondered what his cousin the lieutenant wanted with Brabazon.

When the lieutenant entered the room, he looked surprised at seeing Dick.

"Dick, old man!" he said, "I did not expect to see you here. Have you cut the old shop?"

"Yes, but you astonish me by coming here. I thought you were at Portsmouth?" answered Dick.

"I left this morning and intended to look you up at your Kemp Town diggings. Did not you know I was engaged to Brabazon's sister? His father, Lord Brabazon, is one of the senior Lords of the Admiralty, and is trying to get me a ship."

Dick whistled.

"That's how the wind blows, is it?" he said. "I see."

Lieutenant Smart went up to Brabazon and shook hands with him, as he did with the other pupils, to whom he seemed to be well known. It was not his first visit to Mr. Markwell's.

"Do you know that cad?" said Brabazon, in a tone of disgust, pointing to Dick.

"Cad!" repeated the lieutenant, in amazement. "He's one of my cousins, and as nice a gentlemanly fellow as ever breathed."

"We don't think so."

"How long has he been here?"

"An hour or two, and that's too long," answered Lawless.

"There must be some mistake, which I can put right. Here, Dick, I want to speak to you," exclaimed the lieutenant.

Dick approached.

"You've been up to your tricks, you young rascal," continued Lieutenant Smart. "Admit it, now, or I'll never speak to you again. Brabazon says you are not nice. Tell us all about it. Out with it—no nonsense!"

"I dare say Mr. Brabazon will find out for himself in time," replied Dick.

"That won't do. Tell us your motive for mystifying them," persisted the lieutenant.

"The fact is, Brabazon annoyed me by his gentility, and all that sort of thing, and I thought I would have some fun with him. If I offended him, I apologize, and am ready to shake hands. I don't want to be on unfriendly terms with anyone."

"Then you're not a cad?" said Brabazon.

"I hope not. I've only being fogging you, and now Smart has let the cat out of the bag, it's no use keeping up the joke."

They all laughed, and soon got into a good temper.

The lieutenant could not stop.

He was on his way to London, and had only paid them a passing visit.

What he had said about Dick put him on a very good footing with his companions.

Mr. Markwell did not suspect his share in unwigging Miss Priscilla.

Everyone thought that it had been insecurely fastened, though she herself had a different opinion; but she said nothing, and had the moral courage to come into the room at tea-time as if nothing had happened, though she looked coldly upon Dick.

Mr. Markwell gave him some books, and being a thoroughly good scholar himself, soon found out what he knew, and what he ought to be taught.

Throwing off the vulgar behaviour he had assumed, Dick soon became a favourite, and so keenly did the young gentlemen feel the satire that he had directed against their gentility, that he heard nothing more about taking the whole of the pavement, pushing people into the street, and similar nonsense.

Each boy had a bedroom to himself, and Dick slept in one next door to Mr. Markwell.

In the night he got up to execute a little scheme that he had concocted.

With the utmost care and gentleness he abstracted from the drawers and cupboards every pair of trousers, and everything in the shape of a coat and hat, belonging to his tutor.

These he put in a cupboard in his own room, and locked the door.

He had previously ascertained that Mr. Markwell did not come down to breakfast till ten o'clock, leaving his pupils to get up their lessons as they liked before that hour.

Indeed, there was not much work done at Mr. Markwell's.

If a boy chose to work, he did so; if he did not, he let it alone.

The next morning Dick was up early and went out for a walk, going to a livery stable, and looking at some traps for hire.

At a hairdresser's he bought a beard, whiskers, and moustache, and wrapped in his great coat, looked quite a different personage from what he had done previously.

He hired a phaeton for two hours, and getting in, drove up to Mr. Markwell's exactly at half-past ten.

Sarah opened the door, but did not know Dick at all.

" Is Mr. Markwell in ?" he asked.

" Just getting up, sir. I hear his bell ringing now for the hot water. Who shall I say?" asked Sarah.

" Tell him an aide-de-camp of the commander-in-chief is here, and wishes to speak to him about placing his nephew under his charge," said Dick.

" Yes, sir."

Sarah went up to Mr. Markwell's room, and knocked at the door.

" Here's a gentleman, sir," she said.

" Who is he?" asked Mr. Markwell.

" Something to do with the commander-in-chief, sir, and wants to place his nephew with you."

" Ask him inside; and, Sarah, where the deuce have all my things got to?"

" What things, sir?"

" Trousers and coats, and bless me, I can't find a boot!"

" Oh! sir, said Sarah, " I know nothing about trousers."

" Send Mr. Lawless to me, then, and make haste," said the bewildered Mr. Markwell.

Sarah went away giggling, and told Lawless that the master wanted him.

Then she went to the door and asked Dick to step inside.

" I can't," answered Dick. " I'm lame of one leg, and can't get in and out without a ladder, and this morning my servant is not with me.

" Tell your master to be quick and come out here, as time presses.

" He may miss a valuable opportunity of acquiring a good connection."

Sarah went to Mr. Markwell's door and told him all this, at which his impatience increased wonderfully.

When Lawless arrived he explained the predicament in which he was placed, and they both searched in every direction for the clothes, which, of course, were not to be found, as Dick had hidden them during the night.

" It's very odd," said Mr. Markwell; " and it's very annoying, as the gentleman won't wait."

" Will a pair of mine do, sir?" answered Lawless.

" Too short."

" Yet you might make shift with your smoking cap and dressing-gown, and a pair of slippers. You could talk to him on the doorstep."

" So I could; a good idea," said Mr. Markwell.

Lawless presented him a pair of trousers, and helped him to dress, as he sympathised with him in his unpleasant position.

The trousers were hideously short, coming down only a little way below the knees; and in a smoking-cap, a dressing-gown, and slippers, Mr. Markwell presented a very eccentric appearance.

" Dear me," he exclaimed, as he was dressing, " how tiresome all this is! Aide-de-camp, I presume, to the commander-in-chief. Bother the trousers, how short they are! You see my advertisements do good. How do I look? Wants to place his nephew. How short this dressing-gown is! I shall be known to the Horse Guards. Do my calves show much? Come along; he's in a hurry.

Great people do not like to be kept waiting."

Mr. Markwell descended the stairs, opened the door, and stood shivering on the doorstep.

"Good morning, sir," he exclaimed. "I am only just up."

"What do you say ?" replied Dick. "Come nearer."

"I am only just up."

"I am rather deaf."

"Only—just—up," shouted Mr. Markwell.

"Please get into the trap," replied Dick, "and sit down for a moment by my side. I am lame and rather deaf, or I would not give you the trouble."

Mr. Markwell muttered something about the nuisance of having such a visitor, and climbed up into the trap, taking a seat by Dick's side.

In his extraordinary costume, he did not recognise him any more than the servant had done.

He took him for an army man, who wished to place his nephew under his charge.

"I have heard of you, Mr. Markwell," said Dick; "and the commander-in-chief wishes to place his nephew under your charge. I am one of his aides-de-camp."

"I thought," answered Mr. Markwell, "that the commander-in-chief was the Duke of Cambridge, and his nephews would be—what would they be? I did not know he had any nephews."

"Oh, dozens," replied Dick.

"Bless me !"

Suddenly Dick jerked the reins, and the horse he drove started off.

"Hi! stop; I'm not dressed!" cried Mr. Markwell, horrorstricken. "Where are you going to?"

"Certainly," said Dick; "if you would like a drive, I will give you one."

"I did not say so."

"Speak louder; I am rather deaf, and the wind's strong."

"For goodness sake, stop the horse."

"How much did you say for the course?" asked Dick.

"I didn't speak of it."

"Quite right. I want to know your terms for a course of lectures. The commander-in-chief's nephew will only have six months to spend with you, then he goes up for his examination."

"Oh, do stop, please—please do! Consider the state I am in, and the figure I shall cut," exclaimed Mr. Markwell, in agony.

They were rapidly nearing Brighton, and the Parade was becoming crowded, as the people turned out on a fine morning to see one another, take a little exercise, and listen to the various bands.

"Speak louder," said Dick.

Mr. Markwell rose, and shouted in his ear—

"Stop."

"All right," said Dick, "I'll make him go faster."

And he whipped up the horse.

"I didn't say that. Oh, what shall I do?"

"Have a cigar ?" asked Dick, taking out a case, and offering him one.

The horse went very quickly, and as they neared the crowded part of the King's Road, the people stared considerably at Mr. Markwell.

"Turn him round," said Mr. Markwell in Dick's ear.

"He won't turn? He's got such a temper! He's got the bit in his mouth! I've lost all control over him."

"We shall be smashed," groaned Mr. Markwell.

"He's thrown me out lots of times. I went through a plate-glass shop-window last week, and the week before I found myself on a dining-room table in a mansion."

"Oh! the vicious beast. My good, dear sir, do please stop; let me get down," exclaimed Mr. Markwell. "Anything is better than running the risk of being maimed, or perhaps killed."

The tutor was too much upset to talk about business, and almost forgot his strange costume in his anxiety to get out of the trap.

Dick pretended to have great difficulty in stopping the horse, but pulled up in front of the Bedford Hotel, where there is always more or less of a crowd.

Mr. Markwell jumped down quickly.

The people stared at him, and well they might.

With his old smoking-cap, his slippers, and his trousers coming down just below the knees; with his dressing-gown, which had come undone, and which he could with difficulty keep the wind from blowing off his shoulders, he presented as funny a spectacle as the Brightonians had seen for a long time.

For a moment he stood as if bewildered.

"Seize him! stop him!" exclaimed Dick, at the top of his voice. "He's a lunatic. He'll do somebody some harm. Stop him! Stop him!"

Two or three of the more adventurous in the crowd made a dash at him.

Mr. Markwell, frightened out of his wits, took to his heels and rushed off in the direction of home.

"Harkaway! Tallyho! Fetch him back," cried Dick. "A madman! a madman! A sovereign for the one who catches him. Hi! hi! hi! Collar the madman! Hi! hi!"

An excited mob set off in chase of the luckless tutor, who soon lost one shoe, and then the other.

One pursuer seized his dressing-gown, and that came off.

This was followed by his smoking-cap, and soon he was being hunted in his nightshirt and the short pair of trousers that Lawless had lent him.

Fear gave him wings.

Dick smiled grimly, and drove quickly to the yard from which he had hired the trap.

Paying for it, he turned up a doorway, took off his false hair, and looking himself again, he walked into the King's Road.

Mr. Markwell had been headed by the crowd, and turning round, was running back again.

"A lunatic! A madman! Stop him! Hi! hi! hi!" shouted, or rather roared, the crowd.

"He'll have a fit," thought Dick.

Mr. Markwell suddenly darted down some steps leading to the beach, and seeing a bathing machine, dashed up the ladder, got inside, and bolted the door.

The crowd, which grew larger every moment, thronged round the machine, and its members discussed the best means of securing the supposed escaped lunatic.

"Burn it down," said one.

"Smash it up with a hatchet," said another.

"He's got a knife. Take care," remarked a third, with a vivid imagination.

The horror of Mr. Markwell may easily be conceived.

To be dragged out in such guise and chased by the rabble, taken for a lunatic, and at last brought to bay in a bathing machine, was like a dream to him.

But that it was a fearful and embarrassing reality the shouts of the ever-increasing multitude proved.

CHAPTER XXVIII.

HENRIETTA'S COUSIN.

THE position in which Mr. Markwell found himself was a most unpleasant one.

He was fantastically dressed; beguiled into the centre of fashionable Brighton, on a false pretence—taken for a lunatic, and hunted into a bathing machine by a wild and frantic crowd.

In the seclusion of his peculiar retreat he could hear the cries of the ever-increasing mob, and their suggestions for getting him out of his harbour of refuge.

What could he do?

In an agony of apprehension he put his head out of a little window at the side, which was opened by a sliding panel, and gazed upon his tormentors.

A stone flung by an errand boy went unpleasantly near his nose, and he beat a retreat.

At this moment the proprietor of the machine came up, and addressing a number of people, said—

"What's all this row about?"

"It's a lunatic," replied the man spoken to.

"A what?"

"A madman—stark, staring, raving mad!"

"Where?"

"In that machine."

"Why, that's my machine!" replied the proprietor, whose name was Pollard, and whose patronymic was painted on the side. "That won't do; I must try and get him out."

"HELP! HELP! GOOD PEOPLE. HI! HI! OH!' CRIED SNARLEY."

No. 7.

He went up the steps and knocked at the door, the crowd admiring his courage as much as if he were a lion-tamer going into a den of fierce animals thirsting for his blood.

"Let me in," said Mr. Pollard.

"I shan't," replied Mr. Markwell.

"Come out then," said Mr. Pollard.

"Not if I know it," replied Mr. Markwell, who thought this was a ruse on the part of the mob to get him into their power.

This was a complication of the situation, and Pollard did not know what to do; to break open the door of the machine would be to injure his own property, and he could not recover damages against a lunatic in an action at law.

He came to the conclusion that it would be best to humour him.

"Do you want to bathe?" he asked.

"Bathe," said Mr. Markwell, with a shiver, "no; who would want to go into the sea such weather as this? It's too cold. If you are a friend, and will come inside and talk quietly, I will tell you who I am and how I came in this plight."

"Who are you?" asked Pollard.

"I don't want the mob to know; come inside."

"I ain't afraid of any number of lunatics," said Pollard to the crowd, who regarded him with admiration.

Some of the more weak-minded said their prayers secretly, as if they never expected to see him again.

The door was opened and Pollard went in, and to him Mr. Markwell related what had happened.

The bathing-machine man recognised him in a moment as a highly respectable gentleman, who all the summer had been a customer of his, and at once believed his story, and agreed to get him out of the mess.

"You must come with me, sir, and put my great coat over you, and let the people believe that you are going to the county asylum," said Pollard.

"Why?" answered Mr. Markwell. "I'm not mad."

"I know that, sir; you are no more mad than I am!"

"It's my firm impression that I'm the victim of a practical joke. It is very odd that the aide-de-camp of the commander-in-chief should behave in such an extraordinary manner, and be unable to stop his horse!"

"Aide-de-camp, my eye, sir!" said Pollard. "It's a plant. But the crowd will hoot you, and make it unpleasant, unless you do as I say. Come with me; I'll tell 'em I've tamed you down and cowed you like, and that you are going back with me to the asylum from which you have escaped."

"So be it," answered Mr. Markwell, with a sigh; "I place myself in your hands."

Pollard led the way down the steps, and on to the beach, keeping a tight hold of the schoolmaster and saying to the people, "He's all right. I've got him, and mean to take him back to his friends."

The crowd made way for them, and hiring a fly, Mr. Markwell was driven to his residence at Hove, where he arrived full of gratitude to Pollard for his clever management of the affair and the loan of his great coat, for which he made him a handsome present.

Quick as Mr. Markwell had been in getting home, Dick had been quicker, and he had, on the pretence of going up to his own room, replaced all his tutor's clothes which he had abstracted the night before.

Miss Priscilla was delighted to see her brother back again, and listened to his story with amazement.

"Who could have played you such a trick?" she asked.

"I know not," answered Mr. Markwell. "That it is a trick I cannot doubt, for no one connected with the commander-in-chief would act in such a way. I fear I have been the victim of some one's pleasantry."

Whether he suspected Dick or not he did not say, and there was an end of the matter.

But though he was disappointed in having the nephew of the commander-in-chief as a pupil, he was greatly surprised in another way, for the Rev. Mr. Lightheart sent him the son of a friend of his, whose name was Horace Stonor, the cousin of Miss Henrietta, Emily's friend and schoolfellow, of whom Dick was so fond.

Horace was not a boy calculated to be popular with Mr. Markwell's young gentlemen.

He was quiet and studious.

He knew his friends were not very well off, and that his success in life would depend upon his own exertions, which induced him to work hard.

Mr. Markwell undertook to prepare him for the university examination, and he hoped to obtain a scholarship, which would enable him to live at Cambridge without troubling his friends.

He was about fourteen, tall, fair, and delicate-looking, gentlemanly in his manner, and submissive.

He did not speak unless he was spoken to, and was generally to be found with a book in his hand.

Dick did not know that he was Emily's friend's cousin, his dear Henrietta's cousin, and, therefore, did not put himself out of the way to be civil to him.

One morning, about a week after Horace Stonor had arrived, the young gentlemen were in the room they used for studying.

Some were reading, others writing, and Brabazon happened to be reading the morning paper.

"I say," he exclaimed, "here's a Horace Stonor a bankrupt. He's a grocer in Eastcheap, wherever that may be. Is he any relation of yours, young shaver?"

Horace looked up, and his face coloured as if he did not like the question.

"Can't you answer when you are spoken to?" exclaimed Brabazon.

"Yes."

"Well, then, what did I ask you?"

"It is my father," answered Horace.

"Your governor! You don't mean to say you are the son of a bankrupt grocer?" exclaimed Chapman.

"I can't help being what I am. I knew my father was in trouble, but they did not tell me he was a bankrupt, though I have heard that is nothing in the City," he exclaimed.

"Isn't it? Bankruptcy means cheating your creditors."

"I am sure my papa would not cheat anybody out of a halfpenny. He is much too honest, and people in trade cannot help being unfortunate sometimes. It may happen that you have taken bills from a man who fails to pay them; so that you, in your turn, cannot pay others to whom you are indebted."

"I know nothing about trade, and don't want to hear a sermon about the commercial morality of grocers," replied Chapman.

"For my part, I wish old Markwell would be more particular about who he takes in. We don't want all the tag-rag and bobtail of the City to associate with," observed Brabazon.

"Have you ever served behind the counter?" inquired Burrell.

"Yes, sometimes," answered Horace.

"How often have you run across the street for change?" asked Dick.

"I don't know. I have gone for change for a note when father hadn't it in the till."

"And they are going to send you to Cambridge! What's the good of trying to make a gentleman of you?" said Brabazon. "Sow's ears don't make silk purses. You'd better go home and stick to your shop."

"They consulted my inclinations, and as my tastes inclined me to a studious life, I was allowed to do as I pleased, and I think your remarks are very rude and unkind," answered Horace, feeling inclined to cry, but not liking to show any weakness of that sort to his unkind critics.

"I shall be obliged to you if you will not address your remarks to me," said Chapman.

"I was spoken to first," answered Horace, with more courage than Dick gave him credit for; "and I am not in the least bit ashamed of my parentage."

"I could stand anything but a bankrupt grocer," said Brabazon, with a sneer.

"What's the price of dips?" asked Burrell.

"If you want to know, you can go and inquire."

"Don't cheek me," cried Burrell, angrily; "I won't be cheeked by an errand boy."

"If you make impertinent observations to me, I shall reply to them as I think fit."

"Will you? Then, perhaps, you will get a slap on the nose for your pains."

"You call yourselves gentlemen," said Horace, with sarcastic emphasis, "but neither your language nor your manner entitle you to the designation. I did expect better treatment from Lightheart, because my father and his were old schoolfellows together, and it was through him I came here; and then again, Miss Emily Lightheart is at school at Kemp Town with my cousin."

"By Jove!" cried Dick. "Is Henrietta your cousin?"

"Yes, she is an orphan, you know. Her father was my father's brother," replied Horace.

"I'm surprised—rather—a few. It's knocked me off my perch, and doubled me up into a cocked hat," exclaimed Dick.

"I thought I should find a friend in Dick Lightheart," continued Horace.

"And so you shall. Did you hear about——"

"Young Henrietta running away to get married? Yes," answered Horace with a smile, "and many a good laugh we had over it."

"Hallo! what's that?" asked Chapman. "Lightheart running away with a girl.

I did not know he was of the spooney order of fellows. We must hear all about that. Enlighten us further, my good grocer."

"Perhaps you will mind your own business," cried Dick, flushing angrily.

"I did not speak to you. Let the grocer answer."

"Stonor, hold your tongue," Dick said.

"Oh! if you are going to be his champion, because you're spoons on his cousin, I shan't interfere. Perhaps you'll be an acquisition behind the counter," sneered Chapman.

"We've had enough about the grocer. Drop it," Dick exclaimed. "The first fellow who chaffs Stonor any more will find out his mistake."

"You were doing it yourself just now."

"Never mind; if you want to have a row with me, I'm ready for any of you."

And Dick glared defiantly around him.

CHAPTER XXIX.

AN ADVENTURE ON THE BEACH.

CHAPMAN was not a coward, but he was impressed with an idea of his own importance, and had imbibed the ideas of the Honourable Henry Brabazon, son of Lord Broadacres, whose gentility had been made fun of by Dick on his arrival at Mr. Markwell's.

He thought fighting low—only worthy of cabmen and roughs.

On this occasion he accepted Dick's challenge, and said—

"If I choose to speak to the grocer, I shan't ask your permission."

"If you utter that word again, I shall pitch into you," exclaimed Dick.

"What word?"

"You know well enough."

"I don't fight. It's caddish, but——"

"Then I do," said Dick, interrupting him, "and that makes all the difference, as you'll find when I prop you in the eye."

"I always said you were not a gentleman," Chapman continued; "you would not use such language if you were; and we might have known what you were by your conduct when you first came here, which you may have thought very humorous, though it did not strike me

as being so; and what I suggest to my friends is that we cut both you and the grocer."

"Oh, you will say it, will you?" cried Dick, between his teeth.

He sprang over a couple of forms and struck at Chapman, who however, was prepared for the assault, and promptly parried it.

Dick was not to be thwarted, however, and feinting with his right, struck him on the jaw with his left, making his teeth rattle like castanets.

He followed up this success by two more blows, the last of which was a knock-down one, and Chapman lay on his back, having very confused ideas of things in general.

"Do any more of you want a taste of it?" he exclaimed, looking round. "I shall be happy to oblige you all, from the Honourable Henry to my friend Lawless."

They shrugged their shoulders and said nothing.

"All right," said Dick, smiling triumphantly, "you know now what you've got to expect if you chaff Stonor."

Chapman was attended to by Lawless, who said—

"Pick yourself up, old man."

With difficulty he rose and sat down, looking furiously at Dick.

"Pull yourself together," continued Lawless; "your time will come."

"I'll fight him with pistols," replied Chapman.

"What's the use of talking nonsense?" Dick exclaimed; "you know duelling is not allowed now, and that men cannot settle their disputes in that way."

Chapman stared insolently at him, and, addressing Lawless, said—

"The low fellow has taken advantage of his superior strength and knowledge of fighting; but if you will join me, we will form a set of our own, and exclude him and his commercial friend from it."

Dick laughed and sat down by Stonor's side, while Brabazon, Lawless, and Burrell formed a sympathising group around Chapman.

"I don't want you to quarrel with your friends for my sake," exclaimed Horace Stonor.

"I feel very sorry that this disturbance should have taken place, though I should not have been strong enough to fight my own battle, and therefore am deeply grateful to you for your championship."

"I have put an end to the annoyance, at all events, and I don't think they will any of them venture to chaff you again," answered Dick.

"Not if they have any respect for your sledge-hammer fists. How hard you do hit!"

"Yes I can slog a little," Dick answered, "and a very useful accomplishment it is, too, I can tell you."

After this occurrence Dick and Stonor became great friends.

The other pupils did not speak to them, which did not annoy Dick much, as he found Horace's society all he required.

There was a fund of information, and a gentle, pleasant mode of conveying it, in the grocer's son which made him a useful and interesting, as well as an agreeable companion.

The winter passed, and the pleasant spring time came.

Dick had made great progress in his studies, and had given Mr. Markwell every satisfaction.

He was anxious to please his father, and make up to him all he owed to his kindness during the disgraceful affair into which Captain Hanger had betrayed him.

The Rev. Mr. Lightheart wrote to Dick, telling him how pleased he was to hear of his good conduct.

Brabazon and the other pupils kept their word.

They ignored Dick's and Stonor's existence, and went about by themselves, as they did before.

The two boys were "cut dead," but their enemies did not attempt to chaff them any more.

Chapman had been taught a lesson, which the others were not slow to learn.

Dick was a dangerous customer, and one not to be trifled with.

Stonor and Dick used to bathe together, and one fine day they were strolling along the beach when a school came up.

"Hold hard!" cried Dick, pressing Stonor's arm. "That's my old school."

"Is it?" replied Horace.

"Yes; let's have a lark with them. There's old Snarley and Messiter. I like Messiter—we used to be chums."

"What will you do?"

"Wait a bit. They're going to bathe. Let them get in. We'll sit down and watch them."

Accordingly they sat down in a secluded corner.

There were half-a-dozen bathing-machines that were drawn up the shelving beach by means of a windlass, which was worked by a horse.

As far as the eye could reach on either side, there were no other machines, and it seemed to Dick that if the horse was got away, it would be impossible to draw up the machines.

The tide was coming in fast and it was rather rough, so that the sea rolled in with huge waves.

Mr. Snarley saw his boys into five machines, which held six boys in each.

The last one he reserved for himself.

He did not get into it until he saw that they were all undressed.

"Snarley's in. Now for it," said Dick.

"Now for what?" asked Stonor.

" Will you do what I ask you ?"

" Tell me what it is."

" Get on that horse and ride away while the bathing-machine man is not looking."

" I don't like the idea, but——"

" Do, just to oblige me," pleaded Dick.

" I will, if you wish it and press me," answered Horace Stonor. " But it is, in my opinion, very foolish to play these jokes, and we may get ourselves into trouble."

" If we do, I have a knack of getting out of it again."

" Tell me what I am to do then."

" Jump on that horse."

" What else ?"

" Ride like steam."

" Where ?" asked Horace.

" Anywhere, so long as the machine-man don't catch you. Get up near the wall. It's better going than on the shingle. Ram into the beast with your heels and hold on by his mane."

The bathing man had gone into a hut he had built to keep various things, such as towels, etc., in.

Dick gave Horace a leg up and away he went, the old horse trotting nimbly along.

The water was rising rapidly, and had nearly reached the floor of the machines.

There was a padlock outside the door of the shed, attached to a hasp and a staple.

Shutting the door, Dick attached the padlock and locked it securely, throwing away the key.

The bathing man wondered at his door blowing to, and tried to get out.

He could not, as he was locked in hard and fast.

Meanwhile Horace Stonor was getting out of sight, going towards the old Chain Pier.

Dick sat down to watch the fun.

There were only a few nursemaids and children about, and one or two idlers, who, not being in the secret of the joke, did not pay any attention to what was going on.

Mr. Snarley saw the water rising in his machine.

He had just got his shirt and trousers on, but to his annoyance his socks began to float on the water.

The door of the machine was towards the water.

Bang went a wave against it, bursting it open.

" Hi ! hi !" cried Mr. Snarley, looking out upon the blank expanse of sea.

The wind mocked his lamentation, and carried it away with a mournful roar.

" This won't do. We shall all be drowned," murmured Mr. Snarley. " Where the deuce is that machine man ? He ought to attend to his business better than this. I won't deal with him any more. Help ! help ! Hi ! hi ! hi ! I wonder how my boys are ! Oh, dear me ! perhaps he has drawn the other machines up, and has forgotten me ! I always was afraid of the water !"

Another wave bigger than the former came with a rush into the machine, and made it shiver again, nearly taking the usher off his legs.

" That's the eleventh. They say the eleventh wave is always bigger than the others. What am I to do ?" said Mr. Snarley.

His hat and coat now floated with his socks, and his boots were knocking about on the floor with the motion of the tide.

The usher grew desperate.

" I will not die like this ! I will make an effort. I will not perish like a rat in a drain !" he exclaimed.

Thoroughly frightened, he managed to climb on the wheel of the machine, and so get on the top of the machine, over which he threw his legs.

" Help ! help ! Good people, help !" he cried piteously. " Confound that man ! Help ! Where is he ?—my boys will be drowned. Hi ! hi ! Oh !"

This latter exclamation was caused by Dick, who, coming near the machine, threw a dead starfish at him.

It struck him on the mouth, and entered the orifice, which was wide open, owing to his bawling.

" Pish !" spluttered Mr. Snarley, picking at the fish ; " nasty—pish ! It stinks ; faugh !—what a bad taste it has."

The boys, meanwhile, were making the most terrible noise, for they thought they were going to be drowned.

Those who could swim got into the water and so gained the shore in their clothes, but they were only about a dozen in number.

"I forgot the boys," muttered Dick, "this is growing serious; another five minutes, and it will be a case with them."

He looked round to see if he could obtain any assistance.

A small crowd had collected, attracted by the cries of the usher.

The situation was becoming embarrassing.

Dick began to see that he had carried his joke a little too far.

It was all very well to have Mr. Snarley in his shirt and trousers on the top of the machine.

But the position of the boys in the machines was growing more dangerous every minute.

Dick turned pale.

He was getting alarmed.

CHAPTER XXX.

RESCUED.

FORTUNATELY, at this critical juncture, a waterman happened to come by in a large boat plying for hire.

Dick ran down to the beach and hailed him.

"Want a row, sir?" said the man.

"Yes," said Dick. "Pull in."

The waterman did so, and got his boat near enough to the beach for Dick to spring on board.

"Where to, sir?" asked the boatman.

"Go to the bathing machines and take the boys out. The horse has bolted, and the man can't wind them up."

This was quickly done.

In less than five minutes four out of the five machines were emptied, and in the fifth Dick found Messiter, his old friend.

"Is it you, Dick?" said Messiter. "I can understand now why we were left in the sea. Where's the bathing man?"

Dick winked and pointed to the hut, from whence the sound of knocking came, as if the prisoner was trying to work his way out with a hatchet.

"In there? What a lark!" replied Messiter.

"Look at Snarley," said Dick. "He'll have a fit. Stay in the boat with me, and we'll row round him."

"All right. You don't know how pleased I am to see you. I heard you were at a private tutor's in Brighton, and thought you would have given us a visit."

"Not good enough, old boy," replied Dick.

The boys were a little wet about the legs, and a good deal frightened, but none of them were hurt in any way, and they stood on the beach, looking curiously at the usher.

When the boat came to the machine, Mr. Snarley recognised Dick. He had been watching the process of extricating the boys with considerable satisfaction, and concluded that it was his turn to come next to dry land.

"Ah, Lightheart, how do?" he exclaimed. "You are just in time to save us from a most unpleasant catastrophe."

"Cat what, sir? It's a big word, and rather too much for me," answered Dick.

"Never mind; I will explain it at my leisure. Let me get into your boat, and then we can row after my hat, which I perceive is going out to sea. Well has the sea been described as a treacherous element; it is so indeed."

"Lie on your oars," said Dick to the boatman.

"Why are you stopping?" continued Mr. Snarley. "You must see my anxiety to get ashore. I am a ridiculous object, perched up here half drowned."

"You can't come in my boat," Dick exclaimed.

"Why not?"

"Because you look very pretty where you are, and it would be a pity to spoil you."

"My dear Lightheart, consider. Oh! what a shock the last wave gave the machine. It will turn over presently, and I shall be struggling in the waves, battling with them for dear life. As you are doubtless aware, I cannot swim."

"Everyone should learn to swim," remarked Dick.

"My education in that respect was neglected; but you are only joking. Take me off, and not a word shall be said about your refusal in the first instance."

"I don't care what you say," Dick replied. "I am my own master now, and you certainly shall not come ashore in my boat."

At this moment, a huge wave sent three out of the six machines rolling on their sides, Mr. Snarley's being amongst the number.

He stood a good chance of being drowned, but Dick stuck a boat-hook into his clothes, and dragged him on board.

"Pull in quickly," said he, giving the boatman some money.

Dick and Messiter assisted the usher to land, and he walked to the bathing-man's hut, intending to remonstrate with him in very strong terms for his bad behaviour.

Just then the door flew open with a crash before a vigorous kick.

One glance showed the infuriated man his bathing-machines on their sides, and in danger of being smashed against the beach.

Running wildly up to Mr. Snarley, he hit him violently on the nose, and sent him rolling over on the shingle.

"I'll teach you to play your confounded tricks upon me," he cried. "Look at my beautiful machines."

"My good man," began Mr. Snarley, wiping the sand out of his mouth.

"Don't good man me," replied the fellow.

"My worthy, but impulsive friend, listen to me. I have cause to complain, for we were nearly all drowned through your negligence, and had it not been for the bravery and presence of mind of this young gentleman, who, I am proud to say, was one of my pupils, we should have——"

"Hold your jaw!" interrupted the man. "Where's my horse?"

And having discovered his new loss, he began to run about like a madman in all directions.

"Good morning," said Dick, "I must be off."

He thought that it was time to look after Horace Stonor, who might be caught on the horse, and shaking hands with Snarley and Messiter, left them to fight it out with the machine-man.

He found Stonor near the old Chain Pier, holding the horse by the bridle, and wiping his face with a pocket-handkerchief.

"What's the matter?" asked Dick.

"The brute threw me off, and I was a good deal hurt," answered Stonor.

"Never mind. Come along with me, and leave the horse. The owner will be here after him soon; and as the machines may be injured, I don't care about being found out, and hauled up at the Town Hall."

They hurried away, and Dick explained to Stonor what had happened after his departure, making him laugh with his description of the comical appearance that Snarley presented when sitting half naked on the top of the bathing-machine.

"I wish I could be as light-hearted and as merry as you," remarked Stonor, as they walked along the Parade.

"What's the use of being miserable?" answered Dick.

"I can't help it sometimes."

"For my part I always keep up my pecker. I have been on my best behaviour, though, since I came to Markwell's, because I wanted to show my father that I could go on well if I chose. Still, to-day I could not resist the temptation of playing Snarley a joke. You don't know what a tyrant he was when I was at a private school. But what's the matter with you? I noticed this morning, after the post came in, and you read your letters, that you were down in the mouth about something. Out with it. You can trust me with your secrets."

"I did not like to worry you; but I had a letter from home."

"Yes."

"My father is very poor. He is trying to pay his creditors in full since his bankruptcy, about which Chapman and Brabazon chaffed me when they read it in the papers. You remember. It was the time when you took my part so nobly."

"That was nothing," said Dick, innocently.

"Oh, but it was, and I have never forgotten it, nor ever shall—all the more because you have suffered for my sake by being cut."

"That I don't care twopence about. What's your grief?"

"My father," answered Stonor, "can't afford to keep me at school. I would gladly go into the shop and make myself useful, but he thinks I know enough, and am old enough now, to get a scholarship."

"I hope you will," ejaculated Dick, sincerely.

"He has set his mind on my being a great swell at college, because he thinks I am clever, and knows I will work. By the way, Henrietta is going to leave Miss Bodmin's."

"Indeed. I wish I was a man and could work to keep her. I'd marry her to-morrow, if I could see my way. I love your cousin, Horace."

"I know you do. She always asks after you when she writes," said Horace Stonor; "and I hope some day I may have the pleasure of calling you my relation, though it is not a cheering prospect to marry into a ruined family."

"What's the odds when you love one another?" answered Dick.

The two boys shook each other feelingly by the hand, and retired into the shadow of a doorway to do so unobserved.

"Henrietta is going to Paris; but she will take a cruise with her guardian, who keeps a yacht, and goes about a good deal, I'm told, so she will have a pleasant time of it."

"Does she really ask after me?" said Dick.

"Oh! yes, constantly."

"Bless her heart. It may have been very foolish of me to run away with her, because we are too young to marry yet; I see that, and I don't think I'm good enough for her. They call me a scamp, but I'll reform."

"I am sure I see nothing objectionable in your conduct," answered Horace. "If you like to amuse yourself now and then, why shouldn't you? You are a gentleman, and can look forward to an excellent future. So long as you do nothing dishonourable, it doesn't matter much."

Dick's face flushed as he thought of the time when he attempted to rob his father.

If he had succeeded then, he would always have been in Captain Hanger's power, and what his future might have been in that case he shuddered to think.

All at once he stopped suddenly.

He trembled and turned pale.

"What is it—are you not well?" asked Stonor, anxiously.

Dick could not speak.

He was only able to look in a dazed sort of manner at a man who confronted him.

CHAPTER XXXI

THE APPARITION.

"SO," said a voice he knew too well, "we meet again, Master Dick Lightheart."

It was Captain Hanger.

Recovering himself by an effort, Dick said, "I wish to have nothing to say to you. Our acquaintance—such as it was —came to an end unexpectedly, and I have no desire to renew it."

"Possibly not; but I want to speak to you, and as we live in a free country, and there is no law to prevent our conversing, I shall take the liberty of talking to you," replied the captain, in his usual jaunty, careless manner.

"Let me pass."

"Not at all. Have you forgotten your theft?"

Stonor stared.

"How dare you speak to me in that manner?" Dick said, angrily. "If you do not mind what you are about, I will do you an injury, and I would any man who attacked my honour, were he as big as an ox. You know very well that I didn't take your cash-box, and you are a villain."

"Pretty language. What would you say if I were to call a policeman and give you in charge, now?" asked the captain.

"You can't do it. Your own character is too well known, and my father would have something to say about the——"

He hesitated.

"About what? Go on."

"You know what."

"The fact is, you are in my power, and you know it. Where are you now?"

"Find out," said Dick.

"I fully intend to do so. Give me

what money you have about you and your address, then you may go."

"This is highway robbery," Dick said. "I am not the stupid fool I was when you first met me. Be off, or I'll get a mob about you."

"Take my advice and don't cut your own throat, as the pig did when he swam across the pond," said Captain Hanger, coolly. "Your father won't do anything to me for helping you in your attempt upon his money, because he respects his own name. But if you don't comply with my demands and give me what money you have about you and your watch and chain, I'll hand you over to a policeman, and it will go hard with you."

A profuse perspiration broke out all over Dick's body.

He was reaping the whirlwind now with a vengeance, and saw that foolish things, whether done in youth or age, cannot go without punishment.

This was the bitter result of his rash and disobedient behaviour when at Mr. Simcox's, and the result of running away from school.

Captain Hanger's confident manner frightened him.

Taking from his pocket one pound thirteen and sixpence and his watch and chain, his mother's present, he gave them to the captain, saying—

"It is all I have."

"All right. I'll give you a receipt on account," answered Captain Hanger.

He took out a pocket-book and hastily wrote on a fly-leaf, "Received on account, from Mr. Richard Lightheart, say five pounds, being part payment for a robbery of my cash-box by him while in my employment."

"There you are, my beauty!" he exclaimed. "And now where are you staying?"

"At Mr. Markwell's, Highfield Terrace, Hove," answered Dick, putting the receipt in his pocket, while his face burned with very shame.

"Ta-ta. You shall hear again from your humble servant," answered the captain.

He walked away.

"What did he say?" asked Stonor, horror-stricken.

With a sinking at the heart and downcast eyes Dick told Stonor everything.

How he ran away from school and met the circus people, and how the money-box was lost, and he was weak enough to go and try to rob his father.

"Oh, Dick, Dick!" cried Stonor, with tears in his eyes. "How could you do such a thing? I did not think you could be so silly, and so—so——"

"Wicked, you mean," put in Dick, desperately. "I deserve all you can say, and I know that you despise me now."

"Not exactly; but I am shocked."

"And you think me too bad to marry your cousin when I grow up?"

"I should like Henrietta's husband, whoever he may be, to be a man of—of——"

"Honour," supplied Dick, with his accustomed impulsiveness. "Say it out like a man. Don't spare me."

Stonor was silent.

"I think I shall go and drown myself in the sea," Dick continued, desperately. "I don't care about living now I have lost your good opinion."

"I will try to think well of you, because you acted on the compulsion of that bad man. Don't be rash, Dick. Your sin has found you out; but it is a dreadful story," continued Horace Stonor.

"Pity me, Horace. I acted foolishly; but I am not bad at heart," moaned Dick.

"I believe you," answered Horace; "we are all imperfect, and far be it from me to condemn you. This man who has just left us urged you to take what you thought your own money, and——"

He stopped abruptly.

The cries of many people startled him, and he saw a fly with a runaway horse coming at full speed up the King's Road.

The driver was vainly trying to stop the horse.

In another moment the maddened animal dashed up against a lamp-post, and the fly was shattered to pieces.

Miraculously, the driver escaped unhurt, but the occupant was thrown almost at the foot of the boys.

He was terribly injured, for he fell on his head upon the curb, and blood flowed from the wound.

"Captain Hanger!" ejaculated Dick.

It was in truth the captain, who had hired a fly to go somewhere, and the horse, being frightened at some noise, ran away, with the disastrous result we have detailed.

The unfortunate man breathed heavily, and seemed dying.

The crowd took him into a chemist's shop, and a surgeon was sent for.

But before he came he had breathed his last.

In the midst of his career and in the prime of life he had been cut off.

But before he died he recognised Dick, who, with Horace, had penetrated to the little parlour behind the shop.

A momentary gleam of intelligence lighted up his face.

"This is a judgment upon me," he murmured; "I have just time to say that I myself took the cash-box from the office. You are innocent."

With peevish impatience, he unfastened the chain of Dick's watch, and handed them both to him.

His strength failed him, or he would have restored the money.

"Say you forgive?" moaned the wretched man, pitifully.

"With all my heart," answered Dick, generously.

His lips moved as if in prayer.

Then the former dull, impassive look of insensibility came over him, and his eyes closed.

The boys remained till all was over, and then took their departure, sad and sorrowful.

"Never mind the money," said Dick. "I have the watch, and you are a witness that he cleared my character."

"Certainly," said Horace.

"He would have been a terrible enemy. I should never have been free from his attacks. How soon accidents happen. Is it not true that in the midst of life we are in death?"

"It is indeed; and now, Dick, try to forget this unhappy episode."

"I will. Only promise me one thing?"

"What's that?" asked Horace.

"That you will still be my friend, and say nothing to my dear Henrietta about what you have heard to-day."

"I do promise, gladly."

The boys shook hands again, and Dick returned to Mr. Markwell's with a lighter heart, though it was many a long day before he forgot the awfully sudden death of the miserable Captain Hanger.

Horace Stonor had letters repeatedly from his cousin, who said she was very happy.

In her last letter she told him that she was going for a cruise in the yacht "Sapphire," which had been built for Mr. Maidment, her guardian.

Dick heard this, and hoped that she would not run into any danger, though he had a strange misgiving, for which he could not account, that some harm would happen to her.

He had made the acquaintance of the coastguardsmen at Hove, and listened with awe to their accounts of wrecks which had taken place on the coast.

Whether it was dwelling upon this that gave rise to an incident we are about to relate or not, we will not pretend to say.

The circumstance may have been owing to that subtle communion existing between the spirits of those who love one another.

But the mystery enveloping the supernatural world is so deep, that it is idle to speculate upon anything connected with it, however strange or extraordinary it may be.

Dick had gone to bed at the usual hour.

The wind was blowing fresh, and gradually increased to a gale, and so furious were the gusts that the casements rattled ominously.

The windows looked out upon the sea, and he could, before he went to sleep, hear the roaring sea beating violently upon the bleak and unprotected shore.

In the middle of the night he fancied he saw a form appear at his bedside.

It was that of a young and beautiful girl; her long hair flowed over her shoulders, and her attire was drenched with sea-water.

The expression of her face was agonizing in the extreme.

She appeared to be the prey of an absorbing terror, and extended her arms to Dick as if imploring his protection or assistance.

He recognised his darling Henrietta.

With a cry, he woke up and gazed around him wonderingly.

Nothing but a murky blackness met his eyes.

The sea still roared, and the wind and the rain beat against the window-panes without.

At that moment he heard the sullen booming of a gun at sea.

It was a signal of distress.

He lay still and listened.

Again and again, at intervals of half a minute, came the dreadful and foreboding sound.

"Some vessel has stranded, and will soon be a wreck on a night like this," he muttered. "I must get up."

Springing out of bed, he struck a light, and, looking at his watch, he found it was half-past two.

Quickly dressing himself, he determined to go to the beach, and speak to his friends the coastguardsmen.

Their station was not far off.

He could not account for his conduct.

At any other time he would have gone to sleep again.

But there are times when we feel compelled to do certain things without knowing why.

We obey a mysterious cause, and are urged on against our will, or perhaps we have no will at all in the matter.

When dressed, he went cautiously along the passage, not wishing to disturb the other sleepers in the house, and stopped before Horace Stonor's door.

His rest was apparently feverish, for he was tossing about in his bed, and talking wildly in his sleep.

"Wake up, Horace," cried Dick.

"What is it?" asked the boy, rubbing his eyes.

"I want you to get up."

"I am so glad you have come. I have had such a bad dream."

"What did you dream about?" asked Dick.

"It is very curious; but I was dreaming about Henrietta. I thought she came to me, and asked me to help her."

"So did I dream about your cousin," answered Dick. "There is something wrong. Get up quickly."

Again the signal gun boomed out, and its sullen noise was carried by the wind shorewards.

"What is that?" cried Horace.

"A signal gun from some ship in distress. I am going to see all about it. Will you come? Yes or no. There is no time to be lost. The coastguard station is not far off. We shall be in time to lend a hand to the poor souls, if we hurry."

"All right!" answered Horace, getting up.

The night was not cold, though the weather was so alarmingly rough.

In a short time, both boys were ready, and descended the stairs quietly, letting themselves out at the front door, and issuing into the street in the grey dawn of early morning, for it was now the beginning of summer, and the nights were shorter as every week progressed.

CHAPTER XXXII.

THE WRECK.

THE boys hastily made their way to the coastguard station.

Men engaged in the service were running about with lanterns.

Approaching one of them, whom he knew, named Simmons, Dick asked what had happened.

"A gentleman's yacht, sir," was the reply, "has been driven ashore by the wind, and as the sea is beating over her, she must become a wreck presently, so we are getting the rocket apparatus ready."

"Can I lend a hand?" said Dick.

"No, thank you, sir, we're not short handed, and you don't understand the process," answered the coastguardsman.

Dick and Horace consequently contented themselves with looking on.

The sea ran very high, and broke in clouds of feathery spray over the doomed vessel, which was just discernible in the dim morning light.

Presently the coastguard fired the first rocket, which, being aimed too low, did not reach the yacht.

The second attempt was more successful, the rocket striking the rigging and enabling the sailors to seize the rope which was attached to it, and make it fast.

Simmons then placed himself in the belt, and was drawn along the rope to the yacht, being completely lost in the huge waves at times, which seemed to engulf him.

But, thanks to his cork jacket, and the excellent working of the apparatus, he suffered no harm other than the uncomfortable drenching of the heavy sea.

The utmost excitement reigned on shore.

In a short time, which, however, seemed an age, Simmons returned with a lady, whom he landed half fainting.

He went back on his errand of mercy immediately, and Dick assisted the lady into the coastguard station, where restoratives were administered to her.

"Is my father safe, and my mother, and my sister?" she inquired, anxiously.

"We trust they soon will be," answered Dick, kindly. "May I ask the name of the yacht?"

"It is the 'Sapphire!'" replied the young lady.

"Extraordinary!" exclaimed Dick, trembling all over; "and you are Miss Maidment?"

"Yes. How could you tell that?" asked the girl, wonderingly.

"Is Miss Stonor on board?" asked Dick, without replying to her question.

"Yes. We only embarked yesterday in the Thames, intending to make our way to the Isle of Wight, when we were caught in this dreadful storm. The yacht became unmanageable, and we were driven on shore. It seems a miracle we should be saved from death."

"Excuse me," cried Dick, "I must go to the shore and look after the others."

He rushed from the house, and went once more to the beach.

It was agony to think that his dear Henrietta should be in danger.

He did not then stay to consider what an extraordinary interpretation his dream had had, though it occurred strongly enough to him afterwards.

Simmons had made three trips to the yacht, bringing safely away Mrs. Maidment, and her two daughters.

"There is one more lady," he said; "we'll have her, and then we must look after the men."

Dick did not doubt that this was Henrietta, and he strained his eyes to see if she were coming.

"It is my cousin's turn next," murmured Horace, to whom Dick related all that he knew.

"I wish they would let me go along the rope," Dick said.

"She is safer with Simmons. He is stronger than we are, and has more experience. Is it not odd that we should wake up with our dreams, and come here to find that Henrietta really is in peril?"

"So strange that I cannot understand it. But, hush! here she comes."

As he spoke they could see Simmons hauled along with a girl in his arms.

He neared the shore, and the boys held their breath.

Suddenly there was a sharp crack, and a despairing cry.

Both man and girl vanished as if swallowed up by the ravenous sea.

The rope had broken.

In fact, the sea had caused the yacht to give an alarming lurch, and the strain was more than the rope could bear.

It snapped in half, and Simmons was struggling in the sea, his lovely burden on his arm.

"Heaven help us! she will be drowned!" cried Horace; "I must save her!"

Before any one could stop him, he had plunged madly into the foaming surf.

Dick was nearly distracted.

Seeing a coil of rope lying on the beach, he tied one end round a flagstaff, and the other round his waist.

"Can you swim?" asked a coastguard, who saw what he was about, and divined his purpose.

"Like a fish," exclaimed Dick.

"It's neck or nothing, sir," answered the man.

"I know it," Dick said, who was very calm now. "Watch my movements· when I grasp the girl, haul in."

"Right," replied the man.

Simmons, who was much exhausted, found himself obliged to drop his hold of the insensible girl, and, in order to save his own life, dragged himself ashore by the aid of the broken rope.

Dick saw this, and the next moment was battling with the waves.

He did not know what had become of Horace, but he fancied he heard him crying for help some distance lower down the beach, where the waves had washed him.

Dick's eyes were fixed upon a pale face and long, fair hair, like tangled sea-weed, which ever and anon appeared and disappeared.

The waves drove him back, and it was with the utmost difficulty that he got into deep water, though he was slightly helped by an undercurrent, caused by the receding of the tide, which was rapidly going out.

His great fear now was that she would sink to rise no more before he reached her.

She was somewhat assisted in floating by the clothes she wore, which gave her a temporary buoyancy.

The coastguard fired another rocket, and the apparatus was repaired.

Simmons was too weak to be of any more use.

He crawled ashore, and was helped by strong arms, more dead than alive, to the station, while one of his companions took his place on the rope.

All this was enacted while Dick was searching for Henrietta.

At length something appeared close to him.

He seized it and found it was the body of the girl he loved, though she was so pale and still that it was impossible to say whether she was alive or dead.

Placing his arm firmly round her waist, he made signals to those on shore.

For a time he did not seem to be heard.

A joyous feeling came over him when he felt himself drawn in.

They had heard his cries, and were pulling at the rope.

By his gallant conduct Henrietta had been snatched from the jaws of death.

He was assisted to the coastguard station, while Henrietta was carried thither.

The usual remedies were employed in cases of drowning.

Henrietta lived, though she remained insensible to the efforts of those about her.

Dick could do no more, or he would have gone in search of Horace.

His strength had departed, and he was as helpless as a child.

Mr. Maidment and one of the crew were brought in, and then, with a horrid crash, the yacht went to pieces.

Those who remained behind, three in number, which included the captain, were tossed about by the waves until they sank for ever.

Soon after the wind went down and the sun rose upon a scene of desolation.

Four corpses were washed ashore.

One of them was Horace Stonor.

Mr. Maidment, congratulating himself upon the escape of his family, went down to the beach.

"Four dead!" he said. "How is that?—there were but three left on board."

"The fourth, sir, is a young gentleman who was at a private tutor's near here," replied a coastguard. "He said something about his cousin being in danger."

Mr. Maidment saw it all then.

Horace had perished because he did not stay to reflect as Dick had done, and courted certain death by his rashness.

They were careful to say nothing to Henrietta about the shocking occurrence when she recovered and was taken with others to the nearest hotel.

The news of the wreck rapidly spread, and several people made their way to the scene to gratify an idle curiosity.

Dick was standing by his poor dead friend, his eyes full of tears, and directing his removal to Mr. Markwell's house.

There was a smile of resignation on his parted lips, and his hands were folded over his breast, either by accident or design.

"He is with the angels now," murmured Dick.

"Hallo! who is this?" cried a voice at his elbow.

He turned round and recognised Brabazon and Lawless, to whom he could not help replying in a severe tone. "It is the boy you persecuted and despised because he was a tradesman's son, but he died in trying to save another, and has gone, I trust, where there is no distinction of class, for in the sight of Him who made us we are all equal."

"You need not preach a sermon," answered Brabazon. "Perhaps we were wrong. Anyhow, I am very sorry for this."

"Tell us how it happened," asked Lawless.

Dick's voice was choked by emotion as he related first his dream and then the episode of the wreck.

He did not dwell upon his own bravery

in saving Henrietta under such desperate circumstances.

He merely stated that she was finally rescued.

"You may as well add, sir, that it was you who saved the young lady," said Simmons, who was standing by with a stretcher on which to place the body of Horace.

"Did you really?" asked Brabazon, looking at him admiringly.

"He will tell you all about it," replied Dick, sinking down on the beach by the side of his friend and crying again unrestrainedly.

"It was a fine thing, sir; as fine a thing as was ever done," cried Simmons. "The rope broke while I had her in my arms, and the sea tore her from me. It wouldn't have done it if I had been strong and well, but I had made three journeys before, and I hadn't any strength left to speak about. However, young master here ties a rope about him, and in he goes. Nothing could have saved her if it had not been for him."

"I'm proud of you," said Brabazon, "and if you will shake hands, we'll be friends again."

Dick extended his hand with a mournful smile.

"This is a lesson to us not to be at enmity with one another," he said, pointing to Horace.

They put him on the stretcher, and he was carried to Mr. Markwell's house, and laid upon his bed.

Mr. Markwell had received no intimation of what had happened, and his astonishment may be imagined.

His first care was to telegraph for the unfortunate boy's father.

A message came from the hotel to say that Mr. Maidment and Miss Stonor wanted to see Dick—the latter being anxious to thank him personally for his courageous conduct.

But Dick made an excuse.

"I should go if I were you," said Mr. Markwell, who was by.

"I can't see *his* cousin, sir," said Dick, "because I cannot forget that it was indirectly through me that he met with his death. If I had not roused him up and taken him with me, he would not have been tempted to rush into the sea and so be drowned."

"You blame yourself without a cause. Be comforted: these accidents are directed by an all-wise Providence. It was not your fault," answered Mr. Markwell.

But Dick burst out sobbing again, and would not go to see Henrietta.

CHAPTER XXXIII.

DICK IS A SCAPEGRACE STILL.

MISS PRISCILLA MARKWELL had been very fond of Horace Stonor, whom she liked as much as she detested Dick.

She did not agree with her brother that Dick was not to blame for Horace's death; on the contrary, she held that it was altogether his fault.

"If he had not got up in the night and worried Horace Stonor into accompanying him to see the wreck, which he heard of through the minute gun, the poor boy would not have been drowned. As to the apparition, that is in my opinion all nonsense, and only an excuse for going out. He is a bad boy. None of the other young gentlemen like him, and I should send him away."

"He was brave enough, for he saved the girl's life," remarked Mr. Markwell.

"For whom he has conceived a foolish attachment. His character came with him," answered Miss Priscilla.

This conversation took place in the study, and Miss Priscilla did not notice that Dick was present.

He had been sitting in a corner, brooding over his grief, and getting up, he walked straight to Miss Priscilla.

"Here is the boy himself. You should be careful about what you say, my dear," observed Mr. Markwell.

"Your remarks about myself, ma'am, are not very complimentary," said Dick, "and I will thank you in future to keep

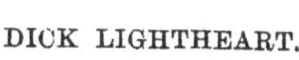

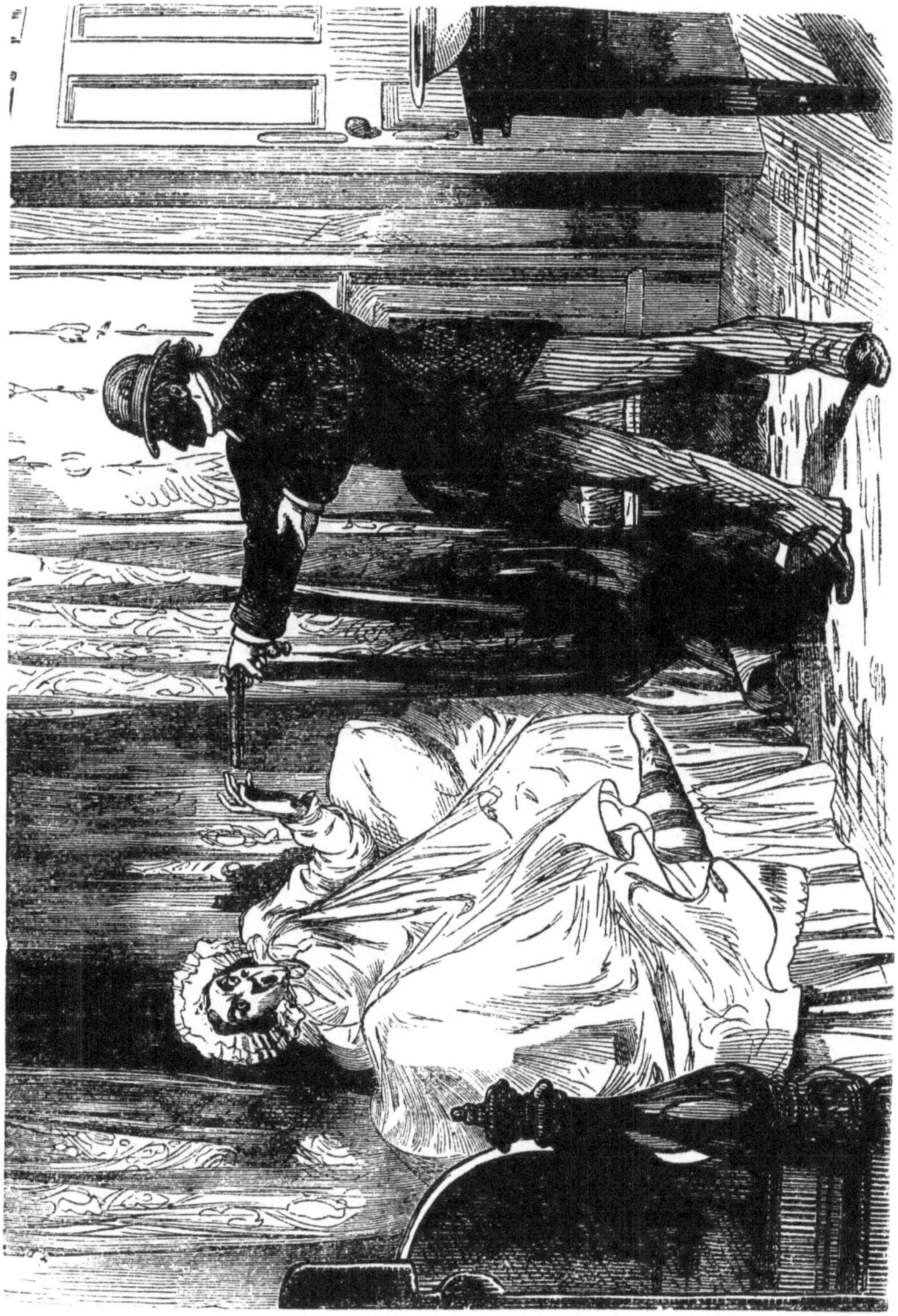

"'TAKE ALL I HAVE,' BUT 'SPARE MY LIFE,' SHRIEKED MISS PRISCILLA."

No. 8.

them to yourself. I recognise no authority here but Mr. Markwell's."

"And that you do not care much about," answered Miss Priscilla. "But I shall not waste my breath in arguing with you."

"Thank you," answered Dick, with a provoking smile.

Miss Priscilla went away, and Dick returned to his seat.

In the evening Mr. Stonor came down from London.

His grief at his son's death was intense, but he was grateful to Heaven for preserving the life of his niece.

By this time the news had been broken to Henrietta, and the father of the dead boy and his niece mingled their tears together.

Mr. Stonor was generous enough to call upon Dick and shake him by the hand, while he thanked him warmly for what he had done.

"Do not come and see Henrietta now," he said. "I wish to spare her any further excitement; but when the holidays come, I shall expect you to visit me at my little place at Wimbledon. You may rely upon Henrietta being there also. Do not blush. I know the story of your running away, and if she likes you well enough, I will do all I can with her guardians to help on your courtship, but ——"

"What, sir?" asked Dick.

"Boys and girls cannot marry. You must remember that. This is an age of early marriage; royalty has set the example. Yet you must be twenty years old at least before you two could marry one another."

"Thank you, sir, for what you have said. Thank you very much," answered Dick.

"My poor boy is to be buried at Brighton. You will follow him?"

"Gladly. We were such friends, and —and——"

Dick broke down; he could say no more.

Mr. Stonor patted him on the shoulder and went away.

In a week from that time Horace was buried in the Brighton cemetery.

The ladies of the family did not follow him, but Dick saw Henrietta for a short time; and although the occasion was a melancholy one, he left her with the fond assurance that he was dearer to her than before.

Dick returned to his work.

The death of Horace healed the differences which had formerly existed between him and the other pupils.

They all became friendly again, but Miss Priscilla's dislike to Dick increased to positive rudeness.

"I can't stand that old girl's cheek much longer," remarked Dick to Brabazon, one day, when the midsummer holidays were approaching.

"I must say she's not so nice in her manner to you as she might be," answered Brabazon, with a smile.

"She has never forgiven me for pulling her wig off," observed Dick. "For though she could not prove that I did it, she had her suspicions."

"That was great fun."

"I'll frighten her out of her wits," said Dick. "Now we are working hard for the examination, you know, we sit up later than she, and Mr. Markwell, too."

"What's the dodge?" asked Brabazon.

"I'll buy a black mask and make a row in the corridor, pretending I am a burglar and bring her out of bed in her nightcap, and then laugh at her."

"Will it be fair?" said Brabazon.

"It will be a lark, and I was always inclined that way."

"But——"

"I don't ask you to help me. You won't be involved in it. I only ask you to hold your row and enjoy the fun."

"All right," answered Brabazon.

With Dick, to conceive an idea of this sort, was instantly to put it into execution.

He bought a black mask to cover his face, and armed himself with the pistol he had bought for shooting cats.

The other pupils were apprised of the joke that he was about to play Miss Priscilla.

They congregated on the stairs.

Dick, about half-past eleven o'clock, went to the corridor, looking very much like a burglar.

He went into Miss Priscilla's room, and standing by the bedside, exclaimed in a stern voice—

"Your money and the key of the plate chest, or your life."

With this he presented the pistol at her head.

Miss Priscilla awoke with a start.

"Oh! dear, kind gentleman," she answered. "Take all I have, but spare my life."

She handed him her watch and her purse which she kept under the pillow, as well as the key of the plate chest.

"It is well," said Dick, in a tragic tone. "Dare to move for the space of two hours, and instant death will be your portion."

Miss Priscilla was in a terrible fright. She nearly fainted.

But directly the burglar's back was turned, she remembered that her brother always kept a loaded revolver in his room, and that he would be terribly angry with her, if she allowed the contents of the plate chest, which were valuable, to be taken away without rousing him. Accordingly she got up, as Dick fully expected she would, and entered the passage in her night dress and nightcap, which was of an old-fashioned kind, something resembling an inverted coalscuttle.

In the middle of the passage Dick flashed his lantern upon her.

"Help! Thieves! Murder!—Murder! Thieves! Thieves!" she cried, at the top of her voice, shrieking loudly afterwards.

In an instant, Mr. Markwell, revolver in hand, was out of his room.

Dick was about to beat a retreat.

But his tutor caught sight of his black mask and lantern, and naturally concluding that he was a burglar who had come to rob the premises, he levelled his pistol at him.

There was a flash, a report, and Dick fell down on the staircase, rolling into the arms of his fellow pupils.

Uttering a groan, he became insensible.

"Where is he?" cried Mr. Markwell, running up.

He saw the pupils holding the supposed burglar.

"That's right. Stick to him; hold the scoundrel. Don't let the rascal go," he exclaimed.

Miss Priscilla had fainted in the corridor, but nobody seemed inclined to pay much attention to her.

"I'm afraid he is hurt, sir," said Brabazon.

"Hurt? Serves him right; one is justified in killing a burglar."

"But he's not a burglar."

"What!" cried Mr. Markwell, in amazement.

"It's Lightheart, sir," continued Brabazon.

"Nonsense."

"It is, indeed, sir."

"How did he come to put on that mask, and take that pistol and frighten my sister out of her senses?"

"It was all done in fun, sir. Miss Priscilla has tormented him a good deal lately, and he thought he would pay her out by frightening her."

"And you lent yourself to this proposition? Oh, Brabazon!" said Mr. Markwell, sadly.

"We didn't know."

"You should have thought of the consequences. But it is always true that one black sheep contaminates the whole flock."

"Shall I run for a doctor, sir?" said Brabazon. "He seems a good deal hurt."

"Do so; pray go at once. We will convey him to his room. Dear me, what a misfortune. We have had nothing but excitement since he came here. Silly, misguided boy! Mr. Brabazon, run, and lose no time," said Mr. Markwell.

Brabazon was off like a shot, and the other pupils, with their tutor's help, carried Dick to his bedroom.

He bled a little from a wound in his leg, but they staunched the bleeding as well as they were able with towels.

When the doctor came he made an examination of the wound, which was merely a graze of the flesh in the region of the calf of the leg.

The charge of powder had not been large, or the consequences would have been much more serious than they were.

Mr. Markwell was very nervous, and did not know how to shoot.

It was a wonder that he hit Dick at all.

They were all thankful that no tragedy had been committed or any dreadful injury inflicted.

As it was, Dick was only ill for a day or two.

He did not mind the privation of staying indoors for a few days, as he was thankful to have escaped with his life.

Mr. Markwell was so much annoyed with Dick's conduct on more than one occasion, that he wished not to keep him under his charge any longer.

"The boy is a scapegrace," ho said to his sister, "and I ought to get rid of him."

"Quite right," answered Miss Priscilla; "I very much approve of your determination. You would have done so before, long before, had you taken my advice."

"The fact is, my dear sister," continued Mr. Markwell, "that I am more fitted for teaching than managing boys. I should like to take a situation as head master in a small school."

"I wish you would," replied his sister. "I am tired of looking after young gentlemen, ordering the dinner, sending their clothes to the wash, and sewing on buttons."

"You have an independent income of a hundred a year, and some money saved, Priscilla. It would grieve me to separate from you, but I should like to see you in a more congenial sphere."

"I should like to have a circulating library and musicseller's business," remarked Miss Priscilla, thoughtfully.

"Let us each follow the bent of our inclinations," cried Mr. Markwell.

"Agreed."

They each took up a newspaper and began to look over the advertising columns.

Some minutes passed.

Mr. Markwell suddenly exclaimed—

"The very thing!"

"How odd," said his sister. "I was just about to make the same observation."

"Have you, too, found something to suit you?"

"I have. Listen."

Mr. Markwell put down his paper, and his sister read him the advertisement of a small but genteel business, such as she wanted, in a fashionable part of Brighton.

"Excellent," he said. "You shall take that, Priscilla; and now, my dear, hear this—

"'Scholastic.—Wanted a gentleman of ability and attainments, a graduate of one of the Universities, accustomed to teach the young. Respondent must be able to take the position of senior master in a small, select, but flourishing school. If he can bring a connection with him, he will find it to his advantage. Apply to Mr. Simcox, Harrow House, Kemp Town Brighton.'"

"You are an M.A. and an LL.D.," said Miss Priscilla, proudly.

"I am," replied Mr. Markwell, "and I will go this very day to Mr. Simcox."

Accordingly, he put on his hat and walked along the Parade to Harrow House.

Mr. Simcox saw him at once.

"My dear sir," said Mr. Simcox, "you are the very man I want. I do not mind confessing to you that my attainments are not extensive. I require a gentleman of superior education to myself to bring my school to that high pitch of perfection it is my ambition to see it reach."

"Have you many boys?"

"Nearly sixty."

"An usher?" asked Mr. Markwell.

"One; a very worthy creature, named Snarley. He has been with me some time now, and we get on very well together; but between you and me and the post, Snarley does not know more than I do. He is all very well for the little boys."

"I perceive. I have been a private tutor, and have a few boys under my charge now, whom I may be able to bring with me; one is the Honourable Mr. Brabazon, the son of a peer."

"Very good," said Mr. Simcox, rubbing his hands. "I like a lord's son. Reference permitted in the prospectus, ver—y good."

"Then there's a clergyman's son."

"Ah, very good. Clergymen are always first-rate references."

"And Mr. Lightheart is——"

"What did you say?" cried Mr. Simcox, nearly bounding from his chair.

"Lightheart! His son Richard has been some time under my charge."

"No wonder, my dear sir, you want to get rid of your responsibility, and are tired of conducting the business of a private tutor, if you have that imp of darkness in your house," said Mr. Simcox, with a groan.

"You know him, then?" exclaimed Mr. Markwell, in surprise.

"Know him! don't I? He was here

for a long while, and nearly brought us all to the verge of the grave."

"Dear me, how strange! I heard he had been at school somewhere in this neighbourhood, though I was far from suspecting that you were his old schoolmaster."

"I do believe I should have conquered him, if he had stayed," continued Mr. Simcox; "Snarley is also of the same opinion."

"Try again. It is a bad thing to be beaten."

"After all," said Mr. Simcox, "he represents sixty pounds a year and extras, paid quarterly with a scrupulous punctuality that is positively refreshing."

"It is a question in my mind," Mr. Markwell went on, "whether a master does his duty to a boy by expelling him. Suppose the stubborn spirit conquered, and a victory obtained, is it not better than casting out the black sheep with a brand upon him?"

"You are right, my dear sir."

"I have advertised for unruly boys."

"So have I."

"Can we not together subdue any number of the most stubborn?" continued Mr. Markwell.

"Let us hope so. Join me in——"

"Did you say a glass of sherry?" interrupted Mr. Markwell.

"Ah, pardon me," exclaimed Mr. Simcox, ringing the bell.

Presently sherry and biscuits stood upon the table, and the schoolmasters regaled themselves.

"Very fine," said Mr. Markwell, smacking his lips; a true dry flavour. Well, as I was observing, we ought to succeed if we unite our exertions. Look at our experience."

"I consider that fortune has done me a happy turn in sending you to me," answered Mr. Simcox.

Their conversation lasted some time, and the preliminaries of the fusion were agreed to.

The two schoolmasters decided to enter into a partnership.

Several other interviews were necessary before everything was settled.

It was arranged that they should begin business after the summer holidays.

Dick went home, as did the other boys, and behaved himself as well as he could, which was not too well.

It was from his father that he first heard of the change Mr. Markwell had made.

"So," said his father, "you will have to go back to your old school, and have two masters to govern you instead of one."

"The more the merrier, sir," replied Dick.

"And you will try to behave well."

"I always do try my best," Dick said.

"Remember that your future prospects in life depend upon your working hard now," continued the Reverend Mr. Lightheart.

"You'll see, father, that I shall grow up such a clever boy that I'll set the Thames on fire," said Dick.

His father smiled.

"Your sisters want to see you," he went on.

"To see me? Why, it's only an hour ago since we met at breakfast, and Emily put a blackbeetle in my tea, or I did into hers. It's all the same."

"A little visitor has arrived."

"Who? Not Henrietta."

"Never mind; go and see."

Dick's face flushed.

He had only been at home a week, and though he knew Emily had invited Henrietta to come and spend a little while with them, he did not expect her so soon.

With a bound he left his father's study and ran to the morning room, where Mrs. Lightheart and the girls were assembled.

In the midst was Henrietta, looking very lovely in her little travelling cloak and bonnet.

Agnes and Emily were kissing her as girls will one another when they meet.

"Mayn't I have one?" said Dick.

"For shame, Richard," replied his mother. "Have you no better manners? Shake hands with Miss Stonor."

Dick did so, and immediately kissed the back of his own hand, making a loud noise.

Mrs. Lightheart heard this, and thought that Henrietta had complied with Dick's request, and kissed him.

"Girls are more forward now," she said, "than they were in my young days."

"Dear Mrs. Lightheart, what do you mean?" asked Henrietta.

"You kissed Dick, unmistakably, and——"

"Indeed I did not."

"Now, Harry dear," said Dick, addressing Henrietta, "don't deny it."

"You impudent thing!" cried Henrietta Stonor, much annoyed. "How dare you say I kissed you?"

"Everyone heard it," said Dick, adding, "If you didn't you ought to, and I'll give you another chance before you're a year older."

"I won't speak to you once all the time I am here, that I won't!" Henrietta said, angrily.

"And I'll help you to pay him out," said Emily.

"Two to one, Emmy, that's not fair; but you're only girls," said Dick, laughing. "Henrietta——"

"Call me Miss Stonor, sir, if you please," she exclaimed.

"You may call me anything you please, so long as you don't call me too late for dinner," said Dick, "but I will humour you before company. The mum's particular."

"Don't call me the mum, sir," cried Mrs. Lightheart. "I'm your mother."

"So I have always been led to believe," answered Dick. "Let me go on with what I was saying. You're pitching into me all round. I was about to inform the charming but somewhat crusty Miss Stonor that I am about to become a neighbour of hers again."

"How is that?" asked Henrietta.

"Mr. Simcox and Mr. Markwell have struck up a partnership. Markwell is to be Mr. Simcox's senior master, and all the pupils are to be at Harrow House, and I've promised to be a good boy."

"I hope you will keep your promise, sir," said Mrs. Lightheart, severely.

"Oh! ma dear," said Agnes, "Richard has a great deal of good in him."

"Thank you, Aggy. I'll remember you in my will," said Dick, with an approving glance.

"He takes care not to let it out, then," remarked Emily.

"Emmy," said Dick, threateningly, "if you don't have some chopped horsehair and salt in your bed to-night, say I forgot it."

"Richard!" cried his mother.

"Yes, marm," said Dick.

"I have told you to address me respectfully. You are, I fear, a bad boy. Try to reform and leave those girls alone; you will wear their lives out. And if I hear anything of putting things in people's beds, I'll tell your father."

"Don't do that," replied Dick, "you frighten me. I have some difficulty in drawing my breath; and you know I was consumptive as a boy. Tell Simcox and Co., but don't—oh! do not tell my father. He might beat me."

As he spoke he made a ludicrous grimace at Agnes, who stuffed her pocket-handkerchief into her mouth, to prevent laughing.

"Well, I will not, as you beg so earnestly," answered Mrs. Lightheart. "I am glad to see that you have yet some feeling left in you. Run away and play. Miss Stonor is fatigued with her journey, and must want to take her things off."

Dick went away, but as he passed his mother, contrived to pin an antimacassar to her collar; it hung down gracefully behind, and a roar of laughter, when he gained the passage, told him that the girls had found out the trick.

"He is the same Dick," said Emily, when they got upstairs.

"And always will be," said Agnes.

"I don't want him to change. He is very nice as he is," said Henrietta. "Though he oughtn't to say he has kisses when he hasn't. If he had really had a kiss, I should not have cared so much."

A form bounded in at the door, strong arms encompassed her, and three distinct kisses were heard.

One on each cheek and one on the lips.

Then the form bounded out again, and Henrietta looked as if she would like to faint.

"Oh," said Emily, "I didn't think Dick would have done such a thing."

"How mean, to listen at the door and then come in and steal kisses like that," said Henrietta.

"He heard you say you wouldn't have cared if he did do it," observed Agnes.

Agnes was always Dick's friend.

"Never mind," said Henrietta, putting her hair in order, "he shan't do it again."

"But then he saved your life, dear," said Agnes.

Henrietta began to cry.

"Don't talk about that, please, Agnes," she said. "I did love Horace, my poor cousin, so much. He was such a good, quiet boy."

Agnes was sorry, and Henrietta's grief soon passed away.

They began to talk about a dozen things at once as only girls can talk.

Dick was satisfied.

He had had the kiss, and that was all he wanted.

"I never saw the girl yet," he said to himself, "I wouldn't kiss if I wanted to. Shan't we have some larks when I get back to Simcox and Co.'s?"

He was rather pleased at the prospect.

Life at the private tutor's had been rather slow, especially after Horace Stonor's dreadfully sudden death.

There was a chance of renewed excitement and fun.

Besides this, he liked Messiter.

It was worth anything to get back to Messiter once more.

And then there was Mr. Snarley.

"I expect," said Dick, to himself, "that Snarley's been getting fat since I left. It isn't good for ushers to be too fat. I shall be doing him a kindness by reducing his weight a little. And won't Mrs. Simcox be pleased to see me? It'll be, ' Hoh, dear me, 'ere's that Lightheart. 'Ow hare you, Richard?' and I shall reply, in the language of the poet, ' Richard's himself again, ma'am, thank you, and as right as ninepence. How's yourself?' "

So it will be seen that the return to Harrow House School was not full of terrors to him.

Quite the contrary.

He rather liked the idea than otherwise.

CHAPTER XXXIV.

DICK FINDS A RIVAL.

DURING the holidays Messrs. Simcox and Markwell had not been idle.

They had a new schoolroom built, and sent out circulars far and wide, which brought them a fresh addition of pupils, so that the school was nearly seventy strong when the boys reassembled.

Mr. Markwell took the highest class in classics and mathematics.

Mr. Simcox had the next, and a new usher named Slocum was expressly engaged for the third form, while Mr. Snarley superintended the fourth, consisting of the smaller boys.

To accommodate the new arrivals, a house next door had been taken, and doors were made in the wall to allow of communication.

One was Mr. Markwell's house and under his care, the other Mr. Simcox's, though they were both united and formed one establishment.

Dick Lightheart arrived early in the morning on the day appointed for the return of the boys.

He saw several old faces, and many new ones.

Among the former was his friend Messiter.

They shook hands cordially and adjourned to the schoolroom, which was in a state of confusion, as there was no work on the first day.

"I didn't expect to see you back again," said Messiter.

"Nor did I expect to come. However, here we are again, and we must do what we can to make our miserable lives happy," said Dick. "How have you been getting on in my absence?"

"Dull as ditch-water," answered Messiter. "There has been no fun, and we have all groaned under the sway of a tyrant."

"Indeed! Who may he be?"

"His name is Armond," said Messiter; "he is a tall, hulking fellow, with long, wiry arms and sledge-hammer fists—an awful bully, and a fellow I'm sure you won't like at all."

"Oh, that's the size of it, is it?" said Dick.

He took up a piece of chalk and began to write on the big slate.

"Simcox and Co., Purveyors of Latin, Greek, and Mathematics," appeared first; then he wrote, "Cocky Armond, B.B."

"That's not a bad name for him. He is cocky," said Messiter, laughing.

"And he shall be called Cocky Armond from this day forth," replied Dick.

"What's B.B. ?" inquired Messiter.

"That's just what I want to know," exclaimed a harsh, unpleasant voice at his elbow.

Dick quietly looked up at the questioner.

"B. B.," he replied, "stands for beast and bully."

"Oh, does it? Thank you for the information, and now perhaps you'll oblige me by rubbing that out."

"Oh, dear, no," answered Dick, coolly.

"Then I shall have to make you."

"Messiter, who is this individual?" asked Dick.

"It's Armond himself," replied Messiter.

"Indeed. Messiter, you've forgotten one thing."

"What's that?"

"Didn't I tell you he should have a nickname? When you have occasion to speak of Mr. Armond in future, you will be pleased to give him his prefix. Cocky Armond sounds well. Repeat it after me."

The new comer stared at Dick as if he did not quite understand him.

He was a tall, thin, dark boy of about seventeen years of age, having a sallow complexion, bad teeth, big heavy eyes, a hanging jaw, and a large bowed nose.

"I don't want any of your cheek, Mr. What's-your-name," said Armond.

"Lightheart — Richard Lightheart. Sorry I haven't a card," replied Dick.

"Well, I don't want any of your cheek, I tell you."

"Don't you? Can't help that. The obligation is on your side. Sorry for you, if you can't see it. I've given you a degree. B.B. Cocky Armond, Esq., B.B. Sounds well, doesn't it, Messiter?"

"Fine," replied Messiter.

Armond was taken a little aback, but he was very angry.

His ill temper increased, as several boys came round, and, looking at the slate, asked one another what the letters meant.

He had held undisputed sway in the school for some months, and was the favourite of the masters.

Tyrants never like being put down.

The popular applause is what they live upon.

"I shall have to give you a licking," said Armond, at last.

"All right," replied Dick. "Knock me down, and see me come up smiling."

Armond tried to give him a box of the ears, but Dick ducked his head, and the intended blow missed him.

"Sold again, and lost your money. You didn't do it that time, Cocky," said Dick, with a provoking grin.

"But I will next," retorted Armond.

"Say which peeper I shall plant a mouse on," continued Dick.

"Make a ring," cried Messiter. "Take those benches out of the way. Clear the room."

The boys set to work in a moment, repeating—

"Clear the room! Make a ring! Mill! mill!"

Dick began to dance round Armond in a manner perfectly bewildering to him.

Then he rushed in, and, with a scientific tap tap, right and left, Dick gave him a reminder on the eye, and what he called "a corker in the mouth."

Thoroughly enraged, Armond swung his big arms round, like the sails of a windmill, and it was clear that if he did hit Dick, that young gentleman would remember it.

At length he succeeded in striking him under the ear with one of his sledge-hammer blows.

Dick spun across the room, just as the door opened, and he fell into the arms of Mr. Snarley.

"What is all this?" exclaimed the usher, looking round in surprise. "You boys, you boys, this will not do."

"Morning, sir," said Dick, recovering himself a little. "It's Mr. Snarley, I think, though my ideas of things in general are rather confused just now."

"Lightheart, as I live," replied the usher. "But I might have guessed it. No other boy would have set the school in an uproar five minutes after his arrival."

Dick sat down on a form and looked at Armond, who was applying his handkerchief to his mouth, and withdrawing it crimson-stained.

"Are you also concerned in this riot, Armond?" continued Mr. Snarley.

"In my position, sir, of head of the school, it is my duty to keep order," answered Armond.

"Very true. Allowance must be made for your position. How did this broil originate?"

Armond had wiped off the slate the words which referred to him, and, pointing to what remained, said—

"Lightheart, sir, had written 'Simcox and Co., Purveyors of Latin, Greek, and Mathematics.' I thought this disparaging, and remonstrated with him, whereupon he struck me viciously. I forbore to hit him again until he had struck me twice, and then I knocked him across the room, as you perceived when you entered."

Dick drew a long breath, and let it out again in the form of a loud whistle.

"What have you to say to this, Lightheart?" asked Mr. Snarley.

"He's told more lies, sir, in two minutes than any average boy will tell in a twelvemonth," replied Dick.

"Stop a bit," said Mr. Snarley, holding up his hand. "I don't like the use of the words 'lies' or 'liar.' Say 'falsehood' or 'storyteller.'"

"I'll call him Ananias, who, the Bible says——"

"Silence! Did you, or did you not, write the sentence on the slate?"

"Yes," replied Dick.

"Did you, or did you not, strike Armond first?"

"I did, sir."

"Then his case is proved."

"But——"

"No more. Not a word!" exclaimed Mr. Snarley; "you are clearly in the wrong."

Armond smiled maliciously.

He knew beforehand that the usher would take his part if he could.

"I will be heard, sir. He pitched into me," exclaimed Dick, "because I wrote something else on the slate, which he has rubbed out."

"What was that?"

"Cocky Armond, B.B."

"What may the enigmatical letters B.B. mean?" inquired Mr. Snarley.

"Beast and bully, sir. I have heard his character, and I took the liberty of christening him."

"You were wrong. Armond is at the head of the school, which has very much changed since you were here before, and Armond was justified in maintaining his authority. We must have discipline," said Mr. Snarley, adding, "What is a school without discipline?"

No one answered him, and he went on.

"As this is the first day of your assembling together, I shall pass over this breach of discipline. Do not let it occur again. Armond, come with me; you must have your eye attended to. Boys, live together in peace and amity."

Mr. Snarley linked his arm in that of Armond, and they left the schoolroom together.

The boys crowded round Dick, delighted with the proof of his prowess he had given them.

"We'll call him 'Cocky' for ever," said one.

"And 'B.B.' too," exclaimed another.

"Did he hurt you?" asked Messiter.

"Rather. He doesn't fight fairly. I didn't expect that swinging round hander under the ear, but I shall be up to his tactics next time," answered Dick.

He had made an enemy of Armond, who was not of a forgiving or forgetting disposition.

"I am glad you have made an example of him," said Messiter. "We all hate him."

"Not more than I do," answered Dick.

"He's sure to get the masters to take his part; they always do, because he's their spy."

"How do you know?"

"Oh," replied Messiter, "he tells them everything. He prowls about the passage at night, and listens at the doors of the dormitories. I know Mister Cocky Armond."

"I'll stop him at that game," said Dick.

"Will you?"

"Yes. This very night, if he gives me a chance."

"And Smith—you remember the fellow we called Smiff'?"

"The man who wasn't all there—had a tile off. I recollect him," said Dick.

"Well, he's a spy of Armond's. It's

all spying here now. We can't blow our noses without someone telling somebody else," continued Messiter.

"That's a nice state of things. It's lucky for you I came back."

"So I think. The school will be as different again, now you're here," Messiter answered.

During the day the boys continued to arrive, and towards evening all had assembled with the exception of a few who were absent through illness.

After supper, Mr. Markwell read a chapter in the Bible, and Mr. Simcox read prayers.

They looked around them with pride, upon the large number of pupils they had obtained, and asked a blessing upon their exertions in the forthcoming half-year.

Then the boys retired to their rooms, which had been excellently arranged.

In Dick's dormitory there were three boys, one of whom was Messiter, another Fowler, and another Smith.

The latter had been put in as a spy upon them, and it was his duty to inform Armond of everything that was done contrary to the rules.

Messiter guessed this, and informed Dick of his suspicions.

"If you are right," said Dick, "we'll make his life a burden to him, and he'll be glad to ask to be removed."

Most of the boys had brought from home some luxuries in their boxes, and these were to be eaten when Snarley, who had charge of their passage, had been round to see that the light was out.

This was duly accomplished as the clock struck ten.

"Now, my boys," said Dick, springing out of bed, "produce the spread."

This was done with a rapidity worthy of the occasion.

The delicacies were temptingly arranged on Dick's counterpane.

All but Smith assembled round the eatables, anxious to begin the feast.

"Where's Smiff? Come along, old fellow, and tuck in," exclaimed Messiter.

"I'd rather not, thank you," replied Smith. "I'm not hungry."

"What's the odds? I am always hungry when there's anything in the way."

"You must excuse me. It's not right; that's another thing. It's against the rules."

"Humbug," said Dick. "Who says strawberry jam? Spread some on a coffee biscuit or some of that short-bread, Fowler. I'll attend to Smiff."

The boys began the feast, and the luxuries began to diminish in size and number.

Two pairs of lighted candles stood on the mantelpiece, which gave plenty of illumination.

"You must have something, Smiff," cried Dick. "It's first night."

"I know that, Lightheart; but it does not make any difference. I would rather starve than do anything wrong!" replied Smith.

"We have too much regard for your health to neglect you. Fowler, hand me that box of tooth powder."

Fowler did as he was requested.

Dick spread some jam on a biscuit, and with the blade of his knife mixed a lot of tooth-powder in it.

"Messiter," he said, "I will thank you for the soap."

When it was given him, he scraped a quantity on the top of the tooth-powder.

"Oh!" he said, looking round, "that citrate of magnesia on the mantelpiece will do; hand it over; and you, Messiter, scrape some lead pencil."

The slate pencil and magnesia were added to the mess, which was all stirred up together.

Going over to Smith's bed with the prepared biscuit in his hand, Dick said—

"Open your mouth and shut your eyes, my dear Smiff, and see what good luck has sent you."

"Oh, don't, Lightheart, please don't make me eat that nasty stuff," pleaded Smith.

"Oh! but you must. We know you're going to sneak, and you must have something to sneak about, you must really."

"Sneak! I'm sure——"

"Now don't tell stories. Lying is worse than sneaking, you know, and it's against the rules. Open your mouth," said Dick.

"I won't," replied Smith.

"I say you must. Make haste, I shall lose my share of the prog; look how those fellows are tucking in. One would think it was the last moment they had to live," continued Dick.

Smith kept his mouth obstinately closed.

"Oh! you won't, won't you?" said Dick, "then I shall have to make you, my boy."

He put the butt end of his knife against the under part of Smith's ear, where the jaw bone ends, and pressing it, Smith's mouth flew open, and in went the mess.

Then Dick kept his mouth shut till he had swallowed it.

"That's Lightheart's patent food for cattle," he cried.

Smith gulped down the last of the nauseous preparation with a shudder.

"You needn't call me names," he said.

"You're an ass," replied Dick, "and that's being a cattle. If you hadn't been an ass, you would have had some of the grub like the rest of us."

"Look out," cried Messiter, in a warning voice.

"What's the matter?" said Dick.

"Dowse the glims. I hear footsteps."

In an instant all was darkness, and the ends of Dick's counterpane were hastily thrown over the eatables, while all crept into bed.

CHAPTER XXXV.

COCKY ARMOND IS MISTAKEN FOR A BURGLAR.

THE boys thought it might be Mr. Snarley who was prying about, or the new usher, Mr. Slocum, anxious to show his zeal.

But Dick and Messiter imagined it to be Armond, and their suspicion was strengthened when after a few minutes had elapsed no one entered the room.

Dick got out of bed and went up to Messiter's side.

"Does Armond come in and kick up a row like a master?" he whispered.

"No; he only peeps in through the chinks of the door when he sees a light, and listens," said Messiter.

"Didn't you bring a cane back with you?"

"Yes; and so did you."

"Where's yours?" asked Dick.

"In the corner, near my bed, and I think you put yours there also," said Messiter.

"Jump out and collar your cane. Give me mine, too."

"What for?"

"We'll go out and fall upon Armond and say we took him for a burglar."

"Bravo! That's an idea," Messiter exclaimed delighted.

"If we don't wallop him within an inch of his life, I'll never play cricket again Come on."

"I should like it," continued Messiter, "he is such a sneak. You know he has a room to himself, just like a master, and no one can tell when he goes in or out."

In a short time they were both armed with short, thick canes..

Without putting anything on, they opened the door suddenly, and rushed into the passage.

As they expected, Cocky Armond was listening, and so suddenly was the door opened that he nearly fell into Dick's arms.

He had put on an old pair of trousers, a great coat, list slippers, and had tied a comforter round his neck.

Seizing him by the throat, Dick cried, "It's a thief, I know it's a thief. Welt him; let him have it, Harry."

Messiter did not want telling twice.

While Dick held Armond, he beat him unmercifully with his cane, and the victim's cries resounded far and wide.

"Let me hold him now," said Messiter, "and you have a try."

"All right," answered Dick.

The grasp was shifted, and Armond, half stifled by the tight grip on his collar, and bewildered both by the sudden attack and the pain he suffered, was unable to make any effectual resistance.

"Do—don't, Lightheart," stammered Armond. "It's me. It's Armond."

"I know better than that, you cowardly thief, to come and prowl about in the night to steal the boys' things," Dick answered.

"Re-really. It's me. It's Ar-Armond," cried the victim, writhing under each fresh stroke.

"Go to Putney," said Dick, incredulously, "you are some discharged servant or other, but I'll teach you a lesson. Armond indeed! I know Armond; we are great friends. I have an immense respect for Armond since he punched my head."

And still the cane came down in a shower of blows, till Armond writhed and twisted like a snake, yelling and crying like a madman.

The boys rushed out of their dormitories, candles were lighted, and the utmost confusion prevailed.

Mr. Snarley, alarmed at the unusual noise, came up stairs with a light in his hand.

"What's all this tumult about?" he asked.

"A thief, sir; Messiter and I caught him in the passage, and we have been cobbing him," answered Dick.

"Surely you imagine a vain thing," cried the usher, who had an inkling of the truth. "Desist from this furious punishment."

"Let him go, Harry," said Dick to Messiter.

Cocky Armond fell down on his knees and began to sob with rage and pain.

Mr. Snarley held the light near his face.

"It is, yes, it is Armond," he cried.

At the sound of the usher's voice Armond recovered himself, and rose to his feet trembling like a leaf.

"How did this happen? inquired Snarley.

"I was walking in the passage, when Lightheart and Messiter fell upon me and beat me like a hound," exclaimed Armond.

"We heard a noise in the passage, sir," exclaimed Dick, "and knowing the lights were all out, thought it was burglars. We came out, and by the moonlight saw a figure in a comforter and a great coat; then we felt sure it was burglars, so we fell upon him and thrashed him to save the house from being robbed; you can't blame us. He shouldn't have got himself up like that; besides, what business had he about the passage after you had seen the lights put out?"

This reasoning was unanswerable.

It would not do for Mr. Snarley to say that he was prowling about as a spy with his knowledge and approval.

So he was obliged to regard it in the light of a mistake.

"It is a sad error," he exclaimed, "and I do not know that I can commend your zeal, Lightheart."

"Won't you do anything to him for this?" cried Armond, still smarting all over.

His vindictive eyes glared at Lightheart, and seemed to flash fire at him.

"I do not see how, in strict justice, I can do so. Dear me, look at these boys congregated around me like sheep. Go to your beds, you boys. Go at once."

There was a scampering, and the passage was cleared of all but the chief actors in the drama.

"Hold him," continued Armond, "while I flog him as he did me. It is all nonsense to say he did not know me."

"Mr. Snarley is too much of a gentleman to treat anyone unfairly," replied Messiter.

"I cannot do as you wish, Armond. Come with me; retire to your room, and you other boys go to yours," replied Mr Snarley. "We must discuss this unfortunate affair in private. Come, Armond, lean on me."

Dick and Messiter returned to their dormitory.

The boys were sitting on their beds, discussing the extraordinary scene which they had just witnessed.

Everyone was pleased, and Fowler was inclined to think it done on purpose; but remembering Smith was in the room, he declared he thought it was a thief, as he wouldn't have said anything before Smith on any account.

The next morning Armond did not appear in school.

He was so sore with his beating that he kept his bed.

When he did make his appearance, he had occasion to pass by Dick.

Lowering his voice until it had a sharp, serpentine hiss, he said—"I shan't forget you, Lightheart."

Dick grinned and rubbed his shoulders as if they hurt him.

He soon found out, however, that Armond was a man of his word.

CHAPTER XXXVI.

THE FLYING TRAPEZE.

THERE was one thing gained, however, by Dick's behaviour.

Armond gave up walking in the passages as a spy at night.

Ten days passed, and in the rapid succession of events which go to make up a schoolboy's life, the beating inflicted upon Armond was forgotten by all but the recipient of it.

His manner was not openly hostile to Dick.

They seldom spoke, but if it was necessary for them to do so, Armond did not display the marked enmity Dick had expected.

Dick had joined the gymnasium class, which had taken the place of the swimming bath class in the winter months.

Twice a week, once in the morning and once in the evening, the boys went to Castle Square and practised at Mohammed's Rooms.

These were famous premises and much patronised by the youths of Brighton.

Dick showed himself a proficient in all sorts of manly sports and exercises.

In leaping, jumping, the horizontal and parallel bars, the flying trapeze and other things, he could distance most competitors.

Armond and he were considered equal.

A match was arranged to take place between them on the trapeze, to decide which could spring farthest through the air.

Dick accepted the challenge, and felt sure of beating him.

"How civil Cocky Armond is to you since that night," observed Messiter.

"Yes; beastly civil. I can't make it out. Can you?" replied Dick.

"I can't, either. You would have thought he'd have been all the more savage."

"I don't quite like fellows who make up to you when they've got spite in their hearts, and they are as full of venom as a toad; but, after all, I'm not much afraid of Mr. B. B."

"Well, look out, that's all," replied Messiter. "It's easy enough to fall over anything in the dark, and he's not the sort of man to work by daylight."

"Who are you talking about?" asked Fowler, who joined them at this moment.

"Cocky Armond, B.B., as Lightheart christened him," replied Messiter.

"He owes me a grudge, I think," remarked Dick. "But I don't fancy he's so bad as Harry wants to make him out."

"Isn't he? You don't know so much about him as I do," replied Fowler.

"Does he hate me?"

"Like steam. I heard him talking to some fellows in the first form the other day, and he swore he'd be revenged upon you for all you've done to him."

"What have I done?" asked Dick, with a smile of injured innocence.

"Oh, nothing!" replied Fowler. "Of course it's nothing to give a fellow a mouse in the eye, and loosen his teeth. It isn't much to give him a nickname, which you have done, for there isn't a boy in the school who don't call him either Cocky or B. B. Of course it's nothing to leather him within an inch of his life! Oh, no! you've done nothing to Cocky Armond, and he's got no right to hate you."

"I don't fear him. A man who has no enemies has no character; a fellow who has any mind and is anything like a fellow must have enemies," replied Dick.

"Didn't you say you knew more about him than most people?" remarked Messiter.

"So I do," answered Fowler.

"Tell us. We won't chaff him."

"Won't you? Promise me you won't tell, and I'll let you know who he is, and all about him."

The boys readily gave Fowler the required promise, and looked at him full of eager curiosity.

"The cook told me," said Fowler. "Before she came here she was servant in Armond's family. You know I often go into the kitchen, and the cook likes me; she gives me bits of things when I'm hungry."

"Never mind what she gives you," said Dick; "get on to Armond."

"I'm coming to him. His father's a cowheel boiler and tripe dresser in Whitechapel, who does a bit of stiff sometimes."

" What's that ?" asked Messiter.

" Lends money on a bill of exchange, and a couple of halves ago old Simcox was hard up, and flew a kite."

" I'm in the dark again," Messiter said.

" What a child you are," said Fowler; " you don't know anything. If you interrupt me like this, I shall never finish my story."

" But what's a kite ?"

" It's another phrase for doing a bill, borrowing money at interest to be repaid in a certain time. Well, Simcox did this, and somehow or other the tripe dresser ——"

" Armond's father ?"

" Yes. He got hold of it in the way of business, and Simcox couldn't pay. It was a good bit; a hundred pounds, I think, and the end of it was that Simcox agreed to take the young Armond into his school for two years until the money was worked out."

" What a lark," said Dick. " He don't really pay anything then."

" He does pay, after a fashion, but not as we do."

" Won't I chaff him ?" continued Dick. " Oh! oh! not at all. Cowheels and boiled tripe. Oh! my."

" You promised you wouldn't," said Fowler.

" I couldn't keep my promise, if I tried. The first time he affronts me out it will come. I shall call him the tripe-dressing charity lad."

" I wish I hadn't told you," said Fowler. " But at all events you won't mention my name or say how you found it out."

" Oh, no, I'll take all the responsibility on myself. Are you coming to Mohammed's to-night?"

" The gymnasium?"

" Yes."

" What's on ?" asked Fowler.

" My match on the flying trapeze with Armond."

" Oh, I forgot. Yes, of course I'll be there."

" If you've got any spare bobs and want to bet, back me. I'm sure to lick him, though he is all legs and wings," continued Dick.

The boys separated, as the school bell rang and they went in to lessons.

In the evening those who subscribed to the gymnasium went to Castle Square, and the trapeze was got ready for the opponents.

Armond made himself very busy in arranging the ropes, of which there were three.

The trapeze consists of two ropes hanging from the ceiling; at the end of these is a horizontal bar.

To this the player holds on by his hands, and swings backwards and forwards.

Then he jumps in the air, catches the middle one by the bar, and swings again and darts forward to the third.

The ropes were placed a good distance apart, and it was certainly a feat to go from one to the other.

The distance from the ground was about six feet, so that if the player fell heavily, he might hurt himself considerably.

They were about to toss for the first trial when Armond said—

" Oh! we won't toss, I'll give Lightheart the first chance."

Accordingly Dick seized the bar, swung backwards and forwards, and looked the very picture of an athlete.

Suddenly he launched himself forth and caught the middle bar.

Then he prepared to fly to the third; a burst of applause had greeted his first successful flight.

Once, twice, thrice, he got close to the third trapeze.

But he refused to take the leap.

All at once, and without any warning, he turned round and jumped back to the first bar. A murmur of disappointment arose.

What could be his motive for such extraordinary conduct?

No one could tell.

He had done the first part of the exercise in a manner which had suggested that he would accomplish the other with equal dexterity.

He was very pale when he gained the ground and trembled a little.

Messiter came up to him and said—

" Are you ill, old fellow ?"

Dick made him no answer.

The attendant, who had charge of the room, pushed his way through the crowd and also came up to Dick.

CHAPTER XXXVII.

THE ACCIDENT.

"WHAT'S the matter, sir?" asked the attendant. "Come over dizzy?"

"A little," replied Dick. "But that's not it."

"Anything wrong with the ropes?"

"I don't know; let Armond go first. I shall be all right presently. It's only a passing faintness; let Armond start."

"Certainly," replied the attendant, whose name was Jackson. "That's fair enough; the gentleman won't mind taking your turn and giving you a little time."

Turning to the crowd of boys, Jackson said—"It's nothing unusual to see a gentleman turn a little nervous at times. It soon passes off, and they get right again."

Armond, however, did not attempt to take Dick's place.

"Now, sir," cried Jackson, who was a tall, thin, active-looking fellow of five and thirty, and had been a private soldier in the army.

"I'm not ready," replied Armond.

"You're stripped. You've got your flannels and shoes on. Cut along. Keep the ball rolling."

"No," answered Armond, who went whiter every moment. "I don't see why I should. It was agreed that Lightheart should go first, and why he should want to back out of his agreement, I can't tell."

"You see he's gone a little queer," said Jackson.

"I can't help that."

"What are you afraid of?—look at me," exclaimed the attendant. "I'll show you how to do the flying trapeze."

As he spoke, he sprang up to the perch from which the trapezist started.

This conversation had been carried on at a little distance from Dick, and he did not hear it.

"Shall I get you a glass of water?" asked Messiter.

"I wish you would," replied Dick.

"Stop a moment then. I want to see this cove perform."

"Which? Is Armond going to do it? If so, I must have been mistaken, though I'll swear I saw——"

He stopped abruptly.

Looking up, he saw that Armond was not upon the trapeze, but that Jackson was.

The attendant was in the act of balancing himself for the final spring.

"Hold hard," cried Dick, at the top of his voice. "For God's sake don't jump!"

Jackson paid no attention to him.

"Stop, I say," continued Dick, in a still louder key. "Some villain's *cut the ropes!*"

The warning came too late.

Jackson had taken the leap.

The next moment the bar he had grasped on the third trapeze gave way beneath his pressure, and he fell to the ground with a dull thud.

He had fallen on his back, and lay perfectly still and insensible.

The blood oozed from his mouth, eyes, nose, and ears.

"Is he dead?" asked the boys, in a fearful whisper.

Armond was the first to run to pick him up.

In an excited tone he cried—

"This is infamous! Lightheart must have done this!"

"Don't you say that," cried Messiter, who was by his side.

"Why not?" said Armond. "Didn't he shirk the last bar, and do all he knew to get me to go on ahead of him?"

"Lightheart has not been here all day, and had nothing to do with the arrangement of the ropes; and you were here this morning in the playhour. So shut up about other people."

"I can't talk to you, now, my good man," said Armond. "Run for a doctor, some of you."

"What's he been saying about me?" asked Dick, who had heard his name mentioned.

"He says you cut the ropes," answered Messiter; "but don't take any notice of him now."

"Won't I, by Jove!" said Dick. "Turn round, you cowheel-peeling, tripe-boiling son of a cent. per cent. bill discounter!"

This was addressed to Armond, who

"'I THOUGHT WE SHOULD FIND YOUR MEMORY,' SAID SLOCUM.'"

confronted him savagely, yet in a shame-faced manner.

This torrent of invective had taken Armond by surprise, for he did not think anyone knew who or what his people were.

"What do you mean?" asked Armond, his under lip dropping a little.

"What I say."

"I think you might have more decency than to attack me just now. You see that I am trying to do the best I can, in the absence of a doctor, for the man wounded through your criminal folly."

"My folly!" answered Dick.

"Yes. To cut the ropes of a trapeze is going a little beyond a joke," rejoined Armond.

"Confound your impudence!" exclaimed Dick, beside himself with rage and astonishment. "Why, I never went near the ropes."

"Why did you stop as you did, and want me to go on?"

"I should have stopped you if you had done so, because I should then have known that it wasn't you who did it."

"Nor was it," rejoined Armond.

"Oh, yes, it was," said Dick. "Your refusal to take my turn quite convinced me of that, my boy. But I'll have it out of you. I'll be upsides with you before I'm done."

"Your violence will not do you any good," said Armond; adding, "When will those boys come back with the doctor?"

"You're nothing better than a charity boy," continued Dick.

"That's low, vulgar abuse, and I shall not lower myself by answering you," replied Armond.

"Does your father pay for you?"

"Yes."

"After a fashion," laughed Dick. "He had a bill of the governor's, which was dishonoured, and you are working it out."

Armond glared at him as if he could have sprung at his throat and strangled him. But he did not.

He was holding, or, rather, supporting the head of the unfortunate attendant in the gymnasium, and, looking up in Dick's face with the sort of mildness the wolf assumes when he wants to humbug the lamb, he said—

"Do confine yourself to the point, Lightheart, if you must talk."

"I am sticking to the point, and the point is your villany," replied Dick.

"Or your own. Who shall say which? How did you know the rope was cut, if you didn't do it yourself?"

"Shall I tell you?" replied Dick.

"If you can."

"When I got close to the third trapeze and was about to spring, I saw, or thought I saw that the strands of the rope had been cut low down close to the bar, and it was God's mercy that I drew back in time."

"A very clever get out, but it won't do," said Armond, with a sneer.

"We shall see, Mr. Cocky Armond," answered Dick. "We shall see, Mr. B.B., Mr. Cowheel boiler, tripe dresser, charity boy, rope cutter, etc."

This wordy war, which was not very seemly in the presence of the wounded man, was put a stop to by the entrance of the proprietor of the gymnasium, who had been advised of the accident, and had brought a doctor who lived a few doors off.

An examination of the attendant's injuries showed that his skull was fractured, and that his system had received a severe shock, though it was not thought that his spine was hurt.

"He will be well again in six weeks or a couple of months," said the doctor. "But he has had a narrow escape of his life. How did it happen?"

A dozen boys volunteered an explanation.

Some said Lightheart did it, others declared that Armond was the culprit, while others again said the rope had broken.

The proprietor and the doctor examined the ropes.

They had decidedly been cut with a knife, and left to hang by a mere thread, so that an accident was inevitable.

A cab having been fetched, the attendant was removed to his home, and the doctor accompanied him.

The proprietor of the gymnasium told the boys to wait until the usher came for them, and then to return home.

"Mr. Snarley," he said, "has only gone to smoke a cigar on the beach. He will be back directly. This is a bad business, boys, a bad business, and I did not think it of any of you."

"Please, sir, I hope you don't think that I would be guilty of such a despicable act," exclaimed Armond.

"I say nothing at present, except that it must be investigated. If the trapeze had been missed in the ordinary way, you would have come down on your feet, and have had nothing worse than a slight shake; but to cut the ropes. Ah, it is a bad business, and some one is the villain."

Messiter was by Dick's side, and he said—

"Go up and speak to him."

"I shan't. I'm innocent, and it must come all right by-and-bye," replied Dick.

"Won't it look well to——"

"You're too anxious, Harry. Let the thing alone. It's all right as it stands. I know what I'm about," interrupted Dick.

Mr. Snarley was much shocked when he heard what had happened, and that one of his boys was suspected of having caused the accident.

He would not believe it, and declared that the young gentlemen of Harrow House School were incapable of doing anything of the sort.

The ropes were shown him, and though they looked as if they had been cut, he was inclined to think that old age had caused them to snap.

He walked home with Armond, to whom he said—

"It never does to admit that one is in the wrong, and, for the credit of the school, we must make them prove it."

"I agree with you, sir," rejoined Armond. "There is no doubt that Lightheart cut the rope to be revenged upon me; but, as you say, let them prove it, if he won't confess."

"There must always be a motive for a crime, and, as you say, he hates you."

"Fiercely; and other boys have told me what he has threatened to do to me."

"I am glad the young assistant was not much hurt. It might have been a serious affair. Fancy his breaking his neck. There would have been an in-

quest, which would have resulted in the ruin and break up of the school."

"I forgive Lightheart for what he tried to do to me, sir," exclaimed Armond, "and have no wish to expose him."

"The affair must be hushed up, and I will get up a general subscription among those who attend the gymnasium, for the injured man."

"A good idea, sir; I will give five shillings willingly.

"And I," said Mr. Snarley, "will head the list with half-a-sovereign. This will pay his doctor's bill and put him all right."

"I hope, though," exclaimed Armond, "that the boys will show their detestation of such a dirty trick by cutting Lightheart."

"I should think they would look very coldly upon him. Boys do not like any underhand work," answered Snarley.

It happened, however, that the school was divided in opinion about the outrage.

Some took Armond's side.

Others took Dick's.

In numbers they were pretty nearly equal, and so it came about that there were two parties, the Armondites and the Lightheartites.

These hated one another, and frequent fights took place.

From the height to which public feeling ran, it was not at all unlikely that some day there would be a battle royal between them.

Time passed, and the mystery was unsolved. One half of the school believed that Dick cut the rope to injure Armond.

The other half religiously held the opinion that Armond had tried to kill Dick by making the last trapeze insecure.

The attendant progressed satisfactorily; the amount of the subscription, including five pounds from Messrs. Simcox and Markwell, was sent to him, and out of the school the affair was forgotten.

At Harrow House, however, the hatred between the Lightheartites and the Armondites rather increased than abated.

Civil wars are always the most cruel and ferocious.

School quarrels are equally prolonged and dangerous.

CHAPTER XXXVIII.

MR. SNARLEY PERFORMS IN PUBLIC.

THE boys worked hard and made great progress in their studies, under the new system of tuition.

Messrs. Simcox and Markwell determined to give them a treat.

Circulars and advertisements announced the fact that the Great Bounce was coming to the Pavilion at Brighton, to give a series of concerts for a limited number of nights.

It would be a good opportunity for the boys to acquire a taste for music and have an evening's entertainment.

Morning school had just commenced.

Lightheart and Messiter were in Mr. Slocum's class, which was called the third form.

They were construing and parsing Latin.

Each had a volume of Cæsar before him, and was apparently taking a great interest in the great conqueror's war in Gaul.

Fowler had just sat down after acquitting himself satisfactorily.

Mr. Slocum's eye travelled round the benches until it rested on Dick, who by hanging down his head, hoped he would not be selected.

Alas! it was the device of the ostrich, and equally inefficacious.

"Lightheart!" exclaimed Mr. Slocum.

"Sir," replied Dick, who not having prepared the lesson out of school, as he ought to have done, scarcely knew a word of it.

"You will stand up and construe, but first of all answer me a few questions. We have this morning met with the phrase *Campus Martius*. What does that mean?"

"*Campus* means a field, sir," replied Dick.

"Very well. Go on."

"Then *Campus Martius* must mean the field-marshal, sir."

There was a laugh at this amongst the better informed, but Mr. Slocum instantly suppressed it.

"Silence there, or I will give you fifty lines all round," he said, sternly.

"Understand, Lightheart, that *Campus Martius* does not mean field-marshal or anything like it. I take it to be the name of a place, which you might call the Martial Field, or Field of Mars. Mars' Field—do you see?"

"Why not Pa's Field, sir?" said Dick, with an innocent look.

"Write out and translate the lesson for that," cried Mr. Slocum, savagely.

"Please, sir, you said it was the martial field and I said it was the field-martial. What's the difference? I only put the cart before the horse."

"That is a stupid proceeding of which only a clumsy person would be guilty. Now, attention. We have in the next line the word *amandum*."

"Yes, sir."

"Now, what is *amandum* ?"

"A man dumb, sir? Why, a chap that hasn't got the use of his tongue—a dumb chap, in fact. You put the cart before the horse this time, sir. I should have thought that any child would have known a dumb man was a cove—I mean a——"

"Si-lence!" said Mr. Slocum, in his most awful tone.

The boys stopped their tittering with difficulty.

It is difficult to prevent boys from laughing when their fancies are once tickled.

They saw that Dick had gone in for chaffing Slocum, and they meant to enjoy the treat accordingly.

"You, Lightheart, will write out and translate the lesson twice. If boys will be funny, they must pay for the privilege."

"Please, sir——" began Dick.

"Si-lence ! Now what is *amandum* ?"

"I don't know, sir."

"Yes, you do. Tell me instantly, or I will have you flogged," cried Mr. Slocum.

His blood was up now, and he did not intend to be beaten by Dick.

"Part of the verb *amo*, sir," said Dick.

"Very good. I thought we should find your memory presently," said Mr. Slocum, with a pleasant smile. "Now go on. What part is it ?"

"What part, sir?"

"Yes. Gerund or supine?"

"Supine, sir," replied Dick, whose ideas about verbs, when he got out of the indicative mood, were rather vague.

"No," thundered Mr. Slocum.

"Then it must be a gerund," said Dick.

"Right. It is a gerund. Now, attention. There are gerunds in di, do, dum. What is this a gerund in?"

"Di," replied Dick; adding quickly, "No, never say die, sir."

"Oh! at it again, are you?" cried Mr. Slocum, getting purple with rage.

"You will oblige me by writing out and translating this lesson three times, in addition to which you will write one hundred times—'I will make no more bad puns.'"

"I call them very good ones," said Dick, ruefully.

"Si-lence! Now, attention! It is *not* a gerund in di."

"Do, sir," said Dick.

"No, sir. How can *amandum* be a gerund in do?" exclaimed Mr. Slocum, with subdued fury.

"Dum, then, sir," replied Dick, getting it right at last.

"The conclusion is inevitable. Now, in order to impress the fact upon your unretentive mind," exclaimed Mr. Slocum, "you will write out——"

Fortunately for Dick, Mr. Simcox's voice was heard at the end of the room, as he stood by Mr. Markwell's desk.

"Boys, I have a word to say to you!"

Mr. Slocum broke off, and forgot to say what further punishment he should inflict upon Dick.

"Bother gerunds!" muttered Dick; "I hate 'em."

"Boys," continued Mr. Simcox, "it is proposed by Mr. Markwell and myself to give you all a treat.

"This resolution has been come to owing to your good conduct during the term which is now approaching its completion.

"The Great Bounce, an artist of celebrity, is about to give a concert at the Pavilion.

"It is proposed that you should attend it in a body."

Loud cheers followed this announcement, and Dick screamed himself black in the face.

Mr. Simcox held up his hand again.

"But," he said, "as we never like to do anything without the permission of parents, as some object to stage plays, concerts, etc., as vanities, you will please write home, ask your parents' and guardians' consent, informing them at the same time that the charge will be a uniform one of half-a-crown, which will be put down in the bill."

Dick bent down and whispered to Messiter:—"I thought he wouldn't stand the treat himself."

"He's too stingy," said Messiter.

"Writing paper and envelopes will be supplied you by Mr. Snarley," Mr. Simcox went on, "and I will sketch a letter on the large slate, which you will please copy."

"Hurrah! Hoo-rah!" cried Dick. "Now boys! Hoorah-ah-ah!"

Unfortunately nobody followed his lead, and he was frightened at his own voice.

"Lightheart," said Mr. Simcox, "be good enough to restrain your impetuosity. Probably the sound of your own voice is more pleasing to yourself than it is to others."

Dick collapsed.

Mr. Simcox took up a piece of chalk and wrote on the big slate—

"My dear father, mother, guardian (as the case may be)—I have sincere pleasure in informing you that our general good conduct and admirable and steady progress in our studies——"

"Especially in gerunds," whispered Dick to Messiter.

"During that part of the half which has already elapsed, has induced our kind and respected headmasters, Mr. Simcox and Mr. Markwell, to propose giving us a great treat.

"The celebrated Bounce has arranged a series of concerts in the great hall of the Pavilion, and we are to attend in a body, if the proposal meets with your approval.

"The small charge of half-a-crown will be made for each of us, which it is presumed you will not object to pay, for this superlative gratification to us. The soothing and elevating art of music is highly calculated to refresh our minds, and I trust, my dear father, mother, guardian (as the case may be), that I shall receive an early reply from you, granting the request which I make to you in this letter.

"I am glad to add that my health is excellent. I am very happy, and feel that I would not exchange the enlightened management, the home treatment, including a liberal diet, and the splendid education I am receiving at the hands of Messrs. Simcox and Markwell for that of any other school in the world.

"I am,

"My dear father, mother, guardian (as the case may be),

"Your ever affectionate

and dutiful son,

"——."

"Isn't the governor laying it on thick?" remarked Messiter.

"Rather," replied Dick. "It's awful rot, though. What's the good of making us tell such a heap of lies?"

"You mean about being happy, and the liberal diet," answered Messiter.

"Yes. If I send for a second cut of mutton, I only get a mangy little slice that wouldn't nourish a two-year-old."

"No talking!" exclaimed Mr. Slocum, as Snarley came round with the paper.

For the next half hour the boys were engaged in the pleasant pastime of writing their letters.

Dick, out of pure mischief, copied the words on the slate verbatim, putting in "my dear father, mother, or guardian (as the case may be")," each time they occurred.

"Have you finished, Lightheart?" asked Mr. Slocum, seeing him sucking the end of his pen.

"Yes, sir."

"Hand me your letter."

Dick did so, and stood by his side while he looked it over.

"You stupid boy!" said Mr. Slocum.

"You should not put in 'father, mother, or guardian.' You have a father, I suppose?"

"Yes, sir."

"Very well, then. Write this over again, and put simply 'my dear father.'"

Dick took it back, and did as he was told, but he kept the first letter, and made the boys laugh by showing it them out of school.

Of course the required permission came from the fathers, mothers, guardians (as

the case was), and the concert was looked forward to with great interest.

"Can Snarley sing?" Dick asked Fowler.

"Not a note. A raven might, and a screech owl might, but Snarley never got beyond the Old Hundredth psalm or a hymn in his life," replied Fowler.

Everybody asked Fowler questions about everything, because he had been longer in the school than anyone else.

"Snarley shall sing," replied Dick.

"Shall! What do you mean?" said Fowler.

"You'll see," answered Dick, with a smile.

When the evening came, the evening on which the concert was to be given, the boys dressed themselves in their "Sunday best," as Dick remarked, and were marched two and two to the Pavilion.

They filed into the seats appointed for them, Dick taking care to obtain a corner near the stage. The Great Bounce divided his concert into two parts—the first was serious and sentimental and made one weep; the second was comic and noisy, and caused one to laugh.

Great was the applause when the curtain fell on the first part.

The boys were delighted, and the Great Bounce received an ovation.

Seeing an attendant come by, Dick put a note in his hand.

"Who is this for?" asked the attendant.

"Our usher, Mr. Snarley, wants it to be given to the Great Bounce himself," replied Dick.

"Mr. Bounce is having a glass of sherry wine in a private room, back of the stage," replied the attendant.

"All the better. Give him the note and say it came from one of our ushers," replied Dick.

The man went away, and knocking at the door of the private room, found Mr. Bounce regaling himself as he had said.

"What's this," asked the great man, who was a stout, good-natured, jolly-looking fellow.

"Note for you, sir."

"Who from?"

"Gentleman name of Snarley; one of the ushers in this 'ere school, sir."

"Wait," exclaimed Mr. Bounce, taking

the note and reading its contents, which were as follows—

"RESPECTED AND ACCOMPLISHED SIR,—I am a humble follower of your art, and my favourite song is ' By the Sad Sea Waves I Left My Loved One Weeping.' You may not be acquainted with it, as it is my own composition; it is, however, my ambition to sing it, during the interval that has to elapse between the serious and the comic parts of your unparalleled entertainment. May I make so bold as to ask you to introduce me to the audience as *formerly a pupil of your own?* I can assure you I shall not disgrace you, as my reputation as a sentimental singer is very high. I shall ever be your deeply grateful and obliged servant,

"SAMUEL SNARLEY."
"Fourth form master at Harrow House School, Kemp Town, Brighton."

When the great Bounce had finished reading the letter, he said—

"Go and ask Mr. Snarley to come to me at once."

"Yes, sir," replied the messenger.

He went back to Dick, who was anxiously awaiting his appearance.

"Where's the gentleman who wrote the note?" asked the man.

"Mr. Snarley, do you mean?"

"Yes."

"He's there. That tall, thin man in a white choker."

"White what, sir? Beg pardon, but——"

"White tie, you fool!" replied Dick. "Cut along—make haste."

The man pushed his way to Mr. Snarley, and touched him on the shoulder.

"It's all right, sir. I'm the attendant."

"All right! What's all right? I was not aware anything was wrong," replied Snarley.

"Governor wants you! Quick, sir."

"Who?"

"Mr. Bounce, sir. He as is performing."

"Oh! he wants to see me, does he?"

"Yes, sir," replied the attendant.

"Where is he? In the private room, I suppose?"

"That's just where you'll find him, sir. Follow me."

"Did he say Snarley? Are you sure that he said 'I want to see Mr. Snarley?'"

"Them was his very words, sir," answered the messenger.

"Lead on, I will follow," exclaimed Snarley. He left his seat and went after the attendant to the private room, which communicated with the stage by a door in the scenery.

Mr. Bounce was standing on the threshold of this door.

He only had to push the curtains a little on one side to be in front of the audience.

"Ahem!" began Mr. Snarley, " a— Mr. Bounce, I believe?"

"That's me," said the great singer, rather ungrammatically.

"I am proud, more than proud, to make the acquaintance of so distinguished a gentleman, whose celebrity has——"

"Cut it short, please; time for the second part will be up directly, and boy audiences are apt to kick up a shindy if you keep them waiting," said Mr. Bounce.

"But, my dear sir, I——"

"Come along this way. Make haste; and, I say——"

Bounce bent down as Mr. Snarley approached him, and added " Don't listen to an encore—that's do it over again, you know."

"Certainly not. I don't quite understand," stammered Mr. Snarley. " But if it is your wish——"

"It is, Mr. Snarley, and now come on, sir; they are beginning to stamp their feet. Come on."

"Come on—as Shakespeare says—come on, Macduffer. No, I don't mean that, it's Macduff. Come on, Macduff!" exclaimed Mr. Snarley, attempting to be jocose, and breaking down lamentably.

"Mind you don't turn out a duffer," said the Great Bounce, adding; " give me your hand. I'll lead you on and give 'em a word."

"Give them what?"

"A little patter; that's what you want, isn't it? Come along."

The next moment, he had pushed aside the curtain and appeared upon the stage, leading Mr. Snarley by the hand.

CHAPTER XXXIX.

AN AWKWARD FIX.

IT was Mr. Snarley's first appearance in public, and he took very good care it should be the last one.

He could not understand why or wherefore he had been led on to the platform.

But as the great singer was with him, he thought it must be all right.

The flood of light which came from the gas lamps nearly blinded him.

For a short time the audience floated before him indistinctly; but after a while he made out familiar faces clearly, especially those of Mr. Markwell and Mr. Simcox, whereon rested a cloud of wonder, not unmixed with indignation.

First of all came the rows of benches, filled with boys who occupied the arena.

Then came the outside public, in the more expensive seats.

All had their gaze bent upon him.

"I wonder what it all means?" said Mr. Snarley to himself.

Leading him to the edge of the footlights, the Great Bounce said—

"Ladies and gentlemen, it is with pride and pleasure that I present to your favourable notice Mr. Samuel Snarley, the respected assistant in Harrow House School, that famous seminary for young gentlemen."

At this there was great cheering among the boys, in which the public joined.

"Go it, Snarley; never say die."

This was from Dick, who was thinking of gerunds.

"Mr. Snarley," resumed the Great Bounce, "is desirous of occupying your time for a few minutes. He is not going to trespass on your good-nature long, but when I inform you that years ago he was a most promising pupil of my own, and that his ability is second to none, you will, no doubt, wish he were here to entertain you in my place."

Pulling the great singer by the sleeve, Snarley in vain endeavoured to arrest his attention.

"He will sing you," continued Bounce, "'By the Mad Sea Waves I Left My Loved One Drinking'—no, that's not it;

it's a fragment of his own composition, and I'm not quite sure of the title."

Here he glanced at the note he held in his hand.

"Oh! I remember now," he added; "it's by the sad sea waves. Yes, 'By the Sad Sea Waves I Left My Loved One Weeping.' Beautiful thing, ladies and gentlemen."

Bending to the orchestra, he said—

"Strike up, music. Anything in two sharps, and not too loud, will do."

A tremendous shout of applause at this announcement rent the air.

The Great Bounce rushed hastily back behind the curtain.

Mr. Snarley stood like one rooted to the spot. He was deadly pale.

He would have run away too, but it was necessary to say something, as he began to see that he was the victim of a shameful hoax.

Though why the Great Bounce should play off his pleasantry upon him he was at a loss to imagine.

"Hurrah for Snarley," cried the boys. "Order, or-der for Snarley's song."

The orchestra began to play a plaintive air.

"My dear boys," said Mr. Snarley, in a dreadfully weak voice.

"Sing, sing!" roared the boys.

Mr Simcox looked at Mr. Markwell, and the latter regarded Mr. Simcox.

"Dear me," said Mr. Simcox, "this is very strange. I did not know that our friend Snarley was a man of musical attainments."

"Nor I," returned Mr. Markwell, "it is singular that he should not have said anything to us about it."

"Or asked our permission," observed Professor Simcox.

"Quite so. It is bold on his part, and I do not think he will increase his authority among the boys by thrusting himself forward in this way."

"I have heard Snarley play the fiddle to a slight extent, and he has followed my lead in the Old Hundredth on a Sunday evening," said Mr. Simcox.

"That's a different thing. His putting himself on a level, as it were, with professionals is intolerable presumption," replied Mr Markwell.

During this conversation the shouts, screams, cat-calls, and cries of the boys, increased alarmingly.

Snarley bowed and put his hand on his heart. The orchestra having played the first bar of the music they had selected as suitable for his song, stopped.

"Order!" cried Dick, "he's going to begin"

Instantly there was a dead silence.

"Gentlemen," said Mr. Snarley, "there is some mistake here.

"I thought so," observed Mr. Markwell.

"I am the victim of a cruel joke," continued Snarley.

"Didn't I say so?" remarked Mr. Simcox.

"Sing! sing!" cried the boys.

"I cannot sing," exclaimed Mr. Snarley, getting in a passion. "I never sang a song in my life. I tell you it's a joke."

"What did you get on the platform for?" cried Dick. "It's all nonsense. No more rot, no more humbug. Give us a hymn if you can't do anything else."

Driven to desperation, Mr. Snarley replied, "I could do a hymn, a trifle of Dr. Watts's, if that would please you, and calm this excitement. Let us say, 'Dogs delight,' or ''Twas the voice of the sluggard,' or 'I have been there and still would go.'"

"Go home and put your head in a bag," said a wag in the shilling seats.

Mr. Snarley attempted to speak again, but his voice was drowned in shouts of laughter.

The absurdity of his proposal was so transparent and mirth-provoking, that the audience found it irresistible.

The confusion now reached its height.

Mr. Simcox, greatly scandalised, said, "Is he drunk?"

"I should remonstrate with him," said Mr. Markwell.

"I will."

Getting upon a chair, the professor said—

"Mr. Snarley, retire. I order you sir, to re-tire."

Amidst renewed howling and cheering, the unfortunate usher made a rush for the curtain.

"Bolted," said Messiter.

"Stole away," cried Dick. "After him, fetch him back. Snarley, sing, sing, sing."

But Mr. Snarley, boiling over with rage, dashed through the door into the private room. The great singer regarded him complacently.

"Well?" he said, "how did you get on? You seem to be a favourite. The boys are making noise enough."

"What is the meaning of this outrage, sir?" demanded Snarley. "Why did you lead me on to that platform, to make me look ridiculous? I am the laughing stock of everybody!"

"Can't you sing?"

"No. I never could in my life."

"Why did you send me this letter?" asked the Great Bounce.

"What letter? Show it me."

Mr. Snarley took the letter which Dick had written and concocted.

The truth dawned upon him.

It was a hoax.

"I did not write this," he said. "It is a device of the enemy. I see it all now."

"Eh?" cried the Great Bounce. "Not write it! Then we have, in the language of the poets, been sold. Awkward rather, very, as it makes me look foolish as well as you"

"I acquit you of blame, sir," replied Mr. Snarley. "But when I discover the delinquent, I will have it out of him."

"Can't talk any more now. Got no time," said Mr. Bounce. "Must go on again at once. Very sorry, but can't be helped."

Showing Mr. Snarley the way out of the room into the hall, he went on the stage, and soon put his audience in a good temper by his comicalities and excellent singing.

Mr. Snarley at once sought the head masters, showed them the letter, and explained how he came to make an exhibition of himself.

"Whose writing is this?" asked Mr. Simcox.

"I know not; the hand is disguised," replied Mr. Snarley. "I wish I did know—that's all."

It was fortunate for Dick that his handwriting was disguised, or he would have been found out.

So perturbed was Mr. Snarley's mind, that he did not think of asking the attendant who had given him the note, and Dick was not discovered.

Dick and Messiter had many a laugh in private over this joke, but they did not take anyone into their confidence.

The incident was soon forgotten by the masters, though Mr. Snarley was often greeted with cries of "Sing, sing."

One day the boys were out walking, and they saw a placard on a wall announcing the last grand *fête* at the Swiss Gardens at Shoreham.

"Look at that," exclaimed Dick.

"ROYAL SWISS GARDENS.

"Positively the last Monster *Fête* of the present season.

"Great combination of attractions, including performances in the theatre, boating on the lakes, swings, bowls, and other amusements.

"Refreshments of the first quality.

"The proprietor has great pleasure in announcing that he has, at a large cost, secured the services of the accomplished and renowned Miss Agatha Mountserrat, who has appeared before all the crowned heads in Europe."

"Why, that's my pretty Polly," exclaimed Dick.

"Your Polly," said Messiter.

"Yes. I saved her from falling down the trap the night I went to the circus with Lieutenant Smart."

"Shouldn't I like to go!"

"Would you?"

"Yes," replied Messiter. "It would be a spree."

"We'll go together," said Dick.

"How? We can't get out, and if we could, we should be missed and flogged when we came back."

"No, we shan't. I've got a dodge," said Dick.

"What is it?"

"I'll write a letter in my father's hand, which I can imitate to a T. It shall be directed to Professor Simcox, and in it he shall ask his permission for me and my young friend Messiter to come and spend the day with him, as he is in Brighton on business, and we are to come to him at the Bedford Hotel."

"Stunning," said Messiter. "But ——"

"There is always a 'but' with you, Harry," exclaimed Dick; "what new croak have you got on now?"

"We've no money. You told me you hadn't yesterday, and you know I lent you my last sixpence to buy tarts."

"So you did; I forgot that. By Jove! that is a lick; we can't go without tin," replied Dick, thoughtfully.

For once in his life he did not see the way out of the difficulty.

CHAPTER XL.

RAISING THE WIND.

ALL the time they were out walking, Dick turned the matter over in his mind.

In the evening he and Messiter were together preparing their lessons.

The hum and buzz of the boy's voices enabled them to talk to one another without being overheard.

Suddenly Dick grasped Messiter's arm and said, "I've got it, Harry!"

"Have you? Mind you keep it then," replied Messiter.

He patted him on the back approvingly.

"Leave off. Don't mess me about," cried Dick. "I'm thinking, and that is—— "

"Such an unwonted exertion that it makes you irritable."

"You shut up. We must raise the wind. To-day is Monday. The *fête* takes place next Monday. So we have got a week to work in."

"Let's write home," said Messiter.

"No good. My dad wouldn't part. He's going on the principle of keeping me short. It's bad for boys to have too much money, he says."

"That's just what mine says, though we are poor at home, and the old boy can't afford it. Still I could get five shillings' worth of stamps out of the mum."

"Try it on then. Every little will help," said Dick. "We ought to have about a sovereign apiece."

"Oh! but wouldn't a sovereign each be a great deal more than we shall want?" Messiter said.

"Not at all. I mean to do the thing like a swell," answered Dick.

"The admission is only a shilling."

"I know that, but we must have reserved seats at the theatre. I will have a boat on the lake, and go to the shooting gallery, and try our strength, and be weighed, and have ices and ginger beer, and a cold collation, as they call lamb and salad, or chicken and ham. I mean to go the entire animal, I can tell you."

"You generally do," said Messiter. "I will leave everything to you."

"Then you'll be right. Don't fluster yourself. I'll pull you through to the other side of Jordan, as the Great Bounce said in one of his songs, and give you such a day's sport as you never had in your life," replied Dick.

"Very well. Go on with your financial statement."

"I shall get over the wall to-morrow, and see if I can catch Emily and Henrietta in the playground at Miss Bodmin's. Girls have generally got money. They save up, and haven't so much opportunity of spending it as we have."

"That's good. You may borrow half a sovereign from each. What else?"

"See this box?" asked Dick, taking a good-sized money-box out of his locker.

"Yes; it's your old money-box. But you've pasted a paper over it; and what is that written on it?"

"Read for yourself."

Messiter did so, and read, "Charitable contributions for the purpose of sending out clothing to the savage tribes who now practice cannibalism and head-hunting, on the coast of Africa, under Oko Jumbo. Collector, Richard Lightheart."

"Oh, Dick!" said Messiter, lost in admiration of the brilliant device. "You are a fellow."

Dick smiled proudly.

"Of course," he said, "I only mean to borrow the money till I get a supply from home, when I will return every farthing placed in the box."

"But who's this Oko Jumbo?" continued Messiter.

"Blest if I know," said Dick. "He's as good a peg to hang the affair on as anyone else."

"Do you think the fellows will subscribe?"

"Yes; I'll make them. Simcox Markwell, Snarley, all of them shall. I'll tell them such moving tales that I'll make them weep, and it will be a case of some coppers in no time," said Dick.

"Why not ask them to lend the money?" said Messiter.

"That won't do," replied Dick. "They would want to know what it was for, and spoil our treat. No, I'll get the coin out of them by the box, and refund when father shells out."

Dick did not exaggerate his powers of persuasion, which he soon had an opportunity of trying upon Mr. Simcox.

When the boys had prepared their lessons, they were allowed to play at dominoes, draughts, chess, or any game they liked, and in which they were proficient.

Putting away their books, Lightheart and Messiter began to play at dominoes.

The game went on with varying success, till Messiter could not play.

"Can't," said he, looking gloomily at sixes at each end.

"Can," exclaimed Dick, playing. "Good, old can-can. Six, two. Go on, Harry. You've got a two. Come in, old man, out of the wet."

Messiter played a two, and Dick played out, crying—

"Domino; you're beaten."

Mr. Simcox came up just as they had finished, and saw the subscription box.

"What have we here?" he asked, taking it up.

"Subscriptions wanted, sir, for the poor benighted savages, deprived of the blessings of respectable raiment," replied Dick.

"Ah! I perceive. South Africans. Very good. Oko Jumbo. Very good. Send out clothing—excellent," said Mr. Simcox, reading the appeal.

"Will you head the list with a trifle, sir?—say half a guinea. It will look well, and the boys will follow your lead."

"Hem! half a sovereign is a large

sum," replied the professor, putting his finger in his waistcoat pocket.

He had a peculiar way of saying "half," and called it "haaf."

"It will be money well laid out. Shall I write your name down, sir?" said Dick, taking up a sheet of foolscap.

Mr. Simcox hesitated, and the man who hesitates is lost.

Dick hastily wrote—"Professor Simcox, 10s.—paid."

The professor dropped the little gold coin into the box with a sigh.

"I am glad to see you engaged in so meritorious an enterprise, Lightheart," he said. "Indeed, your behaviour is much better than it used to be, and I am pleased to behold the amendment."

"Thank you, sir. I'm only a little wild at times, and if there is any alteration in me, it is due to your excellent method of managing the boys under your care," replied Dick.

"I hope I am successful. I try to be, and pray that I may succeed," replied the professor, with a nasal noise something between a whine and a snort.

He passed on, and Messiter remarked—"Can't you talk to them?"

"Like a Dutch uncle. We shall get our expenses out of this box," said Dick.

"And have something to spare for Oko Jumbo."

"I shan't part a rap for Oko. Not if I know it," answered Dick, with a smile.

After this the subscription list filled up gaily; the boys gave their sixpences and shillings, and the masters also contributed.

And Dick said, "It began to look very much like going to Shoreham!"

The next day in the playhour, Dick got hold of the servant, Sam Fuggles, who cleaned the boots, knives, etc., and waited at table.

"Sam," he said, "look over the wall for me and tell me if the old dragon's about."

Sam did so, and coming down, reported the coast clear.

"There ain't no Miss Bodmin about, sir," he said. "But the young ladies is a-skipping and a-playing like so many lambs."

"All right," replied Dick. "Give us a leg up. I'm going over."

"Won't there be a pretty shine if you're cotched, sir?"

"But I don't mean to be. Shove up," replied Dick.

The next moment he vaulted gracefully over the wall and descended at the feet of Henrietta and his sister Emily.

"Oh, Dick!" they cried in a breath. "How could you. If we're seen, we shall be sent to bed without any dinner."

"All the better for your health, my little dears," answered Dick, adding, "Give me a kiss, Emmy."

"I shall not do anything of the sort," replied Emily.

"Harry will, then."

"No, I shall not, either," answered Henrietta.

"You know we're engaged, Harry dear. So you might as well."

"It would look so; all the other girls will see," replied Henrietta.

"Let them; they'll only be envious and wish they had the same chance. Never mind, if you won't, I can't help it. I'll fancy it done, and that's the next best thing. But I say, I want something."

"What?" asked Emily.

"Have you girls got any money?"

"I haven't; Henrietta's got a sovereign, though, she was going to buy something with."

"That's your sort. Lend it me, Harry dear, and look sharp, or we shall have old Mother Frump after us."

"Don't you lend it him. He never pays back again," exclaimed Emily.

"Oh, you base girl," replied Dick, with affected indignation. "What do you deserve? Go, degenerate child, and—and say your prayers."

The girls laughed.

"I haven't got it here," said Henrietta; "it's upstairs in my work-box."

"Get it. Wrap it up in paper, and throw it over the wall."

"How shall I know you've got it?"

"I'll sing 'Bonnie Dundee' when I have it, and you'll know it has been safely landed," replied Dick.

"Run, Dick, the door is opening. It's Miss Bodmin," cried Emily.

"I'm off. Bless you, my children," answered Dick, climbing up a fruit tree, and regaining his own playground before he was observed.

In ten minutes a piece of paper came over the wall, Dick saying, " Dundee, he is mounted, he rides up the street."

He was happy, for the money was coming in, and he was sure of his expenses on the ensuing Monday.

Starting off to look for Messiter, he did not see Cocky Armond who was playing at marbles, and the consequence was he tumbled over him.

" This won't do, Cocky," he exclaimed.

" Why don't you look where you are coming to?" responded Armond.

Dick kicked the marbles out of the ring.

" Can you oblige me with some tripe," he said, " or a cow heel?"

" I daresay you think it very funny to chaff me about what some one told you my father is, but it's not true. He isn't a tripe-dresser," said Armond, flushing angrily.

" Perhaps he can cut a rope."

" I'll tell you what I can do. I can hit you in the eye."

As he spoke, he struck out at Dick, who stepped back.

" You didn't do it, my boy," he said, with a provoking sneer. " Try again."

" What's the row?" asked Messiter and Fowler, coming up.

" Why, Armond's going to give Lightheart a thrashing for cheeking him," exclaimed Conolly, who was an Armond-ite.

" Perhaps you'd like one yourself," said Fowler.

" You can't give it me."

" Can't I? We'll see about that."

In an instant, Conolly and Fowler were fighting, and Dick and Armond also came to close quarters.

" Row, row!" cried Fowler. " Light-hearts to the rescue!"

" A mill! a mill!" exclaimed Gordon, a boy about Fowler's age; " Armondites! Armondites! Mill! mill!"

" Mind your eye," said Fowler, as he rolled his antagonist over.

In a moment, boys came up from all parts of the playground.

The long pending battle royal between the two factions had broken out at last, and through an accident, as is the nature of such things.

CHAPTER XLI.

ARMONDITES AND LIGHTHEARTS.

" COME on, my boys. Who cut the rope? Pitch into the tripe and cow heel," shouted Dick.

The rival parties both took up the cry of " Who cut the rope?" and the battle became general.

Brabazon and Chapman ranged themselves on Dick's side, as they were devoted Lighthearts.

In five minutes the Armondites were getting the worst of it.

They retreated to the schoolroom door, and there made a stand.

Dick rushed in at Armond, who was fighting well. He succeeded in catching him round the neck.

" Now, Cocky," he said, " how do you find yourself? I've put the hug on."

Armond was in chancery, and a shower of blows coming down upon his face like rain gave him a confused idea of things in general.

Armond contrived to wriggle himself out of Dick's grasp and fell to the ground, where he lay still, not attempting to renew the combat.

His followers rallied round his body, and made a desperate struggle to drive back their assailants.

At this moment Mr. Simcox, who had been alarmed by the noise, rushed into the playground.

A melancholy spectacle of black eyes, cut lips, and bleeding noses met his astonished gaze.

" Boys, boys," he exclaimed, in his most awful voice, " what is this?"

Dick was in the act of pitching into a big boy when the sound reached him.

Everyone desisted, as if by magic.

" Please,.sir," said Dick, coming forward with an eye that was beginning to close and a mouth that had already swollen, " it's a new game."

"A *what?*" demanded the head master.

"A new game, sir. We call it Armondites and Lighthearts, but we lost our tempers, sir, and hit too hard."

"How do you play it?"

"Armond and I toss up to choose sides, sir, and then his men and my men try to catch each other. Just like prisoner's base, but we lost our tempers, as I said, and some of of us got into real instead of sham fighting."

Mr. Simcox was only half convinced.

"It is a bad sort of game," he said, "and I forbid you to play at it again. Do you hear?"

"Yes, sir," replied Dick.

"And to show my sense of displeasure, I shall not allow you to go on the beach or out of the house—none of you, mind, until next week. Half of you are not fit to be seen—go and wash your faces; it is nearly dinner time. Get out of my sight, do. I'm ashamed of you, and let me hear no more of Armondites and Lighthearts," said Mr. Simcox.

Armond had risen to his feet, and looked a deplorable spectacle.

Dick had punished him severely.

"Armond," exclaimed the professor, "you should have known better than to engage in sport of this kind. Bless me, what a sight you are."

"He provoked me to fight him, sir," replied Armond.

"Who did?"

"Lightheart."

"Well, well! Shake hands, and be friends! There! Make it up," said Mr. Simcox, "and let me hear no more of it."

"I don't mind, sir. Here is my hand, Lightheart, if you like to take it," exclaimed Armond.

"Thank you, no. I don't mind shaking hands with a sweep or a crossing-sweeper, if he's honest, but I must decline the honour on the present occasion," replied Dick, stiffly.

"What's the cause of this feud between Armond and yourself?" inquired Mr. Simcox.

"He tried to kill me at the gymnasium, sir. You know the story."

"Ah, ah!" exclaimed Mr. Simcox. "That is a disputed point. He accuses you, you accuse him, when, after all, it may have been the fault of an old rope."

"It is too bad of Lightheart to try and injure me again by speaking ill of me!" exclaimed Armond. "He knows very well he cut the rope; but I forgive him, and I should only feel annoyed if he misled you, sir."

"A truly Christian spirit. Very good. I commend you, Armond. Now run and wash your face. This must not occur again. You know the high opinion I have of you, Armond."

"Thank you, sir."

"If you are set upon again, call me."

"I will, sir."

"Do not lower yourself by fighting like a blackguard. Call me. I am headmaster in this school, and you shall see that I will maintain my authority."

Bending a fierce look upon Dick, the professor strode away, leaving Armond the master of the situation.

"You're a nice, whining, hypocritical sort of cur," said Dick; "and, if I had not given you such a hiding, I should feel tempted to soil my hands once more with your ugly mug."

"It will be best for you, Lightheart, to keep quiet. You heard what Mr. Simcox said," answered Armond.

"Get out," continued Dick; "get out of my sight, or, upon my soul, I shall kick you."

Armond thought it advisable to go away, which he did, with a pious snuffle.

But in his heart, the vengeance and hatred that had been for a long time gathering against Dick, increased tremendously.

"He's my enemy," thought Dick; "and anything I can say or do, won't make him hate me less."

The Lighthearts had given the Armondites a thorough thrashing, as the bruised faces at the dinner-table sufficiently testified.

The masters were greatly shocked and scandalized, but, as the whole school was to blame, they couldn't punish so many.

Owing to Dick's clever excuse, not even the ringleaders were singled out.

But pains and penalties were threatened if it happened again.

Even the Honourable Brabazon put his gentility on one side, and received a black eye.

Dick and Messiter were both knocked about, and they tried everything they could think of to get their faces well by Monday.

It was the day of the *fête*, when their great scheme was to be put into execution.

As the time drew near, their hearts beat high.

Dick prepared the letter in imitation of his father's handwriting, and kept it in his desk.

It was his intention to slip it into the letter-box on Monday morning early.

This would make it appear that a servant had brought it from the Bedford Hotel, and had left it, not thinking an answer was necessary.

CHAPTER XLII.

THE "GYM" AT WORK.

ON Saturday Mr. Snarley was in a very good temper.

He went out with the boys to the cricket field and condescended to take an innings, making the wonderful score of 0.

He was loudly cheered when he took his bat back to the tent, where Messiter was scoring.

"Got a duck, sir?" said Messiter, grinning.

"As you say, Messiter," he replied. "Put me down a duck's-egg. I have obtained a cypher. It is the fortune of war. Make a little room on that bench, please. I am inclined to sit down, and have no wish to exert myself much, as on Monday I go out."

"Go out, sir?"

"Yes. It is what I call my holiday. I have asked for a day, and Mr. Simcox has kindly given me one."

"What shall you do, sir?" asked Messiter.

He thought of his intended outing with Dick, and hoped sincerely that Mr. Snarley would not go in any direction where he might meet with him.

"Unfortunately," replied Mr. Snarley, "my friends live in Gloucestershire, so that I shall not be able to see them. I see a *fête* advertised at the Swiss Gardens, Shoreham. Probably I may take a trip down there."

"Oh! I wouldn't go there, sir," said Messiter, quickly.

"And why not?"

"Awfully slow; wouldn't interest you, sir. It's a pleasure garden. I went there once, and didn't care for it at all."

"Well, do we not want pleasure and relaxation when we take a holiday?" said Mr. Snarley. "If the bow is always bent, what happens?"

"It breaks."

"Of course it does. Therefore we must occasionally unstring it. I am decidedly in favour of going to the Swiss Gardens. There will be singing in the theatre. I saw the name of Miss Mountserrat in the bills, and Mr. Slocum, who has seen her, thinks her very nice."

"Dick's Polly," thought Messiter.

"And now let us improve the occasion," continued Mr. Snarley. "In the intervals of scoring you can answer me questions in Scripture history, in which you are very backward, and if you do not improve, you will never pass your examination."

Messiter groaned inwardly.

"Tell me now," said Mr. Snarley, "who was the most merciful man in the Bible."

"Merciful man, sir?—Og."

"Og! Why Og?"

"Og, the King of Bashan, sir, for his mercy endureth for ever," said Messiter.

"Absurd. You have made a mistake; that phrase, which continually occurs in one of the Psalms, has no connection with Og."

Fortunately for Messiter, it was his turn to go in, and, being called by the captain of his eleven, he made his escape from Mr. Snarley, much to his delight.

When the stumps were drawn and the boys were going home, Messiter communicated his news to Dick.

"Snarley's got a day out," he said.

"Well, what of it?" replied Dick.

"He's going to moon about in Brighton."

"All the better."

"He's seen the advertisements of the *fête* at the Swiss Gardens, and thinks of going there to see Miss Agatha Mount-

"'ALLOW ME TO WALK BY YOUR SIDE WHILE YOU PROMENADE THE GARDENS,' SAID SNARLEY."

serrat, about whom old Slocum raves and says he's awfully spooney."

"What! my Polly! Slocum spoons on my Polly!" exclaimed Dick, indignantly.

"You've got Henrietta. You don't want two."

"I don't know. Variety is always charming," said Dick, carelessly. "Suppose Henrietta lets me down, I can fall back on Polly, and *vice versa*."

He did not like the idea, however, of Snarley going to Shoreham.

"Didn't you try to choke him off when he told you?" he asked.

"Yes, rather," replied Messiter. "I said I had heard it was not the sort of place to suit him."

"It's too good for him," replied Dick. "But I'll tell you what we'll do, if he does go."

"What?"

"We'll get old Hopkins, that's Polly's father, you know, to help us, and we'll capture Snarley and put him in a caravan, and make him the wild man of the woods, and show him at a penny a head."

"Oh, Dick;" said Messiter.

"Do you think I wouldn't do it?" Dick asked.

"No, not for a moment. You always do a thing if you say you will."

"He shall be the natural phenomenon, or wild man of the woods, I tell you, caught in his native forests, somewhere up South America way. He has eaten more men than he can digest, and his temper has become worse in consequence!"

"Won't it be splendid!" exclaimed Messiter.

They were walking behind the other boys, who were hastening home, carrying bats, balls, stumps, pads, and other things they had taken with them.

Suddenly a man who leant on a stick as he walked touched Lightheart on the shoulder.

"Hallo! what's your game?" cried Dick.

"Don't you know me?" said the man.

"Hanged if I do! Yet, stop a bit; I've seen you somewhere."

Dick tapped his forehead, as if he was trying to remember.

"I was at Mohammed's place, in Castle Square."

"Of course; you're the gym. You're the attendant—name of Jackson—I know you now; glad to see you about again, my dear fellow, heartily glad!" said Dick, shaking his proffered hand cordially.

The gymnasium attendant smiled, and replied—

"I am the gym, as you call me, and I'm pleased to think I'm getting on so well. My injuries are much less severe than I suspected."

"It's a pleasure to me to see you," continued Dick, "because your speaking to me proves that you don't really think that I did the dirty, shabby trick which laid you up."

"I know you didn't," replied Jackson.

"You can't know it for a fact, but you feel positive it was Armond. Is that it?"

"That's it," answered the gym, "and I have to thank you all for your kind subscriptions. I'm not well off, and my friends are poor. My illness would have been a serious blow if I had not had some money."

"If you want any more I've got some loose cash, old fellow, and you're welcome to it. Perhaps it will do you as much good as Oko Jumbo."

Jackson smiled at this remark, though he did not see the joke, and answered—

"Thank you, I'm all right at present. But I wanted to see you to tell you that I have been thinking a good deal while I lay on my sick bed, and I'm determined to punish Mr. Armond for being the cause of my accident."

"He meant the trap for me," replied Dick.

"I know he meant the trap for you," said Jackson, "but I fell into it. You, too, have fallen in the estimation of your companions, for he has circulated the most infamous reports about you behind your back."

"He can't hurt me," replied Dick. "My friends don't believe him, and he'll be found out some day."

"He's a villain, and you ought to be on your guard, Mr. Lightheart," continued the gym. "A fellow who could coolly and deliberately do a thing like that would do something much worse. He'll have another shy at you."

"Think so?" replied Dick.

"I'm sure of it. However, I'm at work, and if I can bowl him out, I will. I suppose your masters would not keep him in the school if it was proved that he had actually committed such a—a crime. I may call it a crime, because it might have killed you, and very nearly did me."

"I don't know. They might keep him," replied Dick.

"I may be wrong, and I may be right, sir," replied the attendant at the gymnasium, "about my expectation of finding him out. One thing I know I'm right about, and that is your innocence."

"Wire in," said Dick. "I wish you luck, and if ever you're hard up for a pound, come to me, and if I haven't got it, I'll get up a subscription for you. I'm wonderful at getting up subs, ain't I, Harry?"

Messiter laughed, and replied in the affirmative.

He shook hands with Jackson, as they were nearly home, and said—

"I can't ask you in, as it isn't my own house, you understand; and I can't ask you to have a drink either, because our usher would drop down upon me. So you must take the will for the deed. You meet me when I'm out on the loose, and see if I won't do what's proper and handsome."

Jackson declared that he wanted nothing but his friendship and goodwill, and walked back again.

"That gym is a good sort," remarked Messiter.

"First-class," replied Dick. "I'm awfully pleased he doesn't think I cut the rope, and I hope he will find Armond out. For although Mr. Simcox has not accused me of doing it, more from want of evidence and proof than any feeling of goodwill, he and several others believe me guilty."

"Give a dog a bad name and hang him," said Messiter.

"You mean that I have got the reputation of being a scapegrace, and on that account everything that is bad and suspicious is put down to me."

"Live it down."

"I've a good mind to turn missionary," said Dick, "and go out myself to Oko Jumbo."

Messiter laughed at this, and said he thought he would soon wish himself back again.

When Monday came, they were glad to see that the bruises they had received in the fight between the Armondites and Lighthearts had disappeared, so that they could appear in public with a presentable appearance.

Early in the morning Dick slipped the letter he had written in his father's handwriting into the letter-box.

With a beating heart he waited the result.

CHAPTER XLIII.

OFF ON THE SPREE.

IT was half-past nine when Sam Fuggles, the servant, came into the playground where the boys were amusing themselves before ten o'clock school.

"Master Lightheart, sir," he said.

"What is it, Sam?" replied Dick.

"Governor wants you at once."

"Coming, Sam," said Dick.

He guessed what he was wanted for and felt sure that his clever, if not strictly honest, device was already as good as successful.

Mr. Simcox was in his study, the remains of a substantial breakfast were upon the table, and he was reading a morning paper, while he indulged in his early pipe, for smoking was one of his pet weaknesses.

"Oh! Lightheart," said Mr. Simcox, "your father has arrived in Brighton for a day or two, and wishes you to spend a few hours with him."

"Has he been here, sir? asked Dick, innocently.

"No, he has written."

"May I go, sir?"

"You may," replied the professor. "Your conduct has improved lately, and I gladly give you the holiday for which your respected father asks in his note."

As a matter of fact, Dick had not greatly improved, but he had not been found out so frequently of late.

"Thank you, sir," he said.

"Oh! and you may take your friend Messiter with you. The Rev. Mr. Lightheart mentions his name, and prefers a request to that effect," continued the professor.

"Very well, sir, I will tell him."

"You can start as soon as you like, and you must be home by ten o'clock, if not before."

Dick promised to remember this, and, wild with delight, went to seek Messiter, to whom he communicated the good news.

They went to their dormitory and quickly changed their clothes.

Each wore a hat and put on lavender-coloured gloves, and carried a small cane in his hand.

"Oh! my, you are toffs," said Sam, as he saw them going out.

"We mean it this time, Sam," replied Dick.

"If you young gents ain't up to mischief, I'm mistaken."

"Not we, Sam; we're too quiet and innocent," Dick said, with a wink.

"Yes, you are—over the left," replied Sam, grinning.

"Has Snarley gone?"

"This hour or more, sir. He don't often have a day out, and when he does, he likes to make the most of it."

"Perhaps he'll never come back. I had a bad dream about him," said Dick.

"Now I know there's something on," exclaimed Sam. "Oh, Master Lightheart, you are a born imp for mischief."

"Shut up, Sam, you are becoming familiar. Learn how to treat your superiors with proper respect. I shall have to complain to Mr. Simcox of your unseemly behaviour," replied Dick, with mock gravity.

Sam burst out laughing as the boys started on their journey.

"Going to see his father, Master Messiter said," remarked Sam, between explosive bursts of laughter. "So am I going to see my father. There's a game on. Oh, he is a treat, that young Lightheart. See his father! So I should think."

As they walked along the Parade, Dick began to sing "Off on the spree, boys, off on the spree; we'll have a day, boys, down by the sea. Strike up, Harry, you're not half a cock."

Then he went on, humming gaily—

"Shoreham Gardens, have you ever been there? Such tricks, picnics, as are only seen there."

Laughing and talking, they went to the railway station, where they took first-class return tickets for Shoreham.

The train started almost directly, and it was about half-past eleven when they found themselves at the entrance of the Swiss Gardens, and gained admission by payment of one shilling.

They went into the beautiful grounds, and admired the lovely autumn flowers and the various buildings, chiefly made of wood in the Swiss style, and the winding paths, with quaint little bridges over the water, and after they had gone everywhere, they stopped in front of an enclosure where a large balloon lay safely at its moorings.

"Pull up here," said Dick.

The balloon was to ascend in the afternoon, under the skilful guidance of its owner; the car was attached, and seemed capable of holding four people.

At one side of the big balloon, which was called the Montgolfier, were half-a-dozen small pilot balloons.

Suddenly Messiter said—

"There's a pretty girl, Dick."

A glance in the direction indicated by Messiter showed him it was Miss Agatha Mountserrat, otherwise Polly.

Dick was going up to speak to her, when he beheld a gentleman shuffling after her, as she strolled slowly along.

This was Mr. Snarley.

There was no mistake about it.

He had got himself up in a white hat, a blue silk necktie, and yellow-looking gloves, all of which made his rather ungainly figure and features the more striking.

Pulling Messiter's arm, Dick withdrew behind a shrub, saying—

"It won't do to let him see us at present, as it would spoil all our fun."

"So it would," answered Messiter. "What a nuisance he should come here."

"It's a bore, but we'll send him home."

"How?"

"Oh! half drown him or something," replied Dick, adding—"Look, he's speaking to Polly."

"Is that your Polly?"

"Yes. Isn't she pretty?" said Dick.

"I should think she was, too," replied Messiter, with enthusiasm.

Mr. Snarley made bold to address Polly, close to where the boys were concealed.

"Ah! pardon me, my young lady!" he said. "I—I have an appreciation of—ahem!—talent, and—and I have been given to understand that you are—ahem!—Miss Agatha Mountserrat."

"That's my name, sir," replied the divine Polly, regarding the strange scarecrow-like figure before her with considerable amusement.

"Ah, thank you," he continued. "May I—ahem!—if it is not too early in the morning, invite you to—to partake of a glass—ahem!—of sherry, say sherry wine?"

"No, I am obliged to you; another time," she replied.

"At least, allow me to walk by your side, while you promenade the lovely gardens."

"Sir!" said Polly.

Dick turned to Messiter, and said—

"I can't stand this! stay where you are."

He had drawn a small fish-hook from his pocket, in which he generally kept a little arsenal of all the things a schoolboy may or may not want.

With wonderful rapidity he cut the rope of one of the small pilot balloons, and attached the gut of his fish-hook to the end of the string.

Then he crept across the path, till he got behind Snarley, and contrived to stick the hook in the rim of his hat.

The balloon caught a breath of air.

There was a tug, and away went Snarley's new white hat, sailing gaily over the garden towards the pathless sea.

His bald head was revealed in all its shininess.

Dick retreated, and joined Messiter again.

Mr. Snarley uttered a dismal shriek, and said—

"My hat, oh! my hat. Fit for the races. This style ten-and-six. Half-a-guinea gone at one swoop, and I am bare-headed; but how the dickens did it go?"

Polly laughed, and though she had not been inclined to talk to him a minute ago, she now said—

"The pilot balloon must have broken loose, and somehow it caught your hat."

Mr. Snarley at a little distance beheld a shooting gallery.

To rush to it and snatch up a rifle did not take him long.

Levelling the gun at the runaway balloon, he fired and missed.

"Good idea, sir," exclaimed the proprietor of the gallery, "but a bad shot. You'll never hit it; your hand shakes too much."

"Do you try; a shilling for your trouble."

"Spring a bob, sir. Make it a florin."

"Fire, fire, or it will go out to sea, and become the prey of some rascally Frenchman. Don't waste precious time in talking," shrieked Mr. Snarley.

The man ran down the path after the balloon and fired, once, twice, thrice. The third shot hit the side, the air rushed out, and as the prepared paper collapsed, the hat descended with a run.

But not on the solid ground.

It fell on the lake, and began to float round and round in a graceful manner.

"I should like to throw a brick at it," said Dick.

He ran down to the side of the lake, followed by Messiter, and saw a boat moored to the bank.

A written notice stuck on the bows informed him that it was "For the use of visitors. N. B.—Don't pull up the plug in the stern, which is to let out the water when she leaks, and has been beached in consequence."

This was enough for Dick.

He jumped over a seat, and drew out a bung-like plug in the stern.

Then he scampered back, and ran with Messiter behind a couple of friendly trees.

As he had expected, Mr. Snarley had stopped to pay the rifle-man for bringing down his hat, and the man, not able to leave his gallery, had directed him to the old boat on the lake, telling him to row after and recover his property.

Polly had accompanied him to the water's edge, and Dick heard her say—

"I am sorry you should have lost your hat while talking to me."

"What are hats?" replied Snarley, in a tragic voice, "what is the universe in comparison with——"

"If you stop to pay me high-flown

compliments," she interrupted, "your hat will sink, and that will be an additional punishment to you for speaking to strangers in pleasure gardens."

"Angelic being——" began Snarley.

"Don't you make me laugh. I daresay you have got a wife at home."

"Divine creature, hear me swear!" exclaimed Snarley, laying his hand on his heart.

"No; you mustn't do that. I shan't like you if you swear. Look after your hat."

Dick did not like this flirtation, so he threw a stone at Snarley's hat, which, striking it on the crown, made it spin round in a most intoxicated manner.

A hungry-looking swan approached it, as if he thought it was something good to eat.

"My hat; I must have it," groaned Snarley. "Boys are throwing at it, and swans peck it with their bills. Behold me, Agatha, about to embark in that crazy boat, and if you never see me more, drop one tear to the memory of a distracted being with whom to see was to admire you—to admire, to love you."

With this impassioned speech, which he thought would make a great impression upon the fair Mountserrat, Snarley jumped into the boat, and pushing her off with one of the sculls, he drifted towards the hat.

CHAPTER XLIV.

DICK RENEWS HIS ACQUAINTANCE WITH POLLY.

"I SHALL soon recover my hat," said Mr. Snarley to himself.

He settled himself down to his work, and tucked up his sleeves so as to be better able to use the sculls.

"Ah!" he continued, "a pleasant life is that on the ocean wave. Dear me, what a log this boat is. It scarcely seems to me to move a bit."

Polly was regarding his exertions from the bank, and he redoubled his efforts.

"Make haste, sir," she cried; "your hat will sink."

At that moment Dick, who with Messiter was concealed behind some shrubs, threw a stone at the hat, which hit it on the side and made it spin round like a teetotum.

"Some one is throwing stones," said Mr. Snarley. "My dear young lady, can you kindly inform me who is throwing stones at my hat?"

"I can't see anyone," answered Polly.

"It's very odd."

"Why don't you row harder?" asked Polly.

"For the most simple of all reasons, I am unable. Ha! what is this? I perceive water in the boat?"

"Water!" echoed Polly.

"Yes. As I am a sinner, the wretched old tub leaks. What is to be done?"

"Pull harder, sir."

"I am trying to do so. My utmost efforts, however do not suffice to propel the hulk more than a yard a minute. Oh!"

This exclamation was caused by his catching a crab, and falling backwards in the water which had accumulated in the boat, with a great splash.

The sculls fell on either side and floated away from his reach.

When he got up, he was dripping wet, and pale with rage.

"This is too much," he said.

Polly was laughing until the tears ran down her cheeks.

"Here do I come out for a day's pleasure," Mr. Snarley went on, "and I find it marred in this manner."

"Shall I send some of the garden people to your assistance, sir?" asked Polly.

"Do so, if you please, my dear young lady, and I shall be indebted to you. My position is a most unpleasant and even alarming one," replied Mr. Snarley.

She walked quickly away, but Dick, who had left Messiter in the thicket, went after and intercepted her.

"Stop a bit, Polly," he cried.

"What do you mean by calling me —oh! it's Master Lightheart," cried Polly, recognising him.

"Mister, please, Polly. You're Agatha when you're in public, and I'm Mister when I've got a chimney-pot hat on and go out for the day."

"Come with me," she said laughing. "I'm so glad to see you. But there is a poor gentleman in a boat on the lake, and he'll be drowned if he is left to himself. The boat is leaky."

"I know it is."

"*You* know it."

"Yes, I pulled the plug out."

"Oh !" said Polly, shocked.

"It's our usher, Mr. Snarley, and we've been having larks with him. I fastened the pilot balloon to his tile. You let him alone; he wasn't born to be drowned."

"Poor man."

"I want to talk to you, Polly," continued Dick.

"So you shall presently; but I must send some one to the unlucky gentleman."

"Why ?"

"I know that boat well."

"What then ?"

"If you take the plug out it fills in ten minutes. Go round to the stage entrance to the theatre and you'll find papa; promise me you will."

"When I've seen the last of Snarley in his watery grave," replied Dick.

Polly shook her head at him and ran away.

"Don't split about me, Polly," cried Dick after her, "if you do get him out."

She turned round, gave him a reassuring look, and then was out of sight.

Dick rejoined Messiter.

"Well," he said, "how's Snarley?"

"Bleating," replied Messiter; "hark at him."

In fact the usher was roaring for help at the top of his voice.

The boat was nearly full of water, and he sat on one of the seats with his arms round his knees, looking the personification of misery and despair.

Luckily there was another boat in which a gardener was able to pull off.

"Hold tight, sir," said the gardener.

"It's all very well to say hold tight when there is nothing to hold to," replied Snarley, and as he spoke, the boat gave a lurch and capsized.

Snarley was struggling in the water.

He made a frantic grab at his hat, which bobbed away from him like a cork.

Then with a groan he prepared to sink, but at the critical moment the attendant came up with his boat and seized him by the arm and dragged him in.

Snarley lay down exhausted at the bottom.

"I'll bring an action against you all," he gasped; "I'll have the law of you."

"Is that all your gratitude?" replied the man. "Haven't I saved your life?"

"Look at the state I am in. Where's my hat?"

"Bother your hat; here's the land; step out and don't shake yourself on me," the man said.

Mr. Snarley bestowed upon him a withering look and stepped sadly on shore.

He was soaked through and through, and he was hatless.

Old Hopkins, Polly's father, happened to be standing by, watching the fun with some others who had been attracted by the usher's cries.

"What shall I do?" groaned Snarley dismally.

"I can give you a change, sir, while you have your things dried," said Hopkins.

"Do you belong to these gardens ?" answered Snarley. "Because, if you do, I tell you fairly I mean to bring an action against you for putting people into leaky boats."

"I am engaged here, that's all. I've got a show on at the theatre, and if you like to put on some property togs, I'll have your own dried."

"Put on what ?"

"Property togs. Pantaloon's dress, or anything handy," said Hopkins.

"I once had a clown's on," groaned Snarley. "But I see what you mean, and am thankful to you."

"Beggars mustn't be choosers, sir."

"Very truly. Lead on, my friend. You are a good Samaritan."

Hopkins conducted Mr. Snarley to a little room behind the stage of the theatre which he was privileged to occupy.

There was another little room leading out of it, which was called the ladies' dressing-room.

In front of all was a larger apartment, which was dignified with the name of the green room, in which the ladies and gentlemen connected with the theatre waited for the " call."

All sorts of costumes lay about; and there were a sprite, a harlequin, two policemen, a fishmonger, a baker, and a Bond Street swell attiring themselves.

" We've got a bit of pantomime on," said Mr. Hopkins, by way of explanation.

" Oh! have you? " replied Snarley, shivering.

" Where's Groggles?" continued Hopkins, addressing the sprite.

" Blind drunk, as usual, under the bar in the gardens. They poked him under with a broom, to let him sleep it out in the shady cool," answered the sprite.

" Blow Groggles?" exclaimed Hopkins, savagely.

" Nothing wrong, I hope," replied Snarley."

" Yes, there is, sir. I'm manager of this show, and as such I pay Groggles one two six every Saturday."

" And the treasury's never failed at two o'clock," put in the sprite.

" Nor never has since that thief Captain Hanger died," replied Hopkins. " But, sir, Groggles gets systematically drunk."

" What is he?"

" Pantaloon. In real life he's a rheumatic fisherman on the retired list, but it makes him do the 'loon all the better."

Mr. Snarley's teeth chattered.

" It's what I call ungrateful of Groggles; but I'll dock his screw. If I don't—I say, sir, hold those castanets a-chattering. I forgot you were wet, all along of my indignation with Groggles. Take off your clothes and have a wipe with a clean towel; then put on Groggles' things."

" What! the pantaloon's?" echoed Mr. Snarley, aghast.

" They'll save you from a severe cold, and are, at all events, better than nothing."

Mr. Snarley yielded, though much against his will, and giving up his own clothes, which were hung against a fire lighted on purpose to dry them, put on those of the facetious drama.

" It's too bad of that Groggles," continued Hopkins. " Here was he as 'ard up as 'ard up could be, when I fust come here and took the theatre."

" Was he?" said Mr. Snarley.

" And no mistake. What do you think he did?—used to keep a property bloater—wooden fish, you know—on a plate in his room, to let people think he'd had a breakfast, or was going to, when never a morsel passed his lips."

" Really !"

" That's Groggles. He's all bounce and outside show," continued Hopkins.

" And drink," said the sprite.

" Undesirable member of a company, I should think," continued Snarley.

He was now dry and comfortable, and sat warming his hands before a good fire, which, owing to the state of the weather, was more agreeable to him than the rest of the company.

" Not so bad a pantaloon. That sort of talent's scarce in the country," replied Hopkins.

" Is it ?"

" Yes. You don't often get anyone to look the character. But now I come to see you, sir, you seem as if you were a born 'loon."

" I—I !" cried Mr. Snarley. " What do you mean ?"

" I've been connected with the profession, sir, all my life, and done more for it, perhaps, than it has for me, and I know what's what when I see it, and I say you're every inch a pantaloon."

Mr. Snarley got angry.

He snatched up a stick, and his legs being a little shaky, tottered up to Hopkins, saying—

" Take care, sir. Take care."

Hopkins leant against the wall, and laughed till the tears ran down his cheeks.

" You can do it, sir," he cried; " I knew you was an actor. I could see it in your eyes."

" I an actor !"

" Yes. You can't deceive me. You've played low comedy."

" No."

" You have, and you've played farce."

" Never !" exclaimed Mr. Snarley, emphatically.

" And you're well up in comic business," pursued Hopkins.

" I know no more than a baby."

" Yes, you do. Stash it. Modesty won't do in our line. Look here, sir. I'll stand a dollar if you'll take Groggles' place this afternoon, and come in as

Pantaloon in 'Harlequin My Lord Tom Noddy and the Fairy Cabriolet.' "

Mr. Snarley listened to this singular offer with amazement.

He go on the stage !
Take Groggles' place! Play pantaloon!
The idea was enough to take his breath away.

CHAPTER XLV.

CLOWN AND PANTALOON

HOPKINS was destined to be in trouble that day.

No sooner was it discovered that Groggles was drunk and incapable, than a fresh misfortune was heard of.

Lapchin, the clown, had followed suit.

He was reported to be babbling childishly to himself over three of gin in a flowery arbour somewhere in the grounds.

"No one knows what it is to be the manager of a show," cried Hopkins. "I shall turn it up. I'd rather play the fiddle in the street for a living or do the bones with a wandering minstrel troupe."

He rushed out to look for the unhappy Lapchin.

Before going far, he met Dick and Messiter, who were carrying Snarley's hat.

"Gentleman's as was nearly drowned?" asked Hopkins.

"That's it," replied Dick. "Take it to him; we hear you've got him in tow. I rescued it from the waters of the lake; but I say, Hopkins, old boy, don't you recognise me?"

"Give us your fist," cried Hopkins; "you're the young school gent Polly's talked so much about ever since you saved her life when we were circussing?"

"You're right. I am that singularly fortunate individual."

"Blowed if I should know my own father to-day, I'm that upset," continued Hopkins.

"What's up?"

"Up. Nobody's up. They're all down. It's the last day. We close the show to-night, for it's the end of the season, and the blessed company's all getting drunk."

"That's bad," said Dick.

"It's all my own fault. I shouldn't have given them a treasury this morning at nine sharp."

"You paid them too soon."

"I did. They thought I might bolt in the night, and they pressed me for their last week's screws before it was time to pay them. I yielded like a babby as I am, and what's the consequence?"

Hopkins looked round him inquiringly.

"The consequence is, that Groggles the pantaloon is drunk, ditto Lapchin, the clown."

"What will you do?"

"Half drowned gent's dressed up in Groggles' togs, and he's going to play pantaloon," replied Hopkins.

Dick's eyes twinkled with delight.

"Snarley going to play pantaloon!" he said; "never!"

"He is, though. Do you know him?" said Hopkins.

"Rather. He's our usher," replied Dick.

"Oh! if that's it, Master Lightheart, I needn't ask how he came into the pond."

"You mustn't tell him we're here, though; he doesn't know it."

"Hasn't he seen you?"

"Not yet. We're his fate, but it's the awful mystery of the hidden hand—twig?"

"I see," replied Hopkins.

"We're on the spree," continued Dick. "Come and have a drink, old man. Anything you like, from bitter beer, the simple and refreshing bitter, to champagne."

"I don't mind a glass of shammy," answered Hopkins. "It'll square me up a bit."

"Come on, then, and I'll make you happy."

"How?"

"By undertaking to play clown to Snarley's pantaloon."

Hopkins was startled at this proposition.

"I think you could do it. If you'll

come on the stage with me, I'll put you up to the business in ten minutes," he said.

"I've been to pantomimes, don't fret," exclaimed Dick. "It's only having larks with and bullying the pantaloon."

"That's it. Bully him awful!" said Hopkins.

"Won't I? If he don't holloa a rum un when I begin with him, I'll go home and say I've been a bad boy," answered Dick.

"Then we'll leave Lapchin to drink as long as he likes. Let's have the drink and we'll go behind," Hopkins said.

They went to a bar, and Dick ordered refreshments.

Messiter was left eating cold pie, while Hopkins and Dick went to the theatre.

A little information was not lost upon him.

Dick dressed on the stage and painted his face so that Mr. Snarley should not recognise him.

When he was ready, he went into the ordinary dressing-room and found Mr. Snarley getting very jolly over repeated hot grogs, which he took to keep the cold out.

It was now two o'clock in the day, and the first performance had to begin.

Hopkins hoped that Groggles and Lapchin would be sober enough to play by four when the public were next admitted. Messiter, who had been gorging cold pies and tarts, took a front seat in the stalls, and ate nuts and oranges in a reckless manner.

First Miss Agatha Mountserrat did some graceful dancing and sang some pretty songs.

She was a wood nymph, and a satyr, who afterwards became harlequin, followed her about and annoyed her.

At length the bell rang and Dick, preceded by Mr. Snarley, rushed on the stage, harlequin and columbine appearing at the same time.

"Hullo! here we are again, Snarley," cried Dick.

Dick gave him a slap on the face that made him spin round.

"Oh, my eye!" cried Snarley.

"Who told you to speak?" exclaimed Dick.

The look of pain Snarley put on was indicative of an apparent wish to please

the audience, and they roared accordingly.

From that moment, whenever Dick got a chance of kicking or hitting the unlucky pantaloon, he did it as hard as he could.

His bones ached all over.

Pantaloon had to climb through a shoemaker's window, but he stuck after he had got the upper part of his body through.

Dick snatched the harlequin's wand, and belaboured his nether regions till he howled like a bull calf.

When he came off and stood near the clown in the wings he said, rubbing himself dismally—

"What do you want to hit and punch and kick like that for?"

"It's business," replied Dick.

Snarley groaned and was soon engaged in trying to discover which was the hardest, his head or a wooden turnip.

At last it was over.

Dick ran into the dressing-room and put under his arm Snarley's dry clothes, which he made into a little parcel.

He changed his own things in a little cupboard, and then ran out to the stage-door, where he found Messiter.

"How did I do it?" asked Dick.

"Ripping. Every yell Snarley gave was real, wasn't it?" replied Messiter.

"Rather."

"I think he twigged me. His eyes seemed to single me out in the stalls, and once I had a good mind to give him an orange on the nose."

"I don't fancy he did see you. It was your nervousness," said Dick.

"What have you got under your arm?"

"Snarley's dry clothes. Find half a brick," said Dick.

"What for?"

"To tie to them and sink in the pond. Snarley must never see these togs again. Never," answered Dick.

"How will he go home?"

"In his professional attire."

"Oh, Dick," exclaimed Messiter, "how I shall laugh. You'll be the death of me."

"Hope not," said Dick. "You are young, and I have some faint expectation of making a man of you yet."

"Thank you."

They went to the side of the pond, and Snarley's clothes found their last resting-place.

"Now," said Dick, "I'm going to have some dinner in the refreshment saloon. Can you eat anything, or have you choked yourself up with trash?"

"Not quite."

"I saw you gorging into nuts and things, while I was doing clown."

"We must not lose the balloon ascent," said Messiter.

"Not for worlds. What time does it start?"

"Six, I think."

"Come and feed; we've lots of time," said Dick, looking at his watch.

They walked arm-in-arm to the saloon, sat down at a table and called for the waiter.

CHAPTER XLVI.

THE BALLOON ASCENT.

"WAITER," said Dick, "we want to dine."

"Yes, sir; bill of fare, sir," replied the waiter, with a napkin tucked professionally under one arm, while he jingled his money in his breeches pocket with his other hand.

"Ah!" said Dick, with the eye of a connoisseur, as he ran over the list—"Spring soup, er—turbot and lobster sauce, er—ducks and green peas, er—lamb and grass, er—maccaroni au gratin à la tomate, jellies, ice pudding, and er—bottle of Bordeaux, that at 42 shillings, and, er—ice, and plenty of it."

"Yes, sir; directly, sir," said the waiter, hurrying off.

"You can order a dinner, Dick, and no mistake," exclaimed Messiter.

"Don't you wish you hadn't gone in for those pies and things?"

"I've got a corner left. The waiter thinks you're a swell. How he did look at you."

"So I am," answered Dick, complacently.

"Do you think you will have money enough?" Messiter inquired, anxiously.

"Lots. We haven't touched the subscriptions for Oko Jumbo yet," Dick replied, with a grin.

When the dinner appeared, they did ample justice to it.

Dick paid the bill, rewarded the waiter liberally, and, chewing a toothpick, walked again into the gardens.

The balloon was moored by a couple of ropes to the ground, which the car almost touched.

It was a comfortable wicker-work construction, and Dick, with his usual impudence, got in.

"Oh," said Messiter, "come out—do come out, Dick. You'll have the man it belongs to on to you."

"I'll give him five shillings to take me up with him," answered Dick.

"Would you really go in a thing like that?"

"Why not? It's safe enough, and the seat's jolly comfortable."

"Is it?" said Messiter, doubtfully.

"Come in and try it."

With fear and trembling Messiter climbed in, and took a seat opposite Dick.

"Now," said the latter, "what is there to fear?"

"Not much certainly, that I can see at present, but going through the air is different."

"What's that row?" suddenly said Dick.

A great hubbub was proceeding from the back part of the theatre, which was not many yards off.

"You've stolen my clothes," cried a voice, raised in anger.

"Who are you a-talking to about stealing?" retorted Hopkins.

"It's Hopkins and Snarley. Here's a spree," cried Dick delightedly.

"I'll call the police," continued Mr. Snarley, emerging from the dressing-room. "You keep me in here, make me work for you, and try to cause me to become intoxicated on bad gin, while you steal my clothes."

"It's false."

"It's true. I have heard of the tricks

of you strolling players, but I'll make an example of you. Police! Police!"

"You're drunk," said Hopkins; "that's about the size of it, and I shall have to lock you up."

"Ha! ha!" cried Snarley, cutting a caper on the grass. "I defy you, villain, and all your myrmidons!"

He looked extremely comical in his pantaloon's dress, his tight-fitting wig, and his long peaky beard.

"I didn't think I could laugh so much," observed Dick.

"He's tight," said Messiter.

Reeling up to Hopkins, and snapping his fingers in his face, Snarley exclaimed—

"My clothes, miscreant, my clothes."

"I haven't got 'em. They're vanished, and I think I know where they're gone," replied the showman.

"Where? Tell me your suspicions and I'll forgive you," said the usher eagerly.

"Two of your boys are in the garden," replied Hopkins.

"Oh, Agatha's father," groaned Dick, "I didn't think you'd split on us."

"It's all up now," said Messiter.

"We shall be carried back to the house of bondage," Dick said.

"My boys!" said Snarley. "Who, what, where? Name them—explain this mystery."

"One of them is Master Lightheart. He played clown to your pantaloon."

"That accounts for the blows I received. Go on, Mr. Showman."

"They're about somewhere. Now, if any one's had your things, it's them," replied Hopkins.

Messiter had a half-peeled orange in his hard.

"Give it me," whispered Dick.

Taking it from him, he threw it dexterously at Hopkins and hit him on the ear.

"Don't you throw no oranges at me," exclaimed Hopkins, squaring up to Snarley.

"I didn't," replied Snarley.

"It came from the balloon," remarked a bystander.

"Did it?" the usher replied. "Then the boys are there, but how they got into the gardens I don't know—yes, I do—they had a holiday, Lightheart and Messiter. Two twin imps. Mr. Showman."

"Sir."

"Help me to capture these audacious culprits."

"I shan't help you. Go and talk to them; there they are, seated in the car of the b'loon, happy as bugs in a rug."

Mr. Snarley ran to the ropes which shut off the enclosure.

The boys were distinctly visible.

"Ah! you Lightheart. Ah! you Messiter," said Mr. Snarley, with concentrated anger, "come out of that."

"Who are you?" replied Dick.

"Your usher."

"I don't believe you. My usher wouldn't dress himself like a pantaloon."

"It was done to—a—propitiate the father of a lovely girl, the—a—the beautiful Agatha Mountserrat. But no matter. Come out of that and help me to recover my clothes."

"I shan't. You've no right to order me about. I'm not at school now, Mr. Pantaloon," answered Dick.

"Then I will pull you out by your arms and your legs, and I will make an example of you," said the usher.

He climbed over the ropes.

Dick drew a knife from his pocket, and leaning over the side of the car, began to cut away at something.

"Oh! what are you doing?" said Messiter, in alarm.

"Sit perfectly still," answered Dick, who was very grave.

"The thing is beginning to wobble about."

"It will be all right presently. Take up one of those bags of sand at your feet, and shy it plump at Snarley. Make haste."

Messiter did as he was told.

The bag hit him on the nose, and he fell backwards sprawling.

"Give him another."

Messiter did so, and this time he hit him in the stomach.

"Oh!" groaned Snarley, getting on his hands and knees. "What a thing it is to have to deal with a wicked and perverse generation. He has taken all my little stock of wind."

Suddenly the balloon began to rise in the air.

The spectators shouted loudly.

Rushing from the refreshment bar,

where he had been beguiling his leisure moments, the proprietor ran out.

He tore his hair.

He raved and shrieked.

His beautiful balloon was gone, and he might never see it again.

"Give him one on the nob and stop his row," said Dick.

Messiter dropped another bag of sand on the proprietor's head.

It knocked his hat over his eyes, and he floundered about in utter darkness.

"Stop! stop!" cried Mr. Snarley. "Misguided boys, hold your mad career; you will be killed. This is a disastrous day. Stop, sto——"

He fell down again on his back, having been struck by another bag of sand, which this time, falling from some height, stunned him.

All was confusion and excitement in the gardens.

Hopkins took hold of Snarley, and with assistance carried him to a fly, in which he placed him.

"Drive this gentleman to Harrow House School, Kemp Town, Brighton," he said. "He's tight, and we can't have any more of his nonsense here. He'll get locked up."

"Right," said the fly driver.

"Don't you let him get out."

"Not I."

"Tell them at the school that I shall call for the pantaloon's dress to-morrow," continued Hopkins.

The flyman jumped on his box, and Mr. Snarley was driven off to Brighton.

The blow he had received, the excitement, and the spirits he had swallowed, all combined to make Mr. Snarley drowsy.

He did not wake until he was landed at Harrow House, about seven o'clock in the evening.

The flyman knocked at the door, which was opened by Mr. Simcox in person.

Mr. Snarley was roused by the driver and jumped out.

He ran up the steps.

"Who are you, and what do you want here?" said Mr. Simcox.

"Do you not know me, sir?" replied Snarley.

"You are—yes, you must be my assistant teacher. But why this disguise? Once before you returned dressed as a clown. Is this a joke? **Is this done on** purpose, sir?"

"No, sir."

"Are you sober?"

"Stand on one side," cried Mr. Snarley, in a rage, "I won't be kept on the steps for little boys to gibe at."

He pushed his respected head master on one side and entered the house.

"This conduct is highly reprehensible, sir," said Mr. Simcox, shutting the door.

"Do you want to fight?" cried Snarley.

"Fight! Bless me, no."

"Then don't provoke me too far. I can fight, though I've had enough excitement for one day."

"How did it happen?"

"Young Lightheart was at Shoreham Gardens."

"Ah! With his father, I presume," said the head master.

"No; he and Messiter were by themselves, and they've done this for me."

"Where are they now? Why did you not bring them back with you?"

Mr. Snarley laughed wildly.

"Ha! ha!"

"You laugh."

"Yes, at the idea of bringing them back, when they're off in a balloon. 'Up in a balloon, boys, up in a balloon, all among the pretty stars, sailing round the moon,' as the song says."

"Mr. Snarley."

"Sir."

"Again I must ask you, are you sober?"

"Rubbish, I am all right," replied the usher, "though this day I have gone through enough to consign any average man to a lunatic asylum."

He briefly told Mr. Simcox all that had happened.

"Dear me. This is alarming news. The boys will be killed," said the head master.

Mr. Snarley was going to say, "A good job too," but he held his peace.

Simcox led the way into his sitting-room and produced wine and cakes.

The usher drank sherry out of a tumbler, helping himself two or three times.

He had had no dinner that day, and the wine, added to his previous potations, took effect upon him.

"Is this prudent, Mr. Snarley?" Mr. Simcox ventured to remonstrate.

He was filling his glass for the fourth time.

"You be bothered," replied Snarley.

"Do you know who you're talking to, sir?" Mr. Simcox exclaimed, severely.

"If you're game for a dance, fair heel and toe, I'm your man. Come on," answered Snarley.

Receiving no response, he began to dance fantastically.

Mr. Simcox looked on dismayed.

Presently the door opened, and he waltzed into Mrs. Simcox's arms.

Seizing her round the waist, he swung her round and round till he got giddy, and they both fell in a corner.

Disengaging herself, Mrs. Simcox, breathless with indignation, said—"Well, hi never! he's hon hagain."

"It's Mr. Snarley disguised, my dear," said her husband.

"Disguised in liquor, the beast! Send him to bed, and discharge him."

"I must think about it. At present I am in a mist. My head whirls. What will become of those boys?"

In great perplexity Mr. Simcox walked up and down the room.

Mr. Snarley snored pleasantly, and Mrs. Simcox helped herself to sherry to calm her nerves.

CHAPTER LXVII.

A VOYAGE THROUGH THE AIR.

"WE'RE off," said Dick, as the balloon shot up into the air.

Messiter was about to throw out another bag of sand, of which there were several in the car.

"Drop that," said Dick.

"Why? I can just plant a cove below beautifully on the nut.

"It's ballast, and the more you throw out the higher we go."

"Is that it?" replied Messiter.

"I've read about balloon ascents, and you must let me be captain of this ship," said Dick.

They sailed gaily away over Brighton, and then over the open country of Sussex.

At first they liked it.

Their appearance created a sensation everywhere, and the boys turned out crying—"Ah-bah-loon, ah-bah-loon!"

They could distinctly hear the shouts, and even the barking of a dog was audible.

At length there were no boys to shout, and the villages were few and far between.

Still they went on, on, with a pleasant, gliding motion.

"How is this going to end?" exclaimed Messiter, looking glum.

"Blessed if I know," replied Dick.

"Isn't there a way of getting down?"

"I believe so. You let the gas out."

"How?" asked Messiter.

"That is the question. There is, I fancy, a valve in the bottom of the balloon, and if you pull a string, the gas escapes, and you descend."

"Pull it then."

"Where is it?"

"I can see a string twined to one of the ropes of the car," said Messiter.

Dick examined it, and thought that this was the right string.

"Wait a bit," he said, "we won't go down just yet; let's have our spree out."

"I'm getting frightened."

"What at?"

"I don't know exactly, but it makes one dizzy to look over the side."

"Don't do it then," said Dick, who was a philosopher.

Messiter turned his attention to the interior of the car.

At his feet there was a locker, which he opened.

It contained some cold provisions, a bottle of brandy, and a stone bottle of beer.

"Grub!" he exclaimed.

"What sort of grub?" asked Dick.

"A pie, a chicken, part of a tongue, brandy, beer and gin, half-a-dozen of cham."

"That's good," exclaimed Dick. "Haul out the cham, we'll have a bottle."

He quickly opened a bottle and they drank a tumbler apiece.

"What a rage the aeronaut will be in; we've run off with his machine, and we're making free with his grub," said Dick.

" I wish we had not done it," groaned Messiter.

" It's better than being taken back by Snarley ; we're safe enough. It's only the novelty of the thing that makes you afraid. Some day we shall have steam balloons, and it will be as natural for a man to go to business in his balloon as it now is to go in his 'bus."

" You'll go down before dark."

" Certainly."

" Where are we now, do you think?" asked Messiter.

" This is the Thames underneath us ; how quickly we must have gone. It must be the Thames, as it is the only big river we've got, and look at the ships !"

They went on and sailed over part of Essex, which they recognised by its flat, marshy aspect.

" Suppose we try to land here ?" said Dick.

" I shall be so glad. Oh, do try," answered Messiter.

Dick took hold of the string, and, instead of pulling it gently, gave it a jerk.

The string snapped close up to the valve.

He stood with the broken piece in his hand and looked blankly at his companion.

" The beastly thing's broken," he exclaimed, in a tone of disgust.

" Oh, don't say that !" exclaimed Messiter.

" Here's a go ; we're stumped."

" Can't you reach the end ?"

" I could if I were able to fly ; that's the only way. Look what a height it is off."

Messiter began to cry.

The balloon now got into a different current of air.

It left English soil, and the boys could see the blue rolling waves of the sea beneath them.

" We're over the sea. I wonder what sea it is," remarked Dick.

" It must be the German Ocean," answered Messiter, between his sobs.

" We couldn't land now if we wanted to. Open another bottle of fiz, Harry ; it's getting cold," said Dick.

With trembling hands Messiter obeyed, and they drank the sparkling wine in silence.

The shades of night began to fall.

All was dark, dismal, and cheerless.

The breaking of the valve-string was a veritable misfortune to them.

They had delayed the descent too long ; now it was impossible.

Even if they had been able to reach the valve and let the gas out, they could not have descended on the waves.

That would have been to court certain death by drowning.

" Now, Harry," said Dick, " you must show yourself an intrepid voyager, no humbug ; crying won't do any good."

" I can't help it. You do such funny things," answered Messiter. " Who, but you, would have thought of cutting the ropes. and going off in a balloon ? "

" It's one of the penalties you have to pay for keeping my acquaintance," said Dick, coolly.

" I'll——" began Messiter, who stopped short.

" Go on, Harry," exclaimed Dick. " I know what you mean. You'll cut me when we get safe home. Isn't that it ?"

" If ever we do."

" Say your prayers, like a good boy, and go to sleep," Dick continued, wrapping his jacket more tightly around his breast and neck.

Thoroughly exhausted, Messiter sank down on the bottom of the car and tried to go to sleep, which he succeeded in doing.

Dick sat with his arms folded in thought.

The sea was beneath him.

Above was the firmament, studded with innumerable stars.

Occasionally he could see the headlight of some ship ploughing her way to distant lands.

Towards morning a cold rain fell, which wetted him to the skin and chilled him to the bone.

He was obliged to drink some of the brandy in the locker to support himself.

When the rain was over day broke, and the sun rose resplendent in the heavens.

Its warm rays served to dry the boys, and their spirits rose again as they made a good breakfast.

They were still over the sea, and as the wind was fresh, appeared to be travelling at a rapid pace.

" Dick," said Messiter.

Lightheart was dozing in a corner.

"YOU COWARDLY RASCAL,' CRIED DICK."

"Well?" he replied.

"Would the balloon go on for ever like this, cutting through the air?"

"No. It would get rotten and smash up, or a storm might destroy it."

"Where are we going?" continued Messiter.

"As far as I can judge, direct to the North Pole," replied Dick.

"How horrible."

"We shall be picked up some day by some Arctic travellers, in the form of frozen boys, and be talked of as great curiosities."

"Oh, why did you do it?"

"Do what?"

"Start on this mad voyage," said Messiter.

"I don't know; it was an impulse. Frankly though," answered Dick, growling, "I wish I hadn't done it, and that's flat."

"I'd give anything to be at Simcox and Markwell's, if it was only in the black hole. It's dreadful to die so young."

"We're not dead yet, Harry," said Dick, in a cheerful voice.

He was far from feeling merry, but he wanted to cheer up his companion.

"No; but we soon shall be," groaned Messiter.

"Perhaps not," said Dick; "it all depends upon the wind. Wait a bit."

Messiter sighed deeply, and seemed to resign himself to his fate.

Dick, however, took up a telescope he found in the locker, and began to scrutinize the horizon minutely.

CHAPTER XLVIII.

ARMOND'S DIARY.

THE news of Lightheart and Messiter's disappearance in a balloon flew through the school like wildfire.

It caused the utmost excitement amongst the boys.

Dick was a general favourite, and it was hoped that before long he would return.

The croakers, and they were not few in number, shook their heads and declared that they thought the school had seen the last of the runaways.

Mr. Simcox telegraphed for the Rev. Mr. Lightheart, who came over to Brighton and met the proprietor of the balloon at Harrow House.

He was a man of the name of Turner.

Mr. Lightheart was much concerned about his son's safety.

"What do you think will be the result?" he said to Turner.

"It's impossible to tell, sir," said the man; "if the boys understand the valve, they can let out the gas and descend rapidly."

"Would they not have done so before now, if they had this knowledge?"

Turner imagined they would.

"I fear," he said, "that my new and beautiful balloon will be lost, but you, sir, are a gentleman, and will of course compensate me."

"How dare you talk to me of compensation," cried Mr. Lightheart indignantly, "when my boy's life is in danger?"

"But——"

"There is no 'but' about it; you should have exercised more vigilance, and not allowed the boys to get into your balloon."

"When Richard went away in the boat, he telegraphed directly he reached land," observed Mr. Simcox.

"He did, and I fancy he would have done the same thing had he descended. There are telegraphs everywhere," said Mr. Lightheart.

"In what direction would the wind blow them?" asked Mr. Simcox.

"Due north," answered Turner.

"They would be blown over the German Ocean."

"Precisely."

"My poor rash boy," said Mr. Lightheart, "he may be frozen to death amid the fogs and frosts of the North Pole. It is dreadful to think of."

The conversation continued in a similar strain, but without bringing one gleam of consolation to the sorrowing parent.

"You see, sir," said Mr. Simcox, "that I am not to blame. The boy forged your handwriting, or I should not have let him go out."

"I know it; he is a bad boy."

In the course of the day Messiter's father arrived, and he was equally perplexed and anxious.

They returned home in the evening, hoping against hope, but when night fell no news had arrived.

Armond did not disguise his delight at the disappearance of his enemy.

After twelve the boys were allowed to stroll on the beach.

Armond went out, taking with him his inseparable companion Smith.

Smith was his toady, and he confided all his secrets to him.

They sat down together on the pebbly beach behind a bathing machine, which protected them from the wind.

"I'm glad," said Armond, "that the beast Lightheart is gone at last."

"So am I," replied Smith.

"How I do hate him."

"You have cause to. Is there no chance of his coming back?"

"I think not. Neither he nor Messiter know how to manage a balloon, which is a very delicate thing to handle."

"He was very nearly being maimed for life on the trapeze," remarked Smith.

"I meant him to be," answered Armond, incautiously.

"Then you did cut the rope?" said Smith.

"Yes," replied Armond; "you are my friend, and I don't mind admitting the truth to you, because I know my secret is safe."

"Oh, as to that," answered Smith, "I like you too well, Armond, to let on. I never blab about you."

"I know it, and I trust you as a brother. We have worked together ever since I have been at this school."

"You shall have no cause to repent your confidence."

"No fear. You're made of the right stuff. You and I were cut out for chums," answered Armond.

"I hope so."

"When I think of the insults that fellow Lightheart has heaped upon me, it makes my blood boil."

"He called you the son of a tripe-dresser, and a bill-discounter, and Cocky, and B. B., and——"

"Don't go through the list, you only make me mad," interrupted Armond. "I could see him dead at my feet with pleasure."

"He'll never come back, you say, so that is one comfort," observed Smith.

His little, ugly, freckly face gleamed with gratified malignity.

Armond took a book from his pocket, which was secured with clasps and a lock.

"This is my diary," he said.

Turning to a certain page, he added—

"Here is my entry about the trapeze affair."

"Read it," exclaimed Smith, "if you don't mind."

"'Went down to the gymnasium and cut the ropes of the last trapeze upon which Lightheart was to spring a match with me. . . . Was very sorry my attempt failed, and Lightheart was too wary, and would not take the leap. . . . He escaped, but the attendant fell. Bad luck this. Hope for better next time. . . . I hate him now more than ever.'"

"Ain't you afraid of someone seeing it?" asked Smith.

"No. It has a lock, and is never out of my possession. When not in my pocket, it's in my desk, and I have the key of that," Armond replied.

He began to write in it with a pencil.

Smith looked over his shoulder.

"Hear that Lightheart has run away in a balloon, and is not likely to be seen any more.. . . . Hope he won't be. . . . This is really good news."

"It is wicked to hate people," said Smith. "But I think we may be excused for hating Lightheart."

"Ain't it different where a fellow brings it on himself?" said Armond.

"Yes."

"I would have let him alone if he had not molested me."

The voice of Rumcovey the pieman was heard.

"Tarts, cakes, or buns this morning, sir?"

He addressed a young man who had been lying down on the beach almost under the bathing machine, and close to the spot where Armond and his precious toady were.

"Any tarts, Mr. Jack——"

The young man put his fingers to his lips, and saying "Hush," walked quickly away.

Rumcovey looked after him, muttering—

"Something up. No business of mine," and approached Armond, crying, in his monotonous voice, "Any tarts, cakes, or buns to-day, sir. The learned Armond, sir."

"What do you call me learned for?" asked Armond.

"You are the head of Messrs. Simcox and Markwell's school, sir. Tarts, cakes, or buns to-day, sir?" said Rumcovey.

"Treat me." said Smith; "I haven't got any tin."

"Here's sixpence; lay it out to the best advantage," said Armond.

Smith made his purchases and paid Rumcovey.

Meanwhile the young man whom the pieman had first addressed hurried along to the cliff.

He was no other than Jackson, the assistant at the gymnasium.

Jackson, who had been injured by falling from the trapeze.

He had been enjoying a lounge on the beach.

Chance had enabled him to overhear the conversation between Smith and Armond.

This was very important to him.

At last he had found out that his suspicions were correct.

He had all along believed that Lightheart was incapable of doing the shabby action that Armond and his friends imputed to him.

Without losing any time he hastened to Harrow House, and asked to see Mr. Simcox. Mr. Simcox had just been having an interview with Mr. Snarley, who did not get up early.

It was a satisfactory one.

Snarley explained how he had been treated, and Mr. Simcox generously forgave him, and reinstated him in his good opinion once more.

"Well, young man, what can I do for you?" exclaimed Mr. Simcox, as his visitor was ushered in.

"My name is Jackson, sir; attendant at the gymnasium," was the reply.

"Oh, ah, yes. I remember. You were hurt there by some accident. Sad thing. Better now, I hope."

"Yes, thank you, sir. A little stiffness in the left knee, that is all."

"Well, we did all we could for you. Can't do anything more."

"You can do justice, sir," replied Jackson.

"To whom?"

"A young gentleman named Lightheart was accused of being the cause of my accident."

"By whom?" asked Mr. Simcox.

"Some of his companions, of whom Mr. Armond was the leader."

"Well?"

"He didn't do it," said Jackson.

"How do you know that? It may be that if we establish Lightheart's innocence—and mind you, I never accused him, or took up the matter at all—the exculpation will not be of much use to him."

"How is that, sir?"

"He is missing; but go on with your story," returned Mr. Simcox, curtly.

Jackson then related the conversation he had heard between Armond and Smith on the beach.

"Very improbable," replied Mr. Simcox, who, for reasons of his own, wished to stand well with Armond and his father.

"Ask for his diary. If you see the confession in black and white, you'll believe it then, won't you, sir?" said Jackson.

"Yes, very true, that will be evidence; we must get that diary. I will see into it. Thank you for your information; but in future don't you think it would be more creditable to you, Mr. Jackson, not to lie under bathing machines listening to people's conversations?"

Jackson flushed angrily.

"It was accidental," he ejaculated. "I didn't mean to, nor should I have continued to listen unless I had been interested in the revelation; and I think I was perfectly justified in doing so."

"Ah, that's a matter of opinion," Mr Simcox said, stroking his whiskers.

"I can see how it is," Jackson exclaimed, indignantly. "You like this Armond, and you want to make Lightheart the scapegoat."

"My good young man——"

"Don't 'good young man' me!" interrupted Jackson, who was insensible to Mr. Simcox's persuasive tones.

"But listen——"

"I will not, sir, until you have heard what I have to say."

"What is that ?"

"I now know who is the cause of my injury, and if you do not take means to bring the offender to justice, I will."

Jackson spoke with determination, and Mr. Simcox lowered his tone.

"Very good," he replied. "I have no fault to find with the purport of your remarks, though you are a little violent. Call upon me this day week, and I will see what can be done in the interim."

"Thank you, sir. I will be satisfied with that promise."

"Good morning," said Mr. Simcox, ringing the bell.

Jackson did not wait for the attendant to how him out, but opened the door himself.

When he was gone, Mr. Simcox sent for Mr. Snarley.

He wished to consult him as to the best course to be adopted.

CHAPTER XLIX.

DICK'S DESPERATE ATTEMPT.

IT was bitterly cold up in the air.

The balloon seemed to be traversing the icy regions of the North.

Dick's hand trembled as he grasped the glass, and he could scarcely hold it.

But by means of a telescope he was enabled to see that which made his heart thump in his breast.

He saw land!

The balloon was drifting right over against it.

"Now, Harry," he exclaimed, " what's your lotion ?—put a name to it."

"Oh, no, thank you. I don't want to drink anything. My head aches already," replied Messiter.

"Then I must. I want a reviver."

"What for?"

"I've got work in hand," replied Dick.

"What sort of work ?"

"Aerial navigation, my boy. There is land ahead, and it won't do for us to travel any further."

"Do you think you will be able to manage a descent ?" asked Messiter.

"I mean to try."

"How ?"

You see that little bit of string flapping up against the valve?" replied Dick.

"Yes."

"I intend to climb up the ropes which bind the car to the machine, and lay hold of that with my teeth."

"If you slip ?"

"It is all over with me—that's soon settled," answered Dick.

He drank a little brandy, and the boys anxiously watched the course of the balloon.

The land appeared at first a mere speck; it gradually grew larger, and at length they could see they were traversing the region of a huge pine forest.

"This must be Norway," exclaimed Dick.

"Oh! what a way we have come. How shall we ever get back again ?" said Messiter.

"That don't worry me the least little bit. Let us only by God's mercy put our foot on land, and we'll get back again somehow. Never fear."

"Will the trees hurt the balloon ?"

"Don't for goodness sake worry me with your childish questions," replied Dick impatiently. "You're worse than a baby. Of course they will; the trees will smash it up, but what do we care for the bit of varnished silk. It's our lives I'm thinking of just now."

"You must bear with me, Dick," said Messiter; "I know I'm foolish sometimes."

Dick took his jacket and boots off, cold as it was, so as to be able to climb with more freedom.

"If I slip, Harry," he said, "I shall be dashed to pieces, but I'll do my best for your sake as well as my own."

"Never mind me," said Messiter, sobbing again.

"But I do and must. It was I who

got you into this scrape. Shake hands and say you forgive me."

" Willingly."

The two boys shook hands.

" If anything should happen, and if you should fluke out of it after all, say I died in trying to do my duty," said Dick.

Messiter only answered with sobs.

" Give my last love to Henrietta, and my duty and affection to my parents and the rest of the people at home."

Messiter nodded his head.

His little heart was too full for words.

Dick began the ascent.

In that hour of peril he showed all the qualities that go to make a hero.

It was with the utmost difficulty that he contrived to haul himself up the slender cords which bound the car to the bottom.

They seemed scarcely able to maintain his weight.

Slowly but surely he got higher and higher.

At last his head touched the top of the valve.

He was hanging on to one cord now.

Moving his head on one side he grasped the string with his teeth.

Instantly a rush of gas took place, which nearly suffocated him.

He was obliged to let go.

Hand-under-hand he descended the rope, and stood in the car once more.

" That won't do," he said, faintly.

" Can't you manage it ?" asked Messiter, trembling.

" I can do it, but not that way. Find a bit of string, Harry," said Dick.

Messiter gave him some which was in the locker, and armed with this, Dick ascended again.

He exercised the same laborious caution, and was rewarded by once more reaching the valve.

Tying a loop in the broken bit of string, he fastened to it that which he had brought up with him.

Then he slid down, holding the string in his mouth.

Pulling it gently, the valve opened and out rushed the gas.

In less than a minute the balloon began to fall with rapidity.

" Gently, gently," muttered Dick, not pulling so hard on the string.

The gas escaped more slowly.

Therefore the fall of the balloon was not so rapid or dangerous.

" Get ready the grappling i ons," cried Dick.

This was a sort of anchor made fast to the car by a strong cable.

Its use was to enable the travellers to cast it out and check their progress, as it hitched in the branches of a tree.

" Stand by," continued Dick, " and cast when I give the word."

" All right," replied Messiter.

He stood, grapnel in hand, waiting for the signal.

Gradually, very gradually, the huge machine neared the black funereal pine forest.

No sun was to be seen.

The sky was dull and leaden, and there appeared to have been a recent fall of snow, as the topmost branches of the trees were white

" I shall cut the car loose," said Dick.

" Do what ? " asked Messiter.

" Cut the ropes of the car when we strike. It contains food and things that will be of use to us."

Presently they were skimming over the tops of the pine trees.

" Cast !" exclaimed Dick.

Messiter did so.

The grapnel caught in a bough and held fast, while the car settled between two branches.

The balloon, however, tore and rolled in a frantic manner.

Hastily Dick slashed away at the many ropes which bound the machine and the car together.

After a time he cut the last strand, and the huge balloon, like a thing in pain, swayed away into the heavens.

" There it goes," exclaimed Messiter.

The car gave a lurch.

" And there you'll go if you don't watch it," replied Dick.

The boys grasped the branches of the pine, to steady the car, which had settled in a fork.

" Thank God, we are safe," exclaimed Messiter, clasping his hands together in gratitude to Providence.

Dick said nothing, but his lips moved, and the tears came into his eyes, while his limbs shook convulsively.

The danger was over now and the re-action had set in.

His nervous system had been severely tried.

The trembling did not last long; he was soon himself again, and as the depression wore off and a sense of safety and deliverance dawned upon his mind, he gave way to high glee.

"We're all right now, Harry," he said.

"I don't see it," replied Messiter. "We're up a tree, and how to get down I don't know, and where we are when we do get down I can't tell, and how to get home again is more——"

"Shut up," cried Dick; "you're like a dog at a fair, no sooner out of one trouble than you're into another."

"Well, aren't we up a tree?"

"Never mind, we'll get down. Go first."

"No, thank you," replied Messiter. "I'm not going to be eaten by bears or torn to pieces by wolves in a strange country."

"Bosh!"

"It isn't bosh. I'd rather stay here. I'm very comfortable where I am."

"Oh! all right," replied Dick, carelessly. "You've been flying through the air so long that, perhaps, you fancy you're a bird, and have got a nest in a tree. Hadn't you better go to roost?"

"Don't chaff, Dick."

"I'm not afraid of anything living, now I'm out of that blessed bah-loon," exclaimed Dick, "and I'm going down."

Dropping from branch to branch, he soon found himself on the ground.

The trees were very thickly planted together, and they were evidently in the midst of an impenetrable forest.

On the ground between the trees was snow of a considerable depth.

The cold was intense, and the prospect anything but cheering.

"I don't know that Harry hasn't got the best of it up there, after all," he muttered.

"How are you down there?" said Messiter from above.

"Lovely," replied Dick. "There's a Turkey carpet, and table and chairs, and quite a cosy little cottage."

"Is there, really?" asked Messiter, simply.

"Yes. Woodcutters, and all the rest of it. I'm quite one of the family already. They're lighting the fire and getting the dinner ready. Come down."

In a short time the crackling branches showed that Messiter was descending.

Imagine his disgust when he found Dick shivering up to his shins in snow.

"Oh what a story!" he exclaimed; "you said there were woodcutters and a cottage, and how could you sell me like that?"

"Because I want you down here, Harry. It isn't time for thinking. We must put our shoulders to the wheel, unless we want to be frozen to death, and leave our bones to whiten in this forest."

"I'll work, Dick, if you'll only tell me what to do," replied Messiter.

"That's all I want. First of all, we must make a house."

"Out of what? We've got no tools."

"We don't want any," replied Dick; "our house will be one of snow."

"Won't it melt?" said Messiter.

"Not a bit of it. I shall leave a hole in the roof, to let the hot air escape, and you'll be surprised how warm you'll find it. The Esquimaux always live in igloos or snow huts. Fire away. Here is a place between four trees. Let that be the model. Mould the snow hard, and make your walls thick."

"All right," said Messiter, who began to recover his spirits; "I'll take this side. You take that."

"Very well," replied Dick, "and we'll see who is the best mason."

And they began with a will to make a snow house.

"'HALLO! HERE WE ARE AGAIN SNARLEY,' CRIED DICK."

CHAPTER L.

ARMOND'S ESCAPE.

WHEN Mr. Snarley sought the presence of the head master, his face wore a subdued and even grave air.

He had a very bad headache, he was tortured with a fierce thirst, and he suffered all the evils of unaccustomed dissipation in their worst form.

He was ashamed of himself.

Once he had been betrayed into intoxication and he came home dressed as a clown.

Again he had been tempted, and fell, the consequence being that he appeared before Mr. Simcox's astonished eye arrayed as a pantaloon.

He wondered what he would come home like if he did it a third time.

"You sent for me, sir," he exclaimed, as he entered the study.

Mr. Simcox motioned him to a seat.

"I have had a troublesome visitor," he said.

"May I ask his name?"

"You may. It is Jackson."

"I only know one of that name, and he is an attendant at the gymnasium," said Mr. Snarley.

"That is the man."

"Does he want more money?"

"No, he asks for justice," replied Mr. Simcox.

"Upon whom?"

"He alleges that he overheard a conversation this morning on the beach between Armond and Smith, in the course of which Armond admitted to Smith that he cut the ropes."

"Indeed! I always considered Lightheart the culprit," said Snarley.

"My suspicions also pointed in that direction, but Jackson declares that Armond read an extract from a diary he keeps, which fully detailed the crime."

"This is grave."

"Very," replied Mr. Simcox. "Jackson demands that I shall obtain the diary and disgrace Armond, while doing justice to Lightheart."

"It seems a proper request."

"No doubt, and our duty is clear," Mr. Simcox rejoined. "But it is no secret to you, Snarley, that I am under considerable obligation to Armond's father."

"You have hinted as much, sir."

"I owe him money. If he were to withdraw his son, I could no longer work out the sum. I should have to pay, and I am not in the position to do so?"

"Precisely," said Snarley, "I see where the shoe pinches."

"Perhaps Lightheart may never return. He has not been openly accused of, or punished for, cutting the ropes of the trapeze."

"No."

"Therefore he has not much cause of grievance," pursued Mr. Simcox.

"Certainly not," Snarley answered.

"Then again, we have made Armond the head of the school."

"We have."

"He supplies us with valuable information which enables us to know what is going on amongst the boys."

"He is our spy, in fact."

"I do not like the word spy. It is harsh," said Mr. Simcox. "But we will say that he assists us in performing duties that are arduous."

"Quite so; I stand corrected, sir."

"Now, having made Armond what he is, it would seriously embarrass us to disgrace him and humiliate him in the eyes of the school."

"So it would. Let us take no notice of the attendant's communication," Snarley rejoined.

"That course does not recommend itself to me; it savours too much of favouritism. I must see Armond and speak to him, but I think it would be as well if you were to see him first."

"With pleasure, sir."

"If that diary did not exist, there would be no proof against him," Mr. Simcox went on.

"For my part, sir, I don't believe there is such a thing. It is a malicious invention on the part of Jackson."

"Very likely. Go and make your investigations, Mr. Snarley."

The usher departed to do so and found Armond on the beach.

"Morning, sir," said Armond. "Did you enjoy yourself at the Swiss Gardens?"

"Not much. There were causes that—ahem!—interfered with my pleasure. By the way, Armond, it is a bad plan to keep a diary; don't tell me you keep a diary."

"Why, sir?" asked Armond, surprised.

"Mr. Simcox has been told that you have written incautious admissions in a book."

"As to what?"

"That unfortunate affair of the trapeze ropes."

Armond turned deadly pale.

"Who is his informant?" he asked.

"Jackson, the attendant at the gymnasium. The fellow says he was lying on the beach this morning, and he heard you reading a confession to Smith. It is an absurd story, is it not?"

"Ridiculous," replied Armond, going whiter still.

"Mr. Simcox is determined to sift the matter, and compel the production of the diary; but if you haven't got one and it can't be found, the matter falls to the ground, and there is an end of it. Now the question is, do you or do you not keep a diary?"

"I will gladly give you the keys of my box, my desk, and my locker, sir, and if you can find one, you are welcome."

He handed Mr. Snarley a bunch of keys as he spoke.

"Ah, that is fair and straightforward," said the usher. "I am glad you have met me in this spirit. I will go at once to Mr. Simcox," replied the usher.

"Thank you, sir," replied Armond.

He breathed a sigh of relief.

"Excuse me for troubling you, Armond, but this Jackson is a vindictive, troublesome fellow."

"Let me see him if he comes again troubling Mr. Simcox."

"Your request is a very proper one, and shall be preferred in the right quarter," Snarley replied, shaking his hand.

When he was gone, Armond turned to Smith and said—

"A narrow shave that."

"Very," replied Smith.

"Fancy the sneaking beggar being behind the bathing machine and listening to what we said."

"Fancy," repeated Smith.

"Simcox doesn't want to have a row with me because of his transactions with my father, and he sent Snarley to talk to me. I can see that. Cleverly done, wasn't it?"

"By Snarley, you mean—to put you on your guard?"

"Yes."

"You'll get out of it all right now; but what shall you do with the diary?" said Smith.

"I don't know."

"Throw it in the sea, or destroy it."

"No," replied Armond, "I don't want to do that; there are lots of things in it I want to remember and look at. I shall hide it."

"Where?" said Smith.

"That's the question; tell me a good place."

"You know the old sycamore tree in the playground?"

"Yes."

"There is a sparrow's nest high up in the branches; we might put it there for the present," said Smith.

"A brilliant idea. The leaves will hide it."

"So will the stuff the nest is made of," answered Smith.

"Let's go at once and do it. I can climb up the tree," said Armond.

The boys rose and went home.

There were only a few boys in the playground, playing at marbles and leap frog; and they did not see anything extraordinary in Armond's climbing up the tree.

He soon reached the old sparrow's nest, and safely deposited the diary on the hay of which it was made.

Then he descended, feeling that he had baffled his enemies for the present.

"That's a weight off one's mind," he muttered.

Before dinner, Mr. Snarley sought him again.

"Well, sir, are you satisfied?" asked Armond.

"Perfectly, my dear boy. Mr. Simcox and I acquit you of the base charge brought against you by Jackson," said Snarley.

"Thank you, sir," Armond said, with a hypocritical smile.

"He is a malicious scoundrel."

"Kick him out, sir, if he comes here again telling lies."

"Depend upon it, he will go out quicker than he came in. I congratulate you upon coming so well through the ordeal."

Armond again thanked the usher, and his face was radiant with smiles.

Calling to Smith, he said—

"Make us a back. I feel so jolly that I want to do something."

Smith bent down, and he leaped over him with agility; then he went down, and Smith cleared him, crying, "Tuck in your twopenny," and so they amused themselves till dinner time.

The day passed, and no news came of Lightheart.

All the boys talked about him and Messiter.

Some made bets. The betting showed that the school did not think much of Dick's chance of getting back again.

The betting was six to four against his return.

END OF VOL. I.

The Scapegrace Series

are included in the following volumes:

The Scapegrace of the School. Two volumes.

The Scapegrace at Sea. One volume.

The Scapegrace in London. One volume.

Price of each volume—SIXPENCE.